"Run, lad!" cried the elf, helpless to keep the otter out of harm's way.

"I can't leave you, Jahn."

"Go get help from your father," gasped the elf, the weight slowly crushing him into the dank, smelly leaves.

"I won't," shouted the otter, and leapt at the thick, dark thing that had attacked his friend. He bared his tiny fangs, biting down with all his might, vowing he would never let go—just like all the heroes he had heard of in the lore books who would never surrender when they knew they were right.

The last thing he remembered was a great shout of pain—or was it a high wind howling—as he was flung high into the air. He could hear the elf calling to him from a great distance; then there was the darkness that swallowed him up in a deep, bottomless pool.

Books by
NIEL HANCOCK

THE CIRCLE OF LIGHT SERIES

I   Greyfax Grimwald
II Faragon Fairingay
III Calix Stay
IV Squaring The Circle

THE WILDERNESS OF FOUR SERIES

I   Across The Far Mountain
II The Plains Of The Sea
III On The Boundaries Of Darkness
IV The Road To The Middle Islands

Published by
WARNER BOOKS

The Wilderness of Four—4

THE ROAD
TO THE MIDDLE ISLANDS

by Niel Hancock

WARNER BOOKS

A Warner Communications Company

WARNER BOOKS EDITION

Warner Books, Inc.,
666 Fifth Avenue,
New York, N.Y. 10103

A Warner Communications Company

Printed in the United States of America

First Warner Books Printing: November, 1983

10 9 8 7 6 5 4 3 2 1

For Barry Braden: in hopes that somewhere it is always Europe in 1959, full of Dena and Ferraris; and for Carter Hague, who told me of the Islands.

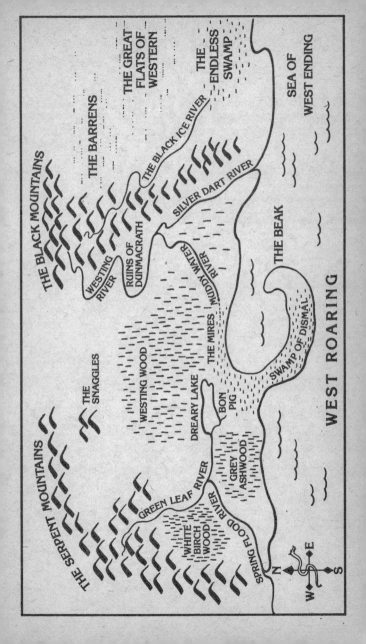

I. THE PASSING OF AN OLD ORDER

A Holt on the Greenleaf

UP the Greenleaf, far above the last of the Aspen and Birch, there was the quiet eddy where Morane kept her holt. It was snug and cheery in its winter coat of snow, safe from all the freezing winds that chased themselves up and down the canyons in the long winter.

Malcom was her mate, but he had been gone on a long ramble that had taken him all the way to the sea, and he had no sooner returned than he patted her reassuringly and was gone again. She could get nothing out of him where he'd been, but she had lived with him for many seasons and knew him well enough to know there was something amiss somewhere, for he stayed only long enough to eat and rest, and he never talked of his winter games, or what good fishing there had been, and he never even remembered to ask her when their pup was due, although she had been dying to tell him that it would be soon.

No matter how brave she had tried to be, she had broken down and wept in loneliness and frustration after his stout gray form disappeared over the last patch of clear ice before the trees, vanishing into the tall stand of beech there.

If it had not been for Ilia, she would have died from the terrible emptiness. It was also Ilia who helped her deliver her pup, who had turned out to be a rolly gray fellow, broad-cheeked, with tiny ears laid back, and the most haunting eyes she had ever seen on any animal in her entire life; and it had been long and full, lived on the teeming Greenleaf and the many other rivers that ran on eventually to the West Roaring.

Morane knew this small pup was no ordinary otter. That frightened her in an odd way she could not explain, for she knew she would lose him to the mysterious call that pulled her Malcom away from her into the long journeys he made with all the strange animals, and the elves, and the others that she had never seen.

Malcom called the elves the Eolin, when he said anything at all about them. He said that they were old friends of the animal kin, or at least animals that yet dwelled below the borders of the Black Ice, and that they knew many things, and would be of great service one day.

Morane tried to get Malcom to bring these unknown friends home, hoping that she might thereby have more time with her mate, but he would only smile and say that they were forever busy on some errand or other, but perhaps one day they would stop for a visit.

She pressed him for names and was amazed at the strange sounds they made on his tongue when he told her.

"They are strange enough to the ear," she agreed. "It's a wonder you're able to remember them at all."

"You won't be likely to forget, once you meet them. I have traveled with them now these past ten turnings, and they aren't the sort of folk you forget easily."

"But why must you spend so much time off on these outings? Can't you tell me anything at all about where you've been? I get so worried when you're away so long."

A slight edge of fear had crept into her voice as she spoke.

"And your pup will hardly know his father."

Malcom gave her paw a hurried squeeze.

"There is no need to worry on that account. He shall have his own errands as soon as he is big enough to begin traveling with me."

"Oh," squeaked Morane, her voice barely a whisper. She left the room and went to the cheery, snug corner where the small otter pup lay sleeping, his tiny paws crossed on his stomach, his ears twitching in the excitement of a dream of chasing a pond crawler through the thin fingers of ice that lay on the frozen surface of the water of the weir.

His mother told him of what the river looked like in the other seasons of the year, when the snow and ice were gone, but he could not imagine it.

Morane reached down to touch the dreaming pup, and his eyes opened a moment. He asked her sleepily if it were time to eat.

"Not yet, dear. Your father and I will wake you."

He mumbled something, then turned over on his side.

She looked down at him another while, then went back to the kitchen where Malcom sat toasting himself in front of the open hearth.

"This tea is just the thing to chase off the chill," he said, trying to turn the subject away from a matter that upset his mate so.

11

She nodded absently, setting the table for their meal, finding it a relief to have something to do with her hands and something to think about other than her small, helpless pup disappearing into the long and lonely woods with his father, on trips to places far beyond anything Morane could conjure up even in her wildest fancies.

"The river will be full this spring," said Malcom, pottering with an old favorite among his pipe rack.

"The snows have been heavy all through the mountains, and I don't doubt but that we'll have to abandon those lower storerooms until sometime after the middle of summer, when the runoff has eased up a bit."

"I'll clean them out and move everything. That will give me something to do."

Morane thought that sounded hopeful, if he were talking of the spring floods and the chance of being about for the middle of the summer. She stirred her porridge until it turned a creamy, rich brown and clung to the wooden spoon in large lumps.

There were good signs about, she thought. Maybe Malcom would spend at least the worst part of the winter at his own hearth, for he had been back now for almost eight days without the least indication of leaving, and he seemed to be taking great pleasure in his pipes and his old worn armchair in front of the fire, where he was forever making entries in his journal, or studying mysterious maps with strange names and lines that crossed and recrossed until it grew so confusing she would have to return to the order and simplicity of her kitchen.

Malcom read to them aloud at times after their evening meal, and the pup's eyes would be wide in wonder at the things his father related in the tales. He would squirm and wriggle on his mother's lap until she would have to put him down on the floor, where he would race about in hard scampers until he tired himself, and then he would lie quietly, listening to Malcom's voice drone on until he would find himself fast asleep.

Sometimes he would awaken to see his mother and father sitting together on the cozy wooden bench before the dying fire, and that made him feel warm and secure inside. He would lie that way, dozing until Malcom would lift him gently and carry him to his own small sleeping hammock.

The time his father spent in the holt was a special treat for the pup, for there were times when he would not see him for

12

long periods of time, and his mother always seemed very sad then. She never read to him from the green-covered books that lined the front of his father's desk.

He could not understand what made the time come when Malcom would suddenly pack his knapsack and disappear, often before dawn, or even sometimes in the middle of a dark, frozen night. There were never explanations. He would know if his father was gone again by awakening to a silent breakfast and hearing the muffled sobs of his mother as she tried to keep her tears from showing behind an upraised paw or teacup.

This time Malcom had been at home longer than any other time the small pup ever remembered, and he was growing close to the point of believing that perhaps all other times were now over, and that everything was going to be different. He would be able to doze in front of the fire always, with the strong sound of his father's voice chasing away all the dark fears that sometimes found him in the quiet part of night, when he wondered about it all, and if he would be alone when he awakened from his sleep.

The Late Arrival

MALCOM had been at home for a longer period of time at once than Morane had ever remembered. She began to think that it might be that at last all the mysterious disappearances were over and they would now be able to carry on a more normal life among the community that dwelled along the banks of the Greenleaf.

She was never one to complain overly much about things that she couldn't change; but it had made her feel uncomfortable now and then when the other animals would ask after Malcom and she would always have to say she didn't know, that he was away on a journey. His trips went beyond the decent sort of outings that the winter animals made; and after a few seasons, no one asked any more questions, except to politely inquire as to when she expected him home.

The Greenleaf and Aspen and Birch were all quiet rivers,

and the animals there had lived for a long time without any unpleasant interruptions. They had grown so used to their uneventful lives that they would remember no other existence; and if anyone drew allusions to an outer world beyond their safe river, they were cut short with a stern look or reproachful word.

It was true that some of their number had been carried off and slain some time before, but the end of that story seemed to have come with the disappearance of the gaunt gray wolves that had been responsible. Since that time, none of the others had ever made a point of recalling the days of terror that had settled over their quiet community.

Malcom was the only one of the entire settlement who continued to harp on the danger they were all still in, and who, when he was at home, would warn everyone who would listen of an impending doom that hung over their entire wood and that would one day strike and sweep them all away like twigs in the spring runoff. There were things they should be doing, he insisted, although none of the others ever paid enough attention to find out what; so it would always end up that he would vanish again and they would have a certain degree of peace and quiet around the wood, which they all knew was the true order of how things should be. They all agreed that there could only be trouble if one was forever talking about it.

Malcom seemed content simply to sit in front of the broad stone fireplace this time, though, smoking his pipe; or sometimes just sitting, staring at the patterns a particular cherry log fire made, with the unlit stump of the pipe clenched in his strong jaws.

There were many undecipherable charts and strange journals that were written in a high, flowery hand, and some others in the small, neat paw of Malcom; and many strange drawings that Morane had to keep picked up and out of reach of her pup, for they were of frightening beasts, some with horrible gaping jaws and wings that looked like the ragged edges of the Great Barrens, a mountain range far off to the south, which Malcom said bordered the regions where the most horrible beasts of all dwelled.

There were also dreadful things that stood on two legs which were bigger and even more frightening than mankind, which were also in Malcom's sketchbook and journals.

He had shown her other drawings of certain clans of men

14

which he said were good and were the friends of all living things.

"Who are they?" she had asked, curious to know what sort of clans they came from, and what made them so different from all the rest.

There were many terrifying stories of what had happened when the settlements of man had been near, and how many of the animals had been hunted and butchered, or slain for sport. Morane was not easily convinced that there were tribes of mankind that were bent upon anything else but murder and mayhem among themselves, or any other kinds that were unfortunate enough to cross their paths.

"These are men from over the High Boundaries," he replied.

Malcom always spoke in terms that she didn't understand or that she was unfamiliar with, and she had no idea where the High Boundaries were or what lands they bordered upon.

"Where is the place you speak of?" she asked.

Malcom smiled and reloaded his pipe.

"Not a place so much, unless you're able to travel that way. More a way of being," he answered vaguely.

"And you say they're not like the rest?"

"Not at all, yet they are from mankind. They are much older and have been about since the Beginning."

This news baffled Morane even more.

"The beginning of what?"

"It's a long story, dear. I'm not too certain that I'd be able to explain it all even if I were to stay home and try for the entire winter."

The tone of his voice turned her next question into silence before she could ask it.

Malcom looked at his mate tenderly.

"I have enjoyed this time here at home more than I can say, Morane. The pup is a sturdy lad, and I can see that you've taught him his lessons well. There are things a mother needs to teach a pup that no one else can do."

Morane's heart pumped faster, for anytime Malcom became serious and talked to her this way, she knew he was on the verge of another journey.

"Are you leaving soon?" she asked, not really wanting to hear his reply.

He reached across the small table and patted her paw gently.

"You are the best, Morane. I could never have found a better mate even if I'd turned the wood upside down in the looking."

15

"Then you're leaving soon?" she pressed.

"Not so soon, dear. There are things that have to be done here and a hundred chores to attend to before I even think of leaving."

Morane stared into the fire, her heart pounding. She had lulled herself into a false security, telling herself that he would stay this time, at least for the winter. That was the worst time of all, although she now had her pup to keep her company through the seemingly endless hours that dragged slowly through the long gray winter days.

A faint, faraway bell rang in the upper rooms of the distant passage that led to one of the outer doors, followed by a drumming sound of the knocking of an impatient visitor.

Morane's eyes widened.

"Whoever would be calling at this hour of the night?"

The noise had awakened the pup also, and he came padding down the hall, half asleep.

Malcom laid his pipe beside the journal he had been reading and disappeared down the maze of passages that wound about the holt and eventually led out into antechambers aboveground, or onto landings that bordered the weir.

Morane went to the table and picked up the journal, holding it closer to the candle. She could make nothing out of the writing, for it was done in a thin scrawl, in ink that ran into different colors over the thick parchment page. There were drawings there too; and lists of what appeared to be names; and a small map at the bottom that bore odd-sounding names, none of which she recognized except for the legend across the blue portions of the chart which said it was the West Roaring Sea.

Her pup had crawled into her lap and was looking at his father's pipe and the heavy journal.

"What's in that?" he asked, reaching out a paw to touch it.

"That is your father's work," she said, somewhat angrily.

He tried to touch it again and this time Morane got up holding the small pup under her arm and marched resolutely into the kitchen to see what she might offer whoever the late caller was, and to get the squirming pup a mug of warm tea to put him back to sleep.

This wasn't the first time that there had been unusual guests in their holt, but it was the first time in a long while since the visitors had come so late. And it was unusual too, in that it was the worst of the season, and there were not many

16

souls about who were active or who made a habit of calling at midnight in the dead of winter.

Only Malcom, she thought forlornly, would be acquainted with anyone of that odd nature.

Jahn Spray

THERE was a fine powder of fresh snow that lay on the moonless ground beyond Malcom's holt door, and it took him a few moments to recognize his old friend, for the cloak and hat he wore were covered with the fine snow, just as if it had been dust on a long, dry trail.

"Well, if you're not a sight," he said, helping his friend to knock the snow off. "I was beginning to wonder if you'd lost your way."

Malcom's voice was light, but it concealed a deep concern.

His friend, a fair elf with sharp features, and taller than Malcom, swooped the hat from his head, knocking it against the door frame.

"May your door be always open," he replied politely, then carelessly pulled the cloak from around his shoulders. "But you had need of some worry, my friend, for there are strange doings in the White Birch tonight."

As the two came inside and shut the outer door, Malcom noticed that his friend was heavily armed, with sword and dagger and a full quiver of arrows for the slim, silver-colored bow slung over his back in a case alongside his knapsack.

At the closing of the outer door the newcomer grasped Malcom strongly, giving him a hug that displayed a powerful grip, in spite of his small size.

"Greetings, Jahn. My hearth is yours."

Malcom returned the hug, and out of old-fashioned courtesy they had not spoken their names outside the safety of a closed refuge. It had not always been the case; and the others of the small community deep in the White Birch Wood no longer thought it necessary, but the otter knew differently and had seen growing evidence of a terrible cloud of doom descending upon the wood and all in it.

In his travels, he had found that it was everywhere. There

17

were many small communities up and down the Greenleaf and Springflood which had simply vanished without so much as a trace, although he and Jahn had found the marks of the wolves and the things that were not man but which walked upright and might once have been of mankind.

"They are prowling tonight, Malcom. I have seen two full bands of them and a pack of the wolves as well. I was lucky to be able to slip through without them getting on to me."

"If anyone could do it, Jahn, it's you. There's not many animals that I know of that are as sly when it comes to getting about somewhere unnoticed."

"These things are no ordinary beasts," replied his friend, taking off the knapsack and laying his weapons against the wall. "They have come up the river on the far side and it looks as though they're on their way toward Salt Creek."

"We should warn them!" said Malcom, his gray whiskers beginning to twitch at his muzzle.

"I have already done so, my friend. That was why I was a bit late."

"Did they heed your warning?"

"The beaver family left, and I think a few of the others. Mostly all I got were disgruntled looks and reprimands for calling so late at night."

"That would follow," snapped Malcom. "I have watched the entire river lose its good sense these past few seasons. No one has any time these days to listen to an old boot like me trying to warn them of a danger that's coming as sure as the sunrise."

"There's no good in blaming yourself. I have found it difficult in every settlement, whether it be dane or delving, animal or fowl, for no one wants to hear bad news or think of anything but their supper."

"Speaking of that, have you had yours?" asked Morane, waiting for a moment before breaking into the conversation.

Jahn bowed low and replied softly.

"May your hearthfire never dim."

"Come along, come along," insisted Malcom. "I have kept you here chattering all the while and you're probably famished. Forgive me."

"I haven't had time to think about a missed supper," said Jahn. "But now that I hear word of it, I am a bit the worse for lack of food."

Morane had heard the talk between her mate and the elf, who was familiar to her, and who had been to their holt on

18

other occasions in the past. She was not overly fond of Jahn, for he was one of Malcom's regular traveling companions. She knew this visit could only mean that she was on the verge of another long vigil, awaiting her mate's return from some journey that he was already busy planning.

"Jahn says he has just warned the folk at Salt Creek about a band of the yellow fangs."

Morane had seated the elf and poured a mug of tea for him, looking at him over the steaming plate of porridge she handed him.

"And did they listen?"

She was torn between being frightened at the news and angry at the elf for bringing it.

"The beavers did."

"They would. If you ever want to meet a sensible lot, it's the beavers," agreed Malcom.

He sensed his mate's feelings and wondered how he would bring up the subject that must be discussed.

"Have you decided yet which way you shall go?" asked Jahn.

Morane's eyes widened and she posed a question with her silence.

Malcom flushed gray and cleared his voice a few times before speaking.

"I think we'll go eastward, toward the Roaring. It's the only way left open, as far as I can tell."

"Is this going to be for long?" asked Morane.

"Not so long, my dear. You and the pup will have a nice time, I'm sure. There are some beautiful parts of the Greenleaf; and the falls at Willow Head are always spectacular this time of year. The ice just hangs out in space at the top and when there's sunlight on it, it looks like nothing you've ever seen."

"Besides it won't be long before the raiders begin to cross the river and then there won't be any getting out at all," added Jahn.

"And there is Cousin Lelia and her pup there at the Fallen Ash. They'll be happy to have the company."

The elf ate noisily for a while, cleaning his plate and finishing his mug of tea.

Morane remained silent, looking across the table at her mate squirming uncomfortably, his attention taken by the fire.

"Jahn will be with us," he offered at last, unable to stand the forsaken look in Morane's eyes.

19

"I'll be with you for a part of the trip, but there are danes I must gather along the way; and I never know how much talking I'll need to do to convince some of them. There are a few of the older settlements up the Springflood, and a few in the Gray Ash Wood, that I don't know for certain will even let me in, much less listen to me."

Morane smiled bitterly and nodded slightly, although neither of the other two noticed.

"Do you think it is time?" asked Malcom, a worried frown playing across his broad, handsome muzzle.

"Everything seems to say so," replied his friend. "The rivers are beginning to be flooded with the debris of all those massacres of settlements upstream, toward the mountains. You and I have seen more than a dozen ruins of what were once active danes or settlements. The elf is not an easy one to catch napping, but there is something loose now that has caught more than one of my poor kinsmen."

"And mine as well. It doesn't seem to be only man, although we have found traces of them, along with whatever else it is."

"The Banskrog," said Jahn. "Black Death. That's what our Old Ones call it. They say that there always comes a time when it comes forth from the tomb and tries to darken the world."

Malcom mouthed the word around as if tasting it, his whiskers wrinkled.

"It is an awful sound," he agreed.

"And an awful time. I don't remember reading much about it, for it was too horrible to describe, although some of the Old Ones used to tell stories around the fires. They also told some wonderful tales too, and said it was all a part of the way of things."

"They sound awful to me," said Morane sharply. "Better leave alone those ideas and not look for the worst, if you don't want to find it."

"Sometimes the worst finds you without any warning, no matter how hard you've tried to overlook it," replied Jahn softly. "Some things will be as they will be, no matter how much we would wish it another way."

Morane rose abruptly from the table, replacing the elf's empty plate with a dish of dried apples from her root cellar.

"She isn't going to make any trouble," whispered Malcom to his friend. "I've seen her like this a hundred times. She always goes right ahead and does whatever needs doing, but you hear a lot about it."

"I understand. I didn't think she would be too taken with the trip. I also know she doesn't care for the likes of an elf, but I always thought she would go along."

He tasted an apple, nodding his approval.

"And there really is no choice," he went on. "We have to find safe haven for the Pipe of Ring Parath until the time comes when whoever is to carry it comes forth to claim it."

As Jahn spoke, he reached into the folds of his tunic and pulled out a small, finely stitched leather case, putting it on the table beside his dish of apples.

"There is a lot more to this than a simple otter can fathom," said Malcom, looking carefully at the small object.

"There's a lot more to it than any of us can understand. It has been going on now for a long while. We've only begun to come across some clues to it all."

"You think all the beast raiders and all the other signs are a warning the Banskrog has come from sleep again?"

"The Black Death is upon the world again. She will swallow us all if we sit by and do nothing."

Morane had returned to the table and now sat holding her pup on her lap.

"That's all fancy talk and it gives you two the perfect excuse to be off somewhere at the blink of an eye or the twitch of a whisker. I think perhaps there may be other answers to those signs. It need not be this Black Death you speak of, Jahn."

"I wish that were so, Morane. There would be nothing that would give me half so much pleasure as to think of how delightful it would be to return to my own dane and winter by a snug turf fire. I could catch up on all the things I've been meaning to do these past seasons."

"Then why not do that?" she asked stubbornly.

The elf smiled sadly and the deep gray-blue eyes reflected the stillness of a time long before, when the Eolin had come down from their High Danes to help a troubled world and to learn the secrets of the life there.

"I would do so, Morane, and will one day, when the time has come."

"The first trip we took together, he was given the pipe here," explained Malcom, seeing his friend withdrawn and far away in his thoughts.

21

"And who would give him that?" she asked, unimpressed with the worn case that lay on her clean tablecloth.

"It was given to him by one of the ancients that guard the ruins of the old danes at Dun Macrath."

Morane was unmoved.

"There are no folk that live at Dun Macrath anymore."

"Not as we know them," said her mate. "But I was there with him. The strangest things began to happen. When we made our camp for that night, we slept in the ring of walls that had once been the dwelling of the elfin queen in those days that were long ago."

Jahn took up the story then, in a voice that was almost a monotone; and he spoke as if in a trance.

"There were stars blowing by above us and the night was full of a brilliant light that seemed to come from inside the trees and rocks themselves. There was a sound of voices and singing; and the sweetest sound of all was that of a reed pipe, played by one who seemed to know all sorrow and all joy by heart."

"But there was no one there," protested Morane.

"None that our eyes could see at first. As we watched, the walls were made whole again and the glory of the olden times was before us. There were golden drapes at every window and silver tapestries on every wall, woven by hands that could sew and shape the very air itself."

"And the elves," broke in Malcom. "They were everywhere, all tall and glorious and terrifying to look upon."

Morane looked sharply at her mate, for she had never heard him say anything of this tale before. It frightened her slightly, seeing him in such a state.

"The Queen was a tall woman who was dark-haired and so beautiful you could not look full upon her without disappearing. She wore a gold-colored dress and the five-pointed star was upon her head, glittering against her dark hair like stars against the night. She reached out and touched my arm and handed me this case."

Jahn's hand went out to the worn leather object on Morane's table.

"There was a voice then," said Malcom. "As plain as you or I are talking."

"'At the distant islands there will be heard the Pipe of Ring Parath. It will signal an end to sorrow for a time.'"

Jahn paused.

"Then there was another vision that came and all the lights

22

and sounds disappeared and we were in the cold room of the darkness again; and an old hag sat across from us at the fire. She said that whoever opened the case of the pipe would be he who carried it to the islands and that it would be known one day in midwinter in a place by a river."

"That wasn't very helpful."

"More helpful than you might think," said Jahn. "For we have traveled up one end of the wood and down the other every winter. We have set the test to every likely soul, animal, dwarf, or elf, who has come to our attention or that we've ever heard of."

"And you mean to say no one has ever been able to open it?" asked Morane.

"No one has ever done so," replied the elf. "And everyone who has tried has fallen into a deep sleep for a time; and when they have awakened again, they remember nothing at all of who they were before or what had happened to them."

Morane's paw had crept to within an inch or so of the case but stopped as the elf finished his speech.

"But that's awful! What happened to them?"

"We always warned everyone of the risk before we allowed them to try the case. They knew the danger involved. Some say the Eolin are the forgetful people, and that any who share their affairs in any way become like them. The ones who tried to open the case were made like the Eolin themselves, for it is said of our kind that we came from the High Danes and then forgot the old ways and the secrets that would have carried us safely home again."

"There is a story that goes like that among the animal lore," said Malcom. "And all the other lores too, I suspect, if you studied them closely. But most everyone has forgotten it and so no one remembers anything except what they see about them. And now I see the raiders and wolves from beyond the borders and know that many of the animals have slipped back into the old darkness."

"That's all a fine tale to spin by the fire," said Morane. "But I don't see what it has to do with anything about going off in the dead of winter to heaven knows where, dragging all our belongings and a pup not even yet big enough to be safely out on his own alone."

Roused by his mother's angry tone and looking about the warm hearth for a plaything, the pup's eyes fell on the worn leather case on the table. Before anyone could move to stop him, he had reached out a stubby little paw and dragged it to him.

Morane cried out in alarm and tried to snatch the dreadful object away from her baby, but it was too late. In the next instant the room was flooded with a brilliant white light and a sound that began beyond the lowest tide of the sea and went beyond the highest peak of the ancient shoulders of the mountains, filling the minds of those there with sights and visions that dazzled them into a reverent silence.

Soldiers of Dun Macrath

MORANE could never be sure that what she saw was real, but her mate and the elf Jahn both assured her they saw the same visions and heard the same music. Her life had never been touched before by anything very out of the ordinary, and she considered herself a very practical, level-headed animal, not prone to wild ideas or hysterics. She knew a good number of her friends who were forever going on about one thing or another, but she always remained a solid rock in her even outlook on life; and in the end, it was she who would be there still, the one remaining calm voice amid all the chaos. There had been the scare of the savage beasts from The Barrens, when every family on the Greenleaf had lost someone; and other less serious times, of course, but Morane had always been the one the other animals came to for advice or consolation.

It had been a long while since the wood or river had been upset in its routine, and there had been a long absence of any of her friends at her door, wringing their paws or wrinkling their whiskers, voices beseeching her to hear out one sad tale or another. And now she wished she had someone to go to with this incredible tale, to talk to about the impossible things that had gone on in her very own kitchen.

She remembered, and Jahn told her he had seen it too, a long silver-white river of fire that poured from a tall urn shaped in the manner of a great bird in flight, and a sound of a distant wind blew through the small kitchen. Grim, armored warriors with gleaming mithra and silver caps rode forth from the blowing clouds that appeared from the rampant river. These soldiers were mounted on powerful steeds that were neither horse nor any other animal that Morane had ever seen, for they had long necks and legs and thick, muscular bodies which were covered with armor, just as their riders were.

Malcom had tried to pull Morane and the pup to him in order to shield them from the strange intruders, but he found he was unable to move or call out, or to do anything at all but stand helplessly before the visions that appeared to him.

Jahn had broken into an unknown tongue and seemed to be talking to one of the armored riders who had drawn up his steed and hovered in the seething tempest of the thunderous white fire storm that blew in streaming sheets of blinding light about him. As Jahn spoke, the reply was heard from the messenger who wavered in the air before him, and a new sound was heard of a fine, high pipe, which made their hearts both terrified and joyful beyond thought at once. The pipe played on until at last the riders vanished into a golden stream of fire that billowed like clouds over a faraway range of mountains where there was light reflected from the high peaks of ice that glimmered there.

Very slowly the visions settled into a thin, silver-white cloud that covered the kitchen like a fine mist on a late spring morning, between the cold and the warmth of a new day; and then there was nothing except their startled faces looking wild-eyed and strained, amid the echoes of what they had just seen and heard. There in the middle of the floor was the chubby otter pup holding the Pipe of Ring Parath, which was a silver-pearl color, set with a row of dazzling blue stones that still glowed and shimmered with the colors of the fire of the vanished river.

Morane swooped down on the pup and picked him up to inspect him for any injuries. She moved to take the pipe from him, but a hidden light in the small otter's eyes began to show through the smile he wore, and she did not try to touch the pipe again.

He replaced it in the case that he had opened and set it carefully in front of Jahn.

"I think he wants you to hold it for him," said Malcom, finding his voice at last.

"What were they saying?" asked Morane.

"They were the army of Dun Macrath," replied the elf. "The ancient elfin hosts that battled the Banskrog in the last

25

wars. They were unable to find rest or return to the High Havens until the next bearer of the Pipe of Ring Parath was found."

"So it is you?" asked Morane, slightly awed by the whole affair.

She had carefully checked her kitchen over with her eyes to see if anything had been trampled or broken by all the strange doings, but everything was as it was before except for the odd sense of age that had come over her pup in that short passage of time.

The elf shook his head slowly.

"It is only for me to carry it for the one who shall receive it."

"Then who will it be if not you?"

Jahn studied his friends for a moment, a strange look crossing his fair features.

"Your pup."

Morane's heart faltered and she gasped aloud.

"He's not! He'll have nothing to do with that business. That is an affair for an elf!"

Malcom tried to calm his mate, although he was also shaken by the news; his whiskers wrinkled into a worried frown.

"I'm sure there's nothing more to it than a short chore, if it has to be done at all," he said. "And I'm sure that it would be just as easy for me to do it, if it comes right down to it."

The otter looked at his friend hopefully.

"Surely there is no service that the pup could do? He's too small to be of use. It wouldn't be right to expose him to any danger."

"He's in no more danger than the rest of us now," replied Jahn. "But don't worry, my friend. The pup has nothing to do as yet except to grow strong and healthy. The faithful Jahn will carry the pipe until the time comes that is written."

That answer only partially satisfied Morane and she pressed the elf further.

"Then you will carry it and there might be no need for him to ever have anything to do with it? He is so small. It will take him another season or two to even be big enough to be alone, much less be drawn into doings beyond the Greenleaf."

"We'll all be beyond the Greenleaf by then," said the elf softly. "We shall be a good way from here and all the life you've ever known here. And your pup is no ordinary otter. I

26

think you already know that by what you've seen here in your kitchen."

Morane grew angry.

"He will have nothing to do with any elf affair; and I don't know whether or not I'll be gone from the Greenleaf! I have seen no reason to give up my holt now or to start off on any wild trip in the middle of snowtime for any reason at all. You and Malcom are perfectly at liberty to do as you please; but you've guessed wrong if you think you'll draw my pup and me into your silly schemes. All the neighbors talk enough about your doings as it is. I, for one, won't give them any further gossip to spread about."

She stopped abruptly with a snort.

"The idea of it all! Taking a half-grown pup and setting off in the worst of the season to who knows where, spouting some half-baked story of seeing visions in my kitchen!"

"You have never been one to hold back your ideas about anything," said Jahn evenly. "And that is a good thing. I understand your fear for your pup and your reluctance at leaving your home. Those are natural things. I would never want to have to reach a time where I dealt with any who did not have those feelings. It still remains, though, that there are forces at work who don't give a good hang about what we want or don't want. The Banskrog is loose and there are no more choices to be made on our own. There will be no one who may stay safely by his fire anymore and no hope for the newborn of any kind until this threat has been met and dealt with."

"What he says is true, dear," said her mate. "We have seen the truth of it on every journey; and we've watched the plague of trouble spread everywhere and heard from those even farther beyond our small boundaries that it is the same in all those places."

"Then it will just have to wait until the thaw," snapped Morane peevishly, feeling betrayed by Malcom for taking the elf's side of the argument against her.

"If we wait until then, there will be no hope of escaping, Morane. The numbers of the raiders and wolves have grown so that there will be no way out before long. Even now we should be on our road and not arguing here about the matter."

"I've said my piece," said Morane. "You and Malcom are free to leave whenever you wish. I can't keep two grown souls from plunging off in the blackest part of the night in the middle of winter, but I don't have to be party to the insanity."

Malcom looked at the elf, and his glance asked that he be left alone with his mate. Jahn noisily excused himself and said he wanted to take a look around outside.

The sharp cold of the night beyond slipped into the room through the open door and Morane shivered, either from the frozen chill that had crept in or from her own dark thoughts; she could not tell which.

"There's no sense in your trying to bring me around to your way of thinking. My mind's made up."

"I know this has all been sudden, dear. I know how upsetting it must be. I don't like to think about leaving our holt or going off in high winter with the pup, but the situation is one that demands drastic action or none of us may be around to see the thaw."

Morane laughed bitterly, holding back the tears.

"It's easy for you to talk about leaving and no cause to worry. That's all you've done these past turnings. More often than not, you're away on one of your endless outings somewhere, so it probably doesn't mean anything to you."

Malcom tried to take her paw, but she turned her back to him and pulled away.

"It's easy enough for you; but I've never had a choice in your doings, although I could have wished for you to spend more time at your own hearth instead of dragging around in the woods with your friends, stirring up trouble and bringing home all these tales about beasts and raiders and Black Death."

Malcom shook his head.

"I haven't purposely done any of these things, Morane. They are not my doing."

"But you don't have to go out looking for them!"

"They would find us whether I go out looking for them or sit by the hearth without moving a paw. And if I didn't know all the things I have found out on my journeys, we might not live long enough to see the pup grown."

"We may not do so if we go wandering off in the dead of winter following after an elf," she snapped. "And he is to have nothing to do with that pipe!"

Her voice rang with finality. As she spoke, she turned toward the small otter, who was playing quietly on the floor in front of the fire. Morane reached to pick him up, but his eyes met hers, and there was another moment of strange visions and old memories that were stirred from their sleep, memories from days far away in the silent times when the play was written by the High King who directed them all.

Malcom was speaking, but she did not hear him, for the music of the pipe had filled her thoughts. There were more of the armored elves that stood before her inner eye, and they were speaking too; and then there was a darker one who had on a helmet of gleaming silver-mithra, but she could not see who it was until the warrior lifted the visor. Although the features of the fierce-looking soldier were not familiar, she knew it was her own pup.

There were many around him, and a great thunderous noise of many voices rose and fell on that unseen wind. There was the noise of the pipe above it all and then she could make out what was being said; and as she mouthed the words aloud, it startled her into her own kitchen once more.

"Olthar," she repeated.

"What is it?" asked Malcom, a frightened look darkening his muzzle. "You haven't heard a word I've said and you've had the strangest look."

"I've seen our son. He is the Olthlinden."

Malcom fell back into one of the bright-colored chairs by the hearth.

"I never dreamed," he began. "When I saw the visions before, I knew; but I was afraid to believe it. I don't want it to be my son."

Malcom shook his head, bewildered.

"I had no idea. Even when Jahn sought me out all that time ago, I had no notion as to why an elf would want anything to do with our kind. They are such a secretive bunch for the most part. But he always said our fates were one and that we had a long path to go between us, and that there would come an hour when I would understand."

Morane was crying silently, her shoulders hunched in pain. The small animal at her feet hugged her then and Malcom squeezed her in a strong embrace, although he was very near tears himself.

"The Olthlinden," he said aloud, although mainly to himself. "I had always thought that that was only an elf's tale; and that even if it were true it would be someone else who would bear the burden."

Morane looked up hopefully, the tears still streaming down her muzzle.

"We could not let anyone know! We can go away tonight

and find a safe place on another river in another wood where no one knows us."

Her voice wavered and she began sobbing again.

"Oh, he's so small, Malcom. He's only a pup!"

The two otters held onto each other for a time; and the young one sat at their feet looking very much a young pup in his size, but his eyes were already old and full of a secret knowledge that made his gaze as sad as the sorrow that one saw in the eyes of the elves.

Another frozen breath of the night outside entered the room and Jahn stood beside them.

"We must take the Olthlinden away from here now," he said in a low voice. "The Banskrog has spies in every wood. I am afraid there were others about who might have seen or heard the messengers of Ring Parath."

"We must pack some things," began Morane, trying to regain control of herself, looking about to try to decide what to pack and what to leave behind.

"All we shall have need of is a knapsack or two and cloaks and food. The rest we shall have to leave."

"All my beautiful things?"

"I'm sorry. We have a need to go lightly. There are friends that are waiting for us not many hours from here. We can stay there until we've rested, then you and Malcom can go on to the cousin you spoke of. That will be safe enough until I have gathered the Eolin and we have banded the clans."

Morane had picked her youngster up and was on her way to the cupboard to see what she had there for the journey that she had resigned herself to make, when the first sounds of the other voices reached her.

The King of the Shanoliel

AT first it seemed as though a great wind had sprung up from beyond the icy hills of winter, from over the green fields of the spring that was always blooming in the gardens of the Upper Meadows, and the sound of it at once lifted the heart and overpowered it. Morane had never heard singing like it, nor the music that accompanied the voices. It was hard for her to tell which was the instrument of the throat and which the pipe, so well was it done. Gently yet fiercely did it come into her kitchen, filling the room with the wonders of its spell.

The pup began to dance in awkward, rolling steps, and Morane could not tell if he were laughing or crying, but neither could she sense that even about her own feelings. At one instant she was full of a joy that she could hardly contain, and the next brought the bottomless sorrow of a gypsy far from home, alone in a wilderness that had no end.

She saw Malcom and Jahn go to the outside door beyond the kitchen hallway; and after another moment, the music grew louder and she knew they had opened the entryway and whoever had been singing fell silent. Picking up the struggling pup, she crossed the room and stood at the foot of the hallway, staring dumbstruck at the scene that spread out beyond the outer door which framed the vision she saw.

The darkness outside, which on a normal midnight was so dense it would make one giddy and uneasy if out in it, was aglow with flickering lights, burning like crystal sparklers reflected on the frozen, snow-blanketed landscape.

Jahn had stepped out to meet the leader of the group gathered there and spoke in a tongue she could not understand. He was greeted in return by an elf somewhat shorter than Jahn, dark-haired, with a long, dark beard tinged with gray. Morane remembered this elf particularly because he wore a rich purple-colored cloak which was edged in gold and white, and when he spoke, his voice sounded like one of the reed pipes that had been playing before, when the singing had filled the air.

Malcom turned to her, his expression dazed.

"As far as I can make out, it's the King of the Shanoliel," he breathed. "They say they have come to pledge their service to the piper of the Ring Parath."

"Jahn?" she asked, still not comprehending.

"Our pup."

The young otter squirmed down from his mother's grasp and scampered past his father and Jahn, racing about the feet of the elf in the regal cloak. He laughed and reached down to take up the small animal. When he did so, the others behind him sent up a cheer, and the sound of the pipe came clearly again, making Malcom's hackles crawl on the nape of his neck.

As the elf put the youngster down, he spoke once more, this time in the tongue common to Morane.

"It is truly the Olthlinden. Young Olthar shall be the very one to carry our light until such time as we can join the Emigren who have already crossed over the Dark Sea."

Jahn turned to the otters to explain.

"The Emigren are the most ancient of the Eolin, who went back to the Upper Danes before the gates were closed."

"We have waited a long and weary wait," said the elfin king. "There have been false starts and rumors from time to time, but they all have been merely the wishful thinking of one mind or another. Until now, we have had no proof of ever being closer to returning."

Malcom regained his voice, and questioned the elf.

"But why an animal to carry the pipe? Why don't you simply take it with you now and be done with it? And why haven't you shown yourselves before now? Jahn has carried it for more than a few seasons."

"But there was no one who was the Olthlinden. We dared not show ourselves until that had been decided."

"But we're just simple otters. We don't know your laws nor the things you have to do. We will only be in the way or cause trouble."

"We have dealt with your folk for many lifetimes, my friend. We are familiar with the nature of your kind. It was in a battle long ago that the deed was written of what would come to be. It was given that a high king of the Eolin would be in league with the descendants of the animal kings, and in that time there would be a shroud over all the wilderness of the Lower Danes."

"The Banskrog," exclaimed Jahn.

"The Black Death. It was said that it would be rampant once more and spread to every corner of these places we know or dwell in. And in the secret pages of the lore of the Eolin is written the names of the animal lords and those of mankind who have become Elders of the Circle along with the dwarf lords who will join themselves in the struggle to keep the Light from perishing."

Morane finally overcame her shyness and fear, stepping forward to try to capture her pup.

"We'll all perish from the cold first, if we stand about outside like this."

She looked at the gathered crowd of elves and wondered if there was enough room in her holt for all of them, and if she

32

would ever find teacups for that large number. Her good manners won out over her reluctance, and she insisted that they all crowd in as best they could around the fire to carry on their discussion.

The elfin king, who said that they might call him Duirn, which was the only name he could give them other than his true name, which could only be spoken in the High Tongue of the Eolin, laughed. In the wink of a whisker, there were long tables set and spread with mugs and plates; and there were pots of steaming tea and loaves and cheeses and fresh fruits the likes of which Morane had never seen.

There were walls around the night then, and the darkness was lighted by the elfin lamps, which gleamed and shone like the very deep-blue fires of the distant stars, and which the elves did, in truth, call starlamps. Instead of frozen snow and ice, there were white carpets of spun elfin cloth and the air about them began to smell of sweet incense. The long-forgotten smells of summer drifted over them and made them forget the cold and bitter season outside.

"Come, come and join us," said Duirn, raising a hand once again; and the music began, only softly, and the elves began to sing a very wonderful song of greeting that made the hearts of all there glad and full of strength and cheer.

The young otter, who was the center of attention, danced and rolled about the fine, soft floor the elves had made, and all those present clapped and urged him on. There were many who hugged or patted him as he passed by. Morane's heart ached with love for the small pup who had filled her life in its most empty hours, and who now stood upon the point of leaving her behind, along with that part of him that was the sort of love for someone that never goes away, for it is the most secret part of all and lives on in the heart forever.

Malcom came to stand beside her, and Jahn joined them.

"Let us sit down before they think we are without manners," her mate finally managed, for he was going through the same emotions at watching his young pup cavort and mingle among the gathering of elves. They treated him as an equal, and the otter pup seemed to know everyone, although before that night, Morane knew he had never seen an elf in his short life except for Jahn.

Malcom and Jahn were led to a table and seated. Morane was placed in a seat of honor next to Duirn, who held the young otter pup on his lap.

"Now we can be comfortable and discuss what we must and

33

decide anything that might need to be decided," said the elfin king.

"You were telling us why it is an animal that should carry the object so dear to the Eolin," reminded Malcom.

Duirn stood, and Morane took her wriggling pup.

"There were black deeds done by those of elfin blood long ago, in another time when the Banskrog was again over the world. There were ancient kings who fell under the thrall of that evil, and in doing so, they gave up the right to certain powers and certain tokens which have been in the care of the Eolin since the First Ancestral Beginning. Because of greed and forgetting the true nature of the Light, those ancient forefathers of ours caused the split between races of elf and dwarf, animal and man; and the Law is written that in order to regain our true homes in the Upper Danes, we must patch the rift of all the factions that now stand divided. Hence an animal must carry the elfin secret of power until such time that it is no longer necessary."

"Why must it be him?" asked Malcom. "Surely there are a dozen other worthy animals in this community alone."

"But they are not the Olthlinden," replied Duirn gently. "We did not choose your pup. It was decided by the High King himself."

"The Olthlinden," said Jahn, "is the one who is designated to lead the Eolin. In days of old it has always been kept within our own kind; but twice now in these last times of trouble, we have had others from beyond our ranks."

"There was Aline Haydil, who was the Lady of Wicker; and then there was Yvan Earlig, the Hero of the Promise," said Duirn.

At the mention of these names, the elfin host stood as one and began to sing a lament that bordered on tears but yet was full of hope. There were elves there who played upon harp and lute and reed pipe, and when the music played, all other thought vanished. It was difficult to say if it went on for a single moment or for days.

When the song was done, Duirn turned to Morane.

"We shall escort your party to the safety of the Wood of Westing and the ancient halls of Dun Macrath. The pup shall be schooled there in all he needs to know and we shall all have the time to learn the ways that we must learn to survive the Banskrog."

"But my lovely holt," began Morane, knowing that there was no use in arguing with the elfin king.

"We shall have one prepared exactly as you like," he soothed.

"But it won't be mine," she wept.

"Oh, but it shall, Morane. There are ways we have learned of the workings of the heart. You shall hardly know you haven't lived there all of your lives before. And perhaps that is so."

Duirn looked at her then, and his eyes were a deeper blue-gray than a late autumn day. She thought she saw all of her thoughts there but couldn't be sure; and after a long time of seeing the things there she needed to see to be reassured, she forgot her sadness at leaving the holt she had dwelled in with her pup for a time. She knew that the changing of the places where she dwelled made no difference, that the true home was safely warm and forever in her heart of hearts.

When she came from that deep pool of thought and was aware of her surroundings again, Malcom and Jahn were talking to Duirn about the dangers that lurked in the woods all about them. Jahn was reporting what he had seen of the raiders from beyond the Serpent Mountains.

"We shall have need of secrecy, then," Duirn was saying. "It may be that the wisest move of all would be toward the Westing Wood and the old danes there."

"It will take us across the trail of the Serpents," argued Jahn. "Those hills are full of the raiders."

"There aren't many places left that aren't," added Malcom.

"Then we shall travel by the old Eolin road. It is protected still by the spirits of those who have gone before and who cannot depart for the High Havens until they have served out their time and the Upper Gates have been opened again."

"What road is that?" asked Malcom, his muzzle drawn into a questioning frown.

"You have probably seen it a hundred times in your travels, my friend. Sometimes it appears to be a trail that perhaps some animal has made; or then again, it might not appear to be anything at all more than a rough clearing in a wood or a ford at a stream. It ran from one end of The Barrens all the way to the Serpent Mountains, where there were dwarfish delvings once, and then down beyond the Great Western Flats, where it is said to go underside, all the way to the Sea of West Ending. It also touches the Greenleaf and runs down to the Lake of Dreary and the Dismal Swamp."

"But I've never heard of a road like that, Duirn," said Jahn. "And I know most of the old lore as well as anyone."

"You do indeed, Jahn, but there are some parts of our histories that have had to remain secret until the time was such that what had been unknown could be opened to those who had a need to know. The Eolin road is so ancient and so treacherous to use that it has been closed off to many travelers for a long time. Sometimes it is a devious route if you don't know the nature of the ones who built the road and laid it out. They were the first of the long line of the Eolin who were already under the sway of the Black Death, and they devised means by which they could protect themselves. Some of those means could be dangerous to folk who might use the road innocently, for the snares that were laid to deter the forces of the Banskrog are still there, and they would trap the innocent traveler along with one who might use the road for a more evil purpose."

"Is there no way we could go by a safer route? We don't want to put the Olthlinden into more danger than we need to."

"Your concern is well taken, Jahn, but from what you say, and by what we already know, there is no other door left open to us."

"We could just stay on here," suggested Morane. "After all this talk of all the dangers there are involved to get to somewhere else, why wouldn't it be just as simple to stay where we already are?"

Duirn was on the point of reply, when he suddenly fell silent and looked away for a long moment or two, lost in thought. Jahn was about to tell Morane that there was no other solution left to them, when the leader of the Eolin spoke again.

"I think there may be some merit to what you have said, Morane. Especially so since the Olthlinden is so small and not exactly seasoned in the ways of the world that we live in today. It might be a far wiser thing to go on with our plan of using the old road and carrying out our intent just as if we had the Olthlinden with us, for that would draw all attention away from here. It might also draw off these new raiders that have come into these parts. We might lure them into the Westing Wood to boot. That is an old wood, and there are still some of the relics of the days before there were other living things about. They are friend to the Eolin, but a dark fate awaits a stranger lost among them or one who isn't aware of the danger in making the wrong replies."

"What relics are those?" asked Malcom, a shudder of fear crossing his heart.

He had been twice into the fringes of the Westing Wood and other than the threat of the wild beasts or other expected dangers, he had never suspected anything amiss.

"They look like trees to the untrained eye," replied Duirn. "Sometimes they appear as oak or ash, or once in a great while, holly or yew. They can take any form that pleases them, but few do, and they mostly dwell there in their most natural form, which resembles a tree."

"I've heard some strange yarns about the Westing Wood," said Jahn. "That is perhaps an explanation."

"The wood wasn't always there. There was a time when a great Eolin dane was in that part of the world, but the lure of knowledge and lust for power caused an end of it all, and the Eolin who lived there were lost. They are still there in one form or another, awaiting the gates to the High Havens to open. It is said they have become as old as the others."

"I will be curious to hear more of these tales," said Jahn. "I can see that much of what I know has come from faulty sources. I am anxious to study these things more closely."

"And you shall have an opportunity to do so, good Jahn. You are to be the tutor and guide of our small Olthlinden here, since you are also charged with protecting the Pipe of Ring Parath until he can carry it. That is only as it should be."

"But I had hoped to go with you," protested Jahn.

"Not yet, my good cousin. There will be a time."

"Then we shall stay here?" questioned Morane eagerly, hardly daring to believe her ears.

"For the time being, yes. We shall be in touch. Keep to your own parts and on no account go beyond the Greenleaf or toward The Barrens. We shall put the spirits of the Eolin at sentry duty there, and once they are loosed, it would not bode well for any to run afoul of them."

"But what about the other animals there?"

"We shall warn them, Malcom. Rest easy on that account. The Shanoliel have never willfully or knowingly harmed a friend."

Duirn made a slight motion of his hand and the grand hall was gone. The friends found themselves once more outside, beneath the pale light of the stars reflected on the snow.

The elfin king bowed low to the sleeping pup, who had grown tired and climbed onto Morane's lap once more.

"Farewell for now, Olthlinden. We shall greet the time when it is written that the bearer of the Pipe of Ring Parath shall lead the armies of the Eolin against the fortress of the Banskrog, and the stars shall be blown away on the death of that passing, to be renewed again by the breath of the High King."

The Eolin raised their starlamps in salute and withdrawing as they had come, faded slowly into the darkness with a faint silver glow that lasted in Malcom's eyes long after the elves were gone.

He came to himself later when he felt Morane's paw firmly grasping his own. He turned to look down upon his mate and the sleeping pup that was no longer a simple otter but the small figure of one who would play an important role in the unfolding events that had come upon them by surprise in their easy lives, events that would sweep them all away into a maelstrom of war and revolt and terror, in the form of the Banskrog, the Black Death, that hung over the light of day and promised to drag them all into the awesome, yawning whirlwind of destruction.

He squeezed Morane's paw in return and helped her put the youngster to bed, trying not to imagine all the difficult times that lay ahead for them all, animal and dwarf, human and elf alike.

A Messenger by Firelight

IN the long weeks after the night of Duirn's visit, Malcom and Jahn went over their combined lore books, comparing maps they had either drawn themselves or gotten from others they had met in their travels. There were many evenings around the cheery hearth when Jahn would read aloud of the exploits of the Eolin or some doings from the old days at Dun Macrath, or a story or two he had heard of dwarfish doings.

Malcom found an old, worn scrap of parchment tucked into one of his knapsacks as they sat cleaning gear and drinking steaming mugs of blackberry tea one night. He had hardly given it a second thought as he removed it and laid it aside.

"What's that?" asked Morane, sitting next to her mate, with the sleeping pup on the floor in front of her chair.

"Oh, a scrap of something, I suppose."

Morane put down her mending and picked up the worn, tattered fragment.

At first it looked as though it were nothing more than what Malcom said, for the ink, which had once been blue, had darkened and run until it was difficult to see any order to any of the scratchy marks, which were in a broad, ugly hand, as if they had been done in a great hurry.

She turned it first one way, then another, then she turned it over, studying it closely, her natural otter curiosity aroused. There seemed to be a pattern to the markings on one side, and she got up to stand nearer the candles on the mantel of the fireplace.

"See if you can make any of this out, Jahn," she said finally, exasperated by her failure at being able to make anything of the strange glyphs. Morane, once her interest had been awakened, had never been one to drop anything until she had found out everything there was to know.

The elf put down the bow he was waxing and came to her side. His fine-boned hands held the parchment gingerly, and he peered closely at the stained marks on the bottom.

"It looks as though it might have been a map or chart of some sort. See? There's the legend at the bottom where they always put it on maps. It looks like it was done in some rush, though."

"That's what I thought."

"It's not elfin," went on Jahn.

Malcom lowered the gear he was cleaning and looked at the two before the fire.

"I don't know why all the big mystery. That was given to me by the lads up in the region of The Barrens two or three summers ago."

"When you were gone for so long I got worried?"

"That's the trip, dear. It was much longer than I had prepared for; and if it hadn't been for the lads in the river there, I'd have been a stump up for sure."

"What lads are those?" asked Jahn.

Malcom knitted his whiskers into a frown.

"Funny blokes, living up there on The Barrens. You'd think that all the nasty louts coming across the borders would have been enough to make them think of other quarters, but they've stuck. I think that fact alone makes them stay on, just knowing that it would be easier and safer to move on."

"What sort are they?"

"Waterkind. I don't know of any other animal that can be so long-necked."

"Well spoken," said Morane quietly, looking away from Malcom's gaze.

"But what reason did they have for giving you this?"

The elf held up the tattered parchment.

Malcom frowned, growing perplexed.

"You know, I can't recall. We had sat down to tea, I remember, and had a visit, exchanging what news we had of distant friends. We made a few comments on everything in general, and then I think I left."

"They gave you no reason or clue to what it was about?"

"Not that I can remember."

He thought longer.

"Or that may have been the visit before. I keep getting them confused."

"There was one trip that you came back from very quiet, and it took two days to get anything out of you at all. I thought you'd been hurt somehow, but that wasn't what was wrong. You just sat in your chair there and stared away into the fire."

Malcom's brow darkened and he took the mysterious parchment back from the elf, turning it one way and then another, finally spreading it out before him on the floor next to the sleeping pup. He reached up and took one of the tapers off the low table beside him and held it up so that he could see the faded marks of the old map more clearly.

One side had been an attempt, it appeared, at writing instructions, for there were references they could make out of directions and distances marked off in marches; and the other side was the roughest sort of chart, with clumsy efforts at noting rivers and mountains.

None of it was to scale or anywhere as neat and orderly as an elf chart or even one of the many maps that Malcom drew for himself of where his travels had taken him. There was a sense of urgency to the ancient paper that made him believe that whoever had drawn it had been in grave danger, and that they had had to do as best they were able in a short time.

"Does this look anything at all like the woods beyond the Serpents?" asked Malcom at last, his mind full of strange, disturbing thoughts.

"I think it's more likely down toward Dreary Lake, or perhaps the Dismal Swamp. See the notation there about the bog?"

Malcom looked again at the scribbling along the edge of the map.

"You're right, Jahn. I hadn't been able to make that out." He frowned again.

"When I was given this, one of the chaps said something about the notion that I would need information one day, and I would find it where I least expected it. They said something else about taking a trip to a place I had no idea I was going to, and that I would need to be able to show someone."

"That confuses me more than the map," said Morane. "What could any of that have to do with what place this map was drawn of?"

Malcom looked down at the sleeping pup.

"Call it what you will, I just have a feeling that this all has something to do with what has happened to us since Duirn's visit and the whole business of Olthar being the fellow to carry this Pipe of Ring Parath. Even then, as I think back on it, there was something in the way that this chart was given to me that begins to fall into place now. It was as if they knew all along."

"There are those waterfolk who are friends of the Eolin, and who share the powers that way. It must include you too, Malcom, for you and Morane have been the guardians of the Olthlinden all this while and not even known."

"I knew Malcom should never have taken up with all these strangers," said Morane, half lightly, although there was an edge of bitterness to her voice.

Jahn's gray-blue eyes sought hers, and he smiled sadly.

"There are some parts that we don't get to choose, Morane. I know the pain you are feeling and the fear for the welfare of your pup. That is a natural thing. And I don't know why we're all caught up in this affair, except that a time has come that has caught us, and these are the roles we must play out whether we like them or not."

"Morane is not feeling herself, with all the worry at this business," began Malcom, but Morane cut him short.

"I'm perfectly myself, thank you," she snapped, not realizing until she spoke how angry she was.

There had been a slow, simmering unrest troubling her for a long time, and it now came out in a torrent.

"You've spent all your time roaming around one place and

another, and you haven't had to see the pup grow or take care of him, or do any of the walking the floor late at night because he was afraid of the dark and couldn't sleep, or worry over him when he was sick. It's easy for you to be so indifferent to what all this means. Duirn says he is the Olthlinden! Easy enough for him, for that means the elves don't want anyone of their number to have to do the job of carrying this pipe of the whatever funny name, and it's all well and good for a simple otter to do it, because they don't have any better sense."

She halted to get her breath and went on before the stunned Malcom or Jahn could speak.

"Not only an otter, but a baby at that. It would have upset me enough if it had been you, Malcom. But this is beyond any good sense, and I'm surprised that you've just let it go on! He is your pup, too!"

Jahn shifted uncomfortably in his chair, and the map was forgotten for the moment.

"I understand your feelings, dear," began Malcom, but Morane picked up the small otter pup, flung the parchment into the fire, and left the room in a flood of tears.

Malcom sprang forward to retrieve the map, but it was bone-dry and vanished like kindling.

"I don't think she wants to hear about your understanding," said Jahn at last, in a soft voice.

The otter's eyes had clouded and his muzzle wrinkled into a frown.

"Well, that's that," he said finally. "This is all such strange doings. It's hard to balance any of it."

"Perhaps there is no balance. It may be that it is just a rough spot that has to be gotten over."

"I wish there was something I could do to make Morane feel better."

He laughed shortly.

"I wish there was something I could do to make myself feel better, like getting that map back."

Jahn nodded his agreement.

"They didn't say anything about all this business, and what would happen to Morane and me when they came to tell us that the pup was the Olthlinden."

"There would have been no use."

"Except we might have been warned and tried to prepare ourselves for it."

"I don't think you could, Malcom. There never seems to be

42

any warning to any of these feelings. We don't ever know they're there until they've ambushed us."

"I still wish there was something I could do to ease Morane's pain."

"I think I shall scout around outside and get some fresh air," said Jahn. "There was something about the chart that's right on my fingertips, yet I can't seem to remember what it was I'm trying to place. It looked an awful lot like some charts I saw once in an Elder's library in my old dane."

"But how would my cousins have gotten it? And from whom? And why would they have given it to me?"

"Those are questions we shall have to ask Duirn when next we see him."

"That doesn't help now."

"Then go see to your mate. I'll be late, so don't wait up for me."

Malcom sat glumly on the floor before the fire looking at the burnt pieces of the parchment, yet not seeing them. His thoughts were heavy and sad, of Morane and her words to him and the mistaken idea she had about his not loving the small chubby pup that now was the center of so much attention from forces far beyond the realm of a simple animal who had tried to make do with his life on the river and to live every day as best he was able.

He did not hear Morane come in, nor was he aware when she sat beside him.

A faint echo of a reed pipe had begun somewhere nearby, and his ears began to search for the melody it played, although it was faint and hard to trace. It seemed full of golden light and deep blue sounds, and he strained harder to find the elusive song.

There was a change that came over the fire then; and the flames burned into a white tower of moving silver-gray clouds that turned and spun themselves into shimmering forms and shapes that held the eye, and the music grew louder, taking on a more definite form. He did not feel his mate take his paw in hers, for at that moment the fire began to speak, slowly at first, in a deep, rough-edged voice, as if it were coming from very far away, echoing loudly in the small otter holt. It then grew clearer and softer.

After another moment, Malcom could make out the words clearly.

"The tidings we bring you are grim, although there is no need to fear the news or to despair at the outcome of this venture. We are with you on your errand and will help you keep the Olthlinden safe until he is of age to carry the burden he must carry to deliver the message to those who yet dwell upon the Lower Meadows who have lost hope, and who have been beset by the Banskrog."

"What is it?" whined Morane, afraid of the voice and the knowledge that it was something else to do with the fate of her baby.

"I couldn't hear what it said first," replied Malcom, becoming aware of her presence and giving her paw a reassuring squeeze, although he felt none too calm. "It must have something to do with the parchment that you threw in the fire."

"I wish I'd never seen that chart. It kept you away then, and now it has caused the fireplace to start talking."

A blue-gray cloud appeared in front of the hearth, beginning to form itself into a solid shape that took on the appearance of an otter, sleek and gray, in an odd garb that looked as though it were made of a shiny metal that reflected some invisible sun.

"It's the fellow that gave me the chart!" cried Malcom.

"The same, cousin. My name is Bor Asa in the old tongue. You may call me Bors, for it is shorter and easier to remember."

"But you're only smoke," said Morane. "What use could you be?"

"More than you may think, my lady. We are an able ally. We have been called upon in many battles long before you moved about on these fields of the Wilderness."

Jahn, coming in the kitchen hallway, was startled speechless by the apparition that stood on the hearthstone speaking to his two friends.

"Come in, good elf. We are discussing the things that need it."

"You're the one who wrote the message on the chart!" stammered Jahn.

"Always leave it to an elf to get to the bottom of a secret in a hurry," replied Bors, his handsome gray muzzle showing plainly against the darker shadows of the crested helmet he wore.

"His name is Bors," explained Malcom.

"I thought so. I was getting a strange picture in my mind of someone in armor writing a note or drawing a chart. There was a name,-but I couldn't quite catch it."

"You wouldn't have had not the lady thrown the old message into the fire as she did. The flames freed us from the parchment, and we were able to reach you easier."

"How can you help us?" asked Malcom. "If you're nothing but smoke and ash, what cause can you serve?"

"To educate the Olthlinden. That is our single purpose now. Once that is done there will be no need for us, and we shall be able to ford the Last River."

"But how will you educate our pup? That would take a live being, and take a long time at that."

"You must bring him to us," replied Bor Asa. "We shall teach him all that he shall need to know if he is to carry the Pipe of Ring Parath. That is a difficult and dangerous task, and he must know the secrets of it."

"No! I won't have my baby given over to cloud people," cried Morane.

"It is for his protection, my lady. If he does not learn the powers the pipe holds, it would be very dangerous indeed for himself and all concerned."

"You won't get him," persisted the distraught animal. "He's too young to be anywhere but here in his own holt where he belongs."

A series of changes swept through the room then; and the air grew very still and very cold, and a high, chilling cry sounded from the bottom of a dark place that lay at the depths of all silence. A shroud of gleaming black shadow loomed out of the cloud on the hearth, reaching for the three terrified friends, who stared helplessly, unable to move from their seats.

"This is one of the faces of the Banskrog," came the voice of Bor Asa. "It is growing beyond the borders once more, and it is the reason the Ring Parath were given the pipe that is to be delivered to those mortals left here in the Wilderness again. It is one of the High King's tokens that He has created to help contain the Darkness when it overflows its purpose and would sweep all into its power."

Bor Asa let the next visions speak for themselves. They all displayed clearly what happened to those who fell under the deadly thrall of the Black Death.

"If there is to be any hope at all for these Lower Meadows, it is in the voice of the Light and those who carry the secret keys to the High King's Home. The Olthlinden must be taught of these things so that we may all one day exist free of the threat of this darkness that surrounds us even as we speak."

There were other visions, and the room was suddenly horribly hot and Malcom could barely breathe.

Morane screamed in terror, and the elf was unable to move a hand to fend off the dark claw he saw groping for the otter through a fiery cloud. At the moment it reached her, all visions and noise disappeared, and only the voice of Bor Asa was left.

"You must bring the Olthlinden to the Yew Grove on the next day of the new spring. We shall begin then."

"Wait!" called Morane. "I don't want him to be taken from me!"

There was a silence; then the fire was once again only a regular fire, burning low and emitting a few sparks that crackled onto the floor and extinguished themselves.

"He won't be taken from you," came a far-off voice, barely discernible. "You shall never be away from him, in a way."

Morane strained to hear the words, but there were no more. She slumped back in her chair, exhausted from the ordeal of the visions, yet somehow reassured that the abrupt changes in her life would not be so terrible as she had expected, although she was still not at ease about any of the doings that had overtaken her previously simple, carefree life, where her only problem had been her long-absent mate.

From the looks of the signs, it was going to be far from simple or easy, and a long cry from peaceful. That, she sighed to herself silently, was probably the price she had had to pay for ever taking up with an otter like Malcom, whom she had been warned about by her parents. There never seemed to be an end to the goings-on that surrounded her and she suspected, truthfully so, that she would have been sorely disappointed if her life were anything other than what she had.

"I must remember to say what I feel," she said resolutely. "And not hold back or do something just to please somebody else."

Malcom asked her what she meant, but she nodded and smiled and said nothing.

II. TIDINGS OF ANOTHER SPRING

The Winds of Change

THERE were many moves that the young pup of Malcom and Morane remembered in those dim, early years. Jahn the elf had gone with them across the Greenleaf into the hills beyond when the beasts from the Serpent Mountains had at last found their small community. They had been lucky to escape, for many of the animals in the neighborhood were slain, and the forest was overrun with the wolves and their companions, the horrible creatures from the boundaries.

These were times that the pup liked, even though they were in grave danger always, for sleeping in the soft hemlock boughs or ferns, or the sweet-smelling balsam woods, delighted him, and it always afterward made him think sleeping indoors was stuffy and uncomfortable.

There were always the lessons which the dutiful elf would give, no matter how much he wanted to play or explore. Jahn would drag out the lore book or recite to him the history of this clan or that, and ask him endless questions about everything. The young otter liked the stories the elf told, finding them oddly familiar, although he could not say why; but there were other things to do on early summer mornings than sit and listen to the sleepy elf start on the family orders of an animal tribe that had once lived in the Wood of Westing.

"You'll need to know this one day," scolded Jahn. "My chore of teaching you all this isn't any easier than yours of learning it. You sit down there and finish your breakfast, and I'll finish my story!"

Reluctantly the pup sat, although hopeful that the lesson would soon be over. He tried hard to listen to Jahn, who had begun in earnest relating the origins of the fourth tribe of the Shanoliel, but there were ants near where he sat, and he was soon engrossed with watching them, long lines of them, struggling to load the queen's storehouses for the coming winter.

His nose was pressed almost to the ground, and twice one of

the insects marched boldly across his muzzle, never breaking its stride.

"Hello," said the pup.

"No time," replied the ant. "More of this, more of that, more of something else. We have no time. Winter is on the way."

He was on the ground again, struggling purposefully away, carrying a huge something of a brown nature which almost covered him entirely.

"You're not listening," chastised the elf. "You haven't heard a word I was saying."

"Yes, I was," protested the pup.

"What was the name of the fourth king of the Shanoliel?"

"Drane Elir," replied the otter, although he had no idea at all where that name had come from, unless it was possible to listen to someone without knowing you were doing so.

Jahn was quite startled himself, for he hadn't gotten to the point of introducing the fourth king of the Shanoliel, and had not mentioned the name. He asked the question to try to keep the pup's attention from wandering.

"How could you have known that?" blurted Jahn.

"I don't know. It just sort of said itself."

"But I haven't gotten to the fourth king yet."

"You were trying to trick me!" accused the otter.

"I was trying to get you to listen to your lessons. We don't have from now on to cover all this history. I don't really see what good it's going to do anyway, since you never listen."

Jahn was feeling the welling up of a small splinter of resentment which had been lodged in his heart when he found he was to be unable to go with Duirn, and that his task was to be to stay with Malcom and Morane to educate their pup, the Olthlinden.

No one referred to the small animal by his name for fear that someone would overhear and his presence would be made known to the agents of the Banskrog. Duirn had warned them of this danger and cautioned them about it every time he had sought them out.

"You shouldn't try to trick me."

Jahn felt a twinge of guilt at the ploy he had used on the pup, but he felt justified in his reasoning, for it was important that the pup be taught his lessons properly.

"If you want me to pay more attention, tell me stories that are interesting."

The remark was made simply and innocently, with no rudeness to the elf implied.

Laughing suddenly, Jahn bowed low to the young otter.

"You have given me the lesson for today, my young friend. I owe you amends for my rashness and for thinking that I have the only thing of import that needs knowing."

Sensing that the elf had eased up on the boring lecture, the young otter chittered excitedly.

"Can we go up the river to the old ruins, then? I'd like to look at them again, and they're part of what you need to teach me! You said so yesterday."

"We couldn't stop yesterday."

"I know. But today is fine, and we don't have anything else to do."

"Let me tell your mother, then. She'll worry if I don't."

"She's with my cousins. It'll take too long to find her. Come on! We can be there and back before supper."

"We should tell Morane," argued Jahn, looking back toward the newly built holt that Malcolm and Morane had constructed.

It was roughly done and nowhere near as nice or comfortable as their old holt on the Greenleaf, but it was snug and kept them warm and dry, and was laid out in such a way that it was big enough for the elf to move about in more freely without constantly having to stoop over. That made the roof a bit high for the otters' liking, but otherwise it would have meant building a shelter for the elf as well. None of them wanted to risk the chance of being in the grave danger of being attacked while apart, so compromises were made all around and it was decided they would all dwell together until such a time that the peril was past or until there was a change of design in the plan to educate the pup.

After the massacre at the settlement on the Greenleaf, Morane had no longer doubted the great danger they were in, but once they reached the safety of their new river home and began to go about the ordinary tasks of living there, she had fallen again into the habit of thinking that it was all going to be all right, and that the beasts which had attacked them on the Greenleaf would never find them in their new surroundings.

Jahn and Malcom had exhausted themselves trying to explain to her that the holt was merely a convenience, and that there was little likelihood that they would be staying longer than the winter. Morane had found an ally in the form

50

of her cousin Willow, whose pups were almost the same age and often played with Olthar, even though Morane's chubby son did it mostly from good manners and never seemed to enjoy the games as another otter might.

Morane had worried to the point that she had finally decided in self-defense that whatever danger there had been was over, and that she would set herself the task to make an ordinary home for an ordinary otter pup. Jahn knew that it was fear that drove Morane to continue with her charade of a normal life for her baby, and he tried to keep his lessons to the pup as quiet as possible, and as much like simple history as he could make them. He felt he was doing exceptionally well, for his pupil had finally rebelled at the boredom of it all.

It was true that they had found a safe haven far up the river away from the marauders and seemingly out of harm's way, but there were already signs even here that Malcom and Jahn knew were the omens of worse to come.

The first clue as to the impending danger was the fact that of all the animals that had settled there, each and every one had been driven there from somewhere else. It only followed that sooner or later the very thing that had found them before would do so again.

Morane told no one of the pup's strange guardians, saying no more about Jahn than offering the simple explanation that he was a friend of her mate, and that they sometimes traveled together. It wasn't unheard of, and although some of the other animals stayed away from the elf, it was more from shyness than fear. It was known to all the animals even then that the Eolin were friends to all except the Banskrog and any of those who followed the Darkness.

"Come on!" shouted the young otter, scampering away before Jahn could decide whether or not he should tell Morane they were only going for a brief jaunt and would be back for supper and most assuredly before dark. There was nothing for him to do now but duck his head and make a dash to catch up with his small charge, for the pup was away and swimming hard underwater.

Cursing at Duirn under his breath, he used all his cunning elf speed to catch up, following along the bank to keep an eye on the young animal. It was in being careful to do that that he went much beyond the limits of their ordinary trips when they were exploring. When he fully noted his surroundings again, he realized they had strayed into the very eaves of the wood beyond the last growth of the beech and hemlock and the smaller trees, and they were in the hollow caverns of the ancient oaks which grew to great heights and cut out the sunshine until only a dim, golden light reflected faintly on the leaves far above.

This was an ancient wood, the Westing, and it was full of surprises for Jahn, who was a water elf and not as familiar with the nature of trees and woods as were his cousins. The two families of the Eolin, the wood and water elves, had not been upon the closest of terms for quite a number of lifetimes, owing to misunderstandings and bitter feuds that had been the making of long-perished members of the two races.

Jahn could see, standing in the ancient temple of the ageless trees, that what the water elf felt about rivers and streams and the sea was just the same as what the wood elf felt when standing in a growth of timber that was beyond all time, and which made one automatically speak in a whisper.

The river had narrowed and narrowed again until it was no more than a few yards wide, which is what eventually drove the otter pup to the surface and into the eerie quietness of the deep green wood where he saw his friend Jahn beckoning him to come to him at once.

The elf wasn't afraid yet, although he knew there were things in this wood that would certainly be frightening. It was not in the way a beast raider or wolves would affect him, for this was a fear that was deeper still, below the awareness. There were the beings in these parts that Duirn had spoken of, the old ones who had been from the First Beginning. There were others as well that no one knew much about, except that they were dangerous. They were complete monarchs of their domains and as such were cruel and pitiless and completely without reason.

Jahn motioned for the pup to come to him more urgently. He hoped they were not so far into the inner wood that they would not be able to backtrack and find safer ground. He wanted to keep the young otter as quiet as possible so they could perhaps escape unnoticed.

"What is it?" chirped the pup loudly.

At the sound of his own voice and the unbroken, terrible stillness that lay over the wood, he fell silent, scurrying nearer his friend.

"What is this place?" he asked in a more subdued tone, barely above a whisper.

"We've gotten too far into the inner wood," replied the elf, his own voice also lowered to a breathless croak. "And what we need to do now is to go back just the way we came just as quickly and as quietly as we can."

In more normal times the pup would have argued with the elf or demanded more reasons for doing a thing a certain way, but this time, upon looking around him, he simply nodded weakly.

Sometimes the headstrong youngster drove Jahn into near frenzies of impatience; but looking at the small, frightened animal, he suddenly remembered that regardless of the heavy burden that was Olthar's to bear one day, at the bottom of it all it was merely a pup who now held up a stubby paw to take the elf by the cloak.

"It's not as bad as it could be," Jahn began, trying to reassure his small student; but at just that moment an even denser silence fell and there was no wind stirring through the ancient cathedral of the dark, huge trees. A cloud seemed to have passed over the sun, for the faint light that had been filtering through the thick umbrella of leaves above shadowed twice and then faded completely, leaving nothing but a halo of strange, glimmering silver radiance in the clearing.

The pup began a low whine of warning, whirling this way and that while Jahn tried to catch him to hold him away from any danger.

All the stories he had heard from Duirn ran through his head at the moment and he knew there was nothing he could do against the powerful beings that lived in the heart of the Westing Wood; but he determined that at least they would perish with dignity, if perish they must. He drew the small elfin dagger with his free hand and clamped the struggling pup firmly to his side, waiting.

At first there was nothing that could be detected, although the elf knew they were watched from all sides. His attention was distracted somewhat by the fiercely wriggling otter, who at that instant freed himself from Jahn's grasp. Exasperated and frightened at once, the elf made a lunge at the youngster and missed, losing his balance as he did so, falling forward onto the moldy floor of the ancient forest.

There were the rotting trunks of long-dead trees and the leaf fall of years beyond counting. The sunlight never reached this deep cavern below the giant tree's upper tops, so that it was damp and full of decaying smells, some sticky and pleasant, and some that turned the elf's stomach. These were woods that perhaps might delight his woodfolk cousins, but they frightened and repulsed him.

All these thoughts ran through Jahn's head in the blink of an eye. He was on the point of getting to his feet again when the cruel pressure began on his back, forcing him flat down on his stomach and pushing his face into the slimy mold of the pungent earth. It was not anything like a hand, for it was too large and almost covered him completely, yet that was the distinct impression it gave him in the midst of his fright.

There was no struggling against the pressure of the hard object that was slowly crushing him into the earth, and there was hardly time to cry out a warning to the pup to flee.

"Run, Olthar, run, lad! Get back to the river!"

The youngster, seeing his friend being crushed under what looked to him like a huge, gnarled tree, froze in terror for a moment, but that soon passed. He raced to the elf's side, although there wasn't much left to see of him, except his nose and forehead and the smashed green hat.

"Run, lad!" cried the elf, helpless to shoo the otter away.

"I can't leave you, Jahn."

"Go get help from your father," gasped the elf, beginning to be unable to talk from the weight that was slowly crushing him into the dank, smelly leaves.

"I won't," shouted the otter, and leapt at the thick, dark trunk that seemed to be attacking his friend.

He bared his tiny fangs and latched onto a thinner branch of the solid mass, biting down with all his might, vowing he would never let go unless he was killed, just like all the heroes he had ever heard of from the lore books, who would never surrender if they knew they were in the right or if they were trying to save a friend or a kingdom or the Light.

The last thing he remembered was a great shout of pain, or it might have been a high wind howling, as he was flung high into the air. He could hear the elf calling to him from a great distance; then there was the darkness that swallowed him up in a deep, bottomless pool.

In the Westing Wood

IT was a long time before Jahn realized that he was conscious and looking into a darkness that was outside the hazy gloom of his awareness. The unrelenting pressure was gone, leaving nothing but a sore back to mark its presence, and the smelly forest floor was replaced with the sweet-smelling scent of balsam and pine.

At a distance, he could see a misty, translucent lightness against the backdrop of the dark shadows behind, which he assumed, and rightly so, to be trees, and very tall ones at that. He followed the dark line of their shadows up and up, until at last he was able to detect a faint blueness, and in a cold distance of sky, a single star, faintly breathing.

There were sounds now, and he suddenly leapt to his feet.

He was alone and very sore from his ordeal of the mysterious attack, but he called out, very softly at first, then more loudly, as his concern for the pup grew. A bitterness descended upon his heart then, as he stood alone and lost, for the disappearance of the small animal meant he had failed in his job as guardian. Morane would never forgive him, if he ever saw her again, and the Shanoliel would be waiting for another long line of lifetimes for the proper one to carry the Pipe of Ring Parath.

At that thought, he reached into his cloak for the worn leather case that held the pipe, and his heart stopped. A low moan escaped his lips, for the case was gone.

He frantically searched through all his pockets and the secret folds of his cloak, and patted the ground in the semi-darkness, hoping he might only have dropped it nearby; but as his mind worked, he knew it was useless to search further. The pipe was gone and so was the pup. He began to realize that he was in a different place than where the strange attack had taken place, so he could not search the ground there, where the pipe must have been jostled out of his cloak.

A long, dreary feeling of dread and loneliness overwhelmed Jahn. The crestfallen elf sat back down heavily in the sweet-smelling bed of balsam and pine and hung his head wearily.

There would be no need of his going back to the settlement of Morane and Malcolm, for he would never be able to face his friends again after what had happened. There would be no future for him to return to the elfin danes of his old wood, or of any wood, for elves would only greet him with anger or pity or indifference. There was no place for him to turn, he knew, and no direction to set his feet, for all paths led only to despair and heartbreak and finally death.

Jahn cursed his luck bitterly at having survived the attack of the giants in the Westing Wood, wishing with all his heart that whatever it had been had finished the job, and he would be done with it all and wouldn't be faced with the dreary prospects he faced now. He had been humiliated and defeated. That rankled the elf so badly that it began to make him angry, which he had not been in a very long time; for elves, when they are angry, are very dangerous indeed.

The more he thought of it, the more cowardly the attack on him seemed, for anyone of any decency at all, except the beasts from beyond the borders, would have the common courtesy to at least attack face to face. That was a tactic he credited to the marauders who came from below the boundaries, yet he knew it was none of them in the old wood, for there was nothing that would be allowed in there but the strange beings who had dwelled there since there were histories to write or speak of.

Jahn put his head into his hands and tried to piece together his racing thoughts and to turn the rage he felt into some direction that would lead to action that might allow him to at least move toward a solution to all the riddles he was faced with. The pup was gone, as was the pipe. He didn't even know if the young otter was safe or not, or if the pipe had been merely lost or taken by an enemy.

All the while he had been thinking his dark thoughts, the white haze at a distance had begun to take more distinct shapes and forms, until at last he was able to detect something vaguely like an elf, although much larger, and then there were other forms there too, of animals that he was familiar with, and some others he had never seen or heard of.

A shroud of silence cloaked him then, just as it had in the inner wood. The wavering, ghostly forms began to draw nearer to him, even though he could not detect any outward form of movement. A great fear such as he had never known choked his breath off. He felt as if he were strangling, and his eyes bulged, his heart hammering in his chest.

These phantoms came on until Jahn was surrounded by their misty shapes. He grew cold and his teeth chattered, for it felt like a night in midwinter, and he even thought he could see flakes of heavy snow drifting down through the air to cover the ground at his feet.

His anger was ignited again at the thought of being captured by an enemy in the state he was in, which caused him to find his voice and cry out brashly.

"You have me at a disadvantage, friends. I am unarmed, as you can see. If it is the custom among your kind to slay helpless victims, then set to! If not, give me something that I may defend myself with, and I'll try to make a fair accounting of myself."

His voice seemed to be absorbed by the mist, and he wasn't sure that the things, whatever they were, had understood him.

The figure that looked like a large elf began to evaporate, then it ballooned up again in the form of a great horned stag.

These changes were startling to Jahn, but he tried to hold his ground as best he could under the circumstances. He spoke again, directing himself to the newly appeared specter of the huge animal.

"I can't call you by name, for I know it not. I am Jahn Spray, son of the Eolin, friend of all save the Banskrog. I have come to these parts with no harm in mind for anyone, to simply watch over the otter pup Olthar, who is disappeared, to my discredit. If you object to my presence on these terms, then I am obliged to say that it is my own misfortune which has delivered me into the hands of such enemies."

When the elf was badly frightened, he took on a calm air about him and became extremely formal in his speech.

The silence fell thickly about him again. There was no indication that the spectral white mist forms had heard or even acknowledged his presence. A fine white snow began to lodge on his shoulders and cover the ground all about him, but the elf did not move or notice, never taking his gaze off the form of the stag.

As he stood waiting for some sort of reply, Jahn racked his brain for any clue as to what these phantoms might be and how he might best deal with them. He could come up with nothing that was of any help to him, so he began again with all the courage he could muster.

"I know not your names, nor your purpose. Mine is to find my young charge, an otter pup by the name of Olthar. It is of

57

the utmost urgency that I retrieve him from wherever he is and deliver him home safely. We shall also be guarded by the Shanoliel, who are protecting us. Duirn is the king whose service I am sworn to. He will not take it lightly that I have been set upon by enemies, for that shall make them his enemies as well."

At the mention of the Shanoliel and Duirn, a slight warmth was felt through the chill of the gathered white mist forms.

Feeling he had gotten some response, Jahn hurriedly pressed on.

"Duirn isn't far behind. He will be looking for us. It would go easier on you now if you would give back the pup and the pipe. Duirn is not one to have as an enemy."

The leaden atmosphere cleared a small bit and there were sounds as if the wind were beginning in the topmost branches of the trees. Jahn could see that the mouth of the stag was moving in time with the strange noise, but he could make nothing of the sounds.

The elf shook his head.

"I can't understand what you're saying."

There were odd noises and creaking sounds that might have been the trees around the glade, but the wraith went on, voicing some tongue that was alien to the elf's ears.

After a time of trying hard to understand the words, if words they were, Jahn asked if there were any there who spoke the old High Tongue of the elves, He asked in that language and spoke it haltingly, but clearly. There were not many uses for the High Tongue, so the only purpose it ever served was in speaking to Duirn once in a great while, when the leader of the Shanoliel was in attendance.

A fuzzy idea had begun to form in Jahn's head.

"Are you the spirits of the Shanoliel which have been set out to guard the wood?"

This question seemed to get no response and left him guessing as to what direction to go next.

"Are you the Old Ones?"

The stag vaporized instantly, and a vast array of dull, grayish forms flickered across the darkness. Then there was a huge gnarled form that seemed to faintly glow with a reddish-gold band of light about the upper parts. It looked to be a tree of sorts, although it was not of a nature that the elf was familiar with.

"What do you wish with the Old Ones?" asked a voice quite

plainly, in a tone that sounded of great age and despair and mockery.

Too startled to reply at first, the elf at last regained his senses.

"My name is Jahn Spray," he began, but the voice cut him short.

"We know who you are."

"And may I ask whom I am speaking to?"

"You may ask, but there is no reply. My names are too long to tell in a lifetime."

Jahn took a step nearer the willowy form.

"Do you have the small otter that was with me before?"

There was a pause, then the voice seemed to be speaking to someone Jahn could not see.

After a time, he asked again.

"We have the otter safely hidden. The others have asked that I tell you that. We had thought at first that you were attacking the pup. That was when you were held down so roughly. It wasn't meant as harm. We were just trying to rid our hearth of any unpleasant sorts."

"I was trying to protect him from you, whoever you are!"

There were more grumbling noises. It sounded to Jahn as though the original voice had been joined by more of the same.

"We shall tell the youngster that you are well. Now you will find your way clear to depart."

"But I can't leave without Olthar! Take me to him!"

"That would be impossible."

"You must take me. I can't return to his mother without him."

"He will not return to his mother again in this life. You must understand that."

Upon hearing these words, Jahn's heart fell. He thought of Morane, waiting by the kitchen fire for the pup to come home to supper.

"Then you must kill me," he said, his voice empty.

There was too much pain there for him to think of, and again he cursed his luck.

"You will not be slain by our likes. That is not necessary."

"Then take me to the pup."

Another voice had joined the first.

"The Eolin have always befriended us. We have no quarrel with you, Jahn Spray, so be off! We cannot take you where we go now. It is given that we shall have the duty of keeping the pup safely, for the times are grave. There is no longer any place that you know where he would be able to live until his errands have been done."

"I am the one who was given the duty of holding the pipe until it was to be given to the Olthlinden. That was set down in the Law."

There were more voices conversing now in the slow, rumbling noises that sounded to Jahn like a thunderstorm in the forest.

At last, and after much foot shifting on his part and another long wait while the being took on a new form to speak, Jahn was addressed in formal tones.

"The elf Jahn Spray has met and fulfilled his obligations to the Eolin and to the Olthlinden. There is no dishonor."

His anger began to rise again as he thought of having to tell Morane and Malcom that the pup had been taken by the Old Ones in the Westing Wood and that there had been nothing he was able to do. That was the truth, but it rankled him badly.

It had been a long time since he had had to face the fact that he was powerless over all of the events that occurred in his life, and he could do nothing about anything except his reaction to them. That was all he could truly control, but he was too angry to remember that now. His ego was too bruised and the genuine feelings at the bottom of his heart were all the things he felt at the disappearance of the pup.

"He's too young to be by himself," protested Jahn. "He's hardly more than a slip of a lad!"

"Young?" questioned the voice, now speaking from the misty figure of a wild boar.

"Not old," explained Jahn. "He's barely three turnings old."

Age was a forgotten subject among the beings that dwelled in the Westing Wood. There was never any reference to it, and they no longer had a word for it. It was not an unusual occurrence for a conversation among themselves to go on for what Jahn would have measured off in turnings, as he called them, which were years by common measure.

"You others may not need anyone to comfort you or tell you bedtime stories, but when you're dealing with a very young pup you will have to know these things. You'll have to be able to play with him as well, and go for long rambles with him, like I was on when you found us. He is also full of questions about everything. In fairness to him, they should all be

60

answered honestly and fully. He also gets frightened easily, as he probably is now, not knowing where his friend has gotten to."

Jahn paused to catch his breath and to see if his speech was having any effect on the ancient beings. There was more murmuring and sighing, like wind through a winter forest, and many rumbling noises, as if someone were disagreeing. This went on for some space of time, how long the elf could not be sure because he became mesmerized by the snoring voices that rose and fell, then drifted easily or faded beyond hearing, leaving a silence so total and complete that he had to clear his own throat nervously just to hear a sound in the vast void that enveloped him.

Without any preliminaries or explanations, the startled elf found himself caught up in what felt like brambles, although he could not say for sure, and there was a queasy sensation of movement. He protested loudly, but to no avail, and the motion increased until he had to simply hold his mouth clamped tightly shut to keep from becoming sick. This went on for a time, up and down, his hands and face scratched by the rough limbs and branches that enclosed him.

Somewhere in his mind the idea formed that he was held in some great fistlike affair, although it was certainly not the ordinary idea of what a fist was, but rather what one would look like if you imagined a being large as an oak that had regular branches for arms, and something on the end that might pass for a hand.

Over the sensation of being sick, Jahn felt relieved that his speech had reached the odd beings. He was certain that he was on his way to wherever the pup was held.

As the movements slowed and his stomach left his throat, Jahn spoke again.

"Isn't it about time that someone told me what this is all about? I'm not used to being handled this way. One might have the common courtesy to at least tell me what's going on!"

He doubted that the ancient beings who dwelled in the Westing Wood had any notion of courtesy or any other concept beyond their own codes, whatever those might be.

There was another long, uncomfortable stretch where he thought he might be sick again, then there was a loud, bumping sound, and he blinked in rapid succession, quite abruptly finding himself being hugged stoutly by the small otter pup, who was on the verge of crying, but working very hard at holding back his sobs.

61

Captured

MALCOM had been out all day upon an errand, and it was a worried and frightened Morane that met him at the holt door when he returned home after dark.

"Are they not with you?" she asked anxiously, peering into the shadows behind her mate with such intensity that it caused Malcom to grow quite alarmed, although he tried not to show it for fear of upsetting her further.

"They left early this morning, and I haven't heard or seen anything of them since. This isn't like Jahn. He always has the pup home long before now because he knows I worry so. And if they are ever out after dark, he always tells me they will be late."

"He may have just lost track of time, my dear," encouraged Malcom. "The pup is forever wanting to look into new things. I'm sure they just forgot the time. They'll be along presently. Let's get the things ready for supper. I'm sure that by the time we have the table spread, they'll both be here half-starved."

Morane lingered at the door a while longer, wringing her paws. She could not say what it was that was bothering her exactly about the fallen gloom of the evening. It was the absence of her pup and the elf, she knew, but that was an open reason for anxiety. There was something else she had felt off and on all day. It had seemed to disappear at times, when she went into the garden behind the holt or while she was chatting with one or another of their neighbors, but the minute she was alone again, the feeling of uneasiness returned.

"There's something wrong, I just know it," she murmured softly.

She set out the table for their supper, laying all the regular places, stopping every few minutes to listen to see if she could hear the pup's voice raised cheerfully as he came through the outer doorway of the holt or perhaps the reed pipe that the elf played when they were on their rambles together.

Nothing moved but the wind, which had come up as night had fallen, rustling restlessly through the dark trees. It was not unusual for the wind to be up at that time of year, but there seemed to be something out of the ordinary about it that Morane could not quite put her paw on.

Every few minutes she would leave the snug kitchen and hurry down the passageway to the outer hall, holding her breath and straining to hear any other noise except the mournful sighing of the wind, which seemed to her to be gaining strength.

"There's a storm brewing," said Malcom, going to the fireplace and stoking up the burning wood until it blazed again in a merry, warm shower of sparks. "The lads will be lucky if they don't get soaked."

Pinning down the danger to the risk of being caught out in an early spring rain seemed to Malcom less disturbing than just wondering at all the other possibilities that slowly crowded in upon his agitated thoughts.

He had not forgotten all the many trips that he and Jahn had made and all their grim discoveries. He well recalled their last move, and the ugly brutes from beyond the boundaries, and the savage wolves howling in pursuit; and the close calls that they had had before finally settling into the holt in which he now sat before the fire, warm and safe from the elements. Yet he felt greatly ill-at-ease, with a nagging doubt gnawing constantly at him about the mysterious absence of his pup and close friend.

Malcom knew that Jahn was a most experienced woodsman, and there was no stouter heart anywhere than the one that beat in the chest of the elf, but his mind kept turning to the horrible visions of the half-man beasts with all their great numbers.

Morane had gotten up from her chair for the twentieth time, pacing into the hallway, when they both heard the soft knock at the holt door. They remained frozen for a moment, looking at each other; then the tapping sound came again, more distinctly over the wind.

"It's odd that they would be knocking," began Malcom, already on his way to see to the door.

Morane, suddenly overcome with a sense of fear that almost caused her to lose her balance, hurried along after Malcom, grasping her mate by the paw and holding him back.

"Don't," she was barely able to whisper.

He turned and looked in astonishment at her, but the wide,

horrified eyes and desperate plea in her upturned muzzle shook his resolve.

"I must see who it is, my dear," he said gently. "It may be some news of our two gypsies."

"I'm afraid," she whispered, her voice barely reaching his ears.

He looked at her for a moment longer, patting her reassuringly.

"I must see who it is. There may be news."

Morane burst into tears and fled from the hallway.

With a halting pace, Malcom went to the outer holt entrance and slowly opened the heavy wooden door.

He had half expected to see one of the animals who were their neighbors, or perhaps Duirn, who was always appearing in quite unexpected ways and at odd hours. Instead there was a stocky wood elf, accompanied by a dwarf, both dressed in dark green cloaks and hoods.

They bowed low, introducing themselves before Malcom could collect his wits or utter a word.

"Our service, Master Otter. We have come from a mutual friend seeking counsel. This is my companion, Alar Far. I am Trane."

The wood elf bowed low again.

"Malcom," returned the otter. "May your trails ever end in peace and warm hearths. Come in."

The two did as they were bidden, and entered the holt, making a great noise of knocking their boots clean of mud and taking off their cloaks.

Malcom noticed that they were both dressed alike, which struck him as unusual, one being a dwarf and the other a wood elf. They wore gray tunics and short knee pants with leather leggings over their boots, and each carried a small sword and dagger and had a short bow strapped to his back.

"It looks like rain," muttered the dwarf, Alar Far. "I'm glad enough of a roof this night."

"Very," agreed the wood elf. "Oh, very, very glad."

Malcom called out to Morane that they had visitors, but she made no reply.

"My mate is quite upset tonight," he explained. "Our pup and a good friend have not come home from their daily rambles, and they are quite overdue."

The wood elf looked quickly at his companion, an odd light shining in his eyes.

"They are late you say?"

64

"Quite late. They are never so late as this."

"Then perhaps they have stayed the night with some of their friends," offered Trane.

Malcom knitted his whiskers into a slight frown.

"That would answer. I don't think they would have done such a thing without letting us know, though."

"It may have been the storm," suggested Alar Far. "That might explain it."

The two companions exchanged looks again and seemed to be in great high spirits over something.

"Come in, please," said Malcom, leading the newcomers into the kitchen.

"Morane," he called again. "We've got visitors."

He motioned to the two plates set out for Jahn and his pup.

"You may as well put the food to some use at least. We'll make do for the wanderers when they get in."

A dark smile crossed Trane's fair features momentarily, and it was noticed by Malcom, who thought perhaps it was merely a smile of relief from being out of the weather, next to a warm hearth where there was hot food.

Trane and Alar Far sat down to the table eagerly, making short work of the meal, eating loudly and without conversation. Malcom was kept busy running back and forth filling plates or mugs, and he was wishing fitfully that Morane would return to help him with these guests who had such appetites. When she did, in fact, come into the kitchen, her eyes were red and swollen from crying.

"This is my mate, Morane," introduced Malcom. "She is very upset by the absence of her pup."

The two visitors rose and bowed low to the otter, and hastened to try to allay her fears.

"I was just telling Master Malcom that they have probably decided to spend the night with friends rather than risk being outside. Listen!"

Trane paused, cocking his head and listening to the howling wind outside, mixed now with the sound of hail and rain on the holt roof.

"Oh," whispered Morane, looking to Malcom for comfort. "I hope it is so. I do hope that is so."

She clasped her paws in her apron, and not knowing what else to do to hide her great agitation, she went to the hearth and stirred the porridge and put on more water for tea.

"I'm sure they are in good hands," said Alar Far. "Why, by this time, they are probably as warm and toasty as us."

The dwarf uttered a little bark of laughter that could have been confused with a cough.

"I'm sure they are," agreed Trane. "Things couldn't be better, to my way of thinking. We have traveled all this way for nothing, except that we have had an excellent meal in the process and have gotten in out of the weather."

Malcom turned to the wood elf and studied him closely by the lamplight that filled the room with a warm, golden glow. Trane was slight of build and smaller than Jahn, although the features were much the same. The wood elf was darker and seemed quite restless, his hands being constantly in motion, picking up a fork or knife or twisting his fingers through the folds of his napkin, or fiddling with the dagger at his belt.

Alar Far, the dwarf, was of about the same height, only squat and powerful, his black curly hair hanging down from his head in thick bunches, cropped off crudely at shoulder length.

It was the eyes of the dwarf that began to worry Malcom. They were not quite right in their appearance and gave the impression of seeing two things at once. When Alar Far looked directly at him, he also looked in another direction at once.

It took a short while before Malcom could decide upon which of the dwarf's eyes to look while talking to him, which was very disconcerting. He at length gave that up, and simply addressed the table as if he were finding something of great interest there.

"You said you came from a mutual friend?" said Malcom, growing uneasy.

"Oh, yes, yes indeed," replied Trane. "We have come from a very close mutual friend who feels the importance of the pup a most serious concern and who shares your worry almost as much as his own mother."

Malcom raised an eyebrow.

"And who is this?"

Alar Far interrupted before Trane could answer.

"It is someone who has known you since your old dwelling beyond these parts."

"You are very mysterious, good dwarf. Speak out his name. Is it Duirn or Bor Asa, or one of our cousins from another wood?"

Trane and Alar Far looked at each other again, smiling slightly.

"No, no, none of them. They are all good guesses, but it is not them."

Morane, growing exasperated and short-tempered because of her anxiety, snapped out peevishly.

"Speak a name, if you have one. If you've just said that about a mutual friend to gain a roof and something to eat, no one will hold that against you. We wouldn't turn anyone out on a night like this."

"Do you hear, friend? Oh, good Alar Far, they would not turn us out."

"That's good, Trane. That was very good. Oh, it wouldn't do for us to be turned out."

The wood elf and dwarf broke into a short, ugly laugh.

"No indeed, it would never do."

Malcom, bristling, rose from his chair.

"See here, Master Elf, this is no polite way to treat your hostess. And you, good dwarf, you seem to have forgotten the good manners of your kindred. If you insist on rudeness, then I shall have to ask you to exit this holt immediately."

This was too much for the wood elf, and he burst out laughing, slapping his hands upon his knees.

"We'll have to exit the holt!" he cried, between fits of laughter, then went off into fresh gales of short, choking bursts of amusement.

Alar Far sat red-faced, holding his mirth to himself, every once in a while tipping back his head and giving forth a savage bark that would have sounded to any who heard it more like a snarl than a laugh.

Malcom had at first been angry at the breach of manners by the strangers, but he now began to grow frightened. Blustering to hide the growing unease, he demanded again to know who the friend was who had sent them, and why they insisted upon being so rude.

"Well, aday, rude we are," snapped Trane. "It is all over now anyway, so we can let you in on our little joke."

The wood elf looked at Alar Far, laughing again, a bitter, dry sound that rang in hollow echoes in the warm kitchen of the otters.

"Alar Far and I were sent to fetch your precious pup and his parents to answer to the Queen herself. We've been on your trail now since the night that the cursed Shanoliel first came to you. We had our ears out then and heard and saw much of what was going on, and guessed the rest."

The dwarf coughed out another short bark of laughter.

67

"And here we are with you all tied up in a package as pretty as you please, and from your report of your pup and friend being late for supper, I think I know the meaning of that as well."

"It must be either Olain or Oloth," said Trane. "We came in three parties to be sure we had all the exits of this little hole covered so there would be no chance of a mistake."

Morane had burst into tears and was trying to brush past the dwarf into a side cupboard, but he roughly held her and shoved her back into the kitchen.

Malcom lunged at Alar Far, but he was knocked senseless by Trane, who had drawn his shortsword and clubbed him with the flat of the blade. Morane shrieked, falling on the unconscious body of her mate, sobbing hysterically.

"We have work yet to do here," growled Trane. "See to it that the cages are outside and ready."

"This will be a pleasant surprise for the Protector."

"Oh, yes, gentle dwarf, it will do nicely. We must have them alive to torment the young Olthlinden with. Exquisite, is it not? Such delicious pain, good dwarf. Our queen is very clever in thinking of these things."

"I'll put them in the cages then."

"Yes, good soul, do just that. I'll search the rest of this miserable rat nest and see if there's anything of interest here."

He moved out of the room as he spoke, leaving Alar Far to kick Morane savagely off the fallen body of her mate, and she put up such a desperate struggle that he ended up having to bind her tightly with a length of rope that Malcom had used at times on his travels.

Having fought until she was no longer able to continue, Morane lay panting, helpless and full of such a white-hot rage that she thought she would surely perish on the spot. Her breath caught heavily in her throat, and although she was a gentle, loving soul who had never wished harm upon anyone in all her long life, she wished with all her heart that she could free herself just long enough to plunge a sword into the squat body of the cruel dwarf, and keep doing so until the vile creature could move no more.

Thoughts of her pup being caught by friends of these two drove her into another frantic struggle against her bonds, but Alar Far came back from outside, where he'd made ready one of the cages for Malcom. He gave her a violent kick that caused her to see stars flash across her vision, and she finally could remember nothing but a dark cloud coming nearer and nearer to her, until at last it swallowed her in its terrifying maw and she remembered no more.

Trane and Alar Far finished their work quickly, hauling the two senseless otters outside and shutting them into the cages that the Varad soldiers had carried. The ugly warriors made cruel jests among themselves as they poked and prodded the helpless animals, finally hoisting the cages and setting off toward the east, making their way to their main battle camp, which was at the foot of the Black Mountains.

The dwarf torched the cheerful holt; he and the wood elf waited until they were sure it was burning before they turned their faces away toward their next objective, which was to rendezvous with the others of their party so that the capture of the Olthlinden would be complete; they knew the Dark One would be pleased with their work. They talked between themselves of the great promotions and favors they would enjoy once they got their prizes delivered to Dorini; and talking of these things made them full of great good humor, which they displayed by taking turns at tormenting one or the other of the poor crestfallen otters, Malcom and Morane.

The darkness of that night was nothing to the black despair that had settled over the animals' hearts, crushing all hope from their lives.

The Pipe of Ring Parath

IN the tall shadows of the ancient wood, Jahn lay beneath the shade of a tree reading aloud from the thick book.

They were in the ruins now of the most ancient fortress of Dun Macrath. He had not known where the Old Ones had been bound when they were first acquainted with them, or to what purpose he and the pup would be used. Jahn had not even known if they were to be held forever or freed.

The time had gone on in trickling spurts, made obvious by the pain the pup went through about not being able to return to his mother and father; but as that began to dim, and the Old Ones began to weave their healing magic about the disturbed heart, little by little the passage of time was not so noticeable. Only the news which was brought by one method or another ever reminded Jahn or the otter that any time at all had passed since the day they had first come into the inner sanctuary of the Westing Wood.

The days were filled with sleepy, dreamlike stories told by the ancient beings of the woods, who sometimes used the voice of the wind to speak, or the singing of the birds in the trees, or the sound of the brook running through the deep silence of the rocks. Jahn and Olthar would hardly notice where they were on these enchanted days, and it was all they could do to simply keep their eyes open, so heavy-lidded were they. Many days went by in this manner without any real sense of time passing by at all.

It had gone on like that for what seemed to Jahn a full life span or two when it was announced that they were moving to Dun Macrath. That had at once surprised him and somehow disappointed him, for he had grown used to the lingering spell of the Old Ones, and this move signaled an end to that dreamlike trance, and meant that there was something else afoot.

The pup, once he had gotten over his homesickness and the fear at being away from his parents, grew to love the snoring sounds of the talk of the Old Ones, and he told Jahn that their stories were ever so much better than the ones the elf used to tell.

"They would be, if you could remember them," said Jahn, his feelings vaguely hurt.

"But that's the best. They are wonderful, and I can't remember a thing afterward!" cried the pup.

Jahn thought about that, but had to give it up for it grew too deep for him, and it was difficult to stay awake.

"They say we are moving to Dun Macrath. That means we shall probably see the Shanoliel."

"Will Duirn be there?" asked Olthar.

"I hope so."

"In that case, it will be fun."

"It also means that something else is in the wind."

The small animal frowned, growing more subdued.

"Do you think my mother and father might be there?"

Jahn shook his head, patting the otter gently.

"I don't know, old fellow. I don't know what I think anymore."

"Maybe they can tell us," said the pup.

The Old Ones were always referred to as "them," for the elf

had found out that they had spoken the truth, and that their names were much too long for a mere mortal to ever repeat in a lifetime, even if he were a fast talker and kept at it day and night.

When they had first come to the ruins of the old elfin dane, the wood had been thin and sparse around the outside walls, now broken and tumbled; but with the arrival of the Old Ones, the forest had grown in size into an impenetrable thicket that even the small otter had trouble getting through.

They had said it was a good protection from any intruders. Jahn, who was nimble and very adept at moving about without fuss, knew it was so. Knowing the things he knew about the beasts from the borders and all the other dangers there were, he was glad enough to be fenced in by the ancient beings of the Westing Wood.

"Do you think they might be there?" persisted Olthar, until one of the Old Ones had answered, his slow and ponderous speech becoming speeded up enough so that the mortals could understand.

"Your mother and father will not be at Dun Macrath. They are far away."

"But where?" continued the pup.

"It would do you no good if I were to give the answer, small one. There will come a time for it. It is not now."

No matter how he pressed or argued, there was no further word on the subject and all that came from the snoring, sighing voices of the Old Ones was the stories once more of all that had been and was, and on to what would be.

Jahn tried a question of his own one afternoon after the Old Ones had moved them to Dun Macrath.

"Will Duirn return here?"

He thought his question had not been heard, and after a long, silent wait, he was ready to ask again.

"Duirn is always here," came the reply.

"But we haven't seen him," protested Jahn.

"You have not tried."

"What?" shot the exasperated elf, who never grew used to the rambling answers.

"You will see."

Before Jahn could press his question further, the broken walls and turrets of the ancient dane underwent a profound change. From the fallen ruins the sound of the pipe began, which the Old Ones had kept safe. It sounded from everywhere at once, filling the air with that profound, heartening sound that lifted the heart and pulled an exhausted soul from the brink of despair.

They had never said outright that they had the Pipe of Ring Parath, but Jahn knew they carried it safely with them, and was glad of the chance to turn that heavy responsibility over to someone else.

As he and Olthar watched, the same shapes and forms began to grow in the air as had appeared all that time before when he and Malcom had been here, and when he had been given the task of carrying the pipe.

As the images began to settle into place and the walls of the old dane were once more restored, Duirn's voice reached Jahn's ears.

"Well met, Jahn. You have reached us in good time."

"No thanks to us," the elf grumbled. "It seems we've been carted around and about a long way since we last spoke."

"And much has been afoot. We have just returned from the old settlement of Morane and Malcom. The Banskrog has been there before us. There is nothing left of the holt or any sign of any other living thing there."

The pup, his small muzzle wrinkled into a painful frown, looked steadily at Duirn.

"They were not slain. That much is certain. We think they have been taken alive by the beast warriors and are being held captive somewhere. We tracked a group of the raiding party as far as the edge of the Westing Wood, but they went on farther."

Jahn shook his head, his feelings numbed by the news.

"I thought at least they would be safe. I had dared to hope so. It seemed as though it was a cruel enough blow to have lost their pup."

"As long as they are alive, we have hope," said Duirn. "I think I see a method to their actions. Dorini has begun to see that there is a concerted effort being thrown against her now. Before it has been random, and there has been a long period where she has had everything her own way."

Jahn looked at the otter to see how he was taking the news of his parents' capture by the Darkness.

"You believe they are still alive then?" he asked, wanting to reassure himself as well as Olthar.

"From all the signs that were left around the holt, it can only be that they were taken prisoner. There were others in the settlement not so fortunate. We found their remains where they were slain on the spot."

Duirn paused, a dark frown spreading across his fair features.

"I am afraid the Dark One knows of the Olthlinden, and who and where he is."

"Or was," corrected Jahn. "And would have been, if it had not been for our meeting with the Old Ones in the Westing Wood."

"Exactly. It was as I had feared all along. Someone was watching the night I first came to you, and when Dorini heard of it, she began to search about for the reason that all the fuss was being made over a simple otter family."

"Do you think we are safe here?"

"For the time being," replied Duirn, who was alone this time, and had no court that followed him. "But we must begin to think of somewhere else to keep the pup until the time comes for us to move."

The wind sighed, and many groans and creaking sounds arose from the thick wood that surrounded Dun Macrath.

"I don't think the Old Ones agree with your plan. They protest almost violently for them. I haven't heard such an uproar the whole time we have been here."

The noise increased, and the wind began to fairly howl through the high windows and archways of Duirn's spell of the ancient ruins.

"I shall attend to them now. Excuse me."

In an instant, the leader of the Shanoliel vanished into thin air, taking with him the outward illusion of the old halls as they had been in the golden days of the Beginning when all things were still new and the Darkness had not yet begun to spread its shroud over the infant worlds.

The pup grasped Jahn by the hand, struggling to keep his voice steady.

"Do you think it's true, Jahn?"

"If Duirn says so, it is. But there is hope, if they yet live."

A strange look passed over the young otter's innocent features then, and his eyes seemed to harden.

"We shall have to save them. I am going to grow to be a strong warrior so I can rescue them from Dorini."

Jahn didn't know whether to laugh at the pup's seriousness or to weep at hearing the bitterness in his young friend's voice.

"Well," he said, "it would have been better to have had a little more time as a youngster, but since it has come to this, I guess there's no helping it. It has been a long haul since all this started, and I guess there aren't too many folks anymore who get to avoid dealing with what's going on in the world now."

"Will you come?" asked the small animal, his eye studying his friend.

Jahn looked steadily at the pup, his heart torn by the likeness he saw there of Malcom, his old traveling companion.

"For as long as I am able to be of use," he replied. "And for as long as you'll have me."

"Then that will be for as long as we both shall live," replied Olthar, and Jahn saw the strange look that Morane had seen long before. It was at once old and ageless, wise and innocent, and it made Jahn's heart remember all the sadness and joy there was or would be on the road home to the Upper Meadows.

As the elf stood thinking these things, Duirn reappeared, bringing with him all the past glory of the ancient dane of Dun Macrath. The three once more stood in the splendid white feast hall, drowned in the soft golden light and surrounded by the woven tapestries that moved and trembled in a life of their own, telling of the long, proud history of the Shanoliel.

Their king seemed more drawn, and older.

"Well, I have found out some news, right enough, but it is not the best."

Duirn paused, studying the otter.

"The Banskrog does have Morane and Malcom for certain. The Old Ones have heard it from the other, younger trees, who have heard it from the very forest that surrounds the holt of our young friend here. The Old Ones heard the gossip days ago, but were not going to tell it yet. They saw no need then."

"And now?" asked Jahn.

"I have an idea what the Dark One has in mind. It is ever the way she works. If you have powerful enemies, you find ways to immobilize them by having some hold over them so that they lose their will to fight."

Jahn clenched his fists and ground his teeth in helpless rage.

"It is a cowardly way to deal," he managed at last, suddenly remembering Olthar, and not wanting to upset him any more than necessary.

"It is all right, Jahn. I understand why the Darkness has taken my parents. It shall not keep me from doing everything

I am able to save them, if ever a time comes that I shall be able to try."

Duirn smiled at the otter.

"There shall be a time, and not long hence."

"Then I will welcome it."

"What did the Old Ones say about staying here? Is that what they were upset about?"

"They feel it is getting too dangerous to stay in the Westing Wood. They are never in any danger, for there is nothing that can harm them, but they say that the real threat for us is to be cut off and surrounded by the Darkness so that we can't get free. I think I understand their point. We could go on staying here, but when the time came for the Olthlinden to carry the pipe into battle, there would be no chance to escape. I can go and come as I please, for that is the right of the Eolin, but I cannot take the Olthlinden or even you, Jahn."

"Why not?" questioned the pup. "You bring all these other spells and travel as freely as you please."

"It is the Law, my young friend. I can only take those with me who already have the powers to do so on their own. Otherwise I would lose them all, if I abused them. Everything would be in a fair mess if that were the case; for I would surely make a mistake somewhere and create much unnecessary pain and suffering for someone."

"Then what are we to do?"

Jahn's face had taken on a worried frown.

"If we can't stay here, then where shall we make for? Do the Old Ones say where we should go?"

"Toward the sea," replied Duirn. "They say the way is toward the West Roaring."

Jahn shook his head.

"That's a big stretch of water. Do they say anywhere in particular?"

"The Beak. That's all I could get out of them."

"The Beak?" echoed Jahn and Olthar together.

"I can draw you a chart of the land that lies between here and the sea. There is nothing that says I can't do that or that I can't help you with scout reports of the enemy, and shoot a little fireworks once in a while to perhaps ward off some of the louts who might see fit to set upon you."

"Are we to leave so soon?"

"The Old Ones feel the danger is growing every day. They listen to the other tree souls who are spread all around, and it seems that there are many of the beast armies afoot and closing in on the Westing Wood even now."

"We aren't very well armed to deal with all of that," said Jahn darkly.

"You will have the pipe. That is the main thing you shall need to keep you safe."

"The Old Ones hold that."

"No longer."

Duirn reached into his cloak and drew forth the small object, handing it carefully to the pup.

Jahn looked in amazement at the leader of the Shanoliel.

"He is to carry it? So soon?"

"The time has come," said Duirn gently, a strange light shining in his eyes.

"All this time," mumbled Jahn, shaking his head. "We had never dared dream it, but now it is upon us. No fanfare, no great moment, just three friends in the ruins of Dun Macrath. All at once it is begun."

Duirn laughed, a sound at once full of tears and joy.

"It is begun," he repeated, as the small animal took the pipe and held it to himself, looking earnestly up at his two companions.

Jahn thought he could see many things in that small face, and there were things there that frightened him and made him sad, but mostly it was all a sort of feeling that made his heart sing and the weariness drop away.

"The Olthlinden," said Duirn, bowing low.

"The Olthlinden," repeated Jahn, bowing in his turn.

When he looked up again, there was only a faint trace of the small pup he had come to know so well. It was as though the accepting of the pipe had aged him in the passage of those few seconds, and his eyes were as old as Duirn's.

"Well, it is done," said Duirn. "I shall see you next as soon as I find a way out of the woods that will be the safest for you."

With no further word, the two companions were left alone, Olthar holding the pipe and lost in his own thoughts, and Jahn torn between feelings of overwhelming joy and bitter grief.

An Erling Warrior

IN a quiet circle of the Westing Wood that was at the very forest's edge, near the beginning of a forlorn, waterlogged place called The Mires, Duirn and his elfin host poised to strike at a large war party of Varad soldiers. There were hundreds of the ugly, savage warriors, along with their wolves, who roamed about behind the raiding parties in huge packs to feast off the slain of the battles.

There were also some new soldiers in attendance that the elf had never seen before. These were even larger than the Varads and kept to themselves.

Duirn studied these new enemies closely, noting that they were armed with larger swords and longer bows. The arrows that were in the quivers of the beasts must have been three yards long, and their tips were savagely barbed and jagged so that a wound from one would almost certainly be fatal.

They numbered fewer than the Varads, but it was still upsetting for Duirn to see them. He could only conclude that if there were a few here, there would be more elsewhere, and that as time went on they would go on growing in numbers, just as the Varads had.

"What do you make of those new creatures?" asked his friend Emeon.

"I don't know what to make of them. Have you ever run across them in any of your forays?"

"Never. I thought we had reached the worst with the Varads."

"The Banskrog never sleeps, my friend. The Darkness goes on, no matter what you or I would like to think. We shall see much worse before this is all played out."

Emeon smiled sadly.

"Isn't that exactly what we've been saying for all these turnings? Just when we thought it couldn't get any darker, it always becomes pitch-black."

"I can see no way through down this path for the Olthlinden. We have run across more war parties than I remember seeing since the last battle of Dun Macrath."

"Should we try a route toward the Serpent Mountains? If a way were clear there, he might cross and go down the Black Ice all the way to the sea. It would mean a trip though the Endless Swamp, but that might be a road safer from discovery than some others. The Varads don't seem to favor that part of the country with their presence very often."

"And rightly so," mused Duirn. "There is nothing there for them to kill, nor any hope of victims."

He paused, deep in thought.

"That might serve. We shall see what lies in that direction after we have upset our ugly friends at their breakfast here."

"Shall I signal the attack?"

"Is everyone in place?"

"The bowmen are ready."

"Let's set to, then. I have an old ache that won't go away until these woods are cleared of this foul breath of the Banskrog. Yet I feel I have become a part of it too, with all this killing."

Emeon studied his friend, looking at the haggard, drawn lines of worry in Duirn's face.

"We are all weary of this. I long for the day when we will be quits with it. There is a part of me that feels as if it will never be clean. Even the slaying of these poor foul things leaves me with the cold shudders late at night. If I could only hate them, it would be better, yet I can't help but pity them. The Dark One has turned them to her own will, and they can't truly be held to fault."

"Only long enough to kill you," said Duirn. "We shall be in dire trouble as warriors if we keep up this line of talk. Our task now is to see if we can't make it unpleasant for those lumps out there. We might even draw them off so that Jahn and the Olthlinden could get through to the sea."

"Why didn't you just take him yourself?" asked Emeon.

Duirn met his friend's even gaze.

"Because it cannot be done that way, good Emeon. I wish that matters were so simple. I had thought of it, but the Elders of Dun Macrath told me that if any of the Eolin attempted to take charge of the pipe, or to try to interfere in the doings of the Olthlinden when he finally came, the end would not be reached that was written. How easy it would be to try to become the ruler of the Olthlinden and to use the Pipe of Ring Parath to my own end. I think that is what has happened on more then a few occasions. I can see how easy it would be to try to influence the youngster, and how easy it would be for me to try to put the pipe to uses of my own design."

"It might help us rid the Westing Wood of this plague," insisted Emeon.

"You see? That is my thought exactly. But the fate of the pipe is more important than a part it might play in cleaning out our wood. It is more important than even you or I could dream, although we might go on doing so for another hundred lifetimes."

"It seems we have been waiting that long already," replied Emeon, his voice growing very distant, as if recalling the pain of each of those long years.

Duirn gave his old comrade a gentle clap on the back.

"We sound as if we were already beyond usefulness and in the High Danes. Let us get on with our business. If we talk this way too long we will never finish our tasks here."

Emeon turned obediently and disappeared from his view.

In another few moments the sun would break the horizon; the wood was already gray with the milky light that gathered strength in the dark shadows between the dim treetops and the sky above.

Duirn checked his equipment and loosened his sword, which had been carried into so many frays he had lost count. As he looked about him again, he thought he heard the beginning of the war pipe, and as always, his blood ran cold to hear the terrible call. He found himself blowing out wildly on the silver-tipped stag horn, the notes high and true, and he was racing through the wood toward the Varad camp, his sword gleaming a pale, deadly silver-white light that cut through the gloom of the new morning in a terrifying arc.

The Varad war horns answered now, and the sounds of battle being joined reached his ears, growing on the wind until there was no other thing in existence but the deafening clamor of the struggle. The war pipe called louder still, and the noise of the frenzied elves broke again and again like the wild crashing of waves on the shore, and the din of thunder rumbled across the wood, the noise mingling with the battle sounds until it was all one long, rumbling roar that swept away all before it.

The rain came in sheets, and the unearthly gray wraiths moved about in that watery light like ghosts, the combat never ceasing; until finally during the most frantic part of the battle, the tide turned for the outnumbered elves, who had used the element of surprise as their main weapon. All of Duirn's hosts were well seasoned against the Varads, and had been at the center of the desperate task of keeping the Westing Wood clean of invaders since the fall of Dun Macrath.

In a savage struggle with one of the new warriors that he had seen, Duirn stumbled across a prostrate form that he mistook for one of his own clan fallen in the melee. He stooped quickly and found that it was an elf, knocked senseless by a blow.

His friend Emeon was suddenly beside him and drove a swift blade through the beast's defense, felling him like a log.

"Quickly! Here is one of our band wounded. Let's get him to safety."

"It is all over, Duirn," replied Emeon. "They are fleeing. We have broken their defense."

Duirn stopped and looked about him, having to squint to see through the blinding sheets of rain that fell in such strength that they stood to their ankles in a muddy brown sea.

He and Emeon managed to drag the unmoving elf from beneath the pile of Varad bodies that surrounded it, but Duirn could not recall the face of the senseless warrior, although it could have been because of the blood and the heavy downpour, which seemed to be getting heavier all the time.

"We shall have to make shelter for the wounded," called Duirn, shouting to make himself heard over the noise of the storm.

"They are setting up already," returned Emeon, turning aside to listen to a report from one of his orderlies.

"We need to get this settled as quickly as possible," went on Duirn. "We shall have to pursue these lumps for a while, until they think we're breathing down their necks all the time. It might keep them too busy to notice Jahn and the pup."

The two had reached a high, grassy knoll above the rampaging floodwater that rose higher and higher all the while, and there they found shelters had been erected to protect the wounded. The healers of the elfin clans were there and already at work.

"We'll leave this lad. He'll be in good enough hands here. Come, Emeon, let us see to the rest of this fray and see what we may do to help bring it to a successful close."

Emeon had stooped to lay the wounded elf's cloak closer about him, when he suddenly stopped short, gasping aloud.

"What is it?" asked Duirn, alarmed by his friend's face.

"Look!" was all Emeon could manage. He held open the cloak, revealing the uniform of the Banskrog which the injured elf wore.

"It's hard to believe," said Duirn, shaking his head. "I have heard tales all my life of the defectors, but had supposed it was all in the past."

"I wonder if there are any more here?" asked Emeon, his voice taut as a bowstring, his eyes gone a strange shade of green.

"We shall hear soon enough if there are. We'd best warn the healers that this is an enemy. Send someone in to stand watch here."

Emeon was gone in a flash, leaving Duirn alone. He stood quietly, looking at the injured enemy who was one of the deserters of the Eolin. Duirn's thoughts turned to the long struggle, and he remembered the stories he had heard from those who had known some of the Erlings, as the deserters were called.

"It all begins to repeat itself," he muttered aloud, suddenly feeling very old and very tired.

His mind was full of the memories of endless battles and the endless losses, yet nothing ever seemed to change.

"I need a rest," he muttered aloud, turning to leave the cot where the wounded Erling warrior lay. "It will do me good to see the sea," he said finally, drawing himself up a bit and beginning the process of cheering his thoughts, bending his attention to other things.

A cry from behind caused him to move to his left just the slightest bit in a faint motion. It was a movement from long seasons spent in battle. He could not have said what exactly it was, other than another sense that could detect danger. It began to grow stronger the longer one was in a place where danger attended every step of life. There was a tearing hiss as a throwing dagger tore the air and buried itself in the tent wall next to his arm.

Two orderlies had leapt upon the wounded Erling, who had thrown the knife, wrestling him back to the cot.

"I've seen you," ranted the wounded wood elf. "You are the accursed Duirn. My glory would be great if I had managed to control my blade! You have sold out the last of the elfin clans you shall ever betray!"

Duirn had heard the ravings of many of his enemies, but it

81

was the first time that he had heard such cutting words from one of his own kind.

The orderlies had tied the wounded Erling warrior to his cot, but his eyes were still wide in rage and hatred, and there was nothing they could do to stop his mouth.

"You have betrayed every last one of us," he shrieked. "If I had but known sooner, I would never have followed your wily ways. It was only good fortune that led me to the truth."

Duirn sat down a small distance from the cot and studied his adversary.

"Have you a name?" he asked firmly.

The leader of the Shanoliel had grown in aloofness, and his eyes were a deadly blue-gray.

"Trane. My name is Trane. It would have been Trane-Duirn-Slayer if I hadn't been so weak of arm."

"It would have been Trane-the-Foolish if you had succeeded. Why do you bear me such a grudge?"

Trane's eyes flashed with violent rage.

"He asks why I bear him a grudge? I would bear him more than that, and will, if I ever escape from here."

He thrashed about wildly, but the orderlies had tied him well.

"There will be no escape from here, Trane. We shall put you into the Ancient Sleep if you are too difficult or dangerous for us to hold."

The Ancient Sleep, which was a term the elves used for a spell that rendered one into a coma-like sleep that lasted for as long as the user wished, seemed to hold no terrors for Trane.

"You would do me a better favor if your bungling army had killed me outright. I don't want your mercy or pity!"

Emeon had come in at the moment and stood staring at the scene before him. He glanced from the thrown dagger stuck in the tent wall to the struggling Erling warrior and guessed what had happened.

"Our friend here had a present he wished me to have," explained Duirn. "And I have been listening to the fact that I am a traitor to all elves. I have obviously committed a grievous wrong to this fellow, for he has changed sides."

"I have heard the true tale of the way you were crowned King of the Shanoliel, and of all the innocent blood you spilled in getting that gory crown. The wood elf was lucky to have escaped alive after your purges."

"What history do you speak of?"

"As if you didn't know! I speak of the great purges of the days before you were crowned King of the Shanoliel. My kindred, the woodfolk, were not sided with those that would see you crowned and were killed for their actions."

"You have heard a strange history, Trane. It does not seem akin to any I have ever heard," said Emeon.

"It is because you are deaf, or because you are in league with their murderer," spat Trane.

"We are the ones who picked you up off the field and brought you here. We thought you were of our band."

"More harm to me," snorted the Erling. "If I had looked more like a Varad or Worlugh, I would have been left where I fell and would have escaped."

"Or died from your wound," reminded Emeon gently, although his patience was thin and his anger flared every time he realized how close the enemy soldier had come to slaying Duirn.

"It would have been more honorable than to be held captive by such a butcher as Duirn."

"It seems the butcher is at least a slight bit lenient to let you go on this way after your attempt on his life. Any other would have had you killed on the spot."

"He's too cowardly to do it to my face. He can only give his orders when he is away from those who would look him in the eyes while he does it."

Trane struggled weakly, but fell back exhausted.

"But we know a surprise," he laughed. "Oh, we know a surprise or two that may be better than putting our knife in his back."

The Erling warrior was growing delirious from his wound, and Duirn signaled to the healer to look at the wood elf.

Trane's voice grew higher-pitched and drifted in and out of bits and snatches of speech.

"He's going into the battle sickness," reported the healer. "It is not a dangerous wound, but it was a hard knock on the head. I'm surprised that he was able to come back to consciousness so soon after such a blow."

Trane ranted on, falling into a burbling howl, while his eyes rolled wildly.

"How long will he be like this?" asked Duirn.

"It's hard to say. I've seen it last as long as a week, but seldom longer. He seems in good shape other than the blow on his head. If a fever doesn't set in, he should be mended as

83

good as new in a few days. You can talk to him then, I would say."

Emeon followed Duirn out of the shelter, his brow knitted together into a worried frown.

"That was a close squeak, Duirn. It frightens me to think that there are even those of the Eolin who now fight for the Banskrog."

"That is what makes the Darkness so terrible. Those you would never think of as your enemies are suddenly just that. It was like seeing the elf there among the fallen Varads! It never occurred to me that he was there as one of their fellows, and not because he had been trapped and slaughtered."

"This has come to a sad day," replied his friend.

"I have heard the stories of the Erlings," said Duirn. "There have been those from the beginning that have found one reason or another to turn their backs to their own kind. Perhaps some sort of misguided impression drives them. They may think they are actually helping. From what Trane says, that is the case. He seems to have gotten the idea that I have killed off his kin, the woodfolk, in order to become King of the Shanoliel."

"Where would he hear a tale like that?" asked Emeon.

"I have an idea, but we shall hear it all from him firsthand when he recovers enough. He's sure to tell us everything, judging from the hatred he bears me. He won't be able to resist."

The friends walked on some little distance in silence, each deep in his own thoughts, their hoods pulled over their heads to keep off the driving rain.

At length, Duirn turned toward the shelter that had been set up for his commanders, increasing his pace.

"Come on, Emeon. Let's see to it that Jahn and the pup might have a chance to get away from Dun Macrath. If we press the attack now, we may yet clear a way for them."

Duirn flung back the shelter flap as he spoke, and was followed inside by Emeon.

The rest of the night was spent in planning their next foray and listening to reports from scouts, but Duirn's mind kept returning to the injured Trane and the hatred that he read in the wood elf's look. He could not be sure, for the Erling had become delirious by then, but part of his rambling had sounded like he was speaking of captives, and it sounded very much to Duirn that he had said otters, but he could not be sure. He was distracted, making his commanders repeat everything at least twice before he understood what they were saying.

A slow-growing idea was beginning to form itself in his thoughts, an idea so grim that he hoped for all their sakes it was not true. If it were, he knew the Upper Danes were as far away as ever.

Swept Away

A LEADEN gray sky hung low over the wood, making it impossible to see the sun. Rain fell in tiny pattering sounds that grew in volume until it seemed there had never been a time that it was not pouring down in the milky-white sheets; the forest floor began to run like an angry river.

It had been days since Duirn had left them at Dun Macrath, and Jahn had waited for a sign before he moved, but none came. The pup had grown impatient, hounding the elf every hour to make a move in some direction.

"This rain is the perfect time to go," argued the otter, not very put off by the water. "It is enough to keep the Varads in camp. It is difficult to see anyone moving about in this downpour."

Jahn argued against it at first, although he found himself weakening.

"And what direction do you think we'll go? You've never been to the place that Duirn says we must reach."

"We can ask the way," replied Olthar.

Jahn laughed at the innocent answer of the pup.

"Who would we ask? A passing Varad?"

"Elves!" persisted the small animal. "I am sure we will run into others along the way."

"Duirn and his band, perhaps. There are no others about."

"You haven't heard of them. I'm sure they are there. And it will do us no good to go on staying here now."

"We are to wait for Duirn to tell us which way is the safest."

"Well, if he finds us gone, then he will just have to catch up to us. That should be no problem for him."

"It might be a problem for us when he finds us. It is not a good thing to ignore the orders of the Shanoliel King."

"You are an elf, I am not. And I hold the pipe," reminded Olthar.

Jahn looked steadily at the pup, who was caught between innocence and adulthood, at once charming and impetuous, vain and overbearing.

This was the difficult part of the task, Jahn realized. He must try to impart fairness to Olthar, as well as a sense of justice; and the knowledge that just because one was powerful that didn't give one the right to force those who were weaker to do a thing they did not want to do.

"We shall have to talk about the pipe," said Jahn evenly. "We haven't had a chance since this all began. Now would be as good a time as any."

"There is nothing to talk about, Jahn. Duirn gave it to me to carry. It has been long enough that we have wasted here."

"Perhaps not long enough, if I detect anything from the tone of your voice, lad."

Jahn had seen the very thing at work in himself when he had carried about the pipe. There was a small part of him that was the seed of the Dark One, that wanted to lord it over all the others, to impress everyone with the importance of his journey and the thing that he carried. He was torn by those feelings early in the time that he and Malcom had traveled about searching for the rightful owner of the pipe.

That all seemed so amusing now. He had been with the father of the very one who was to carry it, and the two of them had never had any idea of that at all. That always seemed to be the way of things, he thought, studying the sturdy young otter before him, his eyes blazing with impatience and the first flood of the feeling of power surging through him.

Jahn hoped that he would at least be able to cool some of the foolishness before it got to a point where it might be dangerous.

"We shall leave here, Olthar, and in good time. But I think we should sit down inside these old elfin walls so that I may tell you a story about how the pipe was taken from the hands of an elf and given into the keeping of an otter."

There was just enough pup left in Olthar to respond to the authority in Jahn's voice, and his ardor to leave immediately was quelled to a slight degree. He allowed himself to be led into the driest part of the ruins, where Jahn sat him down.

After looking off into an inner distance for a time, the elf became aware of the otter squirming about restlessly in front of him.

"This all happened a very long time ago," began Jahn.

"All your stories happen a very long time ago," replied the youngster, not trying to conceal his impatience.

"This is also about an elf who was very impatient. We shall see and hear what has happened as a result of that. We will see how all the elf's distant cousins have been forced to pay for his rash actions."

Olthar rolled his eyes in exasperation.

"In the years of the Beginning, when all things were in harmony, the Pipe of Ring Parath was given to the elfin lords to make beautiful music and to be a source of joy to all who heard it. There were other kinds. Each kind received a gift from the King of Windameir Himself, so that the followers would not forget the country they had come from, which was the Upper Meadows of Windameir."

"You've told this story before," reminded Olthar.

"But not in detail," scolded Jahn. "Just sit still a bit longer and you shall hear the difference."

The elf paused, found his place in the story, and went on.

"The High King knew that the things His followers would run into on the lower boundaries would be sad and sometimes frightening, but He loved all His creation so much that He allowed them to go on exploring to their heart's content. He knew that it would make them more aware of what they had in the High Meadows when they returned, so He permitted them to go. The High King also knew he could change that by simply willing that it were not so; but He never did. He gave all his creatures free will so that they were allowed to decide anything they wanted. Sometimes this began to get them into great trouble and caused a great deal of pain to themselves and others, but it all went away as soon as they remembered who they were and turned back to the High King's Law."

The elf stopped speaking and checked to make sure Olthar was listening.

"Now this went on for a very long time; then it came to be that much changed in the Lower Meadows of Windameir. There were new players who came onto the scene. Among these was the Dark One. This had never been before. The Upper Gates were always left open and unattended for the longest time, so that any of the wayfarers who had crossed the boundaries could return Home as they pleased."

"This is still the same as you've told me before," complained Olthar. "We have had this story twice, at least."

Jahn ignored him.

"Then one day, some of the travelers returned through the Upper Gates and spent a time resting there. One of the wanderers saw that his fellow had brought back a beautiful stone from the Lower Meadows. 'What is it for?' asked the other. 'To give to the High King as a present,' was the reply.

"Now the traveler then strangled his fellow and took the stone to give the High King himself, hoping to win great credit and esteem.

"The High King knew at once that it had happened, and so closed the Upper Gates. He saw what had happened to those who went beyond the Fields of Light. It was then that He called forth the Dark One and set the High Dragons at the gates. The Dark One was to make sure that all those who escaped her were truly ready to come back to the Upper Meadows. Only those could return who had been tried and tested and who wanted only to be next to the High King. They were to be the only ones allowed back through the Upper Gates."

"It's just like you told me."

"Almost. I haven't told you all of it. And then the Dark One went out on her own and decided that she would rule the Lower Meadows forever, keeping all those who were there as her prisoners, never allowing them to return to their true Home. That was what led on to this trouble. After a long while, she found out about the pipe and all the other tokens the High King had left below to call His followers Home. She decided she would have them all. The Dark One lured the ancient One-Who-Fell into her trap and was at the point of taking control of the pipe when the Elders of the Circle took it and put it into the keeping of the Shanoliel. It would never be of power again until the time came for it to call forth the High King's followers. In order for it to do so, it had to be carried by one who had not the guilt of the treason of the elfin clans, who had been betrayed by one of their own."

"I know all that," argued the pup. "You have told it to me over and over again."

"Now it is in your keeping," continued Jahn. "It will bring you great power and there will be many who follow you. Many will try to take it from you. The Dark One is looking for it at this very moment. It is a dangerous journey that we are embarked upon, not a romp through the wood. We have to be careful from now on. If the pipe were to fall into the wrong hands, it would be a disaster for many of those who yet dwell here in the Lower Meadows."

"And the elves wouldn't be able to go back into the High Danes," finished the pup.

Jahn had to look at him twice to see whether or not he was being rude, but there was nothing to be read from the pup's eyes.

"That is true. It is also true that all kinds benefit from the power of the pipe. Any who hear it are given the secret of remembering where they have come from, and the desire is given to them to want to return."

"Then let's go and do that," cried the pup, jumping up from his perch.

"As soon as Duirn comes," answered Jahn calmly.

"He may not come for a long time," argued Olthar.

"Then we shall wait for a long time."

Jahn was growing angry at the obstinate otter.

"You must learn to be more patient. If Duirn said to wait for him, he will return as quickly as he can. He wants us to be on our way to the sea as quickly as we can."

"Then why didn't he take us with him?" asked Olthar, whirling on his friend. "I have seen all the mysterious things that he can do. I've seen all the elf work he does. Why could he not simply take you and me to the sea?"

"If you were not carrying the pipe, he would be able to do just that. He would be able to simply take us to the sea with no fuss or bother."

Olthar was silent for a time.

"Then he is jealous because he had to give the pipe to me! If he could take us, but won't, what other reason is there?"

"You know that's not the reason."

"He wants to try to make me give it back."

"He wants nothing of the sort and you know it."

"Then why would he go and leave us behind if it was so dangerous?"

"Because he said he can find a safe way to travel for us."

"Or he can wait until he thinks I am frightened enough to give up the pipe."

Jahn shook his head in amazement.

"That's not the truth."

The elf had been aware of a reluctance to give up the pipe

each time he and Malcom found someone who had been willing to try to become the one who carried it, and he remembered the relief he had felt after each one had failed. That was a strange thing, and he knew it was dangerous to one who could not overcome it. It frightened him to see the pup this way, although he knew he had to go through this process of testing.

"If it is not the truth, then why are we staying here in the place where the elves used to live? Why can't we wait somewhere else?"

"Because it's safer here," returned Jahn, knowing it was futile.

The pup had gotten off the rock he was sitting on and moved to the archway of the ruins. Outside, the milky-white light was dimmed by the falling rain, which had continued in its intensity, now drumming loudly on the shattered roof over their heads, and pouring noisily through the chinks between the stones to gather in puddles at their feet.

Jahn watched as the small animal stood outlined against the light, staring into the gloom beyond.

"If I leave, you'll have to follow," he said, not looking at the elf.

"I hope that's not what you plan to do. It would be very dangerous to expose the pipe to capture like that."

"It would be no worse on the move than it is here."

"You forget we have some protection now. The Old Ones are all around us."

The pup turned, his small features drawn into a frown.

"There is nothing to be done here. There is no hope of finding my mother or father again, or reaching the sea, or taking any kind of action in any direction."

"The waiting is always the worst, old fellow. That is true no matter who or what you are. Duirn has been going through a wait so long that we wouldn't have any idea about how awful it must be. The Eolin have been waiting since the Upper Danes first closed to be able finally to go Home. It has been a weary wait, no mistaking that."

Olthar gazed at him a moment.

"And you, Jahn?"

"I have had a long wait, too."

The pup's impatience seemed to be cooling somewhat.

Jahn had forgotten for a moment the pain the youngster must still be going through, caused by the sudden removal from his family; then he had been given the added burden of carrying the pipe. That fact alone isolated him more than any other; for no matter how many friends he would surround himself with, the task of carrying the pipe was endured only by the one who held it.

"We shall be on our way soon enough," resumed the elf. "It is only a matter of time before Duirn sends us word or comes himself to give us a route that will be safest for us to take."

"What if something has happened to Duirn?" asked the small animal bluntly.

Jahn had not allowed himself to think that anything could ever happen to Duirn, the leader of the Shanoliel, and he was frightened slightly by the realization. That question opened up another picture entirely, one that he did not want to deal with or dwell on. If that was indeed the case, then he came face to face with the fact that he had no plan beyond what Duirn had said. He had not given himself the leeway to try to decide what had best be done in the remote instance that the Shanoliel should fail, or be destroyed by the Darkness.

"What will we do if Duirn doesn't come back?" repeated the otter.

Jahn found himself suddenly very angry, which acted to cover his fear.

"That is a silly thought. Nothing has happened to Duirn. Nothing could happen to him after all this time."

He stopped himself from going on, then lowered his voice.

"And if it did, I don't know what we'd do," he admitted, a worried frown masking his fair features.

Jahn turned over every thought or idea he had on the subject of what they would do without Duirn, but there were no answers. Everything hinged on the leader of the Shanoliel coming back to Dun Macrath to instruct them on what must be done next.

He laughed bitterly.

"I am a fine adviser," he snorted disdainfully. "Here I am without an answer to a plain possibility, and can see no way clear that I'm going to have one."

Olthar, returning to his former good-natured self, came to the elf and gave his hand a short pat.

"I know you have been without your family for a long time, Jahn. You must understand what I feel now. I have held up knowing that we would soon be on our way and I could set out to search for my mother and father, or perhaps find news of them. The Old Ones said that it was for my own good that they are keeping me, but I wonder at that. I don't think they understand what it feels like."

"They are a strange lot," agreed the elf. "I dare say they don't know what it's like to be carried away from home."

Jahn broke off his thought to listen to some vague, disturbing sound that had crept into his consciousness. He could not put his finger on what it was exactly, but it was a noise that was not a part of the rain.

"Do you hear anything?" he asked the pup.

"The rain."

"No, different."

They both held their breath and tried to concentrate on the sound, but it was difficult to separate it from the noise the falling rain made.

"It's getting louder," reported Jahn, after straining for a long while to listen.

"Water," repeated the small animal.

Jahn's features clouded as he tried to piece together the bits of information. The rain had gone on for so long that he had a difficult time trying to remember what it sounded like when it was not raining, and what it looked like to see sunshine instead of the low gray clouds that seemed to hang over the very treetops of the woods.

As he thought these odd thoughts, the dull roar of the rain began to grow louder still, and there was a faint noise of explosions that crackled through the sodden air.

"What in the name of Eolin could that be?" cried Jahn, going to stand at the broken doorway, gazing anxiously toward the sound of the rising noise.

As he moved, he noticed for the first time that the water in the ruins was above his knees. The pup had difficulty in trying to walk, finally giving up and swimming to the excited elf.

The explosions grew louder still, while the milky-white light turned another shade of gray. It was roaring steadily now, coming over the noise of the rain and drowning it out.

Every hair on the nape of the elf's neck stood straight out. Without realizing he had done so, he reached down and picked up the otter pup, holding him tightly to his chest. The pup was so amazed by the move that he offered no resistance, and the two of them turned their heads toward the crashing roar that came on toward them.

In a split second, Jahn saw it all and clutched the pup desperately in his arms. A wall of gray-brown water with a frothing dirty white maw broke over the tops of the trees in the direction of the Serpent Mountains, and he realized that the explosions he had heard before were the bodies of the trees being snapped by the horrendous force of the tons of water rushing on blindly toward the sea.

Jahn thought swiftly of the Old Ones, and wondered if they would drown but that thought was quickly erased from his mind, for the next instant he and the small animal in his arms were buried by the raging torrent, and a peaceful oblivion slowly lured him into its depths, pulling him away from the terrifying power of the rampaging flood that roared across the Westing Wood, sweeping all away before it.

Gone were the ruins of Dun Macrath, and with it, the ancient beings who had moved to circle the old dane. There was nothing left behind but a vast brown river moving slowly on toward the distant coast.

Disheartening News

DUIRN sat across the fire from the prisoner, eyeing him carefully. There was no way of knowing what went on in his thoughts from looking at the bandaged features, but the eyes seemed to constantly dart from one place to another, never meeting anything for more than a moment before rapidly turning away. When confronted with the frank gaze of Duirn, the wounded elf shifted uncomfortably, looking quickly toward the blazing fire.

There were others there, among them Emeon, who sat next to Duirn. Outside the shelter, the steady drumming of the rain went on monotonously, as it had for days on end.

The shelters were all covered with a spongy gray silt that had come with the rain, as if wet ashes had been dumped from the sky with the downpours. No one could explain the gray ash, and it quickly covered the shoulders of the trees and lay in thick coats on any of those who had to be out in it for more than a few minutes at a time.

"It is a bad omen," said Emeon. "I have never seen anything like this. It can only be something that bodes us ill."

For the first time, the prisoner spoke.

93

"It bodes you ill, indeed, you ignorant wretches. You have been duped by the forces of the ones who follow the evil Elders. You have struck against the rightful ruler of these three worlds, and now you will pay. The Protector's time is rising. All who have been against her will pay dearly for their treachery."

A guard moved to silence the prisoner, but Duirn motioned for the wood elf to be left alone.

"We are listening to you, brother. Your cause is known, but why you have chosen as you have is yet a mystery to me."

The prisoner rose shakily, bowing as best he was able.

"You are speaking to Trane, of the Legion of the Black Ice."

"How do you come to be traveling with such lovely companions, Trane of the Black Ice?" asked Emeon.

"I travel with whom I please. It is more freedom than you can claim for yourself."

"That may be as it may be."

"I travel with the Legion of the Black Ice to free all my kinsmen from the tyranny of the Elders and the High Traitor, who has declared war on the rightful ruler."

"You have yet to say who your leader is, Trane. Is it someone we know about?"

"As well as I know about you, Duirn, who have sold out your own blood to rule the Shanoliel."

"You amaze me. How came you to know I am Duirn?"

"By your crown, and by the fact that the stories of your treacherous dealings describe you exactly. I would have known you anywhere."

"That says much to my credit, then. Who is it you follow?"

The wounded Erling rearranged the bandage on his head so that he could speak more easily.

"You may not remember the old danes on the Black Ice River. They were beyond your borders and no one ever made any effort to try to help our settlements. We were the lower brethren, the renegade outsiders who insisted on living where we wished to live, and living as we desired, without all the rules and regulations that plagued the rest of elfdom. No one took any notice of our absence, nor tried to befriend us. We were shunned because of our beliefs and treated as animals, simply because we held viewpoints that were different than others'."

Trane stopped speaking and breathed deeply before going on, gathering his strength.

"We managed to get by somehow, even though the times

94

were difficult. Then came the famine that struck the lands beyond the Black Ice, and our danes were all starving. We sent for aid across the Serpent Mountains, to appeal to our kin that dwelled in the more prosperous lands, but all we heard from the stragglers who returned was that they had been ambushed and slain at will. There would be no aid from that quarter. That was the end of any kinship that might have existed between us. We took whatever road we could take then, until our salvation appeared in the form of one who cared for us and gave us a home, and helped us to rise above those who would have slain us."

"You are speaking of the Banskrog?" asked Duirn.

"That may be what you call her. In our tongue, she is Protector. She has kept my kinsmen from disappearing from the history of elf lore."

"How strong are your bands?"

A sly leer crossed the wood elf's face.

"I give you no information, Duirn. You will find the strength of our armies when you encounter their wrath. They will sweep you under like deadwood on a river."

Duirn rose from his seat at the fire and motioned for Emeon to follow him. Trane flinched, drawing himself into his cloak, thinking he was going to be beaten, but the two companions hurried past him out into the gray downpour that rolled on outside the shelter.

They crossed to another tent, where the leader of the Shanoliel took out a packet of maps that were held by a thick coil of twine, laying them out flat on the field desk. He unrolled a number of the charts until he came to one he spread out carefully, laying a heavy ring upon one side to hold it open, then studying each detail of it as if he were trying to commit it all to memory.

"What is it, Duirn?" asked his bewildered comrade.

"It is a chart of the lands that border the Great Wilderness. There," he said, pointing with a stab of his forefinger. "There is the Black Ice."

"I have heard tales of kinsmen who long ago lived over the Serpent Mountains, but there have been no reports of them in so long I had begun to think that they were only tales and nothing more."

"Do you believe his story about their being murdered by members of our danes? Could that be?"

"He may believe them. I think he does. He certainly has enough steam behind his hatred for us. Yet I cannot ever remember any of his kin being refused aid simply because they were woodfolk. It isn't done."

Emeon fell into silence and pondered a moment.

"Is there any way we could find out more? Would anyone know of these stories now?"

"I shall send for old Banon. He has been with me all my life, and he was with my father for all of his. He seems to grow younger instead of aging like the rest of us."

Duirn sent a page to fetch the old one, continuing with the study of the map while he waited.

"That must have been a hard life, living on the Black Ice. That is not good country."

"I have never seen beyond the Serpents, but from what I have heard, I certainly have no desire to do so."

"The woodfolk have always been a strange lot," mused Duirn. "They have ever gone their own way. It's a well-known fact that they never had much love for the water elf. Yet I never thought the day would come when we would be openly at arms against each other."

Emeon shook his head sadly.

"I have seen some sorrowful things, but this is one of those that really pull at my heart. I wonder where it shall all end?"

His comrade's gaze grew distant and he turned his face away.

Banon entered at that moment and came to join them.

"Greetings, Duirn. Good health, Emeon."

"Ours to you, Banon. Come and help us with a problem here."

"I shall be happy to do so, if I can," chuckled the old elf. He had hair and beard of a fine silky white that, rather than give him the appearance of age, made him appear more noble and dignified. His clear blue eyes were sharp, and they crackled with a dry fire that lit his face above his whiskers and spoke of an honest heart and a kind hand.

"You are looking at a strange part of the country there," he said, glancing at the unrolled map of the Great Barrens.

"Do you know any stories about it, or of the ones who have dwelled there?" asked Duirn.

"That is a big country, and a big question. Ask me more precisely."

Duirn then related to the old elf all that Trane had said, and when he had finished, Banon seemed to be far away, drifting in another time and place. He remained that way for a long time after Duirn had stopped speaking, and Emeon

96

was on the point of turning to look a question at Duirn, when Banon began.

"There was the dane of Eloia and Rogin, which was high up the Black Ice. It flourished for a long while there, until they were driven into the Great Barrens by the beasts. They perished there. Then there was another greater dane of woodfolk at the Wide Crossing. That dane still exists, for all I know. I have not had news of it for a long while, since it is no longer possible for the two clans to communicate. This dane was formed when I was but a small flan. It was a great settlement, and I have heard that there were enough woodfolk there to fill that side of the forest with their offspring; it went on in such a way for a long time. I can't remember who the leader was at that time, but of the waterfolk, the leader was an elf called Hamon. He had a great following also, and lived just across the Serpent Mountains from the woodfolk dane."

Banon drew his breath for a moment, thinking again, then proceeded.

"The two danes had commerce, and there were those who visited between the two danes freely. It was still in the time when our two kindred clans were as one, and not divided.

"This went on for a long while, until the Dark One moved once more. There are tales of treachery then, for her armies slew waterfolk and made it appear they had been killed by woodfolk; and wood elves were killed, and it was made to appear that waterfolk had done the deed. That was just in two danes. The Dark One did the same all across these woods and mountains and seas, until the Darkness had turned brother against brother, and kindred against all others."

"Then his story is partially true. At least as he has his facts," said Emeon.

"To him it is all truth. The Dark One is so subtle in her works that all she needs is a small chink in the wall and she can work all her worst from that. I think we all carry her seed within us, and it cries out to be heard."

"You speak the truth, Duirn. That is all part of the plan. And we have all answered that call in some life or other. That is how it was written to be played. The poor fellow you have caught is but trapped in his own role. It is sad, but there is nothing to be done about it. You might turn him loose when he is well enough to travel alone. He should be able to find his way back to his own kind, with any sort of luck at all."

Emeon looked doubtful at that suggestion, but Duirn nodded.

"There is no sense in keeping him with us unless he wishes to stay."

"Won't he give us away?" asked Emeon, still unsure of the wisdom of the move.

"We are given away already, my good Emeon. We were given away when we chose which side we would fall on in this affair. He has chosen his side and we have chosen ours. There is nothing left but to see where our fates lie."

"I will see this woodfolk, Duirn, if you'll allow me. Perhaps we may piece more of the picture together."

"Certainly. I have a need of all the help I can gather. I feel there is something he knows that would be of aid to us, if we could but get him to speak."

"Perhaps I can use some of my old ways," offered Banon. "They are not the most honest of ways, but often get results. That is what you have need of here."

Duirn smiled, nodding.

"We have an urgent need of results. If it doesn't harm him, then you are welcome to any method you can employ."

"My method won't harm him. It may be the easiest of all, for he won't remember to feel guilty at having given up his information to the enemy."

"It seems strange being thought of as an enemy by one of your own," said Emeon. "I can see that I have yet to experience a few things."

At the entrance to the shelter, Banon paused to look at the gray rain that fell steadily outside.

"Here is another strange thing that I have never seen the likes of. It seems as though the sun has lost its way and will never find us again."

"I don't like it. This rain is going to fill all the fords of the rivers and flood most of the wood if it doesn't let up soon."

"That might be good in a way, Emeon. If the fords were flooded, that would slow down the flow of the beast warriors from across the boundaries."

"In that case, let it rain," replied his friend.

Duirn grew more serious then.

"It might also cover the trail of the Olthlinden, and let him reach the sea unnoticed."

He looked to Banon a moment.

"That is another thing that is heavy on my mind, old friend. I have sent a party to tell Jahn and the Olthlinden of a safe passage through the wood, but I've heard nothing back.

It has been long enough now that they should have been to Dun Macrath and returned."

"The weather, most likely. It is slow traveling in weather like this."

Duirn could not read the old elf's eyes, but he did not press further, choosing instead to cling to the fragile hope Banon had offered.

They crossed quickly to the shelter where the prisoner waited, entering silently. Banon took a seat beside the others and watched the eyes of the captured elf as they moved evasively from one figure to another, finally settling on the fire.

No one spoke. Emeon was about to ask a question, but Banon raised a hand for silence.

Duirn was staring into the fire as well, and after a long period of silence, he thought he began to see strange forms in the blazing wood. Then an odd music began to fill the shelter with the sounds of reed pipe and lute. Duirn began to feel very drowsy and had a hard time remaining awake. He took his gaze off the fire and looked up at Trane.

He could see no difference at first. It seemed that the elf was merely staring into the fire to avoid everyone's eyes, but as Duirn looked more closely, he detected that the wood elf's gaze was glassy, and that his body swayed slightly back and forth.

At that moment, Banon spoke, not in the voice of an old elf, but rather in a voice that seemed to come from the fire, or the air, or the sound of music; yet at the same time it came from all of those places at once.

"You are far away, Trane, in the shelter of friends in your old dane on the Black Ice. What is my name?"

The wood elf formed words with his lips, but no sound was heard.

"Speak louder, Trane. I cannot hear you."

"You are Stane."

"Yes, Stane. I am Stane. You are safe and may tell me everything that has happened to you. Are you injured?" asked Banon, his voice again coming from everywhere at once.

"I am injured," murmured Trane. "The infidels have hurt me."

"Who are they?"

"The waterfolk."

"Did you go into the battle with the waterfolk alone?"

"With the war band of Varads and Worlugh that the Protector sent. I led the first band."

"Are there others of us here?"

"Others?"

Trane's body shifted as if he were struggling, but he became still after a time.

"There were others. We were caught in an ambush. I am wounded."

"Did the others come from the Black Ice?"

"Yes. They came from many other places, too. Alar Far is from the delvings. There are those who come from The Barrens."

"Is Alar Far a dwarf?" asked Banon.

"He is the earthfolk."

Duirn looked at the old elf.

"They even have some of the dwarf hordes with them. The Dark One has done her work well."

Banon raised a hand for silence and turned to Trane.

"This is a prisoner we have, Trane. It is Duirn, of the Shanoliel. We have captured him at last."

A savage glint came into the glazed eyes of the wood elf for a moment. The guard behind him moved closer, in the event the prisoner tried to attack Duirn.

There was a shriek of laughter then, thin and high.

"We have him? By the Sacred Stone, this will make the Protector happy. She has wanted him for a long time." Trane rubbed his hands together gleefully. "Oh, he'll jig a long mile before we're through with him."

The wood elf laughed another long, high-pitched laugh.

"Now we have the animals that spawned that filth they call the Olthlinden, and the King of the Shanoliel. Not many will be able to hold against us for long with these prisoners safely in our hands."

Duirn's ears picked up at the mention of the animals, and he whispered in Banon's ear.

The old elf was quiet for a moment, then took another tack.

"Where do we keep the animals? Are they safely guarded? We wouldn't want them to get free."

"Oh, they won't get free. They are in the Protector's care. She knows how to handle things so that there won't be any getting free of her."

"Do we also hold the Olthlinden?"

Trane's shoulders fell, and he gasped aloud.

"We could not catch him. We thought to have had all of

100

them, but the infernal pup escaped with a wretch of a water elf."

"That was bad luck."

"Bad luck, indeed. Alar Far and I were held accountable. We were lucky to have been let off so easily."

"But now you have Duirn, so the Protector will be pleased with you again."

The wood elf smiled a broad, ugly smile.

"Yes. Now the Protector will be pleased with me again."

"Where do we hold the animals? Is it on the borders?"

"She holds them in her palace. They will not escape."

"Are the rest of our forces crossing the borders to attack the danes there?"

"We go across the borders in great numbers every day. The Protector has sent many more of her new soldiers with us. They are good fighters, but I don't like to be in their company when we are in camp. They eat their slain enemies. I suppose it is all right for them, but I don't care for their company outside a battle."

Duirn had heard all he wanted to hear and signaled Banon that the interview was over.

He led Emeon through the falling gray rain until they were in the shelter that held the field desk and charts. Unrolling another map, Duirn spread it out carefully, scanning its surface.

"If what Trane says is so, Malcom and Morane were captured at their old settlement as we had suspected."

He poked a finger to a spot on the map.

"Then they were carried off by Trane and his companions and turned over to the Dark One."

He made a trail across the lines of the chart.

"They would most likely have gone that way, I think. It is the easiest road."

"Are you thinking of trying to rescue them?"

"I think we will be hearing from the Dark One soon enough. They will be held alive until she can confront Olthar with them. That will prove to be a dangerous meeting, I fear."

"I can hardly think what one would do in a case such as that," replied Emeon softly. "I don't like to think what I would do if it were my own decision."

"We shall at least be prepared for it," went on Duirn. "Better to know ahead of time how things stand."

"We shall have to tell the pup that we know for certain that the Dark One holds his mother and father."

"We shall, indeed, once we are with him again."

"Should you go back to Dun Macrath to see what has happened and find out why the scouts haven't made their report yet?"

"I don't think that will be necessary. I think I hear them returning. Come."

Duirn led the way into the drizzling rain and found the scouts he had sent returned and looking for him. They gathered the elves and took them into the cheery blaze so that they might dry themselves out as their leader give a full account of their story.

Duirn and Emeon grew serious and very still as they listened to all the exhausted elf had to report.

III. THE LONG PATHS OF SUMMER

Coney

A GRAY, flat landscape stretched out before the otter's eyes for as far as he could see in any direction. He stood beside the unmoving elf, holding onto his hand for lack of anything else to do. It seemed to him then that they had been in the raging brown flood of water for days. There were tree stumps and boulders that had been washed along by the power of the water, and it had only been due to the small animal's water sense that either of them had survived at all after the first rush of the towering wall had swept them away into its foaming, irresistible current.

After they had been ejected onto the surface, Olthar kept a tight hold on the elf with his powerful jaws, guiding him as carefully as possible around logs and stones, keeping Jahn's head above water. That had gone on until the pup's strength started to fail, and he began to doubt that they would ever reach dry ground or be able to rest again. The thought of drowning had not occurred to him until the very last when he could no longer force his spent limbs to keep moving. The fatigue had been so great all he could think about was to stop moving and just let the water close over him; then he would be able to sleep, long and undisturbed.

It was at this point that he released his hold on Jahn and stopped struggling to keep the two of them afloat. He was taken quite by surprise then to find his stubby paws firmly on the bottom and that he was able to walk, although his exhausted limbs protested feebly. In spite of some slipping and falling, Olthar finally managed to drag the motionless elf to a patch of ground that stood above water, and there he lay down beside his friend, too tired to care about anything further.

After a time, he came to himself again, looking around and checking to see that Jahn was alive and breathing. In the course of all these small things, he began to take in his surroundings more carefully. The light was still the same pale gray, making it impossible to tell whether it was morning or afternoon; but after remembering back and deciding that it had been morning when the flood had swept them away, he reasoned that it must be afternoon.

Down just at the horizon he could detect the faintest trace of a pale fiery orange crack, as if a strip of cloud layer had been penetrated by the unseen sun for a moment, and as Olthar watched, that pale band of light began to grow slowly, until at last there was a flowing curve of light across the lowering sky that continued to broaden steadily. In this faint gloom Olthar made the elf as comfortable as he could, putting the soaked cloak beneath his head and trying to clean the caked mud and silt from Jahn's eyes and nose and mouth.

The pain began then. He became aware of the bumps and jolts he had received when washed into the floating trees and banged roughly into the tumbling boulders that were rolled about like toys by the fierce current of the floodwaters.

There was no landmark that looked even remotely familiar, and the flat sheen of the pale light reflected off water for as far as he could see in every direction, as if the world were nothing more than a vast, dirty gray lake.

As he continued to stare about him, dazed by the bleak picture, he caught sight of something gliding very slowly by. It was unrecognizable at first, but when the shapeless mass got closer, Olthar saw it was the bloated body of a Varad warrior beaten into a pulp by the fury of the rampaging flood. As he watched the grim lump float past, he caught sight of others, Worlugh among them. They continued past at a steady rate until he lost all count, finally giving up trying to determine how many there were.

A realization came over him then of how much danger they had been in while they remained in Dun Macrath. Thinking of the old elfin dane, he wondered what had happened to the Old Ones who had stood guard around the ancient settlement. He could not believe that they could have survived the storm's onslaught, but he did not like to think of anything happening to them, either.

Olthar remembered the Pipe of Ring Parath then, and he froze with fear until he realized the case was snug against his body, held by its thick strap. Upon reassuring himself, Olthar turned to the elf once more, who had by then begun to flutter his eyes and spew up dirty brown water.

The elf was a sodden mess, battered and bloody, his fair face swollen to twice its normal size. His eyes were blackened and it was difficult for him to open them to more than a squint, which he did, turning a relieved look on the otter.

A feeble hand found Olthar's paw.

"Well, old fellow, it looks like we found a way to get out of Dun Macrath without waiting for Duirn."

Jahn tried to sound cheerful, but as he looked from Olthar to the surrounding grim landscape, his voice faltered. The faint golden twilight that Olthar had seen was rapidly fading, and they were surrounded on their little dry spot by a seemingly endless expanse of dark water. They were hungry and cold and without any glimmer of hope.

"This must be what we used to call Dreary Lake," said Jahn at last, after staring about him forlornly. "It could go on just like this for miles."

"I could touch bottom," said Olthar softly.

"But for how long? And where would we go, even if we could walk on the bottom? I have heard stories of this place. There is quicksand, and there are things that live in these foul waters that would make you shudder to think of them."

Upon that thought, the two companions looked about them apprehensively.

"I saw some dead Varads. There were a lot of them."

"That is some good news, then."

"What do you think happened to the Old Ones?"

The elf screwed up his battered features in thought.

"Do you still have the pipe?"

Olthar held out the small case.

"I strapped it around my back," he explained.

"I don't know how anything could have withstood that flood, but they have been around since the Beginning, so I'm sure they have survived worse than this."

As the elf finished speaking, the looming black shadow of a floating object neared their haven, appearing out of the growing twilight. It was bigger than the bodies of the Varads and Worlugh, yet it seemed to be as grotesque in its shape. There was something about the object's movement that made it seem as though it were steering straight for the small island on which the two friends sat huddled.

Jahn struggled to his feet and drew his short elfin dagger.

"Maybe it's just an old tree," whispered Olthar.

"Or maybe it is one of those things that live in Dreary Lake," said Jahn, brandishing his hopelessly small weapon.

As the object neared the friends, an odd, echoing voice was heard from the center of the dimly outlined shape.

"Come aboard, come aboard. It has been a long time since

I've had so much of a swim. We'll be this side of where we're bound before long. Come aboard."

"Are you from the Old Ones?" asked Olthar.

He had never heard any of the ancient beings talk quite like this before.

"I am one of them. Not quite so old, though. They sent me when the floods abated, for I am the best of the lot when it comes to dealing with water."

"Where are the others?"

"They have gone back to where they dwelled before you went to Dun Macrath."

"Were any of you hurt?"

"There were a few that may have lost a limb or two, but they'll soon be put to rights. Nothing like mending for a thousand turnings. Does the job every time."

"I wish it were that easy with an elf," mumbled Jahn, feeling the full extent of his injuries as he began to try to move about.

"Oh, I expect it is the same with all things. It just seems to be different to you fellows, moving around as you do all the time. If you were sensible like our lot, you'd stay put and see it all through from start to finish and that would be an end of it."

"I wish we were sensible like your lot. Do you have a name we can pronounce?" asked Jahn.

The tree-being began to make the sounds of a winter storm, trembling and shaking as he did so, and was ready to go on when Jahn stopped him with a cry.

"Enough, enough. I did not think you would be able to give us simple folk anything like a handle we could mouth properly. We shall give you a name."

"Me? You shall give me a name? Very unusual, I should say. Most out of the ordinary run of what is done and not done. I don't know that the others will approve of this at all."

"They will by the time you get around to telling it to them. It's the only solution to a thorny problem."

"I am not in the least related to any sort at all that might be a thorn bearer. All my roots lie in the cone-bearing direction."

"Let's call him Coney," put in Olthar. "Otherwise we'll be forever trying to decide."

"That's a rabbit," protested the newly dubbed Coney.

"Well, you have no worry that anyone will mistake you for one."

"This is highly unusual," complained Coney. "But we have much to do and a long way to cover before I shall be able to return to the order. Now let us see if we can't do something about getting from here to there. Dear me, but that name does rankle my bark. I shall have a most difficult time with it."

"You can pretend we never gave it to you once you return to your friends," offered Jahn.

"Or you could give them all names that would be easy to pronounce. That way you would be able to talk about a lot of other things rather than always be going on for days and days trying to say all of your name."

"It couldn't be done," blustered Coney. "Why, the very foundation of our order rests firmly upon the names of each and every one of us. That would be high treason, that would."

"Let's not dwell on it then," said the elf, clinging to a large branch near what would have been Coney's head. "We are bound somewhere, but you didn't say where."

"The Beak," replied Coney. "I was told to take you to the part of the wood that runs down by the sea. That's all they told me. The Beak. I can't remember ever having been there, but all the others say that at one time we stood there as a great forest for a very long while. We only left when there were too many other settlements beginning and we were being murdered in droves. We left then, and traveled to other places, but the same thing always happened."

Olthar was having a difficult time not falling asleep, and had wedged himself into a snug crook of a branch, half listening to the tree talking and being lulled by the sound the water made. It was an old familiar sound and told him of all the lake and what was in it and where it ran. There were frightening things that were there, but he rested securely in the warm hollow of the Old One's branches, feeling that strength generate through the long trunk. He heard the echoing voice rise and fall like trembling leaves in the rain or the powerful creak and moan of a giant tree moved about in a strong wind, and it made him feel as though he were safe at last and could rest.

Olthar's thoughts had run to his mother and father, and he wondered where they were. He felt a terrible loneliness despite all the Old Ones had said. Jahn had helped him by telling of his own separation from his parents, but that did not stop the pain or fill up the emptiness. It was the first loss the pup had felt, and the Old Ones had tried to give him a solid footing to put it on. They told him stories and gave examples of many conditions which he would face, but they all left no real impression on him.

He began to listen to Coney's voice again, which was now telling of the order's move to the inner Westing Wood.

"That was the one place where no one ever disturbed us and haven't done so yet. Even when they did threaten us, we quickly overwhelmed them. At long last we were driven to protect ourselves in order to continue living. That was a terrible thing to be faced with, for there are no stories of violence in our entire history until these last turnings."

"I'm glad you've fallen to the right side. I'd hate to have you or your order as enemies."

"I find it all rather a chore," explained Coney. "There was always time before to stand and ponder any question at all until you had it worked out. It didn't make any difference what problem you chose, there was always time to sort it properly and to look at it from all angles."

What sounded like a long sigh escaped the Old One.

"Now there's never any proper time to do anything. Before you know it, you're off wandering around one end of the wood or another, gabbing like a magpie and not even a decent spot of good earth to get your roots into."

Jahn laughed lightly.

"I can fit myself into that picture. Elves and Old Ones aren't so far apart on that question."

"The elves have long been friends of the Old Ones. It was only that fact that allowed you to be brought into the order."

"I thought maybe it had something to do with the fact that none of your lot had any idea what to do with an impatient otter pup."

"Otters are more in favor with the order than those beastly beavers. They are the one part of the animal kingdoms that we have never allowed into any of our secrets."

"I've had good friends that are beavers," protested Olthar. "They were always good friends to me. I wish I knew where they were now."

"Wherever, it is better that they aren't here now," replied Coney stiffly.

As the three friends went on, the light disappeared completely, leaving a dark, starless heaven above them and a pitch-black lake all about them. The Old One was quiet for a time, and all that was heard was the soft ripple and splash of water lapping at his sides and the distant rumble of thunder somewhere far off, very faint and muted.

"At least it has stopped raining for a while," said Jahn, after a long period of silence. "I might be a new elf if I could have a fire and dry clothes."

Olthar, who was not bothered by the wet, shrugged.

"A fire would feel good."

A trembling shudder rippled through their friend.

"That's the sort of talk that will get you nowhere. Fire is a dangerous, deadly thing. Let's speak no more about it while I'm here, or I may be prone to tip you both over and go back to where that sort of nonsense is never talked about."

"We meant no harm, Coney," said Jahn. "We would never think of using any living wood for a fire. There is that timber which does not belong to the Old Ones, and feeding a fire is its use in the world. You must concede that."

"I will, but not many in these times know the difference. If we had not taken to defending ourselves, it was cut and chop just as quick as you please. No one ever bothered to see whether they were disturbing one of the order, or simply cutting up a log for firewood."

Before Jahn could reply, another distinct sound echoed across the gloomy night, rising on the darkness, then falling, only to rise again.

"Hush," snapped Jahn, quieting the pup before he could ask his question.

"It is wolves or I miss my bet. They aren't far off."

"We are very near the edge of the lake," said Coney.

"How could that be? I looked in all directions when there was that bit of light just before sundown. I couldn't see anything that looked like land."

"It doesn't look like land. It is mostly all swamp through these parts. But there is a shore near us now."

"We don't want to go anywhere near the wolves. That would be a fine welcome, to escape drowning just to be gobbled up by the wolves."

"They are going to the lake settlers' camp," said Coney.

"Who would live out here?" asked Olthar, shuddering.

"These are folk from an old race. They have lived upon these shores for a very long time. They were here when we moved from the sea."

"Are they friendly?"

"They are humans," replied Coney, as if that answered the question.

"Should we warn them?" asked Olthar.

"That would be difficult without going ashore."

Olthar was quiet for a moment, then he unstrapped the pipe from his chubby body.

"I shall blow them a note; then we will cry out that they are in danger."

Jahn was on the verge of reaching out to take the pipe from the small animal, then remembered that it had been given by Duirn himself; it was no longer Olthar the pup, but the Olthlinden that he traveled with.

A long, high note reached through the darkness, rippling the black water around them and splitting the air with a clean, wavering sound. It was followed by another note, lower and fuller, then a dozen more. It was a sound that gave the elf chill bumps. The hackles on the nape of his neck stood straight out, and Coney trembled below them in every limb and branch.

Olthar found the tune he was exploring, and as if by some remote memory, it came into perfect harmony within him what the pipe should say. His stubby paws found the right notes, and it went on for a time that way. He began to sway in time to the music, which wound out through the dark night, and as he watched, there sprang up signal fires all along the surface of the water.

That was what it looked like to Jahn until he saw that there was a long finger of land there. The fires lit up the dark outline of the crude shelters behind, which danced crazily in the flickering light and shadows that played against the darkness beyond.

There were other shadows there too; grotesque forms that moved in jerking motions before the fires, and long, dark shapes that flared out over the black mirror of the water. Many voices were raised then, all calling out in a tongue that sounded familiar to Olthar; yet he could not clearly understand what the words were.

Jahn strained his senses to the fullest and found that the tongue was similar to a lower dialect of elfin speech, and he called out as loudly as he could to the people there that they were in grave danger, and that a hunting pack of wolves was on the way to attack their camp.

The fires were built up higher, raising long arms of flames darting brightly into the night, casting more shadows and bringing more voices to join the din, which seemed to cause a strange chain reaction across the darkness. All along the low shoreline of the lake new fires blazed up on and on until there was a line of lights reaching all the way out of the elf's sight.

Olthar played on, a strange sadness sweeping through him now, and the music of the pipe wove stories in his head that were at once grand and sorrowful; and all through the notes he found his heart following along timidly, for there were visions in the song that he did not want to face.

Then there was a great clamor on the shore. The turf fires blazed so high that the darkness surrounding the three friends was broken, and they glided silently into the landing place dug out by the strangers that dwelled in those fierce, marshy lands. It was a sight that caused the people lining the bank of the lake to fall into a hushed silence as they watched; and the silence was not broken until Olthar, his eyes shining, put the Pipe of Ring Parath to his lips again and blew such a song of greeting that the lake dwellers burst into cheers and tears all at once.

The darkness of the place seemed to brighten then a small bit, and Olthar, as if he had intended to do so all along, strapped the pipe securely to his back and scampered ashore into the waiting throng, all of whom began to dance with delight as he frolicked among them, not stopping until a rather severe water elf stepped sternly forward to announce their arrival in a formal voice.

A Marshland Girl

IN the thin smoky light of the gray, murky shroud of the departing night, the three strange arrivals from the lake stood peering at those who had come to welcome them.

Olthar, who had danced among the tall humans, now grew shy and held back behind Jahn and Coney, floating still at the water's edge, and appearing to all who viewed him as merely a torn piece of driftwood that had been washed away in the disastrous floods that had struck after the long rains.

As their eyes grew adjusted to the dim light, they saw that the low shoreline that had not been visible in the darkness took a distinct shape, winding out over the muddy waters of the lake like the dull brown body of a snake. There were tall shelters on the shore, built on stilts so that they might be kept dry, with roofs of thatched reeds woven into thick mats. Jahn saw that the settlement was built after the fashion of old water elf danes, and he thought he saw a likeness to his own sires in the fair features of the humans who now advanced on their small party.

"Welcome, friends. Our humble hospitality is at your service."

"We offer our service to you," replied Jahn. "We are come to warn you that there is a hunting pack on its way to attack your settlement."

"We thank you, friend. A wolf pack would have a difficult time finding a safe way to reach us. Unless they have learned to use boats, we have nothing to fear from their quarter."

"My brother is forgetting his manners," said a tall, dark-haired girl, stepping beside the man who had spoken to the elf. "My name is Linne, and this is my brother, Largo. We are all that is left of an old family who once dwelled here when these horrid waters were yet beautiful and the times were more kind to all who followed the Light."

Jahn bowed low to the girl and her brother. Olthar followed his lead.

"My name is Jahn. This is my good friend and companion Olthar. Behind me is one we call Coney."

"I see no others," said Linne.

"It may seem a bit strange to you, but perhaps it won't if we explain further how we got this far and how we have come to be in your fair presence."

"Come then, let us retire to a more comfortable place rather than standing outside here. You look tired and hungry. Come."

Linne led the two companions from the water and was surprised when Olthar raced back to the floating tree, where he seemed to be in conversation for a short time.

"What is wrong with the waterkind?" asked Largo. "Is he short of his wits?"

Jahn watched the otter returning, wondering how he would explain the Old One.

"He is a very strange fellow. It would take a long time to explain it all," began Jahn.

"We will eat and rest first, then you can give us your tale. You are injured, good elf. We will see to it that you get tended to."

Jahn had forgotten his ordeal in the water with all the

113

excitement of the meeting with the humans. He was suddenly so faint and so weary he felt he could hardly take another step farther.

"See to the otter. Keep him with me. I am trying to help him reach The Beak," mumbled Jahn, feeling his senses slipping away.

There was a cry of dismay, then concerned voices hovering over him, although he could not open his eyes to see the faces. He heard Olthar's distress whistle in his ear. He tried to reach out a hand to reassure the small animal but found he had no strength to do so, and the voices faded away into a blurry blue-black silence.

Olthar, standing over his friend, looked about in bewilderment until the dark-haired girl bent over the elf and laid a cloak across his shoulders.

"We will take care of your friend. He needs rest and food."

A great weariness overcame the otter and he began to shiver uncontrollably.

Linne reached down and picked him up, ignoring his feeble protests.

"We shall look after you as well, my little one. Stop acting up so. You can hardly wiggle."

"I'll have them prepare a room for these two," offered Largo. "It looks as though the omen we have been looking for has arrived at last."

Olthar's eyes were closed and he was limp in the beautiful girl's arms, but he listened carefully to the humans. There was a part deep within him that feared all who were of the strange race, although he knew he felt he could trust the heart of the one who called herself Linne. It was a kind of knowledge that he didn't know he had, but he let himself stop struggling. He felt the comforting warmth of the girl, knowing that she was a friend of all who followed the High King.

"Omens or not, they need rest and food and a healer."

"I've sent for the Crone."

"Good. Let's get them back to the shelter. We need to send out the other sentries as well. We may as well reinforce the South Dike. That is the most likely place that invaders would try to cross."

"Perhaps, Linne. But you must leave the defense of Lothean to me. You tend to our injured guests."

"I am capable of doing more than that."

"We won't go into it again, Linne. I have spoken my mind on that."

114

"And I have spoken mine, brother. You can't keep treating me as though I'm your helpless sister. It is time I took my own place in the workings of Lothean."

The young man reddened as he struggled to control his temper.

"This is not the time to confront me, Linne. We have injured to tend to and an attack to divert. You go with these strangers and make sure they are well settled. We shall come to a point of agreement on your role as my sister."

"You speak of me as cattle, brother, to be decided on as you might try to decide what to do with property. I have reached my limit with that."

Largo turned angrily, holding his hands over his ears. He stalked away, calling out loudly to groups of men who stood about the circle of shelters.

"Quickly! Come on, lads, we have work cut out for us this night."

Olthar had been awake while the argument had been going on but had kept his eyes closed.

"He treats you like Jahn treats me," he said softly.

"Why, you scoundrel! You're awake after all," she teased.

"Jahn treats me like I know nothing and am too young to do anything on my own."

"Is Jahn the elf?"

"The hardheaded elf. And then there is Coney."

"We only found the two of you," said Linne, walking again toward the shelter where Jahn had been taken.

The healers were gathered there already, and the injured elf had been washed and slipped into a dry cot with thick blankets.

"Coney is an Old One."

"An old what?" asked the girl, pausing to look over her shoulder at the retreating form of her brother, who was leading the others to check the security of their boundaries.

"An Old One. He looks like a tree."

"You mean the tree that you floated here on?"

"That is Coney."

Suddenly Olthar became very agitated and struggled fiercely to get down from the girl's grasp.

"You can't do anything to Coney! Don't let them try to chop him up!"

Linne held on but spoke reassuringly.

"I won't let them do anything to the tree. It's much too wet for firewood, at any rate."

"He's not firewood! He's Coney! The Old Ones can be dangerous enemies to any who try to harm them."

They had arrived at the shelter where Jahn lay, and Linne handed the exhausted otter to an old woman with soft features.

"Here is another one. I think all this one needs is sleep."

The woman tried to take the wriggling pup, but he escaped and crawled into the cot with Jahn, curling up comfortably on the elf's chest.

"Leave him," laughed Linne. "They are the oldest of friends, it seems. I think they will rest better if they are together."

The young woman looked for a long time at the sleeping pair and at last reached down to tuck the otter under the blanket that covered them.

As she did so, her hand accidentally touched the case that was strapped to Olthar's back, and a terrible wind tore through the shelter. A white-hot sheet of blazing light blinded her momentarily, and she was knocked backward painfully to the floor. Olthar was up instantly, baring his tiny fangs and glaring about him wildly.

"What is it?" cried Linne, thinking that some unseen horror had struck them down from ambush.

As the wind and light passed, the otter saw that there was no danger. He felt carefully to make sure the pipe was securely in its place.

"It is all a part of the story we have to tell you," he said at last, yawning again and falling asleep even as he spoke.

Linne's eyes were wide in wonder and awe at the strangers who had come to them out of the vast swamplands. She had begun to think that there were no decent beings left in those wild parts beyond where they lived, for the only intruders who ever reached their settlement were the half-beasts and wolves, who seemed to grow in numbers every passing day. Largo had said long ago that the reason they stayed on in that remote part of the world was because the outer woods and mountains were all filled with the beasts. She had to believe him, for the proof was always readily there, and they had not far to go to prove that there was danger everywhere beyond their borders.

She looked again at the sleeping pair, the elf and the otter, and thought what strange companions they were. The otter had said the other member of their party was a tree and had begged her to not cut it up for firewood!

Remembering that, she made her way out of the dim, cool shelter and found her way back to the landing, where the

116

gnarled trunk lay snugly in the thick mud of the shore. The water lapped quietly against the dark shape, and Linne could see nothing unusual about the uprooted tree that would make it so different from all the other flotsam that had spilled over into the lake from the great flood.

They had been lucky to have had long experience on the lake, and they knew the ways of the water well. At the first sign of the heavy rains, they had prepared large rafts with all their belongings, tethered by anchors of stones to the floor of the lake. If the water rose to a greater height, all one had to do was release more rope to let each raft float higher.

Linne bent closer to examine the tree stump. As she did so, a cold voice, grainy and hard, spoke.

"Stand back!" it rasped.

The girl leapt back instantly.

"Who said that?"

There was no reply, so she walked to the other side of the floating stump and looked carefully to make sure no one was hiding there.

"Stand back!" came the voice.

"Who are you?" repeated Linne.

This time, she moved forward, reaching out a hand to touch the tree.

A great agitation started in the water at her feet, swirling and frothing at the top, and a wind like the sound of a winter storm rushed through the barren limbs of the horizontal tree.

"Stop that! I am your friend. I have the otter and the elf in my care. They said they were with another one named Coney. Are you Coney?"

"No!" replied, the cold, grainy voice.

Now Linne was confused.

"But you are the one that came with the elf and the otter!"

"I am that, no doubt. My name, however, is not Coney."

"Who are you talking to?" asked her brother, Largo.

She had not seen him return.

"I am trying to find out who I am talking to myself."

"There is no one here but this tree stump," observed Largo, peering around carefully.

"This tree stump was just talking."

Largo looked at his sister, barely able to conceal his scorn.

"This is what I mean about you, Linne. You are always full of odd ideas and pipe dreams that you keep confusing with the real world. It is a dangerous habit. That is why I don't want you to take over any duties that relate to our safety."

"You won't let me become a soldier because I am a woman," snapped Linne, her eyes a deep blue that flashed their hurt.

"A girl. You are not even a woman yet."

"If our mother was alive you'd feel different."

"You would, too," argued Largo. "Then perhaps you wouldn't be so bent on dabbling where you have no business. You should be learning to cook and tend the settlement instead of trying to force your way into the life of a soldier."

"It makes the others feel threatened," insisted Linne.

Largo blew up with an oath and stalked away.

"You go right ahead talking to your tree stump. I have important errands to see to."

The young woman was on the verge of tears, but the voice she had heard before came again, only softer and more encouragingly.

"Don't let him upset you. I didn't talk while he was here because he is one of those who might be prone to try to use me as firewood."

Coney floated a bit closer to the landing so Linne would have no trouble hearing him.

"How are my friends Olthar and Jahn?"

"Is that how they are called?"

"Among others. But this time they are Jahn Spray the elf and Olthar."

"The otter is wonderful. I can't say why he makes me feel so good, but there is something in his eyes. When he plays that pipe, I can hardly keep myself from crying and laughing all at once."

"You are very wise for one so young. There is a great errand that he is upon. I have been with him for some small time now. I am taking him to the sea."

"The sea? Whatever would he want to go there for?"

Coney was silent a moment, then asked Linne to come closer to him.

"I will tell you another time. There is something here that I do not like. My sap is all boiling. It only does that where there is great danger. Look to the small one. Stay with the two of them. No matter what happens, you must keep the pipe safe. It is the one thing you must guard as if it were your very life."

The young woman paled at the sudden sternness of the Old One, but listened carefully to everything he instructed her to do.

"What sort of danger? The wolves the small one spoke of?"

118

"More than wolves. My sap never stirs over the presence of the beasts from across the Black Ice."

"Then what shall I guard against?"

Coney floated higher in the water, shaking his outer branches stiffly.

"Treachery from friends," he said quietly, then repeated it to make sure she had heard.

Largo

THERE was no sound in the shelter but the deep, even breathing of the two friends. For the first time in days there was no sound of the rain drumming against the thatched roof, or the splash of the rising water against the already inundated marshland that barely kept its shallow back above the level of Dreary Lake.

The settlement Olthar and Jahn had reached aboard Coney was an ancient one, going back to the times long before, as the Old One had said. In the ancient days the lake had been part of a beautiful inland sea, but as the years wore on, first one, then another of the old settlements vanished in the wars that had begun to rage over Atlanton. As the numbers grew smaller, the survivors began to band together until at last the end of that long proud race was gathered in one small settlement on Dreary Lake, headed by a brother and sister who were the last of the descendants of the leaders of the older order.

Largo and Linne were barely a year apart, but Largo treated his sister as though she were still unable to fend for herself. This was in part because she was his sister and he felt protective of her, and also in part because he resented her spirit and courage, kindness and patience, qualities that he worried he lacked.

Largo was fiercely loyal and concerned with the welfare of those followers who dwelled on his every word, but often short-tempered and cross with those who questioned his judgment, although there was no one who knew him who could call him cowardly. Hotheaded and brash perhaps, and sometimes a braggart, but never cowardly. He saw Linne as a threat to what he envisioned as his manhood. If she had been a brother, it would have all been well understood and easy to deal with; as it was, since she was a female, it was confusing and frightening. Linne never let up constantly pressuring him to let her share in the duties he performed, but that made him feel even angrier, for he was always teased about her.

She had grown into a very beautiful young woman and all the other young men in the settlement could only deal with her by treating her as a girl as Largo did. If they stopped to examine their feelings, they became as confused and baffled as her brother. It seemed easier to just pull her pigtails than to look into her deep blue eyes and feel the flutter of their stomachs and the shortness of breath. Somehow those feelings turned fierce soldiers and good hunters into perfectly clumsy and awkward clods whenever they were near her, which made them feel uncomfortable and somehow lacking.

Largo stood in the silence of the shelter studying Olthar and Jahn. The small animal had made a distinct impression on the settlement by his arrival. It was hard to understand the wild surge of spirit they had all felt when the otter stepped ashore playing the strange pipe that flooded the soul with so many forgotten feelings.

Largo remembered a dream he had had as a child, one of those vivid images that was so real he was never afterward quite sure if it had been only a dream or some dim happening that he remembered years later. The song of the pipe had reawakened that vision; and he recalled it now, standing there in the dark silence looking at the elf and otter curled onto the rough sleeping cot.

There had been a vast army in his dream; and there were many boats with blood-red sails that covered the entire lake. There was someone there who was very important, for all the hosts gathered there lifted their bows and swords and helmets together in salute, and there was a great noise of gathered voices raised in unison as they called out a name over and over. He had been but a small boy when he first recalled this. In the inner desires that drove him, he wanted it to be his name they called, so he soon convinced himself that it was so. He never told anyone of his dream, not even his sister, so no one could ever disagree with his belief.

Even then he was jealous of Linne, for she had always been brave and kind and was well liked by everyone except perhaps the other boys she always beat at their games. The girls of the settlement were alienated by her boyishness but could not shun her because she was the daughter of the chief Elder. They also were envious of her beauty.

Largo had an overwhelming desire to be liked, which often drove him to acts of jealous cruelty to Linne, but she never told on him or complained; the guilt he suffered from these acts and the fact she never once exposed him were later to make him overprotective of her.

He thought of all those things as he remembered the dream that had come to him as a child. It was hard to remember clearly whether there had ever been any real event that might have made him dream in that way. There had at one time been a large army made up of the men of the marsh-lands and lakes that was led by his father, but the long wars had slowly taken them all away. There had eventually come a time when none of the men ever returned home, and there had never been any further word. The settlement had finally given up hope in the end; And when Largo had come of age at eighteen, he was made leader to replace his long-absent father.

A noise made Largo start.

"What are you doing here?" he shot at Linne. She had frightened him and it made him angry.

"I came to see how my wards are doing. We should go outside so we don't disturb them."

"We won't disturb them. I don't think you could wake them now even if you tried."

Linne tried to meet her brother's eyes as he spoke, but he looked away quickly.

"They have evidently gone through much. It is a very strange thing to see elves in these times. I know our father used to speak of an old elfin dane that was near here in the old days, but I can't remember ever having seen any elves."

"They were gone before we were born," replied Largo shortly. "Those were stories of the Four Lake Wars."

"It is still strange to see an elf. I don't think you can argue about that."

"I'm not arguing."

"We are going to wake them up if we don't go."

"There is no one holding you here."

Linne was suddenly afraid to leave the two strangers alone with her brother. Coney's warning had confused her at first, but since she and Largo had stood talking, a vague uneasiness had begun nagging at her. All the past disappointments and cruelty of Largo came into her thoughts; she saw the odd, bright light in his eyes, like the open emptiness of a madman, and it made her afraid. Largo had lived his life in the shadow of his father's legend, a situation which had slowly eroded the insecure boy's self-confidence and turned him into something of a bully.

"I think I'll just stay in case they should wake and need anything."

"I shall see to their needs if they awaken," he said curtly.

Linne could see that he was rapidly losing patience; not knowing what else to do at the moment and not wanting to confront him openly with a very indistinct rumor of a feeling, she left, although she did not go far.

There was a vague sense of foreboding that hung over Linne's heart as she stood waiting outside the shelter. A thousand dark thoughts ran through her mind, and she was on the point of going back to seek Coney's advice when there came from inside the shelter the same terrifying noise that had occurred when she had moved toward the otter pup to make sure he was covered up.

A thin light of understanding began to burn in Linne's mind as she recalled the strange smile on Largo's face the instant the otter and elf made their appearance at the lakeside. She was close to her brother in an odd way and loved him, but she also recognized something else in him that was ugly and misshapen.

A moment after the noise and motion had subsided in the shelter where the two friends lay, Largo came out, ashen and shaking visibly. Linne reached out to try to comfort him, but he shook her arm away violently.

"You traitorous wench! You have set them against me!" he hissed, spitting out the words as if they left a bad taste in his mouth.

"What are you saying, brother?"

"You shall pay for this," he snarled, striding angrily away, his face convulsed in ugly spasms.

Linne watched him disappear, then hurried to the bedside of the otter. She found Olthar awake, watching her from the elf's chest.

"He tried to take the pipe from me," he said calmly. "He was frightened away by the noise."

"My brother is very confused," began Linne, not really knowing how to explain herself.

"He didn't harm me," assured Olthar. "I have heard many

stories from my friend Jahn about this strange desire that people get for the power of the pipe. It turns their minds."

He wasn't sure exactly what he meant, but he was beginning to feel a strange new awareness about the pipe and the responsibility of carrying it. Some of the things Jahn had said began to make sense, and Duirn's tales seemed much more understandable.

Olthar tightened the strap of the pipe case closer to him, feeling it suddenly much heavier than it had been before.

"Can I bring you anything? Are you hungry or thirsty?"

"I would like a drink. I am suddenly very thirsty."

Linne drew a cool mug of water for him from the stone crock.

"I have spoken to your friend Coney," she said, watching him drink.

Olthar looked at her over the top of the cup.

"I have a strange feeling that Jahn and I would be better off going with Coney right now and leaving you all to yourselves."

Linne's face fell. She could not explain why, but she suddenly felt very near tears.

"I'm sorry about Largo. He really doesn't mean anyone any harm."

"Jahn and I only came ashore to warn you of the wolf pack. That has been done. I think when we have some sleep we shall go on."

The otter looked down at the elf, who still slept soundly.

"I don't think I could wake him now if I tried."

"I hope you change your mind about leaving. It has been a long time since we have had visitors. You seemed to make everyone so happy when you came. I have not seen the people laugh in so long I don't like to remember."

"There doesn't seem much to laugh at here," replied Olthar. "It is a gray place. Why do you go on staying here? Aren't there other places you could go?"

Linne shook her head.

"This is where we were when our father left on a raid against the savages. He never came back, but we were afraid to leave. We thought it best to stay in case any of them ever returned."

"And have they?"

"No," said Linne, again near tears. "That was years ago. I don't know why we stay on now. It is harder every year. The

123

food is harder to find and the lake is being overrun by the Bog Hats."

"Bog Hats?" questioned Olthar.

"They are a clan that lives in Dismal Swamp. We have been enemies for as long as I can remember."

Olthar was quiet for a moment, lost in his own thoughts. "Is your brother the Elder here?"

"He has been the leader since he came of age."

"Why does he not move? There are other places that would be much easier to live."

Linne looked away, shrugging her shoulders.

"I don't know why. I thought at first he was still waiting for our father. Then after such a long time, I began to think it was because he was afraid. He has never been beyond our small boundaries here. I don't think many of our settlement have been. Most of those who had traveled went with my father when he left."

Olthar yawned. He felt his eyelids drooping, so he hurriedly mumbled his apologies to the beautiful stranger.

"I shall talk with you further when I am rested. I can't seem to hold my eyes open any longer."

"I will watch over your sleep so that no one bothers you."

"Thank you," he muttered, reaching out a paw to touch her.

He was fast asleep in a moment.

Linne looked long at the still forms of the two sleeping friends, and knowing her brother as she did, she decided to take matters into her own hands. She found the healer, an old woman who had attended her mother at childbirth, and the two of them, carefully tucking the bedclothes about the elf and otter, picked them up easily between them and carried them gently to the landing, where Coney waited against the shore.

"What are you going to do with them here?" asked the old midwife.

"This is as far as you go. Thank you."

"They'll catch cold out here," the old woman warned.

"We won't be staying here long."

The old woman saw that it would do no good to argue, so she left. If she couldn't get the sister to listen to reason, she knew she could convince Largo, who was a sensible lad for all his other shortcomings.

As soon as the old woman was gone, Coney hastened to give Linne his instructions.

"You must hurry and tie them onto me. I shall take care of them. You must come along with me. There have been other things happening on the lake. I am hearing many strange tales now. There is much danger."

"I can't go with you, Coney. I must stay with my brother."

"Then you must warn the others. There is a large party of raiders that are on their way here. I don't think it is the beasts. These are different. I think they're humans."

Linne's eyes widened.

"It might be news of our father!"

"If it's news of your father, it's all bad. I hear only bad talk among them."

"I will tell Largo. Good-bye, Coney. Take good care of your friends!"

The girl's voice broke and she stood for a moment as if torn between going and staying, then turned and fled up the path that led to the settlement.

Coney mumbled an ancient oath that made his limbs tremble slightly, and without appearing to move at all, he shot out into the open water of the lake.

Jahn and Olthar slept on, missing not only the strange noises that the Old One made to himself, but all the strange sights that had begun to appear on the marshy borders of Dreary Lake.

Floods and Dragons

THERE had been a long silence after the scout finished his report to Duirn and Emeon. Banon sat with his head bowed, making it hard to read anything from his eyes.

"It's hard to believe that they could have been lost," said Emeon at last. "Even the Old Ones! I can't believe that they could be harmed by so small a thing as a flood."

"This was no small flood," corrected the scout. "We were able to escape only by the fact that we were near the high ground that borders the river on the east side of the Westing. Even then we had a swim of it. Anything that was caught in that torrent was doomed. I've never seen a wall of water like that in all my days. It was high enough that I could see it clearly above the trees; and it was roaring like the end of everything."

Emeon got up and began to pace restlessly.

"Do you think the Old Ones would have let themselves be caught by such a flood?" he asked at last. "They aren't exactly helpless."

Duirn turned to the scout.

"Did you check to see if they might have moved on to safety before the flood?"

"We had no time," confessed the weary elf. "There were a lot of Varads that had been routed by the water, and we had a tricky time of it just getting out in one piece."

"You did well. I didn't mean to imply that you shirked your duty, Deon," said Duirn.

"There might have been another way the Old Ones could have gone to avoid the flood, but we couldn't get over the river to see, even if the Varads hadn't been there."

Duirn stood very still, gazing away into the distance toward the Westing Wood.

"You shall have to go for yourself," murmured Banon. "There will be no answers for you until you do."

"I don't know that I even want any answers at this point," confessed Duirn. "I am trying not to think of what shall happen to us all if the Olthlinden and the pipe are lost."

The old elf gently grasped the leader of the Shanoliel by the arm.

"None of us want to face that, Duirn, but if that is the way it is to be, then it is best over with at once."

"There are still things to be done," consoled Emeon, although he wasn't feeling at all cheerful.

"I will go back with you," offered the scout called Deon. "I can show you where we were. We can move about from there."

"Thank you, Deon. That will help. Get me some of your best archers, Emeon. Not too many, but enough that we may not worry about Varads."

Emeon bustled away, shouting orders at the top of his voice and calling out names.

"Banon, I would take you, but I need a steady hand here to guide the clan in my absence. I think it might be wise if we were to split our band and plan to meet at The Beak in a week's time. That will give us two chances of running across Olthar and Jahn."

"We will find them, Duirn. This is but a setback for the

126

moment. A few days ago, we were worried about how to get them safely out of Dun Macrath."

Duirn laughed briefly.

"How true. Just when one is ready to deal with one problem, there always is a sweetener to really spoil the tea."

"This may yet work out to our best advantage," went on Banon. "I know Jahn Spray. He is no ordinary elf, when it comes to that. They also have the Pipe of Ring Parath. Just that fact alone argues against anything happening to them."

"It would seem so. I am trying to believe that."

"You just go on trying, my friend. Nothing ever comes of doubting the good of this world. We just have to look long enough to find the point of it all."

At that moment, Emeon returned at the head of a large group of well-armed elves.

"We have enough strength here to stand off anything but a real army of our good Varads."

"Banon is in charge here. We are going to see if we can't find the trail of the Olthlinden. We are to meet at The Beak seven days from now."

Duirn returned quickly to the shelter where his own gear lay and hastily armed himself. He drew on his cloak and was on the verge of departing when he changed direction and made his way to the healer's shelter.

Inside were dark coolness and the sweet smell of herbs and incense. It took Duirn a few minutes to make out anything in the dim light. When he could see satisfactorily, he stepped directly up to the cot of Trane, who lay perfectly still.

"Have you come to slay me?" he asked, without opening his eyes.

"No," replied Duirn evenly. "I have come to see if you are well enough to travel. We are leaving these parts now."

The Erling opened his eyes and studied the Shanoliel King.

"Is this an offer or an order?"

"Neither. I would rather you travel in my group, if you are able."

"What if I refuse to travel at all?"

"Then you will be put into the Ancient Sleep by the healer and we will transport you that way. We are not through with you yet, Trane. You may be our one chance of rescuing the otters from the Dark One."

"Oh, the Protector cares not a whit about the otters or me, Duirn. I will do you no good at all; I will do you harm, if I can. That I can promise."

"I know you will, Trane. We understand each other very well. Still, I feel it is not over yet between us. I shall feel it a good thing to take you with me. There is much to be said for keeping your enemy always within your sight."

"It is a wise thought. I shall also be able to keep my eyes upon you to see what new mischief you are up to. This way I shall be able to report to the Protector firsthand all your actions."

"I have an idea we will be running into her soon enough," said Duirn. "I will send Emeon to you with clothes and gear you'll need for traveling. Make yourself ready."

"Not to oblige you. I shall make myself ready so that I may try for an escape."

"We all have to follow our own hearts," replied Duirn. He had begun to have a strange feeling about Trane, at once very sad and yet satisfied; he began to think that there was, after all, a useful purpose for the Erling warrior beyond even his understanding of the way things were.

Trane glared at the water elf, but his eyes were clouded with a rage and grief too deep to allow him to see the compassion of Duirn's heart.

"We shall follow our own hearts, Duirn. I shall dream of nothing better than to bury my dagger in yours."

"So you say, Trane. It is not for us to know yet how it will all fall out."

Duirn walked out of the shelter into the fine morning air, breathing deeply. There was a new smell that had begun to fill the wind with a promise of new growth and fresh beginnings after the long, disastrous rains had washed clean the old order of things. Somehow it felt like a new start to Duirn, although he could not quite say why. Or it may have been more as if another chapter in the tale had begun, which promised to be a particularly good one.

He gathered his gear cheerfully, wondering to himself where Olthar and Jahn had gotten off to. It had worried and stunned him at first when he had heard the scout's report of the flood; but he had now had time to think on the problem, and a deep sense of optimism had replaced the doubts and fears about the two missing companions' safety. Wherever they were, he felt, they were one step closer to where they needed to be. All he needed to do was find them.

Emeon broke in upon his thoughts.

"I've sent a few of us on ahead to see if they can pick up a trail. The flooding should have gone down enough by now so that there may be a fresh lead as to which way Olthar and Jahn and the Old Ones could have gone."

"Good lad, Emeon. I've decided to take the Erling with us. Will you gather him some gear and see to it that he will be well secured while we're on our journey?"

Although Emeon was surprised by the news of the addition to their party, he said nothing and immediately did as he was bidden.

Banon sought him out next.

"I hear you are taking Trane with you."

"I thought I would spare you that burden, my friend. One of us shall have to deal with him. It may as well be me. You shall have enough to deal with just moving the band to The Beak."

"I shall have no more difficulties than you," objected his friend. "I fail to see the purpose of this needless risk you take. You know he is sworn to avenge himself upon you."

"All the more reason that I should have him with me," countered Duirn. "It may also serve to keep him as closely bound to me as the strongest of chains."

The old elf knitted his brow into a concerned frown.

"You may find it more so than you think, Duirn. When one plays with fire, it is easy to be burned."

Duirn suddenly burst out in a laugh.

"Your warnings are well taken, Banon. I am touched by your concern, but there really is no other choice in the matter. If I were to leave Trane in your charge, I would only worry the more. At least I will know where he is and what he is up to."

The old elf stroked his beard, looking thoughtful.

"You are very much like your father. That was exactly how he would view the problem."

"And how would you view it?"

"I am Banon, not Duirn. I think I should be prone to outfitting Trane with enough food to see him safely back across the Black Ice."

"You have lived for a long time and know many things, Banon. I see what you say is valid. I can't say exactly why I am not willing to do that."

"You are doing what you must, my young friend. You have no choice. No one of us does. We do what our heart tells us and there is an end of it."

"That is exactly what Trane said."

129

"The Erling is very wise, in a way. He is, after all is said and done, an elf."

Emeon interrupted the two friends again to report to Duirn.

"I have equipped the Erling as you wished. He seems well pleased with the arrangement. I wish I could say the same."

"You may find it more to your liking as time goes on," said Duirn. "There are yet things that we don't know about our good Erling that he may be inclined to tell us in the course of a good journey."

"I know you have your reasons, Duirn. I'm just saying that I don't like knowing I'm in the presence of someone who could cheerfully plant his dagger in my back."

"It shall only be for a time, Emeon. As soon as we find the trail of Olthar and Jahn, I plan to give him his freedom. That way we shall have escorted him fairly near the haunts where he will likely be able to find those he prefers to be with."

Emeon's face brightened.

"Well, that's different. I had begun to think that perhaps you were going to try to change his way of thinking back around to our side."

"That would be a tall order, if it were the case," said Banon. "Trane really believes that the Dark One is the Protector and Duirn the murderer. It would take something beyond argument or reason to change his mind."

Duirn's eyes became a darker blue-gray as he spoke, lost in thought.

"I think that Trane is of best service to us by believing as he believes. If he were not the way he is, then there would be a great deal of chaos somewhere down the line. You don't harvest apples by chopping down the tree."

"You are very mysterious," mused Banon. "Is there something that has happened that we should need to know about?"

Duirn shook his head.

He could not find words to explain the vague feelings he had been experiencing. There were the usual visions he saw, but they were common among all elves at that time in the world, so it was nothing out of the ordinary to them. But then Duirn had had one of those very clear days when everything seemed to make perfect sense and every action seemed to be in perfect harmony. It was then that it occurred to him to take Trane upon the scouting trip to try to pick up the trail of the two missing companions. It was as though a long-sought piece of a puzzle was suddenly presented and put into place.

It fit perfectly, making a complete picture out of something that before had been baffling and dark.

Even Dorini had her own dark role to play in the scheme of things. There was no light without the darkness, and no way to learn about the terrible embrace of the Dark One except to have been held in the frozen terror of her unrelenting mind.

Duirn rolled his gear tightly into the clever elfin knapsack and put his bow and quiver over his shoulder where it would be ready for instant use. He went over all the small details of the move to the sea with Banon, although the old elf was more familiar with the charts and the countryside than Duirn was.

They arranged a meeting point at The Beak which was well-known to all the Eolin, for it was a place that was long held to be the very embarkation point for the Upper Havens that their ancestors had once used. That had been in a time when the boundaries were still open and it was possible to travel to and from that destination quite freely.

Banon promised to search his end of the wood on the way to their meeting point and to give battle to any Varad or Worlugh war party he encountered on the way, if the elves were not too badly outnumbered. He tried again to talk Duirn out of his idea of taking the Erling with him on so perilous a journey, but the younger elf was determined.

Emeon had gathered Duirn's party and was on the verge of reporting that they were ready to travel when a distant noise began to force itself into their awareness. It was not quite like thunder but sounded as deeply, although they could see no cloud in the sky or any other omen of an approaching storm.

"What in the name of the High King?" began Emeon, but was cut short by the renewal of the faint rumbling roar, which now had grown in intensity.

"Hush!" said Banon, raising a hand.

As Duirn turned toward the direction the noise came from, his eyes encountered the Erling's face, which had taken on a knowing smile that lit the wood elf's features with a savageness that stopped Duirn's heart for a moment.

"You are doomed, Duirn. There is no help for you now. The Protector said she was going to call down the fate dogs. She has done it!"

Duirn faced Trane calmly, then turned to Banon.

"If what Trane says is true, we shall have to hurry. There will be no time to escape if we don't look to it now. We must

131

use the memory of the Eolin. There will be no mortal way to combat this enemy."

"What is it?" asked Emeon, looking from Duirn to Banon.

The old elf trembled slightly as he spoke, but his eyes were clear and his voice was steady.

"The Dargol Brem."

A look of fear and relief crossed Emeon's fair features. He held out a hand gravely to first Banon, then Duirn.

"It is the time we have awaited."

He turned to the assembled band of elves and brandished his elfin short sword.

"The time is on us, lads! We have heard the first voice of the Dargol Brem! Let us swear again our oath to the High King! Death to the Dargol Brem! Long life in the Havens!"

The fair elves suddenly took on the terrible mien of the grim warriors they were, more dreadful in their appearance for their beauty; and the glen rang with the hollow sound of their ancient battle cry. The war pipes took up the call, their deafening skree tearing at the ears of all who heard, their voices discordant and horrible.

In the blinking of an eye the entire band of Banon's was gone, using the old memory of the Eolin which allowed those elves to travel in ways other than one would normally go by foot. It was the ancient power that some still possessed; others had forgotten or gone over to the Darkness and lost the secrets forever.

Duirn and Emeon still stood listening to the growling peal of thunder, which had taken on a distinct character now. They could hear the grating sweep of the dragon's wings against the air and the roaring of the fierce breath of the beast singing out its death song to all who might cross its path.

Their band waited impatiently, staring at the sky over the treetops, fully expecting to see the arrival of the beast at any second. Trane the Erling was beside himself with rage and frustration. His features were flushed and his eyes bulged.

"You foul traitors! You won't escape so easily. Your powers won't hold when the Protector gets to you. You won't be able to escape her forever with these sniveling tricks. Cowards!"

He tried to go on but rambled incoherently, his eyes starting from his head. He tried to lunge at Duirn's throat with his bare hands, but Emeon moved between them and touched the woulded elf with a small leather pouch that he had withdrawn from inside his cloak. Trane's face froze in a spasm of fear; then a fleeting array of looks passed over his features, from shock, to surprise, to sorrow, to oblivion.

"I had hoped that we could have learned more from him," said Duirn, his face drawn into a worried mask.

"There's nothing for it now, Duirn. We can't take him with us. You know the Law as well as I. It would kill him."

"That might be his salvation," mused Duirn. "Somehow finding death at the hands of his kinsmen might free him from Dorini."

"It is not ours to decide, Duirn. We must hurry or we shall not be able to escape the spell of the Dargol Brem."

Duirn hesitated a moment longer, studying the Erling. He was suddenly sure that this was not the end of the road for their hours together; there would be a time when their roles would be played out to a final scene. Another moment passed in which they could hear the dragon's breathing clearly; then Duirn turned, made a sign to his followers, and the wood was empty of all traces of the presence of his band, leaving only the lone, unmoving figure of the wood elf Trane behind.

Attack of the Bog Hats

LINNE made her way quickly back to the settlement to find her brother, pausing every now and again to try to discover what the strange noises were that seemed to come from first one direction, then another. There were echoes of replies that sounded from farther away across the lake toward the South Dike Gate, which Largo had recently reinforced to hold off any attempts at passing that way into their camp.

The settlement was up in arms, moving this way and that, the able-bodied men and boys hurrying by her in every direction at once. The women had packed stores and herbs for dressings and made ready to move camp at the shortest notice.

"Calen, where is Largo?" she called to an older man who was fastening a thick quiver onto his back.

The man nodded over his shoulder in the direction of the South Dike.

"I think he's taken a group of the lads out there to see what this is all about."

"It's not a wolf pack," said Linne, her beautiful face drawn into a worried frown.

This news startled the man, and he stopped what he was doing to look at the girl.

"Have the scouts seen something else?"

"It's not wolves or the beast warriors," went on Linne, who had begun to help herself to the stack of arms next to Calen.

"And what do you think you're after, young lady?" he asked, taken aback by Linne's actions.

"I'm arming myself," she snorted, her pale blue eyes full of defiance.

"Largo doesn't want you to!"

"Largo doesn't tell me what to do anymore."

"You know the rules, Linne. All the women are to gather here in the case of attack to treat wounded and resupply any who need arrows."

"They shall do that. I am going to find my brother."

Calen saw that there was no use arguing with the headstrong girl. There were other distractions now: the noise of a great number of men shouting at once and the clear sound of the sentries' warning horns floating over the still lake from the South Dike Gate calling out danger and destruction.

"Come on, Calen! We must hurry!"

Linne moved gracefully into a run, causing the older man to have to run hard to keep apace of her. They went swiftly over the concealed pathways that ran through quicksand and low places in the marshy land. Some of the trail was covered by water, and it was only by careful study that a stranger would be able to choose between a safe path and one that ended in a deadly mire that would suck any living thing into its depths in a matter of minutes.

This was all part of the defense system that the settlement had depended upon for a long while. It had been quite successful in keeping away the beast warriors and wolf packs that plagued the rest of the shores of Dreary Lake and had also kept their distant cousins, the Bog Hats, from invading them and carrying all the more peaceful marshlanders into captivity.

Another short call on the warning horn sounded urgently. There were others following Linne now. She had begun to realize that Coney was right. This was something different than they had ever had to deal with before. She could see strange shapes moving in the distance and could hear the sounds of many men joined in battle.

The whiz and snap of an arrow crackled past her ear and for the first time in her young life Linne realized that someone had purposely tried to harm her. She could not see anyone near her, but a moment later Calen stopped and drew back his bow, letting fly a shaft at a clump of marsh reeds that lay off the path to their right-hand side. There was a scream of pain and a body shot upright out of the reeds and vaulted backward into the lake.

"Look to yourself!" shouted Calen. "They are all about us!"

There were three more zipping whirs of arrows snapping past her ear, and Linne saw a half-dozen armed strangers emerge from a low craft that had been drawn in close to the edge of solid ground. She was in the act of stringing an arrow when the shock of an arrow struck her hand, knocking her backward and numbing her mind with pain.

Calen was beside her in an instant.

"Get back to the camp," he growled, helping her to her feet and shoving her back in the direction of their settlement. He wound his neckerchief about her injured hand after making sure she wasn't hurt badly.

"Get yourself tended to, girl. Leave this to the men!"

Linne was on the verge of tears and in no state to argue. The sound of war horns grew clearer all across the lake. There were shouts and the sounds of battle all around her. Her anger began to rise as the pain lessened, but there was no time to protest, for Calen was gone, leading reinforcements toward the South Dike Gate, where her brother was struggling to defend the entryway.

The Bog Hats seemed to swarm from everywhere, shouting and loosing arrows with pale green feathers; Linne was almost wounded again by one of the invaders. He had crept upon her unseen in his small punt, which was concealed with sheaves of reeds all about its edges so that it blended in with the shoreline perfectly; she had not seen the man until she was almost on top of him.

He was small and wiry, but Linne, being badly frightened, kicked him with all her might, sending him stumbling just long enough for her to break out and run toward the settlement. She had dropped her bow in the scuffle, but she quickly drew her dagger with her left hand, yet knowing it would not be of much use to her in her weakening condition. Her vision had begun to blur and she had difficulty keeping her pace.

Stumbling over a fallen defender who sprawled in the path, Linne fell headfirst into the shallow portion of the lake beside the trail, realizing at once that she had ended up in one of the dangerous patches of quicksand that abounded in Dreary Lake and the marshlands that bordered the Swamp of Dismal.

She struggled to clear her cloudy thinking, searching about for anything she might use to pull herself to safety. She had dropped her dagger in the fall; and now she found herself staring helplessly at two of the invaders, who stood above her on the solid ground on the far side of the snare in which she found herself.

"Now here's a pretty bird in the trap," said one, leering at her horribly.

"Nowhere to go, either. I'll wager she'd like us to pull her up out of that mud pie she's gotten into."

"I will shoot with you to see who gets her," laughed the first. "She's the prettiest one I've seen yet."

"You already have two back at the camp! What can you do with another one?"

"We'll shoot for her," insisted the first.

The two Bog Hats took out an arrow apiece and tried to decide upon a target, leaving Linne to struggle vainly to remove herself from the sucking, clinging mud that was very slowly pulling her deeper and deeper into its terrible maw.

She had seen a cow once that had strayed into one of these patches of seemingly innocent mud; she watched in horror as the huge animal had been sucked below the surface in a matter of a few moments, before anyone could rig ropes or devise any means to save her. Linne knew she was not as heavy as the cow, but she could feel the ooze beneath her parting and knew she would soon be over her head if she could not find some way to free herself from this certain death.

The enemy soldiers were occupied with their wager and paid little attention to her, for they were convinced that she was their prisoner already. She cast her eyes all around her but to no avail, until she realized that a slain kinsman might be heavy enough for her to use to pull her weight up and out onto that side of the bog. Now all she needed was to be able to reach some part of the lifeless body that lay there, a long shaft with green feathers sticking up between the unfortunate man's shoulder blades.

She put all her remaining strength into reaching out for

the dead man's arm, which had been flung out in front of him in his death throes; but it was too great a distance for her to bridge. It dawned on her then how quickly the mire had sucked her down. If she had tried to grasp the man's arm at first, she would have been able to reach it easily. Desperately, she turned all her strength into one last effort to lunge forward to take hold of some portion of the corpse, but she fell back exhausted, her hand throbbing wildly now, her thoughts growing confused with the pain and fear.

The sucking, sticky ooze was above her waist now, making it hard for her to move in any direction at all. Largo had told her once that the struggling was one of the things that made you sink faster.

"Largo!"

She didn't realize she had called out aloud until one of the Bog Hats turned to her, his face alight with excitement.

"Oh, we'll largo all right, my sweet bird. You just hold on there long enough for me to find a target."

"There's a couple of the marshers We'll see who has the best eye now."

"I've got the one with the bright red cockade to his cap."

"Done."

The two Bog Hats drew their bows and Linne heard the twang of the strings as the shafts were released. She felt helpless with rage and fear, but she screamed out a warning just as the men released their arrows, throwing them off a slight bit.

"Here, here, now! Stop that!" snarled the first one. "See what you've made me do!"

"Ha," cried the second. "You've gone wide by a dozen hands."

"So have you, you sot."

"We had best pluck this sweet one out of the mud or we're going to neither one have her. She's sunk to her chin while we've been standing here talking."

One of the men quickly inserted his bow into the quicksand immediately behind where Linne was trapped, breaking the suction of the relentless mud. At the same time, the other man sat down on the solid ground at the edge of the bog and extended his bow toward the girl so that she might grab it and pull herself to safety.

Linne hesitated, staring at the two enemies who had her so totally at their mercy; her anger and fear made her burst out in tears, which enraged her more, for she did not want to give the two hateful men the pleasure of seeing her crying.

"Here, here, don't cry, little bird! Grab onto that bow or you will have something to cry over for sure."

"Grab it, girl!" growled the other. "Don't be so uppity about yourself. You could do a lot worse in this world than to be taken to wife by our likes."

Here the men broke out laughing again.

"We'll see which one of us wins the toss, if you'll hurry up and help yourself out of that mudhole."

Her eyes burned with bitter tears. Linne thought for a moment of not taking hold of the extended bow, but she felt another sudden sensation of sinking; and without wishing to, she clutched at the bow and held onto it desperately. The two men laughed loudly at this and began tugging at the trapped girl in order to pull their prize safely ashore.

With a gradual effort, the men freed Linne from the clinging reddish mud. There was a loud sigh, almost as if the bog was lamenting the loss of a victim; and then the girl was clear, having been dragged toward solid ground by the two leering Bog Hats.

She tried to collect her wits and make a plan, but before she was able to catch her breath, she found herself hauled roughly in like a fish on a line and bound tightly with strong leather ties and slung between a stout pole that the people of her settlement had used to cast out their fishing nets.

Linne's mind began to darken with panic. There were the sounds all about her of the fight; men were shouting and there were the screams and cries of her friends and neighbors. While she had been in the bog, she had comforted herself with the knowledge that Largo and the other men would drive off the Bog Hats, who were old enemies from as far back as Linne could remember. That hope had held her sinking spirits up; but now as she lay panting, trussed up tightly to the pole and hung like an animal between the two repulsive enemies, she began to see that this was no ordinary skirmish. The Bog Hats had a large, well-armed party; they had come to take the settlement's women and supplies and to enslave all the men who were not slain. That had always been the way of the Bog Hats. Largo and Linne had known a constant struggle with the fierce clan all their lives, although there had been a period at one time of peaceful coexistence when there had been no word of the troublesome, war-loving people who dwelled upon Dreary Lake's borders. The Bog

138

Hats were mostly settled in the area known as The Mires and farther into the Swamp of Dismal. It was from those places they made their raids. When anyone gave pursuit, the elusive Bog Hats would disappear into the wilderness that abounded beyond Dreary Lake. It was impossible to track them, so the only defense against their attacks had been constant readiness to drive them off. Linne's father had been successful in almost eliminating the raids by the fierce clansmen by building the strength of the marshlanders' defenses. This plan had been effective and had allowed the settlements to live securely for a number of years, until her father disappeared along with a large war band of men who came from all the various settlements on the lake.

It was never known what had happened to the party; but as Linne struggled vainly against her bonds, she thought despairingly that they were probably ambushed by the Bog Hats, just as she had been.

A cold, bleak depression clouded her thoughts, pushing away all hope. She wished she could have had the courage to let herself sink into the mire. Then she remembered Largo, which cheered her for a moment; but that too was dashed when she opened her eyes a brief moment and saw the smoke and fire from the burning shelters and the line of struggling women who were being tied together and herded along toward the spot where she lay.

There was no more resistance. She could see none of the men and could hear no more sounds of fighting. She caught sight of a few of her brother's friends being roughly led along by ropes tied to their necks; and there were many bodies strewn around that she had not noticed before.

It was all over. She was a captive of the savage Bog Hats and had nothing to look forward to but a life of brutal abuse and the worst sort of slavery. Linne wished again she had let herself go under the placid, innocent-looking quicksand, rather than have to face the grim prospects of a life as the forced bride of a brutal enemy warrior.

Cries and shouts filled the air as the victorious Bog Hats gathered their prizes, calling out to each other jeeringly about the turn of an ankle or the color of hair on a captured woman.

"She'll make a good fish bait," called a man to his comrade.

"Aye, here's one that's not so bad."

"As long as it's dark enough that you can't see her," cried another, laughing.

One of Linne's captors raised his voice above all the others.

"Come, come, lads. You shall see the sunshine, the spring-time, the clearest water that you ever laid eyes on. Your heart will break when you see what Ilide and Gorbin have snatched from one of these nasty sinkholes."

Gorbin and Ilide then picked up their prize between them and hoisted the pole onto their shoulders to show off their beautiful prisoner.

Linne was aware of the chaos and confusion of the scene: the screaming, terrified women and the catcalls and ruthless maulings of the Bog Hats, flush with their successful raid. She was pinched and touched and had her hair pulled as the enemy warriors held up her head to look at her face.

The shock of despair began to settle in upon her heart, and the young woman felt a numbness descend over her soul that was as deep and deadly as the quicksand that had tried to swallow her but a few moments before. She became indifferent to the poking hands and insinuating voices, drifting deeper and deeper into a safe haven inside herself where no one could reach or harm her.

The Bog Hats went on arguing and howling loudly with delight at their victory, beginning to round up their prisoners and load them into their boats for the journey back to their own camps far inside the Dismal Swamp.

It was as she was thrown roughly into one of the boats that Linne's glazed eyes fell on a very familiar form. It escaped her at first, but as she looked more closely still, a movement of one of the branches caught her eye, and she would have sworn that the fallen tree was trying to reassure her.

Then she remembered Coney.

In the Swamp of Dismal

THE talk of Gorbin and Ilide turned to many subjects. Linne went from a troubled coma-like slumber to periods of time when she was aware of her surroundings and all that went on. It was such a time now as she lay in the bottom of the boat with her cheek pressed roughly against the wet wood.

"It went off more smoothly than I figured," said Ilide, pausing to rest his oar on the gunwale of the boat.

"He said it would be easy to gain entry by the way he'd leave open for us," replied Gorbin. "I wasn't going to believe him, but it was just like he said."

"It should have been," went on Ilide. "After all the promises that were made to him. He'll be in a real fine state now."

"He wouldn't be if he were in the hands of any of his old friends."

Ilide and Gorbin laughed an ugly laugh that sent chills down Linne's spine.

"Most of his friends will be dead now, so he won't have to worry too much," went on Ilide.

"We'll see how easy he makes new ones in Bonadig. It might not be easy to trust one who has sold out his own kin."

The two comrades exchanged looks and winked.

"There are some things a man doesn't do," agreed Gorbin.

Linne felt that she had to move. Her hands and wrists ached from the chafing of her bonds, and her wound throbbed painfully. She was cramped into the bottom of the boat at such an angle that her back began to feel as though it had been broken. She held her breath and tried to wriggle into a new position without gaining the notice of her captors.

"I'd hate to think of what would happen to one of us if we did it. Famhart would never let anyone go if he caught them."

Gorbin nodded.

"But we don't have to worry. There isn't a Bog Hat among us that would be fool enough to betray Famhart and his magic."

"Isn't there?" asked Ilide. "I wonder."

There was a silence then; and all Linne heard was the steady rhythm of their oars in the water.

"Do you have something on your mind, Ilide?" asked Gorbin, eyeing his friend shrewdly.

Ilide snorted disdainfully.

"I always have something on my mind."

"Anything in particular?"

"Just this. We can turn this here pretty bird into a real treasure trove if we play out our hand right. Famhart is tired of his old wives. He is the chief of Bonadig and all the settlements around. If we bring him a present from this raid, especially a present like this one, we will be able to choose what treasure we may want for ourselves."

"I don't want to give this one up!"

"Dolt! Stupid! Do you think there are no more where this one came from?"

"I've never seen any as pretty."

"Listen, you ox; if Famhart takes a liking to her, he'll take her anyway. If we give him a present, then we can ask for favors. One of those favors will be to govern for him in one of the outer settlements. Then we will be free of his meddling and can do whatever we want."

"I don't know," said Gorbin. "What if he doesn't let us be a governor?"

"We have been good subjects all our lives, Gorbin. You and I have always been trusted with the most difficult errands. We have always done as he's bidden us. If anyone stands in his good graces it's us."

Linne's heart began to hammer as her two jailers talked of their chieftain. She had been frightened enough of them, but somehow the talk of the absent leader was even more terrifying. All sorts of dreadful scenes filled her mind, and she could not dispel the frightening thoughts.

"What settlement would you ask for?" asked Gorbin, after a long pause.

"Which one do you like best?" countered Ilide.

"Goose Creek."

"Then we'll ask for Goose Creek. That's a fine settlement. There is good hunting there and the water is sweet. There is a good crop of women there, too."

Gorbin laughed again.

"Maybe we could have two or three of them to serve us."

"That's the idea, Gorbin. We've done our part all these years to keep the settlements safe. It's high time we got to enjoy the fruits of our labors."

"Hear, hear," replied Gorbin. "I could go along with that."

The Bog Hats paddled on without conversation for a while; Linne could hear bits of conversations from the boats all around her. Once, she tried to make out her surroundings by lifting her head slightly; but she quickly abandoned that idea when she heard Ilide move about in front of her, as if he were aware of her again.

There was nothing to be seen. She tried to remember her geography of the lake, guessing that the Bog Hats had come from the direction of the Swamp of Dismal and supposing that they intended to return the same way. She had not been far into those hostile lands, for the Bog Hats had always been ferocious; and with the disappearance of her father and the weakening of their defense forces, the Bog Hats had grown bolder and bolder, making it unsafe to venture too far into their territory. From what she recalled of the few excursions she had been on, Linne could only bring to mind tall, moss-grown trees, with avenues of water that crawled off in every direction into the wild thickets of clinging vines and water plants. The swampland seemed to have grown continually thicker the farther she had penetrated, so that it was hard to imagine what it would be like in the very heart of that vast, ominous land that had been flooded long ago, where solid ground was hard to find.

Her thoughts then turned to what Gorbin and Ilide had been talking of before. From all she could make out, it sounded to her as though someone in their settlement had allowed the Bog Hats to come into the camp through the South Dike Gate. It was a betrayal by one of her own clansmen! That thought burned her heart with a bitter cry for revenge; but then she recalled that the Old One had said something about that just before she had been captured.

How she wished the Old One and the otter and elf were with her now! Or Largo! It wouldn't even be so hard to bear the humility of being captive of the Bog Hats if her brother were with her to keep her spirits up; they might even plan an escape.

She let her hopes begin to rise as her mind turned over all the possibilities of her chances to elude her captors and somehow organize the survivors of the raid into a new defense force that would ensure their future safety.

Here her thoughts were interrupted by the landing of the boat; Ilide and Gorbin dragged her into a sitting position and offered her food, which she refused.

"I can't eat with my hands tied this way. They're hurting now. I think you've tied the knots too tight."

"Too tight, she says," said Gorbin, turning to his friend. "She says we've tied her too tight."

"We might be tempted to loosen up those knots if the pretty bird would give us her promise not to try to run away. Not that that would do her any good. There's no place to run to but country that the Bog Hats rule."

"She could tell us her name, as well," suggested Gorbin, reaching out to stroke her hair.

"Linne shrugged his hand away in disgust.

"My name is Linne," she replied proudly.

143

A curious look played over the features of the Bog Hat soldiers. Linne was unable to tell if it was surprise or disappointment, or both.

Finally Ilide spoke.

"Well, this points us in a different direction for sure. I can't say that I like it one bit."

"He's going to make trouble," agreed Gorbin. "Now we won't be able to go to Goose Creek."

"We won't cross that off yet. There may be a way of working it all out."

Gorbin brightened.

"Maybe we could tell Famhart that the marshlander was killed accidentally in the raid? Then there wouldn't be any difficulty."

"Except that he wasn't killed in the raid," corrected Ilide.

A sly smirk stole over Gorbin's face.

"It's still a bit before we reach Bonadig. Quite a few things could happen between now and then."

Ilide drew up his eyebrows.

"You mean the marshlander might meet with an unfortunate accident before he reached Famhart?"

Linne interrupted the two at this point by holding her bound hands in front of her.

"I still can't eat like this."

Almost absentmindedly, Ilide undid the leather straps.

"Do you have any particular ideas about how an accident might happen?" asked Ilide, handing a length of dried meat to his prisoner.

"Well, there's plenty of water here. There might be one of the marshlanders in one of the boats who found out they had been betrayed by their leader. He could break free and attack the traitor and they could both drown in the fight."

At the mention of a leader in the marshland camp betraying the settlement, Linne's heart sank; but she clung to a desperate belief that there must be some explanation for Largo's behavior; she was still not sure that the Bog Hats even referred to her brother.

Ilide was looking approvingly at Gorbin.

"That's very good. That's very, very good. Famhart would very easily understand that. No one likes a turncoat."

"With him out of the picture, there would be nothing left to stand in our way to Goose Creek!"

Gorbin turned to Linne and smiled broadly.

"The pretty bird will make a nice prize for Famhart. He's

144

all adither about all his ugly wives. He would be most grateful to two of his most faithful servants for having brought him something so young and healthy and easy to look at."

Linne shuddered beneath the leer of the Bog Hat soldier, trying to keep her dignity by calmly meeting his glance.

"I think you are both wretched men," she said evenly, although her heart was in her mouth and she couldn't hear herself for the noise of the blood drumming in her ears.

Ilide laughed loudly.

"If I wasn't afraid of marking you up before Famhart saw you, I'd give you a taste of what a wretched man I can be, sweet flower. If I had a mind to keep you for my own, we'd soon have that barbed tongue out of you!"

The Bog Hat smiled as he spoke, but Linne saw the dangerous anger of the man very near the surface. His eyes had changed color and his mouth curled down into a snarl.

"Wouldn't she get rid of that tongue if we kept her, Gorbin?"

"Very quickly, I'd wager. Pretty birds who don't have any way of keeping themselves from being hurt learn to sing pretty to them that keeps them."

Gorbin nodded twice in rapid succession as he spoke.

Linne forced herself to eat then, hardly tasting the food. She carefully tried to think of saving her strength so that if a time came that she would find an opportunity to escape she would not be weakened from hunger.

They proceeded on in silence for what seemed a long time then, until a loud commotion in one of the boats ahead of them attracted her captors' attention as they moved along the stretch of water that seemed to be bordered on both sides by reed banks that were very high and lush.

"Hallo, there! Who passes?" called a thick voice from somewhere in the depth of the reeds.

"Arial," replied a man from one of the boats in the front of the procession.

"Hallo, Arial. How does it fare with you?"

"We have captives. We have destroyed the marshlander settlement on Gray Head Island."

"Largo's island?"

"We have him with us. He's going to see Famhart."

At the mention of Largo's name, Linne stiffened. She had listened to the talk between the two Bog Hats earlier, knowing somewhere inside herself that they had been speaking of her brother; but she had tried to blank the thought from her

145

mind. That, along with the shock of captivity, pushed her very near her breaking point.

Now it all flooded through her consciousness.

Largo had long wanted to be a powerful leader like his father; he had gone through the motions of trying to do so, except that he was a weak-hearted young man. He could only call forth any determination when he was beside himself in fits of rage, a quality that made him very inconsistent and indecisive, and which confused his followers to the point of distraction.

Linne knew from her earliest childhood that Largo would need someone to help him rule the settlement; but the threat she posed to his manhood was too great for him to be able to accept her strengths, which were exactly the qualities he lacked. Their father had seen the weak, cruel streak in the son, and knew that there was nothing to be done about it. His only hope was that Linne would be around to temper the fits of rage and the acts of cowardice, and to perhaps lend her even-thinking logic and kindness to the running of the settlement.

And now it was too late; for Largo, in trying to gain the respect of the members of his camp who openly defied him or questioned his authority, had betrayed his kindred to Famhart in an attempt to intimidate or eradicate the rebels.

Linne's heart ached with pain and guilt at what Largo had done; but she still loved the ill-starred young man who was her brother. It seemed that the more hopelessly he became entangled in one tragic affair after another, the more she felt for him.

"Welcome home," came the voice of the hidden sentry. "We shall have a good feast to celebrate this victory."

"There are twenty boats of us," replied Arial.

"I'll count."

"Are there any others out?"

"None. Camwel returned yesterday."

"Good. Farewell."

"Farewell, Arial."

The boats ahead of her glided through what appeared to be a solid reed wall that had parted. After all twenty of the watercraft had passed, the reeds closed again, making it appear as though there was nothing there but solid green growth.

As soon as they passed this barrier, Linne saw they were on a wide waterway that was clear and shallow, with solid

146

ground on both banks. There appeared to be dwellings built on the upper banks, not like the marshlanders' stilted huts but regular shelters that were made of the mud from the wet clay earth, roofed with woven rushes.

Many people began to crowd the shorelines, calling out to the soldiers in the returning boats. Shouts of laughter rang out, while teasing voices asked about the various prisoners. Lynne found the boat she was in suddenly tied fast to a mooring pole on the bank; she was dragged out roughly and stood before a host of Bog Hats, all talking at once and all determined to touch her.

"Here, here, you! Stand back! This is Famhart's new woman. Get back!"

Ilide frowned and turned to whisper to Gorbin.

"We shall have to think of something else to do about the marshlander. It is too late to drown him now!"

"Hush," warned Gorbin. "Someone will hear us."

"We shall just have to take our chances with her. We may not even have to worry about her brother, if Famhart decides that he doesn't want to deal with him as a friend."

"And what if he decides to be friendly? The brother might ask for her to be freed!"

"Then we'll call on the law. It is clear about goods or slaves that soldiers capture in battle. Famhart couldn't free her without giving us something in return. So even then, we'd be all right."

"I still don't like it," mumbled Gorbin. "It leaves a bad taste when you're dealing with a switchcoat."

"I don't like it any better," agreed Ilide. "But it's too late now. We have to go on with it."

He turned and snapped out peevishly at the milling throng that had gathered around their prisoner.

"Get back, all of you! Leave her alone. You'll mark her up before Famhart sees her."

The mob reluctantly stopped their pinching and pawing, but their clamor went on unabated.

Linne was growing truly frightened now, looking on the strange people who controlled her destiny.

They were very similar in size and color; but there was a savage streak in their glances that made Linne's heart pound. She had heard stories of the Bog Hats and how they had slowly gone bad over the years, preying on the more helpless neighbors that still lived on the borders of Dreary Lake; and how they had at one time been a proud, high clan that thrived on trade and commerce with all the settlements all

147

the way from the sea to the Serpent Mountains. Her father had told them tales when she and Largo were still small children; about the powerful Bog Hat kings, when they were still known by their old name, the Boghatians. Largo always liked those stories and had often told Linne that he wished he were one of the old kings.

She shuddered violently, but tried to force herself to hold her head up in the presence of her captors.

"Let's go at once to Famhart," said Gorbin, tightening the bonds on her arms.

"I can walk," Linne said calmly, her voice cool.

"I know you can, little bird, but we don't want you to spoil yourself before our good leader sees you."

Ilide bound her ankles then, and Gorbin picked up his end of the pole. Much to the delight of the mob that was gathered, they hoisted the helpless girl between them and moved off swiftly to the headquarters of Famhart, the King and Elder of all the Bog Hat tribes that yet lived within the confines of the great Swamp of Dismal.

Reinforcements Arrive

ON a deserted stretch of shoreline on Dreary Lake, not far from the beginnings of the Swamp of Dismal, a strange sight was played out under the pale silver light of a full moon. There was the tall shadow of a many-armed giant swaying to and fro in the eerie night; and beside the tall shadow were two very small ones, one of an animal and the other of an elf.

The three of them moved in motions that might have been a dance.

"We shall have to act quickly," said Coney, moving his limbs in a movement that might seem to have been caused by a high wind blowing. "I have heard many things from the swampkind. None of it is good news. Linne is captured and to be sacrificed to the leader of the Bog Hats. Her brother has betrayed his kinsmen; and he is to be murdered secretly."

Coney's voice was harsh with excitement.

Jahn Spray shook his head. He could hardly remember anything of his stay in the marshlanders' settlement except his nap, which was nothing much of a memory at all.

"But we are only two small folk," he observed. "There is

nothing we can do against a well-armed camp of these Bog Hat soldiers."

"You are forgetting you are with an Old One," reminded Coney.

"We don't have anything to arm ourselves with," protested Olthar. "Yet even without that, we must do something to help Linne, if we can."

"We have the Pipe of Ring Parath," scolded Coney. "That is worth all the soldiers there might be in the Bog Hat camp. They might also be surprised to see an Old One upright and moving about. Not many mortal eyes have seen that sight and lived to tell of it."

"I wish we could find Duirn," exclaimed the elf. "He'd help us."

Olthar nodded.

"I am sure the Shanoliel have been searching for us after the flood. They will have gone back to Dun Macrath and found us gone."

"No help to us now," said Coney shortly. "It would be of great service to have the Shanoliel with us; but we must act without them if we are to save the marshland girl before it is too late."

The Old One drew his trunk upright and sank his gnarled roots deep into the soft clay of the lake bank. His limbs waved to and fro in time to an unseen wind; and he seemed to be listening intently to some sort of voices that neither the otter nor the elf could hear.

"There are many disturbing things afoot," he said at last, using the common speech that the two friends understood.

Olthar, his small muzzle troubled with a dark scowl, clutched the pipe case tightly and looked earnestly at Coney and Jahn.

"If we are to help Linne, then we must make all haste. She has been kind to us and showed us good faith. We can't leave her to her enemies."

Jahn was about to protest, but saw the look in the small animal's eye and thought better of it.

There had been many changes that had occurred in his charge since they had been swept away from the old elfin dane of Dun Macrath; and Jahn was not sure that he welcomed the changes or not. The young otter had grown up almost instantly, it seemed, from the moment he had been given the heavy burden of the Pipe of Ring Parath, and the elf could see the aging going on right before his eyes.

Where there had once been the impetuous pup of just last

149

spring, there was now a very much matured Olthar, and his small brow was already wrinkled and troubled. His eyes had taken on the faraway saddened look that hid even in the shadows of smiles: it was the elfin sorrow, a sorrow that would be in all the worlds of time until at last the High King had blown the last winding note and all the lost travelers in all the Lower Wilderness would once more remember Him and be called back to the High Meadows of Windameir to forget all the cares and troubles they had known in the Darkness, and to feel the full freedom of the Light in their hearts once more.

"Do you know where these Bog Hats are, Coney?" asked Olthar, his voice edged with tension.

"I know how to reach them. The brothers in the swamp tell me everything."

"Who are they?" asked Jahn. "The brothers, I mean."

"The spirits of the trees and green growing things," replied Coney.

"Are they Old Ones, too?" asked the otter.

"No, but they have spirits. Even the very lowest orders of things have a spirit."

"And they can guide you to where Linne is being held?"

"The green ones hate the Bog Hats. They say the humans kill even the growing ones among them and let them dry for the fire beast. They will help me find the humans."

"We may as well go then."

"Are we to just show up?" asked Jahn, hoping to have more of a plan than to just walk unarmed into a hostile camp.

"Can you help, Coney?"

"Of course," replied the Old One evenly. "I wasn't intent upon leaving you two to rescue the girl alone."

"I'll use the pipe," said Olthar. "If I try to just feel what it tells me to do, I think we will be all right."

"I wish Duirn were about," lamented Jahn. "I would feel much better if I knew we had a band of the Shanoliel behind us."

"You may come into my upper branches, good elf. I shall hold you safe from harm. The otter will stand before me to sound the notes of the pipe and I will demand the release of Linne. In the confusion I think we shall stand a very good chance of accomplishing our objective. As soon as we have the girl, we shall immediately take to the water again and make our way as quickly as possible to The Beak."

Jahn shook his head doubtfully.

"That all sounds well and good, Coney; but what I am thinking about is a camp full of armed and seasoned soldiers who aren't going to be particularly fond of us running off with one of their prisoners. To my way of thinking, they'll probably shoot us all full of arrows out of hand and that will be an end of the matter."

Coney made a rumbling noise deep in his trunk and shook all his limbs as if he were stretching himself.

"That is as an elf sees it," he replied. "Elves can be almost as dismal in their outlook at times as dwarfs. I have had commerce with both on many occasions in my time. I hardly know which is worse. There are those who think an elf's nature is all fluttering butterfly wings and will-o'-the-wisps, but I can tell you many tales of gloomy elves I have known."

"One of which is here with us now," concluded the young otter.

"There's nothing wrong with being cautious," snapped Jahn. "I didn't say anything about not going. I simply gave my opinion of what was going to be the upshot of it all."

While Jahn had been talking, Olthar had carefully unpacked the last of the travel cakes that Linne had put into his knapsack before she took the two friends to the lake and delivered them over to Coney. He gave Jahn a share and the two sat down to eat while Coney laid out his plan of action.

"I shall use my oldest form when I come out of the lake. You mustn't be shocked when you see it."

"Whatever form is that?" asked Olthar, turning to the Old One with his mouth full.

"This," replied Coney.

In an instant he was transformed into a pale glow of a shape, huge and ominous, with dark limbs that were draped with a coarse-looking moss that looked almost like a beard. The limbs were gnarled and had what appeared to be great claws at the end, which opened and closed menacingly as the two terrified friends looked on at the change that had come over their companion.

Coney's voice boomed out grim and hollow; and the ground all about them trembled and shook, making it impossible to keep their feet.

"This is the form I shall use. It should keep the Bog Hats off balance long enough for us to see to our business."

Recovering from his shock, Jahn nodded weakly.

"That should be enough to do it."

"If it's not, we'll be in hard shape," put in the otter. "When you do that, Coney, I'll start in with the pipe."

"It will give us the advantage we need," concluded the ancient being. "Then there will be nothing between here and The Beak except time and water."

Olthar turned to the Old One, who still remained in the dreadful guise.

"Please, Coney! That is still a frightening mask you're wearing."

In a flash, their friend had taken on his original form.

The young otter went on.

"What I'm thinking about is what we are to do once we reach The Beak. There we'll be just as we are now, except that we'll have a human with us. I still don't understand why we are making an attempt to get someplace when we don't know for sure that help can be found there."

"It will at least be better than here," said Jahn. "I'm not getting any too fond of these creepy waters. I keep thinking I'm seeing things that aren't there; and there are things that change if you look at them too long."

"There are things here that aren't friendly," agreed Coney. "I can keep them away, but they are there. You have been seeing some of them, Jahn."

"What are they?" whispered Olthar, looking about in the eerie silver light.

"Old, bitter things," replied Coney. "They are spirits full of grief or rage that have been trapped without hope of release until they surrender whatever it is that they chose to hold to."

"That is very sad. Isn't there anything anyone could do?"

"It's not so sad, Olthar. It is only a thing they do to themselves."

"Couldn't you talk to them?"

"I do talk to them," replied Coney. "I am talking to them now."

"What are they saying?" asked the elf, full of a strange curiosity.

"They want to drown you."

"Drown us? Whatever for?"

"Because you are an elf."

"What have elves ever done to them?"

"Nothing. It is just that you are alive and free. They hate anything or anyone who is free."

"Do they hate you, Coney?" questioned the small animal.

152

"Me? They fear me."

"Isn't that the same?"

Coney was silent for a time.

"You have begun to learn well, little brother. I see that some of our stories weren't lost on you."

A short, rumbling noise erupted from the depths of the Old One which sounded to the elf suspiciously like a laugh.

"But I know the workings of them well enough. They shall not harm us. I shall call on them to help us against the Bog Hats. It may allow some of them to rid themselves of all their hatred and escape this long and painful lesson they have brought upon themselves."

"That's all well and good as long as they remember to keep us separate from the Bog Hats," said Jahn.

"They won't bother us, Jahn Spray; not as long as I'm here with you."

"Just let us stay close, then," replied the elf, moving a step closer to the Old One.

Having finished their meager meal and made what plans they could, Jahn and Olthar climbed upon Coney again, setting out across the silver-shadowed water toward a distant black line that marked the far side of Dreary Lake and the beginning of the great wasteland of the Swamp of Dismal.

As they ghosted along through the darkness, Olthar and Jahn turned to look behind them from time to time. There were dim shapes there, hardly forms at all yet grotesque and frightening, like wisps of fog that hide a terrible rocky shore from a helpless ship. The otter tightened his grip on the pipe case, shuddering.

"They make me feel funny," he said aloud to Jahn. "I can feel their anger."

"I feel it too," said the elf. "I had been feeling it all along."

"Hush, you two!" warned Coney in a tingling whisper. "Your voice carries over the water. We must be silent."

Falling quiet again, the three slowly and steadily glided across the still waters of the lake, barely leaving a ripple behind to mark their passing.

After what seemed hours, Coney altered his course and began to near a long, sandy shoreline that was bordered on both sides by what looked to be an impenetrable wall of reeds. Jahn stood as tall as he was able on Coney's back, but he could not see anything beyond, except an endless sweep of the water plants stretching on into the darkened horizon.

Coney slowly skirted the sand beach, approaching the thick reed wall from close ashore.

There were sounds then that neither the otter nor the elf had heard before. A faint voice was humming part of a melody that was unfamiliar to the friends. It was joined by others in places, and there were the sounds of silverware on crockery and the noise of mugs being placed on wood. Music from a crude fiddle fetched up a jigging sort of tune, and there was the unmistakable stomp of feet against the earth in time to the music.

A voice almost in Olthar's ear badly startled the small animal.

"I don't see any need for keeping us out here while they're having all the fun," the voice grumbled. "There's no danger now that the marshlanders have been taken."

"They gave us the duty because we didn't take any loot from that lowland camp last week," another voice replied. "It's Famhart's way of punishing us."

"There wasn't anything to take, except a few smelly old fish," resumed the first voice.

"Ugh! And their women were worse! I told the Recorder that we were smart to have left them just as they were. It would only have been more faces to feed if we'd brought them to Bonadig."

"The Recorder is a fat old sop who is married to Famhart's daughter. If you don't give him a little something every time you go on a raid, he'll soon have you out of favor. Just like tonight! Who gets to sit out in the reeds while everyone else is having a good time at the feast? Coldin and Marchal, the two favorites of our fat friend the Recorder!"

The men were silent for a time; the distant sound of the feast drifted clearly over the lake. A woman's scream was heard, followed by a peal of masculine laughter.

"The marshlander woman that Ilide and Gorbin brought to Famhart was a real beauty, wasn't she?" said the first voice, resuming his conversation.

"Too pretty a toy for Famhart, by a long shove," responded the second.

There was another break in the conversation of the two sentries, as the sound of one of them taking a long drink reached the ears of the eavesdroppers.

"Pass me that," said the second sentry. "If we can't join in at the feast table, at least we'll be able to kill the monotony of having to sit out in this weed patch all night."

This speech was followed by more sounds of drinking.

Olthar felt Coney begin to move, barely rippling the water around him. The otter was an expert waterfolk in his own way, and he marveled at how well the Old One maneuvered when afloat. Without speaking aloud, the ancient being conveyed his intent to creep nearer the camp of the Bog Hats.

Jahn clutched his dagger tightly and tensed himself for action. Olthar had taken the Pipe of Ring Parath from its case, holding it ready to his lips.

On they crept, the reeds parting silently before them. It was an unnerving ride, for neither the otter nor the elf could see more than a foot or so in front of him. Coney nudged the reeds aside with his forward progress; but none of them knew when they might stumble accidentally onto one of the sentries, betraying their presence and setting off an alarm that would rouse the camp against them.

The sounds of the feast grew gradually louder; and as they neared the lights and noise, Coney slowed his pace. They seemed to be safely past the two guards who were stationed to watch in the reeds, but they were approaching the main settlement of the Bog Hats: the hour of reckoning was at hand. If they were to do anything at all to help the imprisoned marshland girl, they would have to act soon; and act swiftly and surely.

They passed through another short space of heavy reed banks, then the Old One broke through the last of them, revealing a settlement that ran along both sides of a wide channel. There was a great festival under way, with music and lights from rush lamps and torches; and a great many Bog Hat men and women were singing and dancing before great bonfires that sparkled and reflected off the mirror-dark water.

Olthar felt Coney tensing beneath him, so he put the pipe to his mouth ready to play when the signal was given; Jahn thought fleetingly of Duirn and the Shanoliel, then grabbed firm hold of the Old One's limbs to be ready to do whatever it was he was to do when the excitement started.

And it started the next moment, when Coney came ashore at the foot of a landing that was directly in front of the Bog Hat Famhart's dwelling. Everything from that moment on seemed to happen all at once.

The Doom Snake

THE Dargol Brem felt he had come very close to capturing Duirn and the Shanoliel in his spell. If he had been a bit quicker, he told himself, he would have held the King of the Eolin prisoner, along with the better part of the elfin clans that still moved about on the lower planes of Windameir.

A raging beast when in regular spirits, the dragon was beside himself with the frustration of having let the elves slip away from him. In a moment of passion he thought of killing the wood elf, whom he knew to be a servant of the Dark One; but he thought better of it. Not because he feared any rebuff from Dorini, for he feared no one, but because the wood elf might be able to give him information as to where the others had gone.

He was in a slaying mood and did not relish the thought of having no victims ready to his bloodthirsty whims. Agitated and cross, he flicked his tail viciously and tore down a section of old oaks at a single swipe, breathing heavily as he did so and singeing another stand of timber so badly that there were no leaves left at all, only blackened, naked branches that stood darkly against the sky.

Finding the wood elf in a sort of heavy sleep, the winged serpent began working through a number of spells to wake him, trying each one briefly, then going on to the next. The Dargol Brem were masters of all disguises and all kinds of dark forms and locked the mind of any victim into their own steel-willed control. Even Dorini, the Dark Queen of the Wilderness of Windameir, could not match certain powers of the lords of the Dargol Brem.

There were many names for them: Garoyle Brag, Dargol Brem, the firesnakes, the Purge, the Fire of Doom; they were the distant brothers of the Syrin Brae, the True Dragons; but the rift between the two was unbridgeable. The False Dragons were sworn to death and destruction and ruled the Lower Meadows of Windameir with a steel will that no one could overcome, except those who knew the secrets of the Upper Realms. Once a victim knew the Truth and had the Word, there was no longer any way the Dargol Brem could hold him captive.

It was therefore essential to all the lower dragons that the Darkness of Dorini should prevail over the three worlds of the Lower Fields of Windameir. Since they were dedicated to death and destruction and terror, they gladly joined with Dorini when she had called them down once more. That having been done, even she had no power over them.

The particular beast that landed awkwardly beside Trane was called Rengesbark, although he guarded that secret well. Dorini knew it, but there were few others alive that were able to call him by the right name. When he finally wakened Trane, he was terrible and still did not encourage the wood elf with any sign of friendliness.

"My lord," said Trane, cowering.

"Where have these cursed mites gotten to? Speak, speak!"

A wave of hot, putrid breath that stank of ashes engulfed Trane.

Even if Trane hadn't wished to tell, it would have been impossible for him to resist the power of the dragon; for that part of him that was controlled by Dorini was also the very part of his heart that would have hidden the spark of Light of Windameir, the only thing the lower dragons feared and kept away from.

"I don't know, lord. They put me into the Ancient Sleep and left me. They are cowards and dared not face you."

"They are cowards, true; but wise to flee the doom snake."

Rengesbark erupted into a ragged breath of flame and choking black smoke which nearly smothered Trane.

"We shall find them, O wood termite. Your crafty cousins shall not escape me."

"Oh, never, my lord," gasped Trane. "They will never be able to escape so great a dragon as you!"

Somewhat puffed by this praise, even though it came from a lowly wood elf, the beast exploded into another shower of fire and sparks that ignited the trees around him.

"Rengesbark shall devour them all," he boomed, shaking the ground beneath the Erling's feet.

"Rengesbark!" shouted the terrified Trane, not knowing what else to do, and fearing for his life.

A swift silence followed the dragon's outburst. He eyed the wood elf with cunning eyes which only showed as bare slits in his face armor.

"Come, come, termite! Do you not know where they have gone? Has it perhaps slipped your mind?"

With this, the dragon lifted the helpless elf into the air in a great gnarled talon, holding him dangerously close to the fiery breath that flickered around the edges of his snout.

The Erling was paralyzed, unable to reply; the beast read the elf's thoughts as easily as if they had been written down in pen and ink.

"No! Then I shall have to find them some other way."

Rengesbark prepared to take flight again, casting the terrified Trane aside carelessly.

"Let me go with you, lord," cried the wood elf. "Don't leave me here alone! Help me get back to the Protector!"

The giant winged serpent let Trane grovel in the scorched ashes of the burnt ground for a few moments while he considered.

"All right, termite. I shall transport you back to friends. You perhaps may be of use to me yet. Keep a sharp eye for those traitorous scum of water mites! I shall have them yet, by my oath."

Speaking aloud his thoughts, the beast released a great ugly red tongue of flame that seared the treetops as he lifted himself clumsily above them.

Trane, trembling and clutching the great talon for dear life, could hardly bear to look down. He clung on desperately that way, not daring to open his eyes for the entire trip; even his burning hatred for Duirn was not enough to induce him to peep from his precarious perch beneath the dragon's heavy underbelly. On and on Rengesbark flew, his terrible wingbeat as hollow and dreadful as thunder, his black heart a raging inferno of dark dreams of devouring the Light forever.

He ranged high above the Westing Wood toward The Snaggles, two ugly peaks that marked the northern end of the forest; then back to the very feet of the Black Mountains. There was no sign of the enemies he sought to be found anywhere, and he began to search more randomly. The terrain was much changed and confused by all the great flooding after the long rains, which made it difficult for the dragon to get any sound bearings on his directions. After one last sweep toward the ruins of Dun Macrath, Rengesbark swooped away toward The Mires. If he was unable to find the elves, he knew he would be able to find some hapless victims there, as he had often done in the past.

And it was there that the Dark One had allies with whom

he could deposit the cowering wood elf. They also might have some new sport for him. In older days, he had devastated the lakes and rivers there, turning them into what was known in these later times as The Mires and Dreary Lake. They had been beautiful once, before the wrath of Rengesbark fell like a terrible fury on them, burning away the forests and fouling the waters for such a long while that nothing at all dwelled there for more than a few lifetimes as was marked by the calendars of those caught in the web of the Lower Meadows.

Unknown to the dragon, Duirn and his band were at that moment nearing the burned settlement of the marshlanders, going cautiously along and wondering at the fate of their sometime allies they had called upon at times in the past.

Duirn shook his head, gazing at the wreckage of the settlement of Largo and Linne.

"This is a sad sight, Emeon. I had hoped to perhaps find news of our two wanderers here."

"Bog Hats," said Emeon under his breath. "This is their work, or I'll miss my mark."

The two friends looked at each other with worried glances.

"I had long been intending to do something about that lot. Dorini has swayed them and played them as she would a lute these last turnings. I kept putting off doing anything, thinking they would come to their senses and break off their dangerous ties with her, but I was wrong."

Emeon shook his head.

"You had no way of knowing they would actually go this far."

"I should have seen it. I was so preoccupied with all the doings of the Eolin that I let them destroy some of the very friends we had vowed to protect."

"There perhaps may yet be something we can do. The Bog Hats have their main settlement in the Swamp of Dismal. From the signs here, there were many captives taken."

The leader of the Shanoliel looked away into the distance toward the beginnings of the great swamp, slowly stroking his beard. Evidently having made up his mind, Duirn took a deep breath and showed a slight smile, as if his mind were at last at ease about some bothersome subject.

"Call the lads for a foray! We shall sweep this swamp until we find news of our friends. The Bog Hats have escaped our attention for too long."

Even as he spoke, Emeon was blowing the muster on his thin reed war pipe.

Duirn repeated an ancient verse of the water elf's litany: of the sound of seas and lakes and rain; of the long crash of the hidden falls in the very deepest valley; of the roar of the sea's voice in the dark green halls beneath the ends of the earth. Twice more he called out, and at the moment his words repeated themselves, there were the elfin skiffs that the waterkind had used since the very beginnings of the Lower Meadows, floating lightly at their tethers, ready for use.

These slender craft changed color from moment to moment and could be made invisible to any but an elfin eye; they also had the ability to power themselves without the aid of oars or sail. Each of the boats was named, and all that was necessary was for an elf to call out where he wished to go.

The loading took place instantly. Emeon had rallied all their party, and the elfin band quickly embarked into the waiting boats.

"We shall make for the Swamp of Dismal," said Duirn, guiding his craft toward where he hoped the Bog Hat settlements would be.

The sleek skiff immediately moved forward, barely skimming the surface of the muddy waters of the lake. All the others followed his lead, and soon there was a long trail of the elfin boats following his own across the vast open stretch of Dreary Lake to where it emptied into the beginnings of the Swamp of Dismal.

"When was the last time we were here, Emeon? Can you recall?"

After a long pause, the elf shook his head.

"I can't recall being this way for a long while. There was the last dragon attack, when Collen was lost. That has been a great while."

"Long enough for two or three lifetimes for these humans. That seems a great period to them. They change their minds so easily and forget so quickly."

"They are a difficult race to deal with."

"Some of them are," replied Duirn, thinking back on others of humankind he had known over his very long stay in the Lower Meadows.

"The Bog Hats have long gone over to the Darkness. There's no question of their intent, whatever else we may think of mankind as a race."

"The Dark One has been very busy at her work here. I can remember a time when the elfin high lords sat with the old kings of Boghatia."

Emeon shook his head wistfully.

"I wonder where all this has gotten to sometimes! Here we are perched in a lonesome, inhospitable part of the world on our way to try dealing with an unreasonable bunch of louts who have taken it into their heads that they can do anything they please without ever suffering the consquences. Most likely we shall have a fight as a result of it; and no doubt there will be some of us killed over the whole affair; and then whatever is left of our two groups will go on with renewed hatred at the ills and injustices we have suffered at the hands of our enemies."

Duirn laughed softly.

"You wax eloquent, my friend. You are not far wrong, either. I would add that there we all will be following after our own individual drummers; it is never known of an elf what course he has chosen until he reaches the port from which he will make his departure. Perhaps there will be some of us who will be able to say which one for sure, after our interview with the Bog Hats."

Emeon went on staring at the vast emptiness around him and did not reply. The late afternoon sun was beginning to set; and a pale, round moon hung low over the distant land, waiting to rise.

The elfin skiffs moved on away from the sun and toward the silver face of the moon for a long while. Duirn and Emeon were silent, each lost in his own thoughts, listening to the soft hiss of the other boats moving through the water.

Mile after mile of shoreline, deserted and menacing, passed by; they saw no signs of animals or birds in the last of the marshlands, although they made out the outlines of what must have been large settlements in older, better days. The fading gloom of the setting sun gave way to the inky darkness of evening until the pale light of the full moon rose above them slowly, casting great shadows over the water and making harmless objects seem threatening and dangerous. Their nerves grew raw from the constant vigil of trying to pierce the silver darkness for lurking dangers.

There was a chilly breeze that had sprung up from nowhere, blowing small ripples onto the smooth surface of the lake. It was a strange wind that did not feel natural for that time of year, and it raised the hackles at the back of Duirn's neck. It carried with it a faint odor of burnt ash, and the brow of the Shanoliel King grew troubled.

"We must hurry, Emeon. This wind bodes evil for everyone if it's what I suspect it is."

Emeon glanced at his old friend.

"What do you think? Is it another raid? Perhaps the Bog Hats have left another settlement aflame?"

"Worse. Much worse. I can't think of anything worse to deal with if it's what I fear."

"You chill me to the bone, Duirn. Speak!"

"We have been followed by the Dargol Brem!"

The two friends exchanged horrified looks, then turned toward the direction from which they had just come. At first there was nothing to be seen but the dark, flat mirror of the muddy lake reflecting back the moon. Toward the farther part of the shadowy horizon they could barely detect where the waters of Dreary Lake ended in the solid beginnings of the Westing Wood; beyond that were the invisible shadows of the Black Mountains, which divided the woods from the Great Flats.

Nothing moved but the shimmering rays of the moonlight on the water; a faint burring sound raised itself above the murmur of the wind, flickering about their ears like a persistent fly. And then just at the very edge of their vision, there appeared to Duirn what looked to be an open furnace, roaring and shooting sparks in all directions. It traveled along the treetops where the wood met the beginning of Dreary Lake, leaving a trail of fire and destruction behind it. That part of the sky looked as though a dirty red fallen star had landed among the trees.

"Alert the others," said Duirn softly, never taking his eyes off the distant woods. "We shall have some protection from the spell of the boats. The snake won't be able to see us. If we are ashore with the Bog Hats, we'll have to stand to help our friends the marshlanders; they won't be able to rely on the old ways of the Eolin. They have no spells to help them. We can try to get them into the boats, at least. That is the least we'll be able to do for them."

"What about Olthar and Jahn?" asked Emeon.

"They will have to wait upon us. We can't leave this business undone."

As Duirn finished speaking, the first of the raging blasts from the dragon's mouth slashed across the lake, rocking the boats violently.

Turning toward their old foe, the elves readied themselves for battle. They strung their arrows, specially made for penetrating the thick hides of the Dargol Brem. Being concealed by the invisible cloak of the elfin craft, they would stand a chance of dealing the unsuspecting dragon a fatal blow as he flew above them.

"This would be a great stroke of luck if we were to be able to rid the Lower Meadows of the likes of another of these foul things. Dorini has even on occasion regretted calling them down, I'd wager. They follow no orders but their own."

Emeon blew out a sharp, shrill warning note on his pipe, but there was no need to. The elves were all drawn up facing the beast; they watched it approach, belching flame and sparks into the night. Every eye was riveted to the sight, and every heart beat faster as the roaring grew louder and louder.

Another great searing blast swept over the lake, turning the air into a smothering hot inferno. The elves choked and covered their faces with their cloaks, waiting until the dragon would be within range of their bows.

There was a sudden cry and a horrendous splintering noise as one of the skiffs was sent spinning wildly into the air; the Dargol Brem had used its own spells to creep close to the elfin war band, and with an overpowering blast of its fiery breath, it exploded into view right on top of them.

As the Shanoliel band loosed their shafts, Duirn could see their adversary clutched tightly in the dagon's talon: the wood elf Trane, guiding the dragon's blows onto the invisible elfin craft.

In a moment of black fury, Duirn raised his own bow and let fly an arrow that was directed at the heart of the Erling warrior. He did not see whether or not the shaft struck home, for the next instant the boat he and Emeon were in passed into a thick wall of reeds; there was a great shout raised all about them, and the air was full of the roar and stench of the Dargol Brem and the sound of arrows snapping by. Cries and shouts came from everywhere at once, joined by their own elfin war pipes; and just at the very ragged edge of all that tumultuous noise came the high, pure notes that lifted Duirn's heart from the despair that had gripped him: he rejoiced to the call of the Pipe of Ring Parath.

He clapped Emeon on the back and they both burst into tears and shouts at the same time.

In an Enemy Camp

LINNE had been dumped without ceremony onto the tamped earthen floor of Famhart's shelter while Ilide and Gorbin awaited their leader. The crowd was left outside milling about and calling for music and wine.

The marshland girl's heart was beating so hard she felt it must surely burst. She had exhausted herself in struggling against her bonds and now lay completely spent, awaiting her fate. There was a part of her that was held in reserve, even though her physical strength was gone; and she knew that if they released her from her fetters she would try for Ilide's knife and fight both of them off until she had either escaped or been slain. Death, she knew, was better than a life as slave to another.

There was a smoky golden rushlight that lit the room, and to calm herself, Linne began to study its contents. She was completely alone and unattended, and she struggled briefly against her bonds, but the leather ties only drew tighter, so she ceased her movements and tried to concentrate on ordering her thoughts.

The dim rushlight drew wavering shadows over the walls of the shelter, which were made in the usual marshland way of reed straw and dried clay cut into bricks and laid like stonework. The roof was thatch woven together in bundles, and one wall was covered with thick blankets which had been made by the Bog Hat women, detailing the history of the clan. There were scenes there of what appeared to be the old kings and queens, and scenes of past glories and hunts, all stitched in red and gold and green threads. A low table on Linne's left was covered with a fine cloth and set with many finely wrought glasses and metal cups which appeared to be relics of the ancient kingdoms.

Linne was so intent upon studying her surroundings that it took her some length of time to realize that she was not alone in the room.

She tensed to scream, hating herself immediately for her weakness, but before she had uttered a sound, the man, a Bog

Hat, put a finger to his lips to quieten her. His dark blue eyes were clear and deep, and there was a gentleness in his face that made the girl relax, despite her apprehension.

The stranger cautioned her to silence again and moved toward where she lay. This startled her again, and she had to use every ounce of self-control remaining to allow the Bog Hat to come near her. Not knowing what to expect, Linne shut her eyes as tightly as she could and steeled herself for the worst.

Instead of touching her, the Bog Hat man moved close to her ear so that he could speak without raising his voice.

"Do not be afraid. I am not going to hurt you."

This was spoken in a gentle tone of voice that caused Linne to open her eyes and turn toward the young man. She noticed for the first time that he was no older than Largo, fair-haired and sunburned, with eyes a deep sea blue.

"Who are you?" whispered Linne, barely able to make herself heard.

"I am Famhart."

Linne's eyes widened in terror as she tried to draw back from the youth.

The Bog Hat had laid his hand on her arm gently.

"I am the son," he explained. "I see you have already heard of my father."

Linne almost burst out sobbing, but she held onto what little control she had in reserve.

"Gorbin and Ilide must have told you all about my infamous sire. I can see that you are not going to be won so easily."

"I would rather die first," choked the girl. "Even at my own hand."

The young Famhart looked steadily at the bound girl.

"I believe you would."

"I will show you if you'll untie me!"

"I am going to untie you, Linne, but not until you have heard me out. If you still feel the same after I explain all that I have to say, then you can do what you will."

Linne looked at the young Bog Hat uncomprehendingly.

"It is very confusing, I know. There is much to say and not much time. Please listen closely and don't interrupt until I have finished."

"Where did those who brought me go?"

"Gorbin and Ilide? They are with my father. They are

165

drinking. There are others there with them. It will be a while before they will come to see you."

As he spoke, Famhart undid the leather binding that held Linne's ankles.

He looked earnestly into her frightened eyes.

"Promise me you will hear me out?"

Linne nodded, unable to find her voice.

"If anything should happen before I finish . . ." His voice trailed off and he held out an ugly-looking dagger and placed it near her hands, which he then undid.

The feeling began to course back into her arms and fingers, stinging and throbbing. She moved her wrists and rubbed them, bending and wriggling each finger as if she had just discovered them again. Her gaze rested on the dagger for a moment; she was tempted to snatch it up and plunge it into the young man who stood before her, but when she lifted her glance to meet his, she knew she could not harm him.

"Thank you," she whispered.

"Your brother is safe," he went on, growing serious. "I know they plan to murder him, but so long as you are here, he will be unharmed."

"What do you know about Largo?"

All the painful memories of what Gorbin and Ilide had said came back to her.

"He was tricked."

"How do you mean?" asked the girl, standing and stretching her cramped legs, but never moving beyond reach of the dagger on the table at her elbow.

"Largo and I met a long while ago," he explained, "when we were with very small hunting parties near the border of the lake and swamp. I don't think he even suspected I was a Bog Hat. No one in my band was any older than myself, and almost all the young folk have been doubting this war between our clans ever since we were old enough to be called upon to carry it on."

"You saw Largo then?" asked Linne.

"Yes. We talked for a time, and when I saw that it would be safe to do so, I revealed to him that I was a Bog Hat."

"What did he do?"

"He went for his weapons first, but then thought better of it. We talked for a long while then. We spoke of merging the two clans, marshlanders and Bog Hats, and of making things more the way they had once been. We felt we would be able to do many things if we were no longer always at war with each other. The swamp and lake could once more be safe for anyone to travel and we would be able to rebuild the old settlements and reach out once more beyond our own boundaries."

"Largo never said anything of all this to me."

"No? I am surprised."

Linne's fair face clouded.

"I wonder at that, too. But then he was not fond of having to deal with me. He might have felt it wasn't the sort of secret you could trust a girl with."

Famhart nodded his agreement.

"I can see that that is so. His pride has placed him into deeper waters than he knows."

The youth hesitated, listening carefully to voices that sounded outside the shelter. His features grew disturbed and he darted a troubled look at Linne. She was about to ask him what was wrong, but he raised a hand to silence her.

"Lie back down as you were! Pretend you are still bound. Don't move until I come back."

"But . . ."

"If it comes to the worst, use that dagger to fight for your life. I'll come to your aid unless I am already dead! Trust me!"

With this, the young Famhart vanished through what looked to Linne to be a solid wall with a hanging tapestry covering it.

There were voices then, loud and drunken, and the sounds of singing and shouting outside the Bog Hat leader's shelter. She could make out nothing much but snatches of songs and bits of drunken talk; then there was a voice that sounded like young Famhart's, saying there was food and wine at his house for all. At that there were shouts of cheer and long life to the son; then the procession seemed to wind by, trailing noisy, drunken revelers.

Famhart appeared beside her again before she was aware of him.

"How do you do that?" she asked, once she was over her shock.

"I know this house well, having been raised here," he laughed softly, then grew serious again. "Largo is with my father now. When we met those first few times to discuss the combining of the clans, we had decided to take some of our closest companions into the secret. We didn't know then that we would be betrayed. Largo came to one of the meetings we had arranged and found himself face to face with a Famart,

167

but not the one he had reckoned on. My father had found out about the meeting, had me detained, and went in my stead. He learned of Largo's story from the traitor who informed him of the meeting, and that your father was vanished, so he told Largo that he and your father were working together secretly, and that if he wanted to see him again he would be wise and cooperate fully. That is when I lost Largo. He seemed a man who had taken leave of his senses. I tried to convince him of the truth, that we had no marshlander in any of our settlements that could possibly be his father; but he was determined. I tried to warn him of my father's use of him; but he wouldn't listen. It was as if he had become obsessed with the gaining of his father's approval."

"Even to the point of betraying his own settlement," said Linne quietly. "I feel so bad for him. Maybe there was something I could have done, had I known."

"No one could have done anything. He's even now arguing with my father. Now that he's over the first pang of guilt at betrayal, he's becoming bolder. He wants to be made the head of one of our settlements."

"Does he know I am a prisoner?"

"He thinks Ilide and Gorbin are protecting you. He doesn't know that you are to be given to my father. No one is going to tell him yet."

Famhart looked hard at Linne.

"They are planning on murdering him. They don't have to say anything, but I know. Largo seems to be of no use anymore."

The girl brought a hand to her mouth.

"I can't let him be killed without warning him," she said at last. "He is still my brother. Have you tried to warn him?"

"Yes," replied Famhart. "He is like a man who won't hear. He brushed me aside with disgust and told me I should look to my own affairs."

"I shall tell him," declared the girl. "And I'll tell him what they plan to do with me."

"You? How will you tell him?"

"Bring him to me. I'll tell him the truth."

"That will be hard to do until the feast is over."

"Can you arrange it?"

Famhart shrugged, looking absently about the room; finally, after biting his lip for a time, he agreed to try to bring her brother to her.

"I can't promise. I will try to speak to him again. If he won't listen to reason, I suppose I can trick him into coming along. Everyone else seems to be having good luck running gammons on him."

"Try!"

"Meanwhile, I have to tell you the rest. My father found out about the plot between your brother and me and arranged to lay a snare. That's when he met Largo and began the whole affair that ended with the capture of your settlement. I went on with my plans and have enough followers that we are planning to break away from my father and his old order. They have grown cruel and bitter over all these years. All the settlement members of our age want no more to do with the killing and marauding."

"Where will you go? Won't your father follow and bring you back?"

The young Bog Hat smiled.

"I have found old maps in some ruins that show many places beyond my father's reach. We will go there."

Famhart paused and his features clouded.

"If we do not escape my father, I know how he is. It shall come to killing if I don't elude him. So we must make good our escape."

"When?"

"I had not planned on leaving so soon; but since you have been brought here, it will have to be before my father finds you."

Linne's fair features drained of their color.

"He is my father, but he is a harsh, cruel man. He killed my mother with overwork and despair. She was very beautiful once. She was a captive like you. But my father used her up the way he would use a hound."

Famhart's voice had grown husky with buried emotion.

"I feel it only my duty to get away from him before I am driven to do something to harm him; I can no longer control my feelings. We have been at knife-point on more than one occasion, and he begins to view me as a distinct threat now. Even if I stayed, my life would be worthless. It will only be a matter of time before he has me murdered, just as he will Largo."

"How awful!"

"And sad," went on Famhart. "I wept over it all when I was younger. That seems to be the way of it. The only thing to be done now is to escape him and get beyond his control."

He had barely finished speaking when another loud interruption broke out beyond the room where the two young people carried on their urgent conversation. This time the noise and clamor grew louder; and there were voices that cried aloud to be shown Famhart's new bride. Guffaws and shouts for a preview of the beauty grew more strident until at last there came the sounds of a rough, gravel-voiced individual who was identified by the young Famhart as his father.

"I take this to be well meant, my bucks! We have fared well in our campaigns this day. My tried and sure soldiers have even brought me a pretty to while away my hours this winter."

Here, cries and shouts to be shown the beauty erupted again, accompanied by shrill voices from the women, daring the men to even think about calling an outsider a beauty, as compared to the Bog Hat women. More whistles and shouts came from the men and it was becoming obvious that the potent spirits passed out for the feast were beginning to have their effect. Some of the voices from the crowd had grown slurred and ugly.

The elder Famhart raised his gravel voice again.

"Take it slowly, my bucks. Don't push Famhart. I'll show you my pretty when the fancy seizes me. In the while, there's more to interest you tonight than bothering Famhart. Go on with your feasting and leave me to my business."

Grumbles and complaints were heard among the crowd, but there was a general noise of the gathered group breaking up.

"We shall have to move swiftly now. I shall try to talk to your brother once more. Wait for me here. If I'm not back and they come for you, here is a bolt hole for you to use. It ends right at a landing on the channel's edge. There are boats there. Don't wait for anyone if you have to flee. Make for The Beak. Do you know it?"

"No. Which way?"

"Bear straight toward the moonrise. There is also an old willow that has been growing at the end of the settlement for as long as I've dwelled here. Go in that direction and keep bearing straight on."

"I've never been outside our lake," said Linne uncertainly. "But I will do as you say."

"Good girl. Keep up a stout heart and all will come right yet."

The young Bog Hat paused as he prepared to leave, looking at her for a long moment in silence.

"You are beautiful," he said at last; and was gone before Linne could gather her wits to reply.

Trial by Combat

IN the great hall of the Bog Hat leader, Largo sat sullenly glowering at Ilide and Gorbin. They had told the marshland youth that they had tried to protect his sister, but that she had escaped them; they didn't know where she had gone, or even if she were still alive after the raid.

The young man banged his mug on the table loudly, upsetting a plate onto the floor.

"I won't have excuses. My sister was to have been protected. It was all a part of my pact!"

Ilide's eyes narrowed and he lowered his voice until it was difficult to understand what he was saying.

"If I were in the spot you're sitting, my lad, I'd be a deal quieter about what I said and how I said it. I told you we tried to keep your sister safe, but she bolted from us. If she's come to harm it's her own hardheadedness that's caused it."

Largo darted a look about him. Seeing Gorbin and Famhart glowering, he smiled weakly.

"I meant no affront to you, Ilide. I'm sure you did your best. She always has been a little mule when it comes to her will. I can understand that."

"Did you warn her?" asked Gorbin. "She acted as if there was no word given to her about our raid."

Largo colored deeply.

"I couldn't tell her outright. She would have told everyone, and the whole plan would have been spoiled."

"There is your answer then," said Famhart, speaking very slowly and looking at the marshlander over the rim of his drinking mug. He finished the draft before he went on, wiping the foam from his mustaches with the back of his hand. "We shall set up a search for the girl. If she is to be found, we'll find her."

"Who is this prisoner you have brought for Famhart? Perhaps she knows something of my sister?"

"She knows nothing," said Ilide sharply. "She was caught in a bog when we found her."

"I might know her. You could tell her I was captured, too. She might be able to tell me something."

"We'll see. In the morning, maybe," said Famhart, knowing in his own mind that the marshland youth had served out his usefulness and would have to be disposed of before then.

Largo got up suddenly and began to pace furiously.

"I should go back to see if I can find her. She may be wounded or lost."

"Don't fret yourself, my buck. Someone will see to your sister, if she's alive," said Gorbin, smirking at Ilide so that Largo couldn't see.

The young marshlander paced the length of the room twice more, smashing a fist into his open palm.

"It is true that she bolted. No one can be held responsible for that. She has brought on her own troubles!"

Famhart clapped the young man heartily and shoved another mug of the spiced wine into his hands.

"You're a devil of a fine buck, you are. You've done more for your people than they'll ever know how to thank you for. Your sire would be proud of you if he could see you tonight."

"Do you think so?" asked Largo, looking hopefully at Famhart.

Seeing that he had obviously struck a chord with the youth, Famhart pressed on.

"Oh, no doubt whatever! Why, when he comes back from the expedition I sent him on, he'll drink your health a dozen times over. He'll be proud indeed to know you have followed his wishes so faithfully."

Largo looked questioningly at the Bog Hat leader.

"When will my father be back?"

Gorbin and Ilide winked at each other as Famhart smiled broadly.

"He was sent on a very delicate mission to the sea. I don't know how long it will take, but I have no doubt that he will return soon."

Famhart smiled even more broadly.

"And you'll soon have your settlement, right enough. It may even be more than you had bargained for, my buck."

The three men seemed to find something outrageously funny in the comment, falling into fits of laughter that went on for such a long while that Largo began to think the Bog Hats had become drunk on the spiced wine.

Famhart drew himself up at length, and wiping his eyes with a portion of his cloak, he strode to the door.

"Come along! All of us quick stroke! We shall go out to help celebrate with the Bog Hats."

Largo was pushed along by Ilide and Gorbin, who escorted him on either side, propelling him out into the bonfire-lit night.

"Famhart! Famhart!" chanted the crowd, catching sight of their leader.

There were calls from all sides to drink or eat; and some of the new slaves, who glowered fiercely at Largo, were shoved forward to be shown off to the quick-striding Bog Hat leader. He nodded left and right, accepting a mug from a pair of outstretched hands, laughing and calling out different names. He stopped when he got to the landing where the boats lay moored.

All the firelight from the huge settlement flickered on the face of the dark water; sparks from the burning logs crackled and snapped and sent showers of exploding orange flames into the black sky. High above the Swamp of Dismal, a full moon shone down, flooding the darkness beyond the Bog Hat camp with a misty silver light.

"Come nearer, Bog Hats! Come! Hear your leader speak!"

There were more cries of "Famhart"; a dozen men brought forth a heavily carved wooden table and matching chair and placed it for their leader to sit. Very slowly the gathered throng quieted, with large numbers of coughs and shushings going around before Famhart raised his voice to speak.

"We shall have to hold off our festivities until we have solved a riddle, friends!"

Groans and catcalls filled the air.

"It won't take long, if we get down to it."

"What's the riddle?" called a toothless old man who stood at the front of the crowd.

"Not as good a question as to how you really came to be without all your chompers, Quin, but a riddle no less."

There was a sprinkling of laughter, but most of the crowd quietly sipped their wine and watched Famhart to see what was to come next. They were all familiar with the hard veteran chieftain and knew that he never minced words or bantered idly that there wasn't some mischief for someone afoot; seeing the marshlander beside him, they quickly guessed, and rightly so, that it was something to do about the fate of the quisling who had sold out his own kinsmen.

"Come closer, my bucks! We have a vote to take here!"

Crowding in closer, the throng grew boisterous again.

"What I want to put to the count, my bucks, is this. I have twenty camps and twenty governors. Is my number correct?"

"Aye!" replied the crowd.

"You know it is."

"Twenty-one, if you count where we're standing," cried the toothless man.

Famhart lifted his hand.

"Then here is the riddle. Who is to be let go as governor so that our good friend here, Largo the marshlander, can take over his rightful place?"

A hush fell over the assembled Bog Hats.

Largo, pale and ill at ease, looked quickly to Famhart.

"It doesn't have to be so soon," he stammered. "I can wait until I know how you operate your settlements here." Largo spoke louder as he went on. "Besides, I thought it was agreed that I would have a new settlement."

"You were promised a settlement, my buck. One of the rules of the Bog Hat is that he must earn his way up through the ranks until he can challenge the proper leader for title of governor. It wouldn't hardly be right if it were any other way. If no one respected your word, then you wouldn't be able to keep order very well, now would you?"

Famhart turned to the crowd.

"Would he, my bucks?"

A resounding denial rent the air.

"So! What we have to do is have the trial. But first we need to know who shall defend his governorship. Who will it be?"

A dozen or more men scrambled through the crowd toward their leader, all calling aloud. Largo had shrunk back, but was held in place by Ilide and Gorbin, who were both grinning savagely.

"It is only a fair trial," said Gorbin, who had to shout over the noise to make himself heard.

"I've changed my mind," stammered Largo. "There's no need to go to all this trouble. I don't want to challenge anybody to the right of their settlement. It was never what I meant."

"Do you hear, my stout hearts? Our marshlander says he doesn't want to challenge anyone after all! What shall we do? He won't stand to the challenge after he's called your honor to stake! Is this to be let go by so easily?"

Again a thunderous roar of denial split the night.

The young Famhart, watching from the borders of the crowd, tried to think of some way to help the marshlander

174

escape the wrath of the offended mob. He was thinking of the marshland girl and his promise to try to talk to her brother. There didn't appear to be much that he would be able to do, short of calling his father's hand; he could see the look that he had seen so often before; savage and sly, with a set purpose in mind. He knew the marshland youth had been marked to die and here was that plan already set into motion.

Realizing that he must do something quickly, the young Famhart shoved his way through the crowd until he was in front of his father.

"I should like the honor of the challenge," he said evenly, working his face into an angry mask. "If it pleases you, I will represent your settlement."

"What ho! Look, my bucks!"

The elder Famhart's eyes flashed and he threw back his head and roared out a long laugh.

"Here's my own whelp going to give us sport! Good. Very good. I think this should set us back in the way of a festive mood. Come along! Get out the clan dirks! Draw the ring and let us set to!"

The Bog Hat leader grasped his son in a bear hug and clapped him repeatedly on the back.

"Wonderful sport! Why didn't I think of it myself?"

"You're a cool one," said Gorbin to the young Famhart. "I never would have thought you had this much blood in you."

"More than even you might bargain for," replied the youth, looking away in the direction of the shelter where Linne lay. He knew she would be safe as long as he kept his father occupied. The thing that remained was how to deal with Largo, who was being shoved and led toward the settlement square, where there were men busy at the task of setting out the area where the trial by combat would take place.

As he glanced in that direction, the young Famhart happened to look just a slight bit higher above the rooftops into that deeper darkness that always lingers just on the edge of lighted places. He could not tell if his eyes had been playing him tricks or not, but it seemed to him he had seen a swarm of falling stars bursting over the low horizon beyond the settlement's borders.

He was distracted by Gorbin, who began helping him off with his vest and tunic.

"Don't let this fool lure you into thinking he's not handy with his weapons. Whatever other kind of coward he is, when he's pressed he can fight. He's like one of those water-squirts we catch in the fishtraps every so often. They look small and helpless, but they can rip a finger off before you can skin a bat."

"I'll remember that," said Famhart.

"You're welcome," replied Gorbin snidely. "I might have thought different about telling you if you weren't Famhart's whelp."

"I'm touched by your loyalty, Gorbin. I'm sure my father is, too."

Gorbin smiled a vacant smile and bowed.

Others were pressing around him now; and the youth found himself moving along in the midst of a crowd, listening to an endless spiel of suggestions and instructions on how to deal with the marshlander.

"Cut and slide, that's the thing!"

"Duck by and shoot up as soon as he moves."

"No, no, you'd be sure to get cut on the back like that. Shut up, Tolan! You've never handled a dirk before in your life."

"I'll slice your ears off any day!"

"If I lay down and sit on my hands!"

"Stay outside his guard until you see him tire. Wear him out."

"That's for you old men," snorted another younger Bog Hat.

"That's how we got to be old men, you cockaninny. And plan to get older, too."

There were others pushing and shoving to get near the square, and there was a huge crowd gathered now. The feast had flagged, then picked up steam as the combat drew closer to its onset; more wine was poured out from the kegs that were passed through the crowd, and more fuel was thrown onto the blazing bonfires.

The elder Famhart had arranged himself upon the tall stool that was set out for him at the very edge of the square, where he was flanked on both sides by his most trusted aides. He drew out a little silver-tipped stag horn and blew a note for silence.

"This must be done by the ancient law! Read out the scroll!"

A burly, red-bearded man stepped out of the crowd at Famhart's side. In one hand he held a leather knife case, and in the other was a parchment scroll which he held before him to read. After clearing his throat and waiting for the crowd to quieten, he began.

176

"This is how it shall be. Two dirks of equal length shall be thrown into the center of the square. The combatants will have equal play. There will be no rest or cease until one or the other shall claim victory. No outside aid shall be given. All spectators are to give way if the fight shall go beyond the square. There will be no other weapons used but the dirk."

Here the red-bearded man folded the scroll under his arm and held the leather case before him.

"Here are the daggers to be used. The match will start when the chief Elder shall signal."

"Are the two ready?" asked the elder Famhart.

"The marshlander is ready," called Ilide rudely.

"The Bog Hat is ready," replied Famhart, looking at his son. "So!"

The chief Elder of the Bog Hat clan raised the silver-tipped stag horn to his lips and blew the beginning of the contest between the two young men, who stood naked to the waist, eyeing each other cautiously over the width of the square that had been drawn for the combat. The two dirks were placed in the center in their leather case and the red-bearded man withdrew.

A cheer went up as soon as the crowd saw Famhart pick up his dagger; Largo snatched his quickly and retreated as far away as the edge of the ring of spectators would allow. He was booed and hissed, but the men left off trying to shove him toward his adversary after he turned and slashed viciously at the hands that tried to touch him.

It was all a nightmare to Largo; the firelight reflected off the wild faces of the crowd, making their features hideous; the noise was a dull roar in his ears, swelling in volume, then shrinking away. Famhart kept coming at him with an odd look in his eyes, at once strange and pleading. The marshland youth kept backing away, looking wildly about for a hole in the solid-packed bodies that formed a wall around the square. If he were able to find any avenue of escape, he felt he would just run until he would outdistance all of them. His mind had begun to snap; there were pictures of his father flashing through his fevered brain, pointing an accusing hand at him, glowering with terrible red-rimmed eyes; he saw again the marshland men slain and the women caught as slaves; nothing was working out the way he had planned; and now here was a former ally turned against him, becoming a gaunt murderer stalking him to slay him under the guise of law.

177

Largo threw the dirk as far away over the heads of the crowd as he could. That seemed to him the best solution, and he turned and tried smiling to the Bog Hat mob; but they jeered and hissed and called out for Famhart to finish the marshlander. The red-bearded man appeared in the square again, leading two other Bog Hat soldiers. They held Largo down between them and another dirk was given to the youth; this one was strapped to his arm so that he would not be able to rid himself of it.

"Go on!" called the referee. "It is a fair fight now."

Largo sobbed and thrust against the unyielding mob; but they hurled him back. The shadows began to dance wildly, and Largo saw a dozen huge forms lunge out at him. He whirled, slashing the air left and right, his eyes dilated and his nostrils flared. His lips drew back in absolute terror, giving the appearance of a horrible grin to the taunting throng.

Young Famhart saw the frightened marshlander transformed into a raving madman who was like an animal caught in a trap. If he were to attempt communicating his plan to the crazed Largo, he would first have to subdue him, which was going to be no easy chore.

Largo whirled madly, chasing back the edges of the crowd that pressed too close. A scream of pain tore through the night and a man, holding a slashed arm, staggered back from Largo; three others in the mob then beat the marshland youth back with the flats of their swords.

Largo grew more confused and crazed. Sitting in the judge's seat, the elder Famhart turned to his referee to see if it would be permissible to put a shaft into the raging youth.

The bonfires were blazing high into the night sky, with sparks flying into the dark corners of the crowds; the noise of the cheering, screaming people covered all other sound until at that moment a loud rumble was heard, like the groan of thunder; another bonfire erupted out of the darkness in midair. The shouts of warning came too late to alert the Bog Hats, for in the next blink of an eye, the dragon Rengesbark was exploding into their midst, bringing with him the war band of the Shanoliel, their pipes skreeing a deadly call and their arrows flashing death in the melee. And right at Famhart's elbow on the judge's seat, there appeared a small gray otter, who slowly put a thin pipe to his mouth and began to blow the haunting, dreadful, beautiful call of the Ring Parath.

178

Rengesbark

THERE was nothing in the Lower Meadows that Coney was afraid of except fire. The Dargol Brem was no match for the Old One when it came to wills; but the dragon used fire to a degree that was disturbing to the ancient being. In the initial onslaught Coney had been scorched badly and only kept himself from catching fire in his upper limbs by quickly placing those extremities into the shallow water at the landing of the Bog Hats.

Olthar was at his left, and Coney leaned to the small animal and boomed directly into his ear.

"I am calling the others now," he said. "They shall have to help you here. I must keep myself out of the dragon's way."

"Are you hurt?" cried Olthar, turning to his friend just as the confused battle swarmed over them.

The Bog Hats had recovered somewhat and set to their defense as professional, long-hardened soldiers. Calmly and methodically they formed their ranks and discarded their party mood. The Shanoliel, caught in the furious struggle with Rengesbark, hardly had time to discern between their enemies; there were dragon and Bog Hats all rolled into one vast chaotic mass, fire and thunder and destruction spread in all directions.

Jahn had snatched a short sword from one of his cousins and joined the fray, staying close to Olthar, who was reaching out a hand to touch the Old One.

"I am not able to stay!" cried Coney. "I shall give you all my aid from a safer distance. The fire is too dangerous to me."

Olthar had called out to Coney again, but where the Old One had been there was now nothing but the battling elves and men locked into a furious struggle; and above it all the roar and stench of the Dargol Brem.

"Look out!" shouted Jahn, leaping to knock away a blow that had been directed at the small animal.

"Coney's gone!" cried the otter. "We have to find Linne and get away from here!"

"I'm for that," returned the elf breathlessly, dodging another blow.

A Bog Hat soldier was near Olthar when he spoke Linne's name, and turned around, lowering his weapons.

"Are you friends of the marshland girl?"

"We are," replied Olthar, making ready to defend himself.

"Quickly! We must hurry to help her," said the man.

Jahn and Olthar looked at each other dazedly.

"Who are you?"

"I am Famhart the Younger. I am a friend of Linne's. But she is in grave danger. We must get her away from here!"

"We are all in grave danger," observed the elf shortly. As he spoke, the Dargol Brem's grim tail swiped the ground near where they stood, knocking them all off their feet.

"Look!" cried Jahn. "Look! There is another one off there!"

The elf was wildly gesturing at a point over a dark spot in the swamp, where there indeed did seem to be another of the flying snakes breathing his fiery breath and setting off sparks in that part of the Bog Hats' domain.

Rengesbark had seen the flashing sparks himself; a deep rage built within him as he watched, for he was the sole keeper of this whole end of the creations below the High Gates; and he would tolerate no interloper trying to take over any of his victims or treasures or realms. He had been the one who had left his mark over all the territory he controlled; and he guarded it fiercely from all who would try to take it from him, whether it be dragon, elf, dwarf, or man.

Of all those, he hated the dwarf clans the most, for that unseemly race loved his hoards as much as he did; they were constantly seeking ways to trick him and often did manage to delve into the caves and shafts in which he kept all his pretty trinkets so that he could sleep upon them during the times of his hundred-year naps.

The elves he hated next, for they had much knowledge in the art of defeating him. The worst of the lot were the Shanoliel, who made up the ranks of those who were battling against him now.

He also felt another presence, not quite defined, that struggled to counteract his terrible spells of darkness and disaster that he cast about him like a cloak of black doom.

While the dragon's attention was diverted, Famhart hurriedly led the otter and elf away from the central part of the struggle. The top of the shelter where Linne hid was gone;

nothing remained but burnt thatch and the smoking roof poles.

"This was where she was!" shouted Famhart in a choked voice. "Help me find her!"

Olthar's heart pounded as he hurried through the wrecked shell of the dwelling; from outside there came the increasing sound of the battle as it raged, first from one direction, then another. His thoughts were full of concern about Coney's whereabouts, and how they would escape once they had successfully located Linne. From looking at the ruins left from the dragon attack, he had little hopes of finding the girl alive, which saddened him to the point of bitter despair.

Without fully realizing it, the small animal put the pipe to his lips and blew, not following any tune or melody, but letting the pipe find its own voice. He was immediately cheered; and playing on, he let the notes ripple forth however they seemed to come; the darkness all about him seemed to brighten. Jahn was ahead of him, calling out something he could not hear, but the elf was very excited.

In another moment, Famhart was beside him. Together they were lifting the marshland girl from beneath a heap of rubble that was left from the burning roof, gently laying her where they could tend her wounds.

Before Olthar could reach them, a dozen or more Bog Hat soldiers leapt the broken walls, pursued by a band of Duirn's Shanoliel. A volley of arrows was exchanged; then the two warring parties fell on with such a fierceness that Jahn and Famhart were driven back, leaving the unconscious girl.

Jahn was jumping up and down wildly, darting in and out of the fray.

"The Eolin!" he called, giving the ancient battle cry of the elfin race. After another brief flurry of blows, the Bog Hats vanished into the flame-filled darkness, leaving the elves to a brief reunion.

"Where is Duirn?" asked Jahn of one of the Shanoliel. "Is he with you? How did you come to be here?"

"Duirn is somewhere about, cousin. We shall answer all the rest of your questions as soon as we have finished with this business. We are in boats at the landing. Try to make your way there, if you can."

The elf paused and turned to Olthar.

"Play on, good Olthlinden! That pipe guides our blows. It is the best music we can hear in a skirmish!"

Bowing low to the elf, Olthar began again.

181

"Come on," cried Famhart. "We can get Linne out of here safely now."

"Is she hurt?" asked the otter.

"A knock on the head. She seems to have no hurt otherwise," replied the young Bog Hat.

"I wonder where Coney has gotten to? We need him to leave here."

"They said they have their boats at the landing," replied Jahn. "We shall have to go with them since the Old One had to leave."

"Did you see another dragon? It looked as though there was another one of those foul things out there," said Famhart.

"I wonder," muttered Jahn. "I would not put it past our friend Coney to be at his tricks. The Old Ones are an amazing race. We can hardly know all the things they are capable of."

Struggling to lift Linne, Famhart called for help.

"See if you can help me here, you two! We'll discuss the snake when we get to a place where we might think about it."

Jahn quickly helped Famhart lift the girl from the wreckage of the house; then together with Olthar, he raced ahead to clear the way for the young man, and to protect him while he carried Linne toward the elfin boats that were drawn up at the landings of Bonadig.

A voice from the midst of a hot combat stopped Olthar short.

"Olthar! Here, lad. To me, Jahn!"

Heavy sword strokes rang out and the struggle was so intense that the otter, being short of stature, could not see the one who had called his name.

"It's Duirn!" cried the elated Jahn. "He's here after all!"

"The pipe, lad! Keep up the pipe!" called Duirn, his voice almost drowned out by the roaring approach of the dragon.

Rengesbark had lumbered awkwardly into the air and hung suspended for a moment above the struggling elves and men, still clutching Trane closely in one ugly talon. With a noisy snort of anger, he held the Erling up before his awesome snout.

"Do you see anything that looks like another of the Dargol Brem?" he asked.

"I thought so just a minute past. I could have sworn to it," replied the petrified Trane.

The heavy, armored body of the winged beast slowly lifted a bit higher into the darkness where he could get a more unobstructed view. The arrows of the elves hummed and sang all about him, irritating him further. He swatted viciously with his tail, which was lined with jagged, cruel ridges which were as hard as the treated weapons the dwarfish clans wrought in their under-earth kingdoms. He raked this dreadful appendage back and forth beneath him, upsetting all the elves and knocking them senseless; then clutching the Erling before him, he rose higher into the flaming shadows above the embattled settlement of the Bog Hats.

Rengesbark was aware that the humans in Bonadig were allies of Dorini, but he did not concern himself with that at the moment. What was more pressing to the beast was the presence of another of the Dargol Brem. It was a breach of the ancient law of the lower dragons that only one of them would govern at a time over specified territories. That law had never been broken before to his knowledge, although there were a few bitter disagreements over border disputes that had gone on simmering for ages. These arguments were irritations to the dragons and terror and destruction to all those who were caught up in the disputed territory. Instead of only one of the beasts to contend with, there were two; and if a single dragon was difficult and dangerous to deal with, two of them in a given space were impossible.

Most of the lands above the Black Ice River, the Great Flats of Western, The Barrens, the Black Mountains, and the Endless Swamp were areas where once many settlements of humans, danes of elves, delvings of dwarfs, and communities of animals had flourished and prospered. The coming of the Dargol Brem had marked the beginning of the end to those lands a long time before; and as time wore on and the sway of Dorini grew over more and more of the lands of the Lower Meadows, the dragons began to exert their power over certain choice territories for which they had a fondness.

This fondness, of course, had slain or driven off the inhabitants in such numbers that after a time nothing was left but the scorched and bleak dragon wastes that stretched on as far the eye could see.

"Quickly, quickly! To the boats! The snake is breaking off!" called Emeon, gathering his band to him to fight their way to the elfin skiffs that waited for their masters at the water's edge.

Olthar piped up another refrain which encouraged the elves further; soon they were clear of the Bog Hat main force and began loading quickly into the watercraft, still loosing deadly volleys of arrows at both the humans and the dragon, who hovered in the shadows above them.

"Does he still have that Erling?" shouted Duirn. "Can anyone see if that wood elf is still with the dragon?"

There was no reply, for many of the elves were still occupied with repelling the Bog Hat attacks.

Once they were in the water, the spell of the elfin boats protected them; the humans could not see their enemies. It was as if the elves had simply vanished into thin air.

The only one who could see them plainly was Trane; and he was clutched firmly in one of Rengesbark's ugly claws high above the channel, looking for any sign of another of the Dargol Brem.

Trane's mind raced; his fear of the dragon was growing by the moment, for he knew that he could be crushed in a single instant of anger. Knowing something of the way the dragon thought, he knew there was no predicting what the beast would do next: the total savagery and complete power of the Dargol Brem had made them so temperamental that they might give hoards of trinkets one instant and bite off heads the next.

It was not good judgment for anyone to have any more to do with a dragon than he absolutely had to; it was especially unhealthy for elves, for the Dargol Brem had a great distaste for that race, along with the dwarfs, for they yet held some means of defense that could sting the beasts. There were dragons that had actually been slain by the elves and dwarfs; those were made into martyrs and lamented by their brothers, and the rallying cry of the Dargol Brem was often just the repeating of the names of their fallen.

There was no such brotherly thought on Rengesbark's mind as he scoured every direction from Bonadig; he was certain now that there was another of the order present; and if not that, then something else which was powerful and dangerous.

Lifting higher still, the Dargol Brem lumbered away in the direction he thought he had seen the intruder, leaving the Shanoliel to load their boats with only the Bog Hats to deal with. After the total surprise of both the elfin attack and the unexpected arrival of a long-absent dragon, the human warriors of the elder Famhart were more readily disposed to allow the elves to withdraw unhindered. Their leader had disappeared in the battle and was nowhere to be found; his son had gone along with him. The prisoners they had taken that very day had scattered and escaped, and their settlement was in ruins from the attack of the dragon; it was no happy clan that set about the chore of trying to reorganize their forces and take stock of all that had occurred.

Olthar sat in the lead boat with Duirn; next was Famhart, still holding the marshland girl; then Jahn Spray and Emeon. Their swift elfin skiffs made good speed away from the Bog Hat camp; and Duirn told them that with luck he had pierced the Erling Trane, and they wouldn't have to worry about the wood elf pointing out their boats to the dragon.

"Do you mean to say you tried to put an arrow into him?" asked Emeon, shocked at the news his leader told him.

"I am not proud of it, Emeon. It was something that came over me when I saw what he was doing. I saw the boats we lost, and then I looked up and there was this miserable blot on elfdom's honor. I lost my head."

Duirn stroked his beard in silence for a time, still quite agitated and shaken at the memory of his behavior. His eyes had a strange, faraway look; the companions were afraid to bother him.

The leader of the Shanoliel turned to Olthar at last.

"But at least some good has come of this unfortunate night. We are back where we began: all together. We have the Olthlinden with us now and are well on our way to the place we shall need to be."

"Is it still The Beak?" asked Jahn, not knowing if the leader of the Shanoliel had changed his plans since their last meeting at Dun Macrath.

"Still The Beak, my young friend. There are to be others awaiting us there."

Olthar had placed the Pipe of Ring Parath back into its case and strapped it securely to his back.

"Will I be able to try to find my parents when we get there?"

The leader of the elfin clans shook his head sadly and looked away from the small creature who sat boldly next to him on the thwarts of the skiff.

"We know they are held by the Dark One. I learned that from Trane when we captured him. We thought we might have found out where they were held, but things happened. They are alive, that much we know."

"I shall need to learn to use arms," said Olthar softly. "This is going to be a long campaign. I had thought in my day-

185

dreams it would all be glorious and heroic and I would be able to save everyone with the pipe. I can see that isn't to be."

Jahn reached out and patted his small charge.

"If you have to learn anything at all about arms or their use, it's best to learn it from an elf. There are no better soldiers anywhere."

Emeon nodded agreement.

"Unfortunately, that's true. We have been forced to give up all the other pastimes that we pursue in more peaceful times."

"Pleasant ones, too," emphasized Jahn. "Music and poetry and a hundred other things that could keep you busy from now on if it weren't for all this other unfortunate mess in the middle."

"Dorini is indeed that," said Duirn. "She has given us all her regular schemes and cast of characters; and now she's given us back the Dargol Brem. Just when we thought that whole lot had been dealt with, here they are again worse than ever."

Olthar started up with alarm, looking toward the sky.

"Did you see another one just now? Or something that looked like one?"

Jahn looked up, then studied his friend closely.

"I thought I saw something that might be one. There was the same sort of reddish glow that looked like the sparks the snakes make."

"It has to be something else," said Duirn. "There are few of the Dargol Brem that can bear each other's company in close quarters. I think we'd be in for real fireworks if we saw two dragons in the same territory."

"But what else could it be?" asked Emeon. "It has drawn off the dragon, whatever it was. That much I am thankful for, no matter what the cause."

"You are very welcome, Master Elf," replied a grainy voice out of the darkness next to the boat, which startled Emeon so badly he almost bolted overboard.

"Coney!" cried Olthar. "It was you!"

"As much as I detest fire and anything to do with it, I had to imitate it as best I was able, to convince that flying lump of a toad that there was some competition for him in the Swamp of Dismal. This one is a clever devil. His name is Rengesbark."

"We were so worried about you," said the otter. "I was afraid the dragon had burned you."

Coney rippled with a sound of shuffling leaves that could have been laughter.

"He would have a difficult time holding me still long enough to do that. I am strangely attached to my bark just the way it is."

Suddenly, a soft moan drew everyone's attention to the outstretched form that had lain unconscious in the young Bog Hat's lap until then.

"Linne! Can you hear me?" asked Famhart.

The girl moaned again, but did not answer.

"We have to reach safety somewhere and stay long enough for our healers to tend her," said Duirn, who had moved next to the stricken girl, feeling her pulse and touching her forehead gently with his hand. "She's taken a nasty blow on the head."

He turned to Famhart.

"Is there anyplace near here we might go ashore to tend our wounded and set ourselves to rights?"

"We are almost to the last outpost before we reach the lower swamps. There won't be any of my clansmen this far along the way. I know of an old landing I found once. It was from long ago. My friends and I found it when we were exploring."

"That is where we will make for, then. You just tell the boat how we are to reach it. The others will follow."

Duirn told the Bog Hat the name of the elfin skiff, and the young man gave his instructions; and beneath the fading of the moon in the early morning, the remaining boats of the elves of the Shanoliel made their landing upon the silent shadows of the shore that had begun to take on the distant and distinct salty aroma of the sea.

IV. THE WINTER OF WINDAMEIR

Tales of the Banskrog

THE ancient settlement Famhart had discovered turned out to be one of the forgotten early danes of the Eolin during a time when the ancestors of the Shanoliel were moving from all parts of the Lower Meadows to the ports along the West Roaring, ports from which they would then embark to the Middle Islands and from thence on to the High Meadows. The young Bog Hat had known nothing of elfin lore and had no knowledge of the different races who had dwelled upon the lake or swamp in the earlier days; he had only known of the Bog Hats and marshlanders, for those were the histories most often discussed around the fire. It had not occurred to the young man that his ancestors might have had dealings with elves or dwarfs.

"You have much to learn, Famhart," chided Duirn, as they sat talking over pipes one day many weeks after their escape from Bonadig. Linne sat beside the young man, having been tended by the elfin healers and now quite mended after her harrowing ordeal.

"That seems to be the way of it," agreed the amiable Bog Hat. "But then my father and his friends were never very well versed in anything that didn't appear to be of value to them."

"Knowing one's history can sometimes be more valuable than all the pretty trinkets in the world," replied Duirn, stopping long enough to stir up the fire against the chill that had come with the waning afternoon.

All across the vast swamp there appeared all the signs of fall, and the wind had turned in a more northerly direction, blowing colder every day.

Olthar was returning from a session of weapons instruction with Emeon and sat wearily down beside the fire and poured himself a piping hot mug of tea.

"Your elves are ruining my whole day," he complained. "I had thought of some exploring to find out whether I have any cousins left in this part of the world; but instead, I've whacked and hacked and stabbed away the better part of the afternoon. I can hardly lift my paw to get this mug to my mouth."

"He's coming along," confided Emeon. "There doesn't seem to be a lot of steam behind his strokes, but I expect that is just because he's afraid he'll hurt one of his instructors. His form is good, though. If I could just get him a bit more familiar with the bow, I'd be satisfied to say that our young friend is as handy with arms as any of the Shanoliel."

"And that isn't anything to be overly proud about," said Banon. The old elf had guided his group through the empty swamps directly to Bonadig the night they spotted the fiery trail of the dragon; they had witnessed the attack, but been too late in their arrival to come to the aid of their friends. They had simply followed along after them once Duirn's band had made good their escape from the Bog Hat settlement. It had been a simple matter to find them once the elves had landed at the old settlement pointed out by Famhart.

"What wouldn't I give to forget all this business and return to tending my music," went on the old elf. "There's a dozen things I could think of that I'd rather be after than learning how to shoot a bow."

"That might be so, Banon; but in these hard times, I'm glad enough to know how to protect myself from the Banskrog," said Emeon quietly.

"Aye, the Banskrog," sighed Jahn. "It is always and forever the Banskrog. But we may be seeing an end of that, once the pipe gathers the clans."

"For better or worse," said Duirn. "Once we have the clans gathered and reach a place where we may confront the Darkness, we may yet wish we had never set out at all."

"Do you think we'll hear news of the Dark One soon?" asked Olthar, his small muzzle drawn into a worried frown.

"We have heard from her messenger. The Dargol Brem is a sure sign that his mistress is not far removed."

"I wonder why we haven't heard more from Rengesbark," said Duirn.

"Coney may be able to tell you," said the otter. "I think he is out searching for him."

"You mean he's gone out looking for the snake?" asked Famhart. "I didn't think there was anyone who loved them so much he would seek them out."

Famhart had been surprised daily at many of his discoveries about the elves and all their doings, but the Old One was beyond anything he had ever heard of, even in the tales he had heard as a lad around the late night fires in Bonadig.

"Coney said there was no better way to deal with one of the Dargol Brem than to know as much about him as you could. We are well off, it seems, knowing his name," said Emeon.

"And we have the Pipe of Ring Parath," added Duirn. "The very thing that the Banskrog hates the most. There is no army anywhere that would serve us better than the pipe and the Olthlinden. We also have an Old One with us."

"I'd feel a bit better if we had more bow arms," replied Famhart. "After seeing the dragon at Bonadig, I'd feel a deal safer with all the extra help we could get."

"Numbers mean nothing to the snake," said Banon. "I have had something to do with another of their order long before any of you were around. I was just a youngster myself. Younger than you, my good Famhart. Our dane was upon the Silver Dart, where it runs down from the Black Mountains. It was a pleasant country then, and the Black Mountains were very beautiful."

The old elf's eyes grew dim and misty as he spoke.

"The land was rolling green hills that reached away toward the higher peaks; and when you looked toward the Roaring Sea, it was all stands of old timber and green grass as high as your head."

Banon sat down close to the fire and touched Duirn on the knee.

"Your father and I were old hands in that part of the country. We knew it backward and forward. There were a hundred danes and twice as many human settlements, and there is no way of knowing how many delvings there were belonging to the dwarfs."

"Was this a time when the old kings of Boghatia lived?" asked Famhart. He was eager for any news that would have put him in a better light with the beautiful marshland girl.

"Yes, it was. The King of Boghatia was called Caladin. His was one of the most prosperous of the settlements of humans that abounded around the lake. It was called Clearwater in the time I speak of."

The old elf took up a mug and helped himself to the hot spiced tea on the glowing fire. It was still warm out, although the summer was at an end; and the otter felt, in his oldest form of knowing, that it would be a harsh winter. But for now the wind was merely refreshing and cool and kept the friends sitting comfortably around the low stone hob built roughly of stones to support their cookware.

The elf continued, "At the end of the latter period the Dargol Brem were drawn to all the wealth waiting to be taken. The first of the beasts was slain by the dwarfish clans of a very old delving near the Silver Dart. That really stirred the wind in the Dargol Brem, and soon another of the snakes came; his name was Deolage. He was vicious and cruel and cunning and it was almost the end of all that settled country. The way we see all this land now is but a regrowth of the way he laid it bare. The Black Ice began to run with black mud; the great plains became the Barrens of Western; there was nothing that escaped Deolage's wrath."

"What happened then?" asked Linne, shuddering.

"A great gathering of all the elfin and dwarfish and human clans was called. There was much discussion but no one listened until it was almost too late; the little petty jealousies and power struggles almost caused the complete destruction of every living soul that dwelt within range of the dragon. But at last the clans massed and attacked Deolage in one of his lairs near The Mires. Their numbers were great and they set on as earnestly as they knew how; but in the end, it was a single elf who saved the day. He began by sneaking into the snake's secret sleeping hole while the beast was out fighting the others. The elf was clever and knew he needed a disguise for protection, so he sheathed himself in a silver-mithra robe and wore a fine-wrought mithra crown that had been crafted by one of the finest metalsmiths in the long lines of the Eolin.

"After the dragon had wrecked the defenses of his attackers, he decided to take home his new treasures and to count the numbers in his mind of those he had slain in battle. Coming into his lair, he sensed immediately that someone had been there, but try as he might, could detect nothing out of place. He then shuffled through all the treasure trove, restacking everything and almost smothering the elf in the process. Deolage lay down for a nap on top of all the ill-gotten wealth, and while he dozed, the elf crept near enough the beast to put the mithra shortsword into that unprotected place that lay just behind the dragon's ear. The snake awoke with a start. He screamed in pain and thrashed about, wrecking the place and almost killing the elf again in his fury. At the first lull in the dragon's lashing about, the elf put a tiny reed pipe to his mouth and struck a high note that caused the mithra blade to begin vibrating. It continued vibrating with the music and kept right on until it had worked its way into the dragon's brain. There was the end of Deolage. As the saying goes, it was music to soothe the savage beast."

"Do you think that might work on Rengesbark?" asked Emeon.

"I'm sure it would, my young friend; but who is going to volunteer to get close enough to put the shortsword in?"

Duirn laughed, clapping the old elf on the back.

"My father told me that tale when I was barely old enough to understand any of the things he talked to me of."

"That was a very brave fellow," said Jahn. "What was the elf's name?"

Banon blushed to the tips of his ears.

"His name was Banon," replied Duirn, answering the question for his embarrassed friend.

"I hope we don't have any need for any more of that sort of doings," said Emeon. "Once is enough with any dragon. Maybe Rengesbark found it too hot for his liking and won't be back."

The old elf lifted the tea mug to his lips slowly and sipped at his drink carefully.

"You'll find that where a snake has left its track, it'll be back. They are not ones to forget old ties or haunts. This beast is the very one, I'd wager, that laid waste all this country. It wouldn't let any of its brothers take over what it had once begun."

"Do you think anyone from Bonadig is looking for us?" asked Jahn, turning to Famhart. "I'm not any too distressed by not seeing the dragon; but I'd give a good breakfast to anyone who could tell me what your Bog Hats are up to."

"And I still want to find what's happened to Largo," said Linne. She spoke calmly, but there were deep shadows under her eyes from the lack of sleep, and her fair brow was clouded with worry lines.

"That's as black a mystery as it was the night it happened," said Famhart. "Before anything else occurred, I watched him slip over the edge. It was all too much for him. He didn't seem to be able to bear up under the pressures he found brought against him."

"Largo was always very high-strung. I can see why, knowing the way we were brought up; with all the weight our father thrust onto his shoulders he never had a chance to be a child."

"It's good you were born a girl, Linne. You escaped all that."

"Not really. I was as eager to please my father as Largo, but it was doubly impossible for me for the very reason that I was a woman. He never took any notice, which really hurt me."

"You must have had a strange life," said Olthar.

"Not so bad, really," replied Linne, reaching out and patting the small animal.

"I wish I had more news of my own father and mother. Knowing they are alive and imprisoned by the Darkness is almost more terrible than thinking they are dead."

"You mustn't give up hope there," said Duirn. "Every day that passes brings us another day closer to finding a way to free them."

Olthar studied the elf.

"Do we stay here long?"

"Banon thinks we should go on to the sea. I vote for remaining where we are, at least until we hear word from the scouts we've sent out. It would also help to hear from Coney about what he has found."

"The layover has given us time to mend our wounded, too," added Emeon. "It has been more than a while since any of us were able to put our heads down on the same spot more than a few nights at a time."

"We can thank our good louts out in the other camps for that! They don't make it advisable for anyone to stop off too long without a move."

Duirn unfolded a small packet of charts as he spoke, laying them out before the others.

"So far as we know now, the Worlugh and Varads and Gorgolac have moved across the Serpents into the Westing Wood and the White Birch; they have reached Dun Macrath and the Gray Ash already; they have owned the lands beyond the Black Ice for as long as we can count years."

The leader of the Shanoliel tapped with his forefinger the places that were overrun by the forces of the Darkness.

"We have been steadily pushed to the sea, slowly and relentlessly; I couldn't make much sense of the pattern of things until I took a long look at the lay of the land on these maps. The Banskrog has taken all the settled parts of the Westerlands and occupies everything with her dark armies. We are sitting on a little spit of land that juts out into the sea just like a little bird waiting on the end of a branch for a cat."

Banon was stroking his beard absently, looking at the charts.

"What you say is so, Duirn. I have long wondered at the rhyme to all the ebb and flow of the beast raiders. At first, it didn't seem to be anything but random skirmishers from the borders; then there were greater numbers of them until they began to force danes and delvings to abandon places that had long been safe havens for all."

"The more I study this, the clearer it becomes; I don't know why it never struck me before. We are left with only one place to go; and that is to the sea!"

Famhart looked up in surprise.

"You can't hope to put to sea in your skiffs! They are swamp skiffs! They wouldn't last an hour in rough water!"

Duirn laughed lightly.

"You are quite right, good Bog Hat. They are swamp and river skiffs; but we are water elves and have a whole array of seacraft we can call upon when the need is great. We won't have to drown ourselves in the skiffs."

"But where will we go?" asked Linne. "I don't want to leave here without knowing about the fate of my brother!"

"We shall know all we need to know before we embark, Linne. As to where we will be bound, there is only one course and one destination."

"Which is?" prompted Jahn.

"The route of the ancient Shanoliel. Bor Asa the Navigator laid out that route in the First Returnings."

Banon nodded agreement.

"Bor Asa set the course then; and I can see it must be the same now. Things have a way of rounding out on the same note which they began."

Duirn looked at the small animal next to him.

"We have all that was required of us before we were to make the journey. The Olthlinden is with us, bearing the Pipe of Ring Parath."

"I can't see that I'll be of much use at this point," said Olthar quietly.

"More use than you will imagine, my small friend. Already you've used the pipe to stay one of the Dargol Brem and to call the Shanoliel into battle."

"I had hoped to do more than that," replied the otter, a faint trace of disappointment in his voice.

"You shall have your chances to fulfill all those troubled dreams," said Duirn. His gaze seemed to pierce Olthar's thoughts, and the elf's eyes grew a deep sea blue that was as vast and mysterious as the sky.

"Look!" cried Emeon. "It's our scouts come back! Let's see what they report of the snake."

"And Bonadig," added Famhart.

"They may have news of Largo," said Linne hopefully, although she wasn't sure she wanted to hear the fate of her unstable brother, who had tried so hard to do the very things in life that he was so ill-equipped to do.

The company made room for the returned scouts; and they all sat down in earnest to hear what the travel-weary elves had to report.

But before the scouts had a chance to begin, another visitor made himself visible to the group, rising out of the waters at swamp's edge: it was Coney. And shaking himself mightily in every limb, he quickly ensconced his thick trunk among the friends.

Hydin and Company

LISTENING to his scouts, Duirn grew withdrawn and thoughtful; the news was disturbing and ominous. They had found evidence of the battle at Bonadig, but no sign of the Bog Hats or the dragon. The elves had split up and gone in all directions away from the settlement, exploring as far as they dared; yet there was no evidence of the snake. One party had found the trail of what appeared to be Bog Hat stragglers, although they lost the scent when the survivors, whoever they were, seemed to have disappeared into thin air.

"There were scores of boats in Bonadig," said Famhart. "We lived with boats for as long as we have been in the swamp. Most likely they used boats to leave."

"We found a great number of them sunk at the landings in Bonadig," replied one of the scouts. "There were so many we couldn't see how a great number could be left."

"Do you think it possible anyone could have used the old elfin roads to get away?" asked Banon.

"What roads are they? I've never known any path through the swamp except the water," said Famhart.

"We are sitting in one of the elfin danes from a time so far past there is no telling exactly how old it is; anywhere there is a dane, you can be sure there are more ways than one to reach it, and I'm certain that if we were to explore here long enough, we'd find more ways to come or go than by water."

"We did find traces of the old roads," replied another scout, squatting wearily by the fire with a mug of tea. "They hadn't been used in a long time."

"It disturbs me that you didn't find some trace of the Bog Hats," said Duirn. "I can reconcile the disappearance of Rengesbark: that is in keeping with the habits of a dragon. I'm sure we'll have no trouble discovering him soon enough."

"Do you have any ideas about your kinsmen?" asked Banon, addressing Famhart.

The young Bog Hat frowned and shook his head.

"They are capable of some clever tricks, but I don't know about managing to disappear. I can't imagine what might have happened, unless they were all slain and carried off by the dragon."

A small light lit up in Olthar's eyes.

"Do you remember telling me the story about the old elves in that funny place? When the dragon came and attacked their settlement, and one of the True Dragons came down and carried them away to another land?"

Jahn nodded, a slow look of comprehension spreading over his fair features.

"That could be possible in this case, too. Only it is Rengesbark, and not a True Dragon; and the Bog Hats are the ones that were transported instead of elves."

Banon knitted his brow in deep thought.

"There is an old story that runs that way. It does seem to bear on the case."

"The Bog Hats are allies of the Dark One. If there was any plan afoot to pursue us, then Rengesbark would certainly be used to best advantage."

Having opened up this avenue of thought, the companions suddenly lost the sense of security they had felt just before while sitting at their fire enjoying their tea. The late afternoon sunlight grew pale and weak, leaving them feeling chilled and full of nagging thoughts.

After a long, uneasy silence, the Old One made a rumbling noise somewhere deep inside his massive trunk, clearing his voice.

"You are not far wrong in your suspicions that Rengesbark

is at the bottom of the disappearance of the Bog Hats at Bonadig," he said. "The great worm has been in that area often since we have left; and every time he leaves he takes more Bog Hats with him."

"Then the dragon has taken them," repeated Jahn. "Just as happened in the old story."

"Except that this isn't the Syrin Brae. The dragon has taken the Bog Hats to help mass an attack with the rest of the armies that the Dark One shall throw against us."

Duirn stood and looked at the surrounding empty swamp as though expecting an assault at any minute.

"They are not planning their strike here," assured Coney. "It is nowhere this side of The Beak. I could not even make certain that it would be there, but there are others gathering to make the strike; the ones in the swamp have said as much. The swampkind hate the Bog Hats and anyone else who enters their domain, and now they say the beast warriors are on the move."

Coney shifted his position. He sat at the edge of the clearing, the one tree that was visible in any direction for as far as the eye could see.

"The Dark One has taken a hand in the waging of this battle. I felt her presence strongly when I was in Bonadig and all through the swamp and marshlands on the other side, where there is now a different air about the place, more bleak and foreboding. I could find nothing save a trail of clues that led me on to the worst: that this is to be no small foray. I haven't foreseen the likes of this since the end of the Bitter Winter Wars when the Ellyon was lost."

"Who was lost?" asked Jahn.

"The Ellyon! One of the brotherhood."

"You mean an Old One?"

"Exactly. It was a dreadful thing."

"I didn't think anything could harm you," said Famhart.

"A dragon can, if it is able to counter our spells."

"Is that what happened?"

"The Ellyon that was lost was one of the most peaceful of our order. He did not know what it was to deal with the dark forms and shapes of the Banskrog."

The drift of this conversation led Linne to speak.

"Did you find any sign of my brother, Coney?"

She waited with faint breath for his reply.

The Old One shook his upper limbs in a negative answer.

"He was nowhere to be found. Unless he has gone with the Bog Hats, I can guess nothing of his fate."

"But that wouldn't be likely," argued Famhart. "My father was on the verge of murdering him."

Linne's face fell and her lip trembled. She was very near tears, but fighting hard to keep control.

"I don't know why I'm so upset," she said, her voice breaking. "He was a traitor and responsible for many deaths in our settlements; but I still can't bear to think of him dying."

"There were no bodies anywhere," consoled one of the scouts of the Shanoliel. "If there had been, we would have found them. It is not easy to conceal anything from an elf when he is on a trail."

"What he says is true," confirmed Emeon. "It would take a deal more clever group than a Bog Hat clan to conceal their tracks from an elf."

Emeon bowed to Famhart.

"No offense meant."

"None taken," laughed the youth. "The Bog Hats are sly enough in the ordinary sense of speaking; but I've never seen anything like what I've seen since I've been here."

"You're lucky you're not getting your ears full of all the history of the whole lot," laughed the otter. "When I first ran into these fellows they went to great lengths to make sure they left no story untold."

Jahn chuckled good-naturedly.

"There was just as big a load on my side of it, having to hold you down with one hand and try to read to you from the other."

"You both seem no worse the wear for it. I'd say Coney was the injured party, when all is said and done," smiled Duirn.

The ancient being shuddered and moved his upper limbs.

"Thank you, Duirn. And to think that on top of everything else I am stuck with that wretched name that best describes hares."

"No one could pronounce your real name," said Jahn stubbornly.

"It's quite simple, really; all you have to do is remember to hold your breath on the hissing sounds and stick out your tongue on the floating *u*'s."

Coney was ready to debate longer, but Banon turned his thoughts away to another subject.

"Since we know the Banskrog is gathering forces to strike at us, I think it would be well advised if we call together all

200

the numbers we can. There will be no sense in making a stand in the Westing Wood or the Gray Ash if they are overrun with the beast warriors. I say it is time we gathered our strength to strike the very heart of the Dark One's power. We have the Olthlinden and the Pipe of Ring Parath to guide us; there has never been a more timely moment for the Eolin."

Duirn looked thoughtfully at his friend.

"You are very close to the heart of the matter, Banon; we have awaited the time that would announce a move to end the Banskrog's hold over the Lower Meadows; that hour is now, and it is our responsibility to keep the appointment. It always seems to creep upon those who expect great bells in the sky or flaming clouds to point the way. It never is that simple. It usually starts just like this, with a group sitting around their afternoon tea, talking over matters, trying to decide in what direction to go next."

"I'd settle for a few flaming clouds that would point the way," said Jahn. "Nothing since the flood at Dun Macrath has seemed to follow any logic or order."

Olthar agreed with a series of rapid nods and chitters.

"That flood seems as though it were all part of something that happened to someone else. I can hardly remember what I felt like then."

"If you don't, I do. You had grown a rock for a head and insisted that we leave immediately."

The small animal colored a deeper gray.

"I suppose I was rather hard to handle."

"I don't know what I would have done if it hadn't been for the Old Ones."

Coney responded with a low rumbling noise that was a cross between an avalanche and thunder.

"I was anxious to try to find Morane and Malcom. That is still the first thing on my mind," Olthar explained.

"We have not forgotten that the Dark One holds your mother and father, Olthar. The Banskrog holds many of our loved ones prisoner in her black web."

Duirn looked away toward the invisible sea.

"She has kept the elfin clans trapped here forever, it seems. I am sure that we could find no one who has not suffered under the cruel reign of Dorini."

"It is always the way of it," sighed Banon. "Look at young Famhart here; and Linne, who has lost her father and a brother to the dealings of the Banskrog. One was an honorable loss, the other doubtful; yet her heart feels the same pain at both."

Emeon refilled the old elf's mug for the second time.

"A loss is a loss," he said, "whether it be to a grand cause or a calamity."

"I think our grand loss has been that of vision; in not being able to see the Dark One's strength growing over all these seasons. We were all too overly optimistic about what was going forward. Every day the Dark One's armies grew more powerful as our own defenses waned. She has been subtle and sly. It is a good rule she follows, one that always has some measure of success: never make a move until you have the strength behind it to make sure it works without fail."

Duirn drew circles in the loose, damp earth as he spoke.

"We should have tried holding her in check," said Banon. "If only we had known how far she would go."

Another of the Elfin scouts approached and reported something to Duirn in a low, urgent whisper.

"What is it?" asked Jahn. "News of the snake?"

"Otters," smiled the Shanoliel leader. "They have come to see Olthar! It seems they have heard of him and come to seek him out."

The small animal's muzzle twitched. It was the nearest thing to a smile that Jahn had seen his young friend wear in so long he could not remember the last time.

"Come on!" shouted Olthar. "I want you all to meet my cousins."

Leaping up from the fire and darting away to the water so rapidly that he bowled over two unsuspecting elves who were in his path, the otter exploded into a number of whistles and chirps and chitters that were answered immediately from the rushes that bordered the edges of the landing of the old elfin dane.

"It sounds like birds," said Linne, laughing.

Jahn nodded.

"I have studied his tongue for some time. I can make out some of the noises, but it is a complicated speech. I don't know if anyone other than another animal has ever mastered it."

"There are those who speak it as well as any animal," replied Duirn. "They are the Masters of the Circle."

"Who are they?" asked Famhart.

"Banon can tell you. I think it's quite possible that he has even met with one of their number."

"It could well be so. I've always suspected as much; but one never talks about meeting one of them; it's bad luck."

Changing the subject abruptly, the old elf pointed to the water's edge, where a vast number of otters were surrounding Olthar; their coats reflected the late afternoon sunlight like polished amber, and they scampered and darted with such energy that they would seem to have completely exhausted themselves in their eagerness. Olthar turned and rushed back to his friends on shore, shaking the water out of his fur as he did so.

"Come on, Jahn," he cried with delight. "I shall have my turn with you now. One elf and many otters!"

"All right, all right! But I'm not going swimming," said the elf resolutely.

"Don't be too sure about that," laughed Emeon. "We're all wet enough now and we're not even near the water, except for what Olthar has so kindly brought us."

The high-spirited young animal covered the company with another shower.

"Come on! I want you to meet Hydin. He's come all the way from the Black Mountains."

"I would like to speak to him, too," said Duirn. "If he has come from that far away, he must have news that's fresher than mine about that part of the country."

Olthar paused a moment, growing serious.

"Hydin is from one of the older clans. They don't want anything to do with humans." Here he stopped and looked at Famhart and Linne. "Theirs is an old clan that has spent a long time in the Black Mountains; they have lost many of their number to the beast armies and to the humans who trap them for their coats."

"Surely you can explain that our friends here mean them no harm," said Duirn.

"Oh, they'll come around right enough; but I think it would be best if we go slowly. I'll take Jahn and introduce him, since he is almost an otter anyhow."

"Having paid my costs by tutoring one of the thick-headed beasts," grumbled the elf in a resigned voice.

Banon watched the two friends go.

"Here is a strange thing come to pass. And as all strange things, it is only exactly what has gone before."

"What riddles are you speaking, Banon?" asked Emeon observing Jahn as he was being introduced formally to the head of the otter clan, which was spread out over the dane landing.

"The old tales of when all the followers of the Light gathered themselves to battle the Banskrog. Men and elves and dwarfs and animals all together in a mighty force that kept the Darkness imprisoned for a long, long time."

"Will it ever come to a time like that again?"

"It looks as though it is here," replied the old dwarf, his eyes grown very dim with remembrances of things past and forgotten days that had been recalled.

"I feel bad that they won't come near because of us," said Linne. "I am so fond of Olthar."

"They'll give way," assured Duirn. "It won't take them long to find that they have nothing to fear from our quarter."

"Shows they have good sense, anyhow," said Famhart. "Not easy to run a gammon on them. When it comes to humans I feel the same way: watch and wait!"

Jahn was returning again, the otter racing about playfully at his feet.

"They've come down from all that country Olthar spoke of," said Jahn to Duirn. "They know all the goings and comings there. It is all gone to the Banskrog; nothing but the beast warriors all the way down from the Black Mountains."

"They want to learn the use of arms, Emeon. I told them you would help them. Will you?"

Emeon bowed to his friend.

"It would be an honor. Did any of them bring weapons with them?"

"No. They've been too busy just trying to get down to the sea to be burdened with them."

"How did they find out you were here?" asked Linne.

"From the beasts who have been spying all along the river. It seems the pipe and the Olthlinden are known among the Dark One's armies, and Hydin kept hearing tales of the strange animal and his pipe. The otters learned that the animal was one of their kind, so they kept on following along in our track until now."

Olthar paused and turned to Coney.

"And it seems they met a certain party that I won't name who told them who and where I was."

The ancient being shuffled his limbs serenely.

"Someone has to be on the lookout for what goes on. I dare say it would have taken them a lot longer to find you if I hadn't pointed out the way."

"We shall have to stay on here awhile if we are to fashion weapons for our new allies! Emeon, see if you can scout through this old dane and find where the smiths and armories are. There may even be stores somewhere, if they haven't been raided before now."

"There hasn't been anyone in these waters except a few scouts from the Bog Hats," said Famhart. "And it was said that these old places were all haunted, so no one has touched them."

"Good. Emeon, you go on with your search. Now, Olthar, will you introduce me to your cousin Hydin? I have a few questions I would like to ask."

"He said he will come here. I've given my word he is among friends."

So saying, Olthar scampered back to the water and returned shortly, leading a very subdued and nervous Hydin, who except for the eyes looked to be a replica of the Olthlinden. The shy animal bowed low all around and sat down gravely beside Olthar.

In what seemed a moment, the friends were laughing and talking; and soon Hydin's entire company was stretched out comfortably among the elfin band, talking and chatting as though they had been old comrades long separated.

Looking over the spectacle before him, Duirn knew that here was something that promised to be no ordinary adventure. When his eyes met the calm gaze of Olthar, he suddenly smiled at the young animal, who nodded, somehow seeming far older than his short turnings. There was beginning to grow up a bright aura around his small friend that burned surer and stronger every day.

The Return of the Ancients

IN the remote distances of the high peaks of the Black Mountains, the dwarf Alar Far hummed and chuckled to himself as he went about his task. The shaft he walked about in was in an ancient delving that had been fashioned by his ancestors in a time long before. His eye wandered over the fine carvings and smooth walls as he went, but it was not because he saw the beauty that his sires had created: rather he was humming because he was alive and the king of all that vast domain that ran beneath the Black Mountains. There was no one he answered to but the Protector, and she had been pleased indeed with the capture of the two wretched otters who were the parents of the one who was the Olthlinden. After her anger had subsided over their failure to capture him, the Dark One realized that she held an even stronger weapon: she would be able to use her hostages to gain possession of the Pipe of Ring Parath, which had come back to plague her after all the years of silence when she had grown strong and those who opposed her blindly went on thinking that she was content to remain satisfied with the turn of events in the Lower Meadows.

Alar Far actually danced a few clumsy steps over the water-smooth stone floor as he entered the prison where he kept the two otters, Malcom and Morane. He called out in a cheerful, sweet voice as he entered.

"Hello, my pets. What a glorious day it is up in the sunshine. I enjoyed watching the sun rise just now. Yes, indeed, a glorious morning for those who can see it."

The dwarf cackled at his own humor, then placed the tray of food he carried before the crude cage that he had fashioned out of lumber from the storehouses in the lower delvings.

"Fresh mushrooms from the basement and water that has never seen the day," he said gleefully. "There is also some very good fungus that I think makes an excellent spread for the cakes I've brought."

Alar Far paused, looking with mock concern at his prisoners.

"What? Not hungry? You can't keep your strength up if you don't have something."

Morane stared stubbornly at the loathsome dwarf, refusing to touch the food he had shoved into their cage.

"Now, now, my pets! You won't be able to see your precious pup if you don't eat. I have told you that already."

"I don't believe you," said Morane listlessly. "We have yet to see any proof that you have him. I think you've lied to us."

"Lie? Alar Far doesn't lie. That's very cruel of you to say so. For that you don't get to see your wonderful pup. You have hurt Alar Far's feelings with that remark."

The dwarf huffed up indignantly and rebolted the small opening in the cage door where he had slipped the food through.

"You've been ugly today. I try to take care of you and all

206

you repay me with is a harsh tongue. You will be sorry one day that you haven't tried to make Alar Far your friend."

Alar Far went back along the way he had come, chuckling to himself as he saw the discomfort of the two small animals. They huddled together miserably in the dim gleam of the dwarfish rocklights that were placed throughout all the shafts in the lower delvings.

Morane sobbed quietly into her paws as Malcom paced about the confined space restlessly.

"If he would ever open the door when he puts the food tray in we would be able to get past him."

"We wouldn't know how to get out of this horrible place," sobbed Morane. "Even if we did get out of here, we'd still be lost."

"I know we are in the Black Mountains," argued her mate. "And the Black Ice starts here. That river runs all the way to the West Roaring."

He looked closely at Morane, lowering his voice before he spoke again.

"We can hear the river. All we have to do is get to it and we will be out of here."

Morane stopped crying for a moment, a faint trace of hope in her voice.

"Are you sure?"

"Listen."

The two animals grew silent and concentrated on listening. Very faintly, as if from a great distance, they could hear the sound of water distinctly.

"I heard it when we were first brought here," said Malcolm at last. "I had planned all along to somehow try to make our escape by using it, but this miserable troll never leaves any opening to make a move."

"Couldn't we try the bars again? We might have given up too soon."

"We'd be out of here by this time if we had old Thorton Beaver with us. He would be our only hope of getting out that way."

The cage the otters were kept in had been built in the center of what had once been an arms storehouse in the old delving, and as such it was a small shaft with smooth stone floors and walls. Malcom also gathered from what Alar Far said that it was deep in the center of the dwarfish settlement and far below the outer gates.

Morane had returned to the back of the cage and was

trying to gnaw away at the hard wood that formed the walls of their prison.

"Oh, this is hopeless," she cried, after getting a splinter in her effort to loosen the unyielding bar. She curled up in a ball and began to cry again.

She had spent a great deal of time crying since she and Malcom had been captured, but when Alar Far moved them from the Varad war camp into the depressing shafts of the old delving, she lost all hope and the tears were those of hopeless despair.

The dwarf had gloated wickedly as he guided the Varad warriors along the path down into the mountain, pointing out various things as they passed, or telling them how far underground they were. Even then, Malcom had heard the river and knew that if they were only able to reach it, they would have a chance of survival.

For all the threats of his bringing the Dark One to see them, Alar Far had not done so; the otters began to feel that it was only a threat the dwarf used to try to frighten them more.

"There doesn't have to be anything else to frighten me any more," confessed Morane when Malcom tried to reassure her. "Just being in this hole is enough to do it."

But the Dark One didn't come and the only living thing that the two animals saw was Alar Far, when he brought their food to them.

"Ugh! You wouldn't get fat on that," groaned Malcolm, taking one of the greasy dwarfcakes off the crude tray. "But we have to have something. Try to eat one, dear. We have to hold out until we can find our way to the river. That is all that matters now. If we can once do that, we'll see what next."

Morane made a pitiful effort at eating some of the strong-smelling food, but could only manage a few bites.

"These things smell to high heaven," she said, gagging.

"They aren't exactly tasty, but they will keep us from starving."

"I don't know which would be worse," said his mate.

They ate fitfully in silence for another moment, and were both badly startled by a noise that came from directly behind them, beyond the cage, in an area of dark shadows against one of the shaft walls. It wasn't exactly any noise that they could identify, but more a movement that brushed the air with a static electricity that made their fur tingle.

Trembling, Morane crept nearer Malcom.

There was a long silence then, so long that the otters began to think they had imagined the noise in their weakened condition.

"It couldn't be anyone we would want to see anyway," said Malcom, trying to calm Morane. "If it's not Alar Far come back to torment us, it can only be one of the beast soldiers that brought us here."

The otters spoke in their own High Tongue, afraid that someone might overhear. It was an old animal habit to do so when in danger, and Malcom knew that none knew or understood their language except those who were followers of the Light. The elves knew it, and while some of them could speak it but haltingly, they all understood it. There were also others that Malcom had read or heard of, but he had not met them himself.

Morane went back to nibbling on the pungent, tough dwarfcake that Alar Far had brought.

"I hate this place. It was bad enough when they kept us in the cages in the beast soldiers' camp, but this is awful. I don't know how long I shall be able to take this."

Her voice was calm, which frightened Malcom, for her eyes were wild and she didn't seem to be able to focus on him properly.

"We have to hold on to ourselves," replied Malcom softly. "We'll never be able to escape if we allow Alar Far to destroy our hope."

"I don't care," muttered Morane. "I am tired of all this. I can't stand being here any longer."

Her voice was flat, but her mate felt the hysteria and reached out to touch her; she drew away, cowering in a corner of their small prison cell alone.

"We have to remember Olthar," he said at last, fearing that he was losing her to the blackness and terror of her mind.

A look of bitterness crossed Morane's features that startled Malcom.

"It is all the fault of those elfin friends of yours," she snapped. "If it hadn't been for you carrying on with all their likes, we'd never have lost our pup or been in this terrible place."

"You know that isn't so, dear. Nothing that has happened could have been changed."

Malcom mouthed the words, but there was a thin splinter

of doubt that edged into his thinking, and he wondered if what she said wasn't true.

"I wish I'd never heard of the Olthlinden! If we could have only lived the way we should have, we'd still be together and happy in our old holt."

Malcom shook his head sadly.

"I wish with all my heart that that were so. But I saw long ago that no one was ever going to go on living their simple lives in whatever wood they were in with all the forces of the Dark One moving again. I was a fool to have waited for so long before doing anything."

"And now look what a fine fix we've landed in! I wish Duirn would be as quick to act as he always seemed to be when he was promising his aid to us when we were snug and safe. If he's such a powerful leader, why hasn't he lifted a finger to help us?"

Malcom listened to Morane and realized how greatly she had changed. He had never heard her whine or complain so bitterly and knew the fear and uncertainty were driving her very near the breaking point.

"I'm sure he is trying. I'm sure they are all trying their best."

"They have our pup, so what more do they need with the old worn-out parents? We have obviously served our purpose and can be spared."

Before Malcom could reply, the same noise that had sounded earlier came again, causing Morane to hold her breath. A faintly outlined shadow appeared near the back of the cell that Alar Far had built in the old delving armory; it was too indistinct for the otters to make it out, but it did not move away or appear to be trying to conceal itself.

"You have had your fun and done your work well, Alar Far. What other torments do you want to subject us to? You have succeeded in bullying my wife into hysteria, so you should be pleased with yourself."

Malcom felt a white-hot anger bubbling inside him that was strange and frightening at once. He felt the terrible red claw burning his heart with its grip and his mind burst into the killing lust.

The shadow did not move, but seemed to appear brighter.

"You do not speak to Alar Far, the traitor who has sold out his great heritage."

The voice rang with a stony strength that made it impossible that it should have come from the small shadow.

A glimmering light seemed to pour from the roof of the tunnel then, so bright and powerful it made Morane think it was the sun shining through the very depths of the mountain. Her heart leapt for joy, although she was still frightened by the voice, which seemed to come from everywhere at once.

"Who are you?" managed Malcom at last. "I am called Malcom, and this is my mate, Morane. We are held captive here by the Dark One."

The brilliant light danced across the intricate carvings, which exploded into life on all the walls and ceilings of the old delving.

"The Dark One has held sway in the halls of Lukas Damon far too long. The stench of treachery is so heavy there that I can no longer breathe. I am come to settle our debts with those who have betrayed us. You two may go."

As the voice spoke, a terrible sick motion rocked the otters as they stood trapped in their prison cell. Groans from far inside the bowels of the mountain rumbled and shook, and the glittering reflecting lights that danced along the walls and ceiling began to flicker and gutter like candles in a wind.

"Wait! We don't know how to get away from here," cried Malcom. "We are caught in this cage as well!"

Without the slightest effort, the small shadow figure materialized into a dwarf that closely resembled Alar Far, except the eyes were not so hidden and the mouth was not locked into a cruel sneer. In another instant, the wall of the cell was shattered on the floor at the feet of the two frightened animals.

"You must leave here quickly! The ancient time has come when the clan of Lukas Damon will avenge the treachery that saw the end of our realm."

"How do we get out? We got so confused when Alar Far brought us here."

Above the faint trembling that rippled the floor of the shaft, an angry shriek rose up behind them; turning, they saw it had come from their captor, who stood outlined by the shaft's flickering lights.

"You foul traitor! You will die just like all the rest of your cursed clan, Lukas Damon. You have done your last mischief here!"

Alar Far's features were choked with rage and hatred as he leapt across the shifting floor with a deadly dwarf ax raised above his head.

211

"You shall all die now! You won't escape the Dark One's wrath! Alar Far is the arm of the Protector!"

Morane had moved behind Malcom and trembled violently, caught on the edge of fear and anger. In another moment, she and her mate had burst the bonds of the hopelessness that had held them captive as effectively as the cage Alar Far had built; the white-hot anger exploded into a burning red claw that ripped at their minds, and the two animals lunged straight at the shrieking dwarf.

There was a long moment that seemed suspended as the animals and dwarf rushed at each other; then there came a staggering blow at the very deepest part of the delving's center, which sent them reeling. Before their eyes, a vast abyss started as a small crack in the smooth stone floor and quickly grew until it was so wide Alar Far could not leap across, so he placed the dwarf ax down as a narrow bridge and started carefully over toward the animals. In his rage, Malcom was at the pit's edge instantly, trying to push the head of the ax over the lip of the chasm.

Shrieking wildly and holding on with both feet and hands, Alar Far hurried to reach the safety of the other side. His eyes were red and burned with the dull fire of the Dark One's hold over his mind.

Morane struggled beside Malcom to help him push the blade of the ax over, but the weight of the stocky dwarf was too much for them and they could not budge it. Hand over hand Alar Far came, his cruel smile making his features grotesque; only another few moments and he would be on top of the unarmed animals.

Malcom pushed Morane away and rose up to his full height to meet his powerful enemy. There was nothing left for him to do now but rely on his cunning and animal speed to keep him from harm at the hands of the malignant dwarf.

The second passed, and then another; animal and dwarf were but a breath away from being locked into a life-or-death struggle when the chasm suddenly widened farther, leaving empty space beneath the dwarf ax, which tumbled away so suddenly Alar Far seemed to hang suspended above it, listening to it clatter loudly away into the blackness of the pit, striking sparks against the wall as it fell. Alar Far's rush carried him far enough over to grasp the side of the sheer pit wall, and he clung there for a split second to gather his breath, then began to pull himself up, kicking out with a powerful, squat leg to get a firmer grip.

Malcom stood transfixed, torn between trying to help the struggling figure and biting the hand that reached out near him searching for a hold on something solid. The otter stepped nearer the edge, on the verge of speaking, although he could not truly say what it was he was thinking. As he hesitated, the iron grip of the dwarf closed like a vise around his forepaw, and almost as though in a dream, Malcom bit down as firmly and savagely as all the long histories of the otter family allowed him to do.

There was an agonized scream of pain, and the pressure on his forepaw was gone; in another heartbeat Malcom was peering over the edge of the chasm where Alar Far had been, staring into a bottomless, empty darkness that smelled strongly of deep, dank cellars and sulphur.

Morane had her paws around him then and was clutching him closely in a strong hug.

"You two must go quickly," came the voice from the shadow. "There is nothing left here for the living. The halls of Lukas Damon are at last free."

The small animals turned toward the speaker, but the wraith-like figure of the dwarf was fading rapidly into the dim light.

"Who are you?" cried Morane. "We would thank you for freeing us."

"My name is dust now. I was called Lukas Damon in other times. But you will be able to show your thanks to my kindred, whom you will be meeting soon. Farewell, good souls. Go straight in this shaft quickly. You will find the water there."

There was another guttering light then, and when the two otters looked again, all was silent and growing darker.

"Hurry!" called Malcom. "We must go straight on. This place is dying."

Scampering as hard as they could, spurred by fear and a longing for the outside, they raced away in the direction they had been told. They were still running hard when they felt the smooth stone floor disappear beneath their paws, and then there was a sinking sensation of tumbling through thin air for what seemed an eternity; then there was a loud splash and they felt the icy-cold river swallow them up in a welcoming embrace.

An Uncomfortable Decision

THE days slipped by quickly in the ancient elfin dane. Duirn and the Shanoliel taught the otters of Hydin all the skill of warfare that they had learned over the long years of conflict in the Lower Meadows of Windameir. Coney disappeared on occasion, but always returned with new reports as to the whereabouts of the enemy, or news pertaining to arrivals from other parts. Their ranks were swelled daily by those new arrivals, both animal and elfin, dwarf and human. Their war camp began to take on the appearance of a great settlement, expanding until even the old dane was no longer big enough to hold their enlarged number.

Banon was sitting by the open fire in the early morning hours listening to Emeon drilling Olthar and Hydin in the proper use of the elfin shortsword. Duirn was working on an entry in his journal and marking down notes on a chart of the West Roaring Sea.

"What have you found there that holds your interest so long?" asked Banon.

The old elf had to repeat his question before Duirn heard him.

"The Middle Islands," he replied, pushing the chart toward Banon. "See? They are exactly where Bor Asa said they were in his old logs."

"Were you in doubt of his navigation?"

"No. I had not looked at these charts for a long time. It hadn't struck me that this is where the old roads led. This is the place where the elf has gone in the past on his way to the High Havens."

Banon smiled.

"That is a thought that sounds cheering."

"It has been a long while, Banon. I grow weary of all this."

"You say that exactly like your father used to."

"Do I? I forget that you have been here so many turnings. Don't you grow weary of it?"

"I do, my young friend. But I can sense an end to it now. We have all the signs that have been written and sung about for all this time. The Olthlinden is with us, and the Pipe of Ring Parath. The clans are gathering and we are on the borders of the sea. All the signs that have been spoken of are here."

Duirn watched the young Olthar as Banon spoke.

"Jahn has done well with the lad. His task was no easy one."

"There are no easy tasks anymore. I can remember tasks being easy once, but that was before we came down from the Upper Havens. This has been a hard lesson in the Wilderness."

Duirn searched the old elf's face questioningly, waiting for him to go on, but there was a loud flurry of sword strokes and the two otters followed Emeon to the fire for a tea break.

"You are leaving your guard down too low, Olthar. A Varad or Worlugh is tall and strikes from above. You have to remember that anyone you'll be fighting with is going to be taller than you."

Olthar poured out steaming mugs of tea for Hydin and the elf and sat down wearily.

"It is hard work to learn all this."

"It's hard work to stay alive when you've got a Varad trying to hammer your brains out. The only thing then that is going to stand you in good stead is a good sword and a strong defense."

"But how long do we have to go over it? Hydin and I have been beating each other like this for days."

"Not to say anything of bow practice," added the other otter.

Duirn laughed.

"You were the ones who wanted to learn the art of soldiering. Now you can see that it isn't all a bed of sweetmoss."

"I hardly call being thrashed every day a bed of sweetmoss," shot Olthar. "I'll almost be glad to run into the beast soldiers so I can get some relief from being pummeled by Emeon."

"A Varad won't pull his blows," said Emeon evenly. "If I've hurt you, it's to show you what can happen by making mistakes. In a battle those mistakes can mean the difference between living or dying."

Olthar's attention had been drawn to the charts spread before Duirn and he quickly forgot his aches and pains from the severe training.

"What maps are those?" he asked, pushing his muzzle close so that he could read the legends on the side. "Is this where we're going?"

"In a short while," Duirn answered. He pointed at the dots

215

that represented the islands. "This is where we will meet the forces that are gathering. The Dark One hopes to finish us all for good and have it over and done."

"When are we to leave?" asked Hydin. "And will there be enough boats to carry everyone?"

Emeon laughed lightly.

"The same thing will happen with the boats that happened with the weapons. We found enough to equip all your clan and some to spare. Elves have an odd way of meeting the needs of those shortages in ways that sometimes may surprise you."

"You can say no truer, friend," said Famhart, who had joined the group as Emeon was speaking. Linne stood beside him, looking well rested and recovered from her ordeal at the hands of the Bog Hat soldiers. The care of the elfin healers had worked wonders, and all the fresh bloom of her youthful beauty had returned.

"Well, well, our good Bog Hat has decided to do something else besides wander about looking at a certain beautiful lady who has graced our camp," laughed Duirn. "Welcome."

Famhart blushed, but did not reply.

"You are in time to help us set a date for our departure. We have lingered here a long while, it seems. Our scouts report that the beast armies are coming closer every day."

Duirn paused to look at his charts, then went on.

"We have prepared as well as we are able, I feel. I don't see that there is any reason to tarry here longer. Perhaps we should think of preparing to move."

Banon nodded at the Shanoliel King.

"It is time. I have been feeling it so these past few mornings. Olthar is as skilled as he need be, and Hydin's company is armed and trained. Our clans have had time to gather, and the only thing that remains is to set the date and go."

The old elf looked at each of the others in turn, stopping when he got to Olthar.

"You are the one who gives the final word. You are the Olthlinden. The Pipe of Ring Parath is the key to it all."

For the first time the small animal began to feel the enormous responsibility that the small pipe carried with it. He had had vague hints of the burden before, but now it was all upon him to give the word that would send a vast host into an action that would certainly be the death of many—animal, elf, and man.

Suddenly Olthar felt a great need to talk to his friend Jahn

216

Spray, who had been busy elsewhere since Hydin had arrived. He had not spoken to the elf in private since his time was all spent now in the company of the other otters. He wanted to speak to Coney as well. The Old One was gone on one of his scouting trips, and no one even knew when to expect him.

A heavy pall of gloom settled over the otter's heart as he realized he was all alone in the decision; then there came a faint glimmer of hope that perhaps Coney would be back in time to help decide the matter. All the weight of being the Olthlinden descended upon Olthar in a sickening rush, and he looked at Duirn quietly for a long time.

"I think I begin to see what you have been through all this time, Duirn. I never thought it could be so hard."

The Shanoliel leader smiled sadly; he had that look that Olthar had seen so often in the eyes of the elves, which was at once grief beyond words brightened by a knowledge that it was all as it should be, and that the ultimate end of all things was good.

"It seems we get to try on the costumes of every actor in the play. We are at one time the villain and the next hero. We are also everything in between. It seems heavy indeed, at times like this, when there is nothing more to do but to go on with the inevitable."

"I want to talk to Jahn and Coney first."

"They won't be able to make your decision for you."

"Then Banon can say as well as I. He is the one who has the feeling that we should be leaving."

A small spark of anger was stirring in Olthar's heart at being made to confront the problem at hand. He hoped that by waiting long enough, perhaps Banon or Duirn would give the go-ahead to march and he would be spared that uncomfortable duty.

"I am but an old elf," replied Banon. "I have had my say on many such decisions, and I cannot do so any longer. This choice is not mine to make."

"Then you say, Duirn. You are the one who controls the boats that will take us. All we need to do is know when the boats will be ready for us. That is simple enough. We shall go when the boats are ready for us."

Duirn looked away in the direction of the sea, his brow darkened with concern.

"I think the ships of the Eolin have always been ready. They were made use of many times in the olden days by all the elves who were making the crossing back to the High Havens. All that is required is the words that were given to all the clans of the Eolin when we first came to the Lower Meadows."

"Then there is no decision for me to make," insisted Olthar. "All we need do is go."

"There you have it. All we need do is go. It is very simple."

"We won't have to have a decision if we wait much longer," said Emeon. "The beast armies are closing on us every day. I've heard more tales of Varads and Worlugh these past weeks than I've heard in a long time. Every new group that joins us has another nightmare to tell of."

Olthar looked questioningly at the Shanoliel leader.

"You see? I have no say in this matter."

"You have all the say, Olthar. Without your decision, all this host will be left to their own defenses. The reason we have waited all this time was because we needed the one missing thing to draw us all together. That missing piece of the puzzle was the Pipe of Ring Parath. And the only way we would have that is if there was the Olthlinden to carry it."

Olthar looked about him at the upturned faces of the vast gathering. All those there who were close enough to hear the conversation were gazing upon him with that look of total trust and the unspoken faith that would make them follow wherever he led. It was a terrifying moment for the young otter; his first impulse was to give up the pipe to Jahn or Duirn or Banon and return to his old simple life of being nothing more than an otter like his newly found friend Hydin.

He turned to his comrade to speak, but saw that distance in Hydin's eyes which said we are friends but you are different; we can be no closer, for you are the Olthlinden and I am Hydin. This realization made Olthar feel more alone than he had ever felt in all his short life. It felt as bad as the disappearance of his mother and father, and went deeper still. He found that ache within him that was the empty place his parents had left with their absence, but this new feeling was a bottomless pit which threatened to devour him.

A great anger began to fill him then, at the friends who forced him into the impossible situation he was in; at Jahn Spray for ever having befriended his father, and at Coney for leaving him at the crucial points when he needed the wisdom of the Old One the most. He went on with his list to include Hydin for not standing by him, contenting himself to stay

218

safely back while the big decisions were being made. Olthar had been pacing the whole time he had been thinking and he now found himself outside the gathering of friends around the morning fire, walking slowly along the shore of the lake. No one attempted to follow him or console him, which angered him as well; he also knew that it would have annoyed him as much if anyone had tried to come with him.

He was alone, but didn't want to be; he needed someone, but wanted no one. It was a terrible place to find himself in, and he couldn't seem to get to the bottom of all the feelings to look at the real causes, or to try to decide what would be a solution to the discomfort.

He walked and thought until he was at the very camp's end, where an elfin sentry challenged him until he saw who it was. On the way back Olthar toyed with the idea of simply vanishing; they would all think something had happened to him and he would be free of the suffocating burden that rode heavily on his small shoulders.

A flock of wild water birds was floating on the lake not far from shore, their bodies a starched white against the sunlit water. They had no problems other than food, and he longed to be with them. It had seemed to be a grand thing to have all the attention and to be named the Olthlinden and carry the Pipe of Ring Parath before; now the price was becoming obvious. There was a reckoning due and there seemed to be no way out.

Olthar stood watching the water birds awhile, and after some time had passed, he realized he was no longer alone. Coney was there beside him, silent and thoughtful.

"Hello. I thought you were gone."

"I was," replied the Old One. "I saw you here as I was returning."

"Duirn has told me I must decide when we are to leave for the Middle Islands."

"Have you?"

"No. I don't think it's my place."

"You are the Olthlinden."

Olthar bristled angrily.

"I don't care if I am or not! It isn't fair to make me responsible for everything!"

"The others need that," replied Coney calmly. "They have a hard time imagining the High King, so they must have something more simple that they can relate to."

At the mention of the High King, Olthar remembered as well, and didn't feel quite so alone any longer.

"I don't want to be the Olthlinden anymore. I just want to be one of the bunch."

"You don't have that choice this time."

"Oh, Coney, don't you start in on me, too!"

"I'm not starting in on you," said the Old One evenly. "I have never started in on you. I have tried to explain things to you, and tell you how things are, or will be, but that is only my duty. No one ever said that this was going to be easy."

"Hydin won't be friends with me," lamented Olthar. "All because I am the stupid Olthlinden."

"Hydin is your friend. So are all the others in our camp. You have more friends than you realize. You also have enemies. It is well to remember that. There is no way to be all one or the other."

"I don't mind enemies. At least I know what to expect."

"Don't you know what to expect from your friends?"

"That is a strange question to be coming from you, Coney."

"Don't you think we Old Ones feel any of the things you do?"

"Do you?"

"Yes. But more slowly. Sometimes we feel those things for so long that the Lower Meadows might turn a dozen times on itself."

"But it's different for you. You don't have to be the Olthlinden. It's easy for you. Just like it's easy for the rest."

"They will all help you, if you let them. You shut them out with your self-pity."

"I am not pitying myself," snapped Olthar.

"I'd like to hear what you call it, then."

"It's hopeless to try to talk to you, Coney. You're like everyone else. No one has to carry the pipe but me, when it comes down to it, so no one else has to decide anything to be done. Let Olthar do it, he's the Olthlinden."

"That's what they say," agreed Coney, "because it is the way things are. That is why you are carrying the pipe and they are not. The decisions have to be made, and it might as well be you as anyone."

"Why? Why do I have to be the one? Why not Duirn? He's the King of the Shanoliel and the leader of the Eolin."

"Duirn does not carry the pipe. You carry it."

"What if I give it to Duirn? I can do that."

"You could try to do it, but you couldn't."

"I can."

"Try it."

"I will," said Olthar resolutely, marching stubbornly away toward the camp.

Olthar had gone some distance before he was aware that Coney had not followed, and when he turned to look over his shoulder, the ancient tree-being was nowhere in sight.

Dreams of Past and Future

THE weather had grown gradually colder as the days wore on, and the crisp autumn sunshine felt weak and far away. Duirn and Emeon sat at the fire in the midst of their huge camp, going over charts and speaking to the various leaders of the different groups that had joined the swelling ranks.

There were elves from all the clans, and humans from the marshland camps, along with a sprinkling of Bog Hats, who belonged to the generation of Famhart the Younger. Hydin had brought with him all the animals that were able to escape from the Black Mountains; there were otters and a few families of beaver and hedgehog, woodchucks, squirrels, and a collection of various chipmunks; there were a few solitary badgers who kept mostly to themselves and who were treated with much deference and respect. There were many others who had been slain by the Varad and Worlugh bands, who murdered every living thing in their path in their sweep to the sea.

Included in the last arrivals was a band of dwarfs from the old wood of the far Gray Ash, who had lived in their delvings there until they had finally been driven away by the constantly swelling hordes of the Dark One. It rankled the dwarf leader badly to admit that they had finally had to own defeat and desert their ancestral home.

This dwarf, who was called Gael, sat down wearily at the fire beside the two elves.

"Welcome, Gael. Have you made your arrangements and settled your followers?"

"Your hospitality is very gracious, Duirn. I hope I may return it one day. We have gotten everyone settled in to the

221

new camp and we are reorganizing and taking stock of all we have lost and what we'll need. We are not a race that takes to changes of this nature too readily."

"I don't think any of us take to change readily," agreed Emeon. "I have been living from hand to mouth for longer than I care to remember now, and I still miss my regular meals just like they were always served in my old dane before the wars took it all. I don't think it would take me long to get used to it again, either."

The dwarf chuckled softly.

"Why is it we always seem to set great store on the things we no longer have? It seems the way of everything. If we were still sitting down to a mug of mulled tea in my old delving, I'd probably be complaining about the bad honey or burned dwarfcake."

"It seems to take us a long time to sort out what's important," said Duirn. "We never seem to see a thing for what it is until it is gone from our life for a while."

"If that's the case, I can see a lot of things differently now," said Emeon, sighing. "Everything I can think of has been gone for so long I can't remember a time it was otherwise."

"But you, good Gael, tell me of how you found the countryside. We have spoken of the changes, yet it is always best to hear it firsthand."

The dwarf squatted down by the fire and picked through various maps that Duirn had spread before him until he found what he was looking for.

"Our delving was here where the Gray Ash Wood bordered on the Serpent Mountains. I have watched that country go slowly under the Dark One's hand for my whole life. I suppose it all began long before my time."

"It did. The Dark One has been at work all along, only we didn't always see it."

Emeon made room for Banon to sit down as the old elf joined them.

"We were speaking of the Dark One and the state of affairs in the Lower Meadows," explained Duirn.

"Do we ever speak of anything or anyone else?" asked Banon. "No matter what we talk of now, it always concerns the Dark One."

Duirn gazed at the seated figures around him, then lifted his eyes to look over the gathered army of elves and dwarfs and animals and men.

"There is good come of it, though," he said in a thoughtful tone of voice. "Look at all this."

He motioned with the hand that held his teacup at the sight stretched out before them.

"I never thought I'd see this," said Banon, his old face drawn into a wistful half-smile. "The times have not been so good to the brotherhood of the Lower Meadows."

"All the more reason that it is a change for the good. No matter what the cause, it has given us this. It is a rare thing to find any of us at tea together."

"Speaking of tea, have you seen Olthar? He was trying to find Jahn a while ago. We have frightened him by our decision to let him set the time for our departure."

Duirn frowned slightly, a worried look crossing his face and darkening his eyes for a moment.

"He is so new to all this that it must be a difficult thing to grasp that there really is no choice to be made. All we have to do is simply go along with what is to be done next."

"That is easy for us to see," said Banon. "We have had enough trials to run through it all so that we can see how it works. The pup is not so familiar with either the world or its ways, or himself. He is learning the most difficult way. It is good we have had a quiet time here before the confrontation with the Banskrog. This will give our young friend a chance to touch the root of everything and get himself ready for what must be faced."

"Have you seen the Pipe of Ring Parath?" asked Gael. "I have only heard stories about it. I've talked to a few in your camp who say they've actually heard it."

"You will have your chance, friend. The Olthlinden shall lead us all into battle; the call to arms is blown on the pipe," said Emeon. "It's like nothing you've ever heard."

"That may be so for an elf, but I wonder at the effect it will have on me," replied Gael, his voice tinged with a faint coolness.

"I think anyone who follows the High King can hear the pipe," said Duirn. "There is no difference there. That is why the otter carries it, rather than one of the Eolin."

"Speaking of the Olthlinden, here he comes," said Emeon. "He looks none too happy with affairs as they stand."

"I can't say as I blame him overly much," said Banon. "It all seems so serious for a while."

The small animal came along the water's edge, trudging as though he were on the way to his own execution. His muzzle drooped nearly to the ground and he was a sad sight to those who had never seen him in any mood that slowed his pace and dulled his laugh.

"We must try to cheer him up," said Emeon. "I think I have been much too hard on him in my training."

"You've been easier on him than the Worlugh will be," replied Duirn.

Olthar arrived before anyone could speak further. He studied each face closely as he stood before them, refusing a mug of tea that Banon had poured out for him.

"I need to speak to you alone, Duirn. I have been thinking over what you've told me. I no longer believe that I can carry the pipe. I am going to entrust it to you. An elf should carry it."

"And what will you do?" asked Duirn seriously. "Once you've given up your task, what course will you follow then?"

"I'll join Hydin and his clan. I shall stay, naturally, but I won't be made to decide what shall or shall not be done."

"You can't just give up the pipe," began Emeon, but Duirn stopped him with a wave of his hand.

"It would do no good for him to carry it if he didn't believe that he was meant to, Emeon. There can be no doubt in his mind about that. It would never do to be locked into a death grip with the Banskrog and suddenly decide that the chore of carrying the Pipe of Ring Parath was not the proper thing to do."

"I am an otter," explained Olthar. "I have been thinking about that for a long while now. I am an otter carrying a pipe that has always been carried by elves. It doesn't make any sense."

"Jahn Spray and Coney and I have all told you the reasons that that has to be. We have explained about the betrayal of the Eolin and why an animal must bear the pipe in battle against the Banskrog."

"I shall join your battle against the Dark One, but I won't be used to carry the pipe. That job belongs to someone who knows how to do it."

"You were not feeling this way when the Dargol Brem attacked the Bog Hat settlement at Bonadig. You carried it well then."

"That was all in the heat of battle. I didn't have to make any choices then. All I had to do was start playing."

"And it rallied us," argued Duirn. "If we had not heard the pipe, we might have very well been carried off by the snake."

"Or captured by the Bog Hats," added Emeon.

"I was feeling different then," said Olthar stubbornly. "I talked to Coney and he said that I could give the pipe back to you, Duirn."

"The Old One said that?" asked Duirn, a small note of surprise sounding in his voice.

"Just a few moments ago."

"Where is he?"

"I don't know. I thought he was coming with me, but he disappeared again."

"Well, if you are determined to give the pipe back to me, you shall have to do so by returning it first to Jahn Spray. He has carried it for all that time until you took it, so it must be returned that way."

"I don't know where Jahn is."

"Then we shall have to wait on him." ·

"I want to give you the pipe now. I don't want the burden of carrying it any longer. This way you'll be able to make your own decisions about when we shall move; everyone will listen because the pipe will be back in the hands of those it belongs to."

Duirn smiled a faint smile and refilled his mug.

"Come and sit down here, Olthar. Have some tea with me and then if you still want to return the pipe to me, I shall gladly take it."

"I don't have to have a cup of tea before making up my mind," insisted the otter, but there was something about the way that Duirn spoke that wouldn't allow the small animal to disagree.

The leader of the Shanoliel could be very convincing when he wanted to be, and this was one of those times. Reluctantly, the young animal sat down among his friends, firm in his purpose. He was not sure why it was he was so anxious to return the small pipe in the case around his back, but the growing pressure of seeing all the responsibility had gotten to be too great a load.

Emeon poured out a mug of the spicy mulled tea and handed it to the otter. At the moment Olthar's paw touched the handle, a change came over the fire; there were summer clouds in the sky, and the wind was full of the smells of the fragrant pine and balsam. Instead of the chill that had made the fire seem more snug but a breath before, there was a sultry heat that lay over the dane, making the small animal back away from the gathering of elves.

225

He then looked up, startled to see that Duirn was vanished. Only Emeon and Banon were there, along with some others that he had never seen before. The dwarf Gael was gone, but Jahn Spray sat across from him, his face so haggard that it was hard to recognize his old friend and teacher.

"What is it?" cried Olthar, leaping up and staring about him in disbelief. "Where is everyone?"

Banon, appearing even older, reached out a hand to the otter.

"Here, here, Olthar. There was nothing that could be done. No one could have guessed the Dark One would have attacked us there."

"No one was to blame," went on Emeon. "We came out of the woods on the other side of the river crossing and the Worlugh were there before we had a chance. The Banskrog has grown swift and silent. They even caught our elfin sentries unawares."

"What battle do you speak of?" questioned the confused animal, looking from one of his friends to the other.

"The battle this afternoon," replied Emeon, taken aback by the question. "What battle did you think we spoke of?"

Olthar's mind reeled. He seemed to be trying to remember something that was just at the edge of his memory, but it kept slipping away. There was a vague recollection of the battle and the events that led up to it, although he could not quite focus his attention on a detail that seemed to be very important.

One of the elves that Olthar had not seen before spoke up then, his voice tired and angry.

"If we had had the pipe it might have gone better for us. Nothing has been right since we lost it."

"It won't get any better," added another of the unfamiliar elves. "It has turned out worse than Duirn said it would."

The elf who was speaking turned such a look of hatred on Olthar that the otter felt for a moment he was going to be attacked.

Emeon frowned darkly and held out a restraining hand toward the other elf.

"That's enough of that talk, Halen. We have had some ill fortune, but there is no need to make it worse by fighting among ourselves."

"The ill fortune was ever allowing ourselves to be taken in by this impostor."

"That's enough!" snapped Banon angrily. "You are entitled

to your feelings, Halen; there's no denying that. But you overstep yourself when you begin your accusations. We all do only what we feel we must."

"I have said my say," replied Halen. "You all know where I stand and how I feel. I am taking my band and leaving here. I won't allow my followers to be butchered one by one and do nothing about it. We'll take our chances alone."

"Don't be foolish," said Jahn Spray, speaking for the first time. "If you leave now you won't stand a chance. We will only weaken ourselves until the Dark One can swallow us at her pleasure."

"That looks to me what the Banskrog is doing now," shot Halen's comrade bitterly. "Since Duirn was slain and the pipe captured, there has been only one disaster after another. The Dark One's terms may not be the most desirable, but they are better than living like hunted animals in the wood."

Olthar's mind spun madly when the elf spoke of Duirn's death and the capture of the Pipe of Ring Parath. That was the dark part of the puzzle that he had been missing and trying to remember.

Bewildered, he turned to Jahn Spray.

"What has happened here, Jahn? What happened to Duirn and the pipe?"

His friend looked at him with such pity that Olthar grew more confused than ever.

"You surely can't have forgotten the battle at The Beak?"

"I don't remember. What happened?"

His old friend studied him a long time quizzically, then sighed.

"Well, it doesn't matter. You can't be held to blame for it. I thought so for a time, but I see now that it couldn't be helped. You couldn't carry the pipe anymore. I have felt that feeling in the older days when Malcom and I were traveling together. The burden of it got so great at times I would have gladly given it over to anyone. And then when I finally gave it to you, I missed having the knowledge that I was carrying something of such great power. You can't be held to fault for what happened."

"But I don't know what happened," insisted Olthar.

"You know what happened, but perhaps you don't want to remember it," snapped Halen.

"Enough, Halen! Accusations will solve nothing."

Jahn Spray went on.

"After you returned the pipe to Duirn, it all began to

227

happen, just as it was said in the old tales. The Eolin were not to carry the pipe again because of an elf's abuse of its power in the ancient beginnings. For some reason it was too much even for Duirn. He became determined to lead the Eolin back to the High Havens. The pipe was too much. The power of it slowly began to erode him and he gave in to the temptation to use it for the gaining of personal ends."

"What happened at The Beak was only what was inevitable," added Banon. "There was no way that we were ready to confront the Banskrog there. We were to go to the Middle Islands to join our other allies who would be waiting for us there, but Duirn did not want to wait. Let the elves fend for themselves, he said: the others can do the same."

A very dim memory began to emerge from the hazy thoughts that tumbled about in Olthar's mind. There were confused battle scenes, and the Dargol Brem devastating everything in sight. Torn feelings of confusion and remorse wracked the otter's body, and he could see himself handing the small, worn leather case to Duirn; there was a great fear there inside him, and he gave in to it. He had rid himself of the burden and would not have to deal with it anymore.

A sudden terror overcame Olthar as he sat listening to the gaunt Jahn Spray speak.

"We could not fault you for giving the pipe back. After all, it was still among us. The thought was that Duirn was truly the one to carry it since he was the leader of the Shanoliel. We forgot the truth and the way things were meant to be. We cannot alter the High King's plans."

"And now we shall have to play out this hand as best we can," said Banon. "There will be another time and another chance for us all somewhere."

Olthar was on the verge of speaking, but a feeling of hollow, aching loneliness and failure silenced him. There was nothing to be said to ease the guilt or his shame. His cowardice in giving up the pipe to Duirn had caused the Shanoliel leader to fall to temptation and as a result the Pipe of Ring Parath was lost. The hope of reuniting the Lower Meadows was gone and the Banskrog was triumphant on all fronts. The worst of it all was living with the knowledge of it.

Just at that moment of the ultimate bleak despair of it all, Olthar sat blinking back his tears and saw Duirn's face across the fire, his eyes a deep sky blue, piercing him into that silent place that holds all understanding.

"Now you see why you won't give me back the pipe," said Duirn quietly.

The day was again chilly and the fire felt good as the friends sat warming their hands about it.

Olthar tried to open his mouth to ask a question, but at that moment Jahn Spray sat down beside him, his fair features exactly the way he always remembered them. There were greetings addressed to the elf from all his friends, and he smiled and gave the otter a gentle pat.

"Coney and I have had a long ramble these past few days having a look at things. It is growing a bit too hot for comfort, I fear. Everywhere we've been there have been more Varads and Worlugh. They seem to be gaining numbers faster than we can count."

"I saw Coney," replied Olthar.

"He said he'd seen you," said Jahn. "He was very mysterious about it all. I couldn't get anything out of him."

"There was nothing to get," said Duirn. "We have been trying to decide on a time for our departure. I suppose your report will make it easier for us now."

Olthar looked into the kind, open gaze of Duirn, which was at once full of the grave sadness that lay at the bottom of all elfin laughter and a cheerful note of hope that filled the heart with the strength to go on doing what had to be done.

"I think we had better prepare to leave right away," said the small animal, hearing himself say the words as though he were listening to a total stranger.

"Good lad," said Duirn brightly. "Good lad."

The leader of the Shanoliel rose hastily and began barking orders to those who sat about; before the otter had gotten up from his place at the fire, he fastened the worn case more securely to his back, looking all the while at Duirn and remembering the terrible feelings he had felt at that other place in time.

It turned out to be one of those crisp afternoons that are the more beautiful because there is a promise of snow in the air. Olthar worked tirelessly next to Jahn and Emeon and Hydin loading the gear and preparing for their move to The Beak. Coney appeared just at sunset, but he said nothing and asked no questions about Olthar's giving up the pipe. The ancient tree-being was very cryptic in the answers he gave, but after the others had their supper and settled in for their last night in the old dane, he became suddenly cheerful and sang them tunes from days long gone by, and told stories until everyone was asleep and the fires all burned out.

It was the first time Olthar had ever seen the Old One that way; upon discussing it with Jahn just before they went to sleep, the elf said the only thing he could imagine to account for the behavior was that Coney was happy. The otter thought it might be true, as strange as that seemed, for just before he drifted away into sleep, the tree-being was making snoring noises and shuffling his upper limbs in a way that might have been taken for soft laughter.

It might have been a dream, but it seemed real; Olthar felt the touch of the Old One's mind just at that dark place where fear dwelled and it was as though a light had been let in to dispel all the shadows there.

The young Olthlinden slept soundly between Jahn Spray and Emeon, with the Old One close by; his head rested on the small leather case he had been so hasty to rid himself of, and in the night the pipe played to Olthar all the wonderful music that filled up those dark empty memories of the waking dream he had had at the fire with Duirn. The last song he recalled was the cheerful tune of a clear mountain river on its way to the sea.

An Old Enemy Comes Calling

IN the cold gray of the early morning, before the sun had fully risen, the friends were awake and at their preparations. Their breath hung in damp white clouds in front of them as they loaded and stowed the last of the gear, and the lake itself steamed white mist into the air until it was difficult to see any distance in front of them. Sounds were deadened by the damp, and the water seemed to make noisy explosions as it lapped ashore at the landings of the ancient elfin dane that had provided them with shelter while they prepared to move on to the Sea of West Roaring.

Duirn and Banon headed the party that assigned the skiffs, and Emeon and Jahn Spray helped the large numbers of new arrivals find their transportation, giving each of the elves a quota of those who were to go with them. In this way, all the animals and dwarfs who had reached the old dane late were given transport so that the entire host would be able to reach the sea by water and not have to go by the dangerous overland route, which according to all the scouts was closely guarded by the Banskrog hordes.

The leader of the Shanoliel was worried and frowned as the last of the available boats that were at the landings were filled, and he turned a grave face to Banon.

"We shall run out of space in another load. There aren't going to be enough boats to get us all there."

Banon nodded his agreement.

"I was thinking it was going to be something of a challenge to get all these numbers into the boats we had."

"We could make two trips," offered Emeon. "It would be more dangerous, but not so dangerous as trying to send a part of our number overland."

Duirn stroked his beard and paced back and forth on the stone landing. As he watched, the last few elfin skiffs were filled, and all the others still waiting on shore turned to await instructions from the leader of the Eolin.

"The otters will be able to swim for it," said Olthar. "If we can load the gear into the boats, that will be no trouble for the waterkind."

Hydin spoke up from his place alongside one of the laden boats.

"Give us someone to carry our gear and we'll beat everyone to the sea. A bit of a swim never turned an otter's head."

"No, friend," replied Duirn. "It is an idea, but I think we shall need our strength for other things besides swimming as we get nearer The Beak. That might well work if we had to do it, although I'm thinking along another vein now. Standing here on the dane landing just now reminded me of it. It was under my nose all along, but I just overlooked it."

"Overlooked what?" asked Gael, who was standing amid a crowd of dwarfs that milled restlessly on the landing beside the already filled boats.

"The answer was here all along. I have simply been occupied with other thoughts so much I forgot. The danes of all elves have their own spells, so that it is merely a matter of calling up the elfin skiffs that were from this dane."

"Can you do that?" asked Olthar.

"I may have to try a few of the ancient forms to get the proper key, but they are all similar. I think we shall be able to do it."

"This dane belonged to the clan of Triehart," offered Coney. "I have heard the stones; they tell me things from the old days because I am one of the few beings that can hear them."

"Who was Triehart?" asked Jahn Spray. "I can recollect no one of elfdom by that name."

"Triehart was one of the last of the Eolin who helped those who were returning to the Upper Danes. This very place was one of the settlements that have set many a pilgrim on his way to the Roaring Sea and beyond."

"Were you around then, Coney?" asked Emeon.

"I have been around a long while. I was here before there were any other kinds. It was a different world then."

"Wouldn't it be nice to go back to a simple time like that," said Linne, who stood beside the tree-being, her eyes fixed in a faraway look that did not seem to focus.

The Old One ruffled his upper limbs and grumbled a reply that no one could make out.

"What did you say?" asked Olthar.

"I said it might all be well and good if we never went back to a time as simple as that."

"You surprise me," said Famhart. "I would think you'd prefer to be in a time that was rid of all these goings-on that have taken you from your friends and brought you all the way to the shores of Dreary Lake."

"It was all well and good as far as it went," said Coney. "There was plenty of leisure to ponder over any little idea that might come to mind. I spent a turning or two on almost every imaginable thought that you'd care to come up with; but in the end it was all empty. I have heard all sides of everything, from the beginning to the end and back again. After all that, I was still stuck in the same spot that I'd been in all that while, still arguing or discussing the same things with the same ones I had started with."

"You mean your kind was the first to be?" asked Linne.

"Not the first, but we came in the First Beginning. There are others who came before us, but they have gone now. They were spared, because of their trust. They have gone back to the High Meadows."

"But you mean you wouldn't like to return to how it was, Coney?" asked Hydin. "Surely you don't like all this destruction and disruption that's come upon us?"

"No, I don't say that. There is no seeming sense to any of what is happening now; but it fits me better to be doing this than sitting in my old wood going over the same dry lessons again and again."

"I think he's getting to like this life," laughed Banon. "He sounds as though he's begun to feel some of the things I felt when I first set out to follow this journey through to the end."

Olthar could not be sure, but it seemed the color of the bark of the Old One changed to a deeper brownish gray.

"I don't know whether I would go so far as to say that," mumbled Coney. "I do find it much better to be doing than to be simply sitting like a lump in the old wood repeating my thoughts by rote."

"He has a way of grumbling so you can't understand him when he feels he's been caught out," said Jahn. "I've noticed that of late. When we first met, he wasn't able to wait until he could get shed of us so he could go back to his old wood with the rest of his brotherhood."

"I don't think it would be possible now, even if I wanted to do so," replied Coney. "The countryside is overrun with the beast soldiers, and there are more crossing every day. It is no longer the same anywhere. I have spoken with my brothers every now and again, and they are following the old law that was given to us when we came."

"Which old law?" questioned Banon.

"The law that allows us to return to the Upper Meadows. When the time has come for that, we return to the earth and bloom one last time; but we have to do so in a way which will give hope to any of those who are still following the Light in the Wilderness."

"You know, I never once thought of how you do this, Coney. Now I remember that I haven't seen you in a regular tree form since we first met."

"That's right, Jahn. Coney pulled us out of the flood just before we got to Bonadig," said Olthar.

"I have been freed from the earth to aid you. There will come a time when I shall return to my roots."

The tree-being was interrupted by a scout, who came breathlessly through the gathered friends and took Duirn aside. They conversed for a brief moment in hurried whispers which none of the others could overhear.

Saluting quickly, the scout vanished again the same way he had come, and Duirn raised a hand for silence, his face grown worried and grim.

"We have news of some Bog Hat stragglers, it seems. I think they are led by your father, Famhart."

The young man paled and looked at Linne.

"It is terrible news, if it's true," said Linne. "That means that my brother may still be with them."

"They may just hold him prisoner," consoled Famhart, "if they still hold him at all."

"They hold him prisoner with his sickness," replied the girl wearily. "They have probably promised him something more."

"They might also have found another use for him. That fact alone could well have saved his life, if he is indeed among them."

"What further use could they have for him?" asked Linne.

"As a way to get into the camp. If they know you're here, they will count on your love as his sister to allow him to come with his friends. They can't have much left there in Bonadig. Even the Banskrog seems to be through with them as allies."

"Or they may just be following us to report to the Dark One, my good Bog Hat," said Duirn. "I don't think they would be in a hurry to give themselves into the power of those very folk they have hunted or slain in the past."

"We are too strong for any Bog Hat army now. We have the strength to hold the beast armies if we chose," said Famhart. "My father always plays his odds closely. If he thinks his side might be on the losing end, he'll try to work his way into our good graces any way he can. A trump card would be Largo, if they yet hold him, to be played on his sister's sentiment."

Linne was upset by the news, and began trembling all over.

"I hadn't dreamed it would come to this. I don't know what I'm feeling."

"You won't have to worry, my dear," said Duirn. "We'll know before long what it is they have in mind."

"Whatever it is, it won't have our best interests at heart," replied Famhart.

"It may be they are outnumbered by the beast armies and know we are leaving," offered Emeon. "They may be trying to treat with us so that they can escape."

"I can't see the Dark One turning away her own allies. Yet the number of Worlugh and Varads may be so great now that the Bog Hats are no longer needed."

Banon stroked his beard a moment, deep in thought.

"That may well be what has happened. They may be trying to save their own hides now."

"That's how the Banskrog works," confirmed Coney. "The Dark One sweeps you into her camp, then holds you there for as long as you are of use, then destroys you when you can no longer be of service. These Bog Hats that are left are of no more worth to her now that her other armies are strong enough to do all that she desires done."

"Well, we shall go on with our business at hand," said Duirn. "I need to be busy finding the key to the riddle of calling up the boats that belonged to the old dane of Triehart."

"Go ahead with the order for loading," shouted Emeon. "Get the next wave ready to load. Cast off those skiffs and be on your way. We'll see you at The Beak before long."

All along the dane landings, the loaded elfin skiffs tugged at their painters, awaiting the word to cast off. As Emeon spoke, the gathered fleet of delicate craft shot forward on the silver back of the lake and began to move away toward the distant horizon, which hid the sea from their sight.

A great cheer went up from those on shore as they watched, and the elfin pipes called out the traveling tunes from the ancient days, the same sounds the pipes made to call all those Home to the High Havens; Olthar played a quick reel on the Pipe of Ring Parath that seemed to propel the skiffs forward even faster; there were answering echoes from the lake that lingered on until the last of the first wave of elfin craft were lost from view.

Duirn went on with his work of trying to call up the boats of the dane of Triehart. The task was proving harder than he had anticipated.

"Are you sure this was Triehart's dane?" he asked Coney at last, after a long series of failures with the ordering of the runes.

"It was Triehart's dane," replied the Old One. "It was so until they left and went Home to the High Havens."

"Could they have taken all the boats when they left?" asked Banon.

"Not likely, but I begin to wonder."

Olthar stood beside Duirn and placed the pipe to his mouth again and began a tentative, plaintive air that saddened everyone who heard it. It sounded like the winds of early fall and the calls made by wild swans at the end of summer. He became more sure of it as he played, and moved on to another tune that was somewhat more cheery, although still sad in that same bittersweet way.

There were other reed pipes that joined in then, and the crystal-clear voices of the elves; singing in a deeper bass harmony rang the strong dwarfish chords, and the animals there lent their wild, free songs of the wood and plain and mountain; the volume swelled until the air itself was turning from gold to crimson to blue, and the sky seemed to open its window on the brilliant blue-white stars that hung there.

Tears streamed down every face and muzzle, and just at the instant the crescendo came, Duirn called forth another set of runes, and there filling the landings of the old elfin dane of Triehart the Ageless were the proud skiffs that had once carried so many of the clans before them to the sea and on to the road to the High Havens, which Bor Asa the Navigator had found in those troubled times at the beginnings of the Banskrog.

The skiffs were bright forest green with yellow gunwales and red thwarts; varnished oars of spruce were stowed neatly inside along the oarlocks, and each one of the craft had its name emblazoned in gold script across its transom.

Another great cheer went up from the gathered multitude of elves and dwarfs and animals, and Banon and Emeon were busy with readying the next loading order when a commotion broke out near the far edge of the camp; there were alarm calls and a general stirring in that direction, while the entire host made ready to repel an attack from an enemy that seemed somehow to have come upon them in such stealth that no one had detected them.

After another few moments of confusion, Emeon turned to Famhart and Linne, his eyes wearing a veiled look.

"It is your father, Famhart. He has brought a band of Bog Hats with him."

Linne hesitated, then broke into soft sobs.

"I almost wish they had all been slain," she wept. "Now this means that none of it is over yet."

Famhart gave the marshland girl a clumsy hug, then turned to watch the tumultuous entry of the Bog Hats into the camp. There was no threat of violence, for the enemy band was vastly outnumbered, and atop a sword he carried still in its sheath, Famhart the Elder had attached a dirty white kerchief that fell limply down over his arm.

Escorted by grim elves and dwarfs, the leader of the Bog Hats and his followers were brought to Duirn. The great emotion that had raised their spirits but a moment before was gone, and the King of the Shanoliel looked drawn and weary as he confronted the human who now stood before him.

"Greetings, O exalted one," began the elder Famhart be-

236

fore he reached the elf. A few of those who were closest to him leapt forward as the man lowered the sheathed sword, but Duirn waved them away.

"What do you wish of the Eolin?" he asked quietly. "You place yourself in great peril by coming into our midst like this. We have long met more readily over crossed swords and bowstrings."

Famhart laughed loudly and threw back his cloak in a sweeping gesture.

"Best of friends, best of enemies, I always say, eh, lads? Good soldiers never buckle up at becoming comrades with those that have given them a game, fair fight. There have been bad misunderstandings between us, Master Elf; but I think there has been enough of the bad blood to last us a long while."

Famhart spoke in a grand voice that carried over the assembled crowd, and his eyes took in every object that greeted them; he counted numbers and arms and saw the boats at the landings; his eyes scoured the throngs there and at last fell on his son, standing next to the marshland girl.

"What a stroke of fortune!" he bellowed at this discovery. "My son has been spared! I thought for certain he'd been slain or taken by the snake!"

The elder Famhart made an effort to produce tears, but the effect was more of a horrible scowl.

Linne jabbed the young Bog Hat in the side and nodded toward the two men directly behind Famhart, who turned out to be Ilide and Gorbin, both leering at her and making bowing motions.

"Your son lives, if you speak of young Famhart here," replied Duirn. "No thanks to any circumstances that you might have set into play."

The elder Famhart stopped and looked as hard as he dared at the elf.

"If I recall aright, Master Elf, it was your bunch that laid on first! We have to call the affair as it was."

"And the snake came on us all by surprise," added Ilide.

A voice that had not been heard before now came from beneath a hooded cape that concealed the features of one who stood at Famhart's heels.

"Largo!" cried Linne, her feelings rebelling within her.

"Yes, Linne, I'm safe."

He threw back the cowl that covered his face and smiled at his sister. There were such changes that had occurred in her

237

brother that Linne had difficulty at first recognizing him. There was an ugly red weal that ran from his eye to his chin on the right side, and his gaze seemed to be focused on an object just out of sight behind her. She was torn between feelings of revulsion and love, so she stood without moving until Duirn quietly motioned for her to stay where she was.

"No embrace, little sister? Your own flesh and blood gets a cold welcome."

"There is no welcome here for traitors," interrupted Famhart the Younger. "If you receive no welcome, it is no one's fault but your own."

"You speak very high-handedly, my boy," said the father. "I recall times that you kept a civil tongue in your mouth."

"Those times are long gone, Father. They will come no more."

Duirn went and sat by the fire they had built for warming their breakfast, and beckoned the others to join him.

"You have come to us here to argue more than ill manners or the duties of sons or sisters," he said, pouring out a mug of tea for himself. He did not offer any of the Bog Hats anything to take as refreshments. Jahn Spray had never seen the leader of the Eolin in quite this mood, and he noted that Duirn's eyes were a steel-gray color that betrayed none of his thoughts to anyone.

Famhart's followers moved in closer to circle their leader, who sat down opposite the elf.

"There is no harm in courtesy, even among enemies," he said at last, giving Duirn a reproachful glance.

"Nor is there any harm in caution," replied Duirn evenly. "Speak your mind. There is obviously some reason you have sought us out."

"They've been abandoned by the Dark One, most likely," offered Banon, "and would like to strike a truce so they can get out with their hides intact."

Famhart scoffed, shaking his head.

"There is no talk of any Dark One here. We have always been a poor settlement trying to get by as best we can. Things are different when you are so close to the borders. But we do have a bargain to strike, in exchange for your promise of carrying us safely to wherever you're bound."

"We need strike no bargains, Bog Hat. You have nothing of interest to us."

"We have something one of your party may want," replied the man.

238

"Such as?"

"This fellow who is the brother to the marshland girl."

Linne started to speak, but Duirn silenced her with a single look. She had never seen the elf so hardened or cold.

"What is to stop us from taking the brother and leaving you and the others behind?"

Duirn glanced around him at the gathered elves and dwarfs who waited silently for his command.

"You could take the prisoner, but I know that you wouldn't want him this way. He is completely in my control. I alone can free him from this spell. If you take him by force, I'll never free him."

To prove his point, Famhart snapped his fingers and motioned for Largo to approach. He pointed to the fire and spoke very softly. "Put your hand in and fetch me out a coal for my pipe, lad; I feel like a smoke."

Horrified, Linne watched as her brother, or what appeared to be her brother, moved his hand toward the blazing open fire.

Jahn Spray knocked the extended arm aside, but the young man merely went doggedly on trying to do as he was commanded.

"So this is how you've used your time," said Duirn after another moment, eyes a deep sky blue. "You have been with the Dark One. She has sent you back to bring us this news."

The elder Famhart smiled a wide, wicked smile that showed all his stained teeth.

"We have our leverage, just like you have yours. The Dark One never deserts a faithful ally. The snake has taken us to her, and we have followed her orders well. Now we shall see to our business, shall we, and load these boats! We have a quick job to do to get to The Beak. You see? The Protector knows all your plans. It has been a merry chase, but you'll soon end up rotting in her deepest cells to think about your folly."

"You are a foolhardy man," replied Duirn, "to think we shall let you try to dictate to us through this poor lad. The Dark One knows many things, but she underestimates our intelligence by allowing a buffoon to come slithering into our camp with such foolishness as this."

Duirn made a slight motion with his hand and instantly the elfin host was on the Bog Hat band; in a matter of seconds, the enemy was disarmed and bound by the stout

239

elfin cords that could not be broken or cut by any mortal means.

"Largo, fall on your blade!" shouted the elder Famhart. "Kill yourself now!"

But before the young man could follow his instructions, he was bound tightly, too, and rendered helpless by the cords.

Linne went to him immediately, sobbing as she leaned over the frail shell of what had once been her brother. The young Famhart tried to console her, but her grief poured out in a steady flood.

"I wish he had been killed honorably trying to protect his old settlement," she wept. "At least that would have been clean."

Banon came to try to lift her away from the stammering, vacant-eyed Largo, who writhed and twisted in some inner agony.

"We shall see if our healers can't give him some peace, my dear. We shall do our best."

Linne was immobilized by the pitiful plight of her brother, and cried the harder as she watched the once handsome wretch mutter foul curses at her and struggle to free himself from his bonds.

At that instant, warning cries and the high-pitched skree of the elfin alarm pipes exploded on the morning air from all sides; a hail of ugly black Varad and Worlugh shafts rained down on them from every quarter. The leader of the Bog Hats was bellowing with rage that he was betrayed, and ordering the assault to halt because they were captives of the elves; but the arrows rained on, and the dane was transformed instantly into a beleaguered war camp.

Olthar struck up a violent battle tune on the Pipe of Ring Parath, and the gathered elves and dwarfs and animals leapt to the counterattack; Banon and Emeon went on with the loading of the boats. The Bog Hats were cast aside, and Linne, weeping bitterly, had Famhart help her load Largo into their boat, much against the young man's judgment; but Duirn was busy with other matters, so he could not be asked.

The fighting grew more intense as the embattled host fought its way to the landings of the dane of Triehart the Ageless; then the Varads and Worlugh lost sight of their enemies; there was nothing left but a deserted lake and a dane full of captive Bog Hats. After much struggling to try to cut the elfin bonds, the Worlugh chieftain who had led the assault took out his fury at losing their quarry on the hapless elder Famhart and his followers by slaying them all where they lay.

Olthar and Duirn were in the last of the skiffs which pulled away from the landings, and it was a long while before they were beyond the range of the howls and shrieks of the furious beast soldiers, who loped up and down the landings loosing their arrows into the vast, seemingly empty lake.

Ahead of them, in the direction of the sea, a high white cloud was forming that grew as the escaped companions watched, until it appeared to Olthar that it was a bearded man in a five-pointed crown, beckoning them on toward the setting sun. He could not be sure, but Olthar felt that the face was somehow familiar.

Signs of the Eolin

IT was not difficult to tell that they were nearing the sea; great flocks of circling birds filled the sky, and a tang of salt air bit their nostrils with all the secrets that the ancient ocean held locked closely in its watery being.

They came upon signs of the first group's passing as they went, and it wasn't long before they began to catch glimpses of the leading skiffs in the late afternoon sunlight, which was rapidly flowing into a golden twilight. At times, in odd moments of silence, those in Olthar's skiff could hear the faraway booming that Duirn said was surf on the shore of the West Roaring. His eyes glistened as he spoke, and he seemed to hear something else that the others could not that made him silent and withdrawn. Olthar saw the looks that Banon and Duirn exchanged, and he wondered at the mystery for a time, but quickly forgot when the definite sighting of the leading group was sounded, and they could see the elfin skiffs clearly now, distinct dark shadows on the silver back of the water.

"Do you think we'll catch them before dark?" Olthar asked, hoping to draw Duirn out of his deep reverie.

The King of the Shanoliel did not answer immediately, but continued to stare away toward the sea, his nostrils distended, sniffing the breeze as an animal might.

Olthar repeated his question again, but it was Banon who answered.

"We shall overtake them if they are slowing down to allow us to," he replied. "Otherwise, we shall rendezvous with them tonight on the sheltered side of The Beak."

"Do you think the Bog Hat spoke the truth when he said the Banskrog knows our plan to go there?"

Banon's features clouded and the old elf seemed to age as he spoke.

"The Banskrog has always managed to find out enough from our weaker brothers to throw a surprise or two our way. I don't doubt that our plan to go here is any different."

"Then we shall have to fight to stay there until Duirn can call up the seacraft to help us escape."

"There may be a fight," concluded Banon, "and then there may not. It will depend on what will suit the Dark One."

"At least it will take her armies some time to reach us. Going overland can't be a very quick way to travel here."

Duirn spoke then, and he seemed to come to himself.

"If the Dark One sends her armies to The Beak, it will be to try to capture boats. She has overrun all the countryside there is to control, and she will want to cut off any escape route for any stragglers. The only place left to turn is the West Roaring."

"You mean she can take elfin boats?" asked Olthar.

"No, but there are settlements all along the sea that earn their livelihoods from the sea. She will have no trouble getting her boats from them."

"Will we try to stop her there?"

Duirn shook his head.

"I don't think we would be able, even if we were to try. Our only hope now is to reach the Middle Islands. There will be others there who will aid us."

"That sounds like a long way to go."

"It is, in one sense. The Middle Islands are the old ports of departure, where those who were returning to the Upper Meadows began the last part of their journey. They are still the closest gates that lead on to the upper planes, even though the Darkness has closed off the Lower Wilderness with her attacks."

"Do you think the others you speak of will be there?"

"They will be there. It has been written that it will be so."

"I hope they are," said Olthar. "It is going to be a long journey for nothing if they aren't."

The sun had gone by now, and the breeze off the lake grew colder. A faint trine moon hung low over the water, promising an early moonset and darkness for their movement. In the upper reaches of the sky, a few thin stars had appeared, burning faintly in the deep blue blanket of night. The elfin skiffs moved swiftly and silently through the water, and before him, Olthar could see the line of elves strung out in a wide arc, gliding forward through the night toward the sea. His heart beat faster with a growing excitement, and he turned to Duirn to speak, but saw that the elf was lost in his own thoughts as he gazed at the awesome spectacle that flowed noiselessly beneath the cloak of pale blue light from the waning moon and stars.

Banon raised a hand and pointed to a dark shadow near the lake's edge as they passed, speaking softly as he did so.

"It was an old watchtower of the danes. That was the last post before the sea."

As the young animal turned to study the dark shape, a single brilliant white light flashed for a moment, then was gone, leaving the darkness behind it even blacker than it had been before.

"What was that?" cried Olthar in alarm. "Did you see that?"

"I saw it," replied Banon, who had turned to Duirn.

"Who could be there in the old watchtower?"

"We shall soon find out. They won't be able to see us, so we should be able to clear up this mystery easily enough."

Duirn gave a short, whispered order, and a group of the Eolin swept toward the dark point that had burst into brilliant light for a brief moment. They glided silently ashore and dispersed themselves among the tall reeds that grew there, spreading out in all directions to search the shore. As Duirn followed their progress, another light flared from somewhere ahead of them, burning with the same white-hot intensity for a brief heartbeat, then vanishing as abruptly as it had come.

"I think I begin to see something to this," said Duirn, his face losing its anxious frown.

"What is it? Do you have some knowledge of this?"

"I think I have an idea. Let's go ashore for a quick look and I'll be able to tell you."

The skiff bore away toward the dark shadows on the shore, and Olthar was soon wading through the thick reeds behind Duirn. They left Banon to watch from the skiff and set out at

243

a rapid pace to try to overtake the others in the first party that had come ashore. The King of the Shanoliel was making no effort to conceal his movements or to try to go quietly, so Olthar felt more at ease as he struggled along in the elf's footsteps, but he was curious to know who would be in such a barren place, and what purpose they would be following once they were there.

As they went on, Olthar began to hear the other elves laughing and talking among themselves somewhere within the confines of the ancient elfin watchtower that Banon had pointed out to him. The walls were sheer stone, and rose to a distance of fifty feet or more straight above the reeds. It looked totally out of place, surrounded as it was on all sides by water and marsh reeds. Olthar could see no dry land that looked more than a foot or so above water, and nowhere did he see stones that could have been used to construct such a structure as stood before him.

Duirn was standing in front of a blank stone wall that towered away into the distance of the night sky, looking at some invisible object there that Olthar could not make out. Jahn Spray, who was standing beside him, reached a hand out and touched the smooth face of the stone.

"I have read of these towers that were built in the old times. I never thought I'd live to see one."

"You'll be seeing stranger things than this, Jahn," said Duirn, and touched a place on the wall that seemed to cause the stones to tremble slightly; then a strange door opened there, shaped like a tall mushroom. The laughter and talk of the other elves fell upon Olthar's ear very clearly now.

Stepping inside the doorway, they were greeted by a sea of soft-glowing lights that seemed to float upon the very air; the other group from Duirn's party sat cross-legged in front of a tiny fountain that sparkled and chuckled cheerfully, and filled a small pool that was in the center of the tower. On all sides there were colorful mosaics that covered the inside of the tower cone from the floor all the way to its roof, which glittered in the distance high above them. At the very top of the tower was a golden light that glowed faintly, making it appear as though it was a moon hung forever in a quarter of heaven that kept it always full, and always over the mysterious elfin tower in the very depths of the vast desolation of Dreary Lake.

Olthar stood staring up, his small frame trembling.

"Who built this?" he finally managed to ask, still not able

244

to remove his gaze from the image of the golden moon that pulsed on faintly, sometimes seeming to grow bigger, sometimes appearing to shrink from view.

The King of the Shanoliel gazed about him, a small smile crossing his features; it was the first time since he had known the elf that Olthar had seen this look; for a moment, it almost made the leader of the Eolin appear truly happy.

"It was not built by anyone in particular," began Duirn, trying to find a way to explain to his small friend. "It was begun in earnest by the first Eolin who came and returned from the High Havens. They stopped on their way out, and wherever they camped they built these towers to rest in and to guide them back from their journeys. It was not a well-mapped place, this Atlanton, in the days of the Beginning. No one knew anything of what was here, or what was to be expected. Later on, the Eolin who sought to return to their True Home came upon these towers again and placed all the rest of the things you see here; the walls record the entire rise and ebb of the fortunes of the Eolin; all the long history of the Banskrog is here, and all the dark chapters in our own tales."

Duirn pointed to a portion of the mosaic that was on a level Olthar could see without doing any more than raising himself to his full height: in it he could see the form of an elf in what appeared to be chains, held by a very large, imposing black figure that had no features other than a crude black crown with five jagged points.

"There is the first of the Erlings. We had been in the Wilderness for enough time for the Dark One to start her first attacks on our race. It was not a violent attempt such as the Banskrog has made now. Then it was more subtle, coaxing all who would hear into following along into the ultimate despair of the darkness and terror of what the Wilderness can be."

Olthar grew excited as he looked closer at the mosaic, for there were details to it that caught his eye.

"Is that the pipe, Duirn? Look!"

"It is. It is the taking of the pipe from the first Erling who ever held it. From that time on, it has been a black page in our history; the pipe was lost, to be carried only by the Olthlinden. We have waited a long, grim time for your coming."

The elf held up a hand and pointed to the other, higher parts of the tower.

"The rest of the walls are covered with heartbreak and loss and the waiting."

"But the golden light at the top is there," replied Olthar. "So there must have been hope for all those elves, even in their despair."

"It is the hope of the Return," said Duirn softly, looking down mildly on his small companion.

Olthar felt the thought of the pipe tugging at him, pulling his paw to the case; he removed it and put it to his lips and listened as it began to play a soft, lilting tune that went back to the sadness that had been over all the years the Eolin had been lost in the Wilderness; it broke the animal's heart to hear the low sobbing notes, but as he played on, the golden moon at the tower top began to grow brighter and brighter, until at the last it was a throbbing golden sun that bathed the inside of the tower with a light so brilliant it was difficult to remember that all was dark night outside.

As the last notes died away, the otter replaced the pipe in its case, noticing as he did so that all the elves had been weeping openly; as the echoes of the song died, Duirn drew himself up as if he were just awakening from a long and pleasant dream that had ended all too soon.

"We must get back to Banon. He will be worried about us."

"I wish he could have seen this," said Olthar.

"I think he has already done so," replied the elf. "I think Banon sent us ahead on purpose."

"It makes me sad to think that we won't be coming here again."

"But there will be others," said Duirn. "And look! There at the top! There is a new section of the mosaic added!"

Olthar could not see the forms distinctly, but it looked to be a small animal amid a crowd of elves, and there seemed to be a host of faces beyond; there were scenes there too that portrayed a great battle, but Olthar could not make out the meaning of it all, for it was confused and baffling to look upon. He had no further chance to study it at length; Duirn was calling to him to hurry, for the others were gone and they were alone in the tower.

Olthar gazed up earnestly at his friend.

"I had been meaning to ask you about something, Duirn, but there has been no time before now."

"What was that?"

"About what I saw by the fire that day, when I wanted you to take the pipe back."

Duirn said nothing, but gazed steadily at the otter.

"Would it all have really been as I saw it?"

246

"How did you see it?"

"Well, for one thing, it was awful. You were slain and there was nothing left to even hope for."

The King of the Shanoliel patted the small animal and laughed.

"We shall never know now, shall we? Our path has taken a different turn. Perhaps you glimpsed but another way it might have been; or it may already have been so, at one time or another in our journeys."

Before Olthar could ask any more questions, the elf hurried him out of the tower, where they joined the others; after a short trek back through the tall reeds, they found Banon in deep conversation with Coney, who seemed agitated and anxious that they should go on without further delay.

"What's wrong, Coney?" asked Jahn Spray.

"It's nothing that I can say anything about," he replied. "I just feel the sap running heavy in in my limbs, and whenever that happens I've found that there's always grave danger very near. I'll be able to find out exactly if it goes on much longer, but right now all I know is that I'd feel much better if we'd go on."

"That's enough said for me," replied Duirn. "Jahn, see to it that the others have their orders."

Jahn vanished at once to ensure that all the other boats were prepared to leave.

Olthar told Coney of what he had seen in the tower while they awaited the return of Jahn.

"It was wonderful and sad all at the same time," explained the small animal.

"It sounds much like everything else we know," answered the ancient tree-being. "Always there is the joy replaced by grief, then back to joy. It seems ever the case here in the Wilderness."

"There seemed to be an end to it, though," added Olthar. "The light at the top of the tower was glowing so brightly at the end, it was like it was daylight, and I could feel all the sadness leave."

"Well, that is a good sign, at any rate," conceded the Old One. "I am always glad to hear a cheerful ending to anything that has to do with all this business down here in the Lower Meadows."

Jahn Spray returned at that point, and the companions were busied with the business of departing, so they left off their thoughts for a time and turned their attention to keeping watch over the silent, dark lake and the ominous shadows that made up the changing shoreline; Olthar turned back once to have a last look at the tower of the Eolin, but it was hardly visible at all, even from the short distance they had traveled: he realized then that if it had not been for Banon pointing it out to him, he would not have chanced to see it; the brilliant light that had emitted from it would have gone unexplained, and he would not have seen the amazing mosaic inside, or felt the deep sense of underlying peace that he felt far down in the center of his soul.

He was on the verge of turning to talk to Coney, when he realized that the Old One had vanished again into the gloom of the lake.

"I wish he would stay close," said Olthar peevishly. "Just when I want to ask him something, he's gone again."

"I think he has been hanging about with the elves too long," said Banon. "He seems to be picking up all our bad habits."

The old elf chuckled, but Olthar did not find the truth to be particularly amusing. Before he could say anything further, Duirn broke into his thoughts with the information that the elves in front of them were in sight.

"We shall be up with them in another half hour; it's only another hour or so beyond to the beginning of the marshland that borders the sea."

Olthar's heart raced at the news, for he was already beginning to smell the raw, wild smell of the salt water, and his blood was coursing through him with all the ancient secrets that he and his kind had always held about anything to do with rivers or ponds or lakes; and this was a body of water that was the foundation of all others, and evident even in the tears he wept, salty and hot to the taste and touch.

As he stood staring away into that vast dark memory of a time before there was anything, a faint, dirty orange light crept into his vision, low down on the horizon, just barely perceptible over the flat shadows that marked where water met land.

"What is it?" shot Jahn, asking the question before the otter could find his voice.

"The Beak," replied Duirn. "It can only be The Beak. They have found us out already, it seems."

"Is it the others?" asked Olthar.

"No, I don't think our first party has had time to reach there."

248

"Then who could it be?" asked Jahn.

"There must have been someone there waiting for us," answered Duirn. "And they have warned us in time that the Banskrog has reached The Beak, too. Perhaps we can set on them by surprise, if they are already at the attack. They may not expect us quite so soon."

"This looks like the work of one of the worms," said Banon. "I don't like the smell of it."

"Nor do I, Banon. But we have to have the boats from The Beak or we won't be able to reach the islands."

"We shall do what we shall have to then," replied the old elf. "There is nothing else for it now. In a way, it's a relief to know they are here. Now there is no doubt."

As the warning pipes called to each of the other boats on the dark lake, Olthar could hear the echoes from the boats ahead of them; fainter and farther away, he could hear the barely audible dull racket that came from the distant battle that raged back and forth over the thin splinter of land that was marked on the maps as The Beak.

The dim orange flames off the reflection of the water played across the faces of his companions in the elfin skiff, and for a moment Olthar thought he saw a dark outline of a shadow that could only be Coney, but it disappeared again before he could be sure.

Duirn reached out and gave him a reassuring pat, then set to arranging his battle garb; Jahn Spray did the same, and Banon loosened his own sword and laid out a bow beside a quiver of elfin arrows close to his hand. Olthar felt an old hand at it all by now, and he realized that most of the fear was gone. He wished it were over, but knew that would only happen as it would, so he concentrated on placing the Pipe of Ring Parath loosely in its case and ready to paw; the next breath he was swept into the maw of the battle, for there from the shoreline of the lake was a sudden blazing watch fire that leapt high into the sky with an oily stench, and before anyone of the elves could realize what had happened, the heart-stopping scream of the Dargol Brem sliced through the darkness, and the ugly, grotesque shadow of the dragon lumbered slowly over them, capsizing a dozen of the elfin skiffs; in the next moment, the battle was joined in earnest.

The Pipe of Ring Parath was at his lips, and Olthar began to play.

The Queen of Darkness

TRANE was exultant! The Erling rode like a dark, savage wind down on the surprised elves in the skiffs below, and the terrible din of Rengesbark's leathery wings set off echoes of dull thunder, and the ugly orange tongue of flame exploded into the night like a demon's breath, scorching the air into an oily cloud of doom. The wood elf was beside himself with a blighted joy, and the sweet feelings of revenge he felt caused him to shriek aloud in his passionate delight. The dragon lifted a gnarled talon and crushed to splinters one of the hateful watercraft of the Eolin, and Trane cried out in joy, as if he had been at the most amusing of banquets in the old danes of the wood elf Elders from before the time of trouble.

It was difficult to bear Rengesbark's grasp, and the fear he felt at being carried by the snake caused him some alarm from time to time, but the bitter excitement at seeing the destruction wrought on his hated enemies made it the more easy to bear; everywhere he looked, he saw the hard-pressed water elves fighting for their lives; once the skiffs were destroyed, the Eolin became perfectly visible to the Worlugh and Varad soldiers who lined the shore of the lake.

Trane shrieked aloud again, pointing to a skiff below him, and felt the trembling wrath of Rengesbark as he lowered himself to strike the water where the Erling pointed.

Trane had nursed his hatred carefully, gloating now as he saw the wretched water elf host tossed on the horrible nightmare of the dragon's anger; he had cursed his luck when the arrogant Duirn had left him to his fate beside Dreary Lake, but his persistence had paid off at last: the Protector had rewarded him well by allowing him to direct the doom snake in a final assault on the Eolin armies, where they would be destroyed before they reached the Sea of Roaring.

The Erling's breath came in short bursts of excitement as he saw the destruction of two more skiffs; he watched with glee as the hard-pressed elves scrambled for the shore, where they were beset by those who waited there in ambush. Rengesbark's icy cry pierced through the noise and confusion of the battle, discordant and triumphant. The darkness had broken into shattered patches of orange flames, casting grotesque shadows against the flaming reflections on the lake's surface; in all directions there was nothing to be seen but destruction and chaos, and the fury of the battle raised a dreadful din that threatened to deafen the embattled enemies locked in mortal combat.

As the doom snake wheeled about in lumbering, jerking motions, the wood elf caught a fleeting glimpse of the leader of the Shanoliel, and he called out frantically to Rengesbark.

"They're here! They're below us! It's Duirn and the pipe bearer!"

Trane was beside himself and cried out in a hoarse, hate-choked voice that was heard even above the wing-beats of the dragon.

"You're done for, you foul traitor! No one can save you now!"

In his passion, the Erling could not tell if Duirn had heard him or not, but the dragon now lumbered slowly about in a lowering circle, closing the distance between them. The wood elf lost the King of the Shanoliel for a moment in the confusion and darkness, but he kept his eyes upon the small globe of light that seemed to be coming from the skiff that Duirn was in; there was also a faint, troublesome noise that began growing very slowly, working its way into his awareness.

Rengesbark began to tremble with rage, and Trane feared for a moment that he was going to be crushed; the dragon bellowed aloud in a dreadful voice and sped up his attack on the hard-pressed Eolin.

"The Protector will have that trinket before this night is out! I, Rengesbark, will take that deadly, cursed thing and destroy it upon the sea! It is a splinter that will be plucked from the Protector's side now!"

The music, which until then had been drowned in the fury of the battle, became stronger, rising a note or two higher, until it was audible even over the shrieks and war horns of the Varads and Worlugh, quite pure and clear in its call.

Below, Olthar stood beside Duirn in the pitching skiff, holding onto the gunwale with a paw to steady himself, and blowing desperately on the Pipe of Ring Parath. Jahn Spray and Banon had gone overboard in the first onslaught, and now struggled to keep hold of the side of the boat while Duirn turned the skiff's stem toward the shoreline.

"We shall have to go ashore! That Erling spy is with the

dragon. It's ill luck that my shaft did not find his black heart on our last meeting!"

"Watch out!" called Banon hoarsely. "There are Worlugh on the shore here! Have an eye for a landing!"

A volley of arrows whirred past their ears, falling harmlessly into the lake behind them.

"At least the skiff is keeping us from the beast soldiers' sight," said Jahn. "We will have a chance to land without being seen."

"Where are the others? Can anyone see the others? We must keep together or we're lost!" shouted Duirn, loosing an arrow in the general direction of the black shadow looming dangerously close overhead. On the shoreline, a great barrage of shafts went upward from the elfin host that was already ashore.

The King of the Shanoliel blew out the rallying call on the silver horn about his neck, and felt relieved when he heard the answering notes from all about in the scattered confusion of the battle. He had feared the worst in the sudden first moments of the attack, but the skiffs had done their work well, even beset by the dragon, for most of the elves, although shaken and battered by the dragon's assault, had reached the safety of the shore, where they were able to mount their defense against the beast soldiers; although there were great hordes of the enemy there, it was not so large a force as Duirn first imagined, and the hard trip overland through the endless maze of the Swamp of Dismal had proven to be an effective barrier, even against the brutal Worlugh and Varad armies.

Ahead of him in the harsh glare of the fires started along the shoreline by the snake, Duirn could see that the leading party of the Eolin had been ambushed also, and were fighting their way ashore not far from where he stood. Through the snap and whine of the arrows that were exchanged with the beast armies, the high warning calls of the elfin pipes could be heard from all directions, and as time wore slowly on, it seemed to Duirn that they began to swell in volume, aided by Olthar, who had not let the Pipe of Ring Parath fall silent for a single moment.

"We must gather for a blow to fight our way clear of this," called Duirn to Olthar, turning to make sure the young animal was at his side. At that moment, the darkness seemed to gather strength, and even the light of the fires along the shore seemed to dim. Duirn reached into his cloak and withdrew a tiny starlamp, but its dazzling white radiance was absorbed into the shadow that fell across them; a howling wind began to tear at their ears, making it hard to hear anything at all, forcing them all to turn their faces away from the terrible blast.

A shrieking, rasping cry erupted from the maddened dragon, and the very ground beneath Olthar began to shudder; the Pipe of Ring Parath became red-hot, and there gleamed a terrible blue-white flame from the small object; a sound that might have come from the ending of the world filled the air with a song so horrible to hear that all those upon Dreary Lake, elf and dwarf, animal and human alike, could only fall senseless to the ground and beat the air wildly with flailing arms, their empty eyes starting from their heads; the beast soldiers exulted in the sound, and began to fall savagely upon their hapless victims.

Olthar struggled against the howling, frozen wind that tormented him, finally getting the pipe to his lips, where it took life on its own and a small sound began to emerge, barely audible at first over the deafening roar that swept over the beleaguered armies of the Eolin; then there came the tiny point of brilliant golden-white light that hovered above the lake for a brief heartbeat, then slowly proceeded to grow, looking somewhat as though daylight were beginning to break, although it was not yet past midnight.

The Old One was suddenly beside the small animal, only in a form that Olthar had never seen before; the tree-being was in the form of a human, wreathed in the same golden-white fire that licked at the darkness of the waters of Dreary Lake, and chased away the howling, shrieking blasts of wind that hammered against the walls of night; Coney reached down with a hand and touched the otter on the paw, sending an electric jolt through him that seemed to pull him back from the yawning abyss of the Dark One's mind.

Olthar tried to call out to his friend, but the confusion of the moment made it impossible to speak, and he could not take the ancient pipe from his lips; it now began another shrill call that grew louder and louder, until the night was filled with its strident chords; the stunned hosts of the Eolin began to recover from their stupor and hopelessness, and renewed their efforts to overcome the vicious Worlugh and Varad soldiers who beset them on every side.

When Olthar looked again, the Old One was gone, but the golden-white fire lingered on, and Duirn had appeared from

253

the struggling throngs, his face wild and haggard, urging on his exhausted army.

Not far away, Linne and Famhart were fighting side by side with Emeon the elf, and no one had any time to notice the raving, bound figure of Largo in the bottom of the skiff he had been transported in, or saw the black claw of the wind unravel the elfin knot, freeing the tormented marshland youth. A curious pale green fire burned dully in Largo's eyes as he rose from his knees and vanished into the struggling bands of warriors fighting all about; no one noticed the handsome lad as he made his way toward the otter, now standing beside Duirn and beginning to urge the battle more closely upon their attackers.

Angry arrows snapped and buzzed back and forth all about them, but Olthar was lost in the call of the pipe and was heedless of his danger; in an unguarded moment, Largo was on him, dull eyes glowing a fierce green. His weight overpowered the small animal, and the struggle carried them both to the ground. Duirn, not seeing the attacker, was unaware that his companion was fighting for his life at his very feet.

Largo, possessed by the mind of the Dark One, was like a crazed demon, one hand grappling for the pipe, and the other one closed about the throat of Olthar, who turned loosely in his skin and was trying to find a place to latch onto with his powerful jaws; the two, man and animal, rolled frantically back and forth on the slippery shore of the lake, until Largo stumbled and fell backward over one of the beached elfin skiffs. Freed from his assailant's grasp for a moment, the otter called out loudly to Duirn and Coney.

"Help me," he cried. "Coney! Duirn! It's Largo!"

Coney's voice came from beside the small animal then, although there was nothing to be seen of the Old One's form.

"It is the Dark One, Olthar. She is using Largo's body. She is here among us."

"What'll we do?" shot Olthar, clinging desperately to the pipe and moving out of the reach of Largo, who had regained his footing and pressed forward to attack again.

"This is what we shall do," replied Coney, suddenly appearing in his human form again, and picking up Olthar, he held him close to him within the circle of golden-white light that emanated from the Old One.

The marshland youth, controlled by the Dark One, fell forward as if to attack the two companions, but was hurled violently back as he touched the wall of light that surrounded Coney.

A grating, shrill voice then came from the throat of Largo, a voice so unearthly and harsh that the ears of all who heard were deafened for a time by the horror of the sound.

"Give up your foolish resistance! You cannot hope to overcome me. There is no hope for any of you who continue to thwart me!"

Olthar felt the terrible tug of the black maw that drew him forward toward Largo, although he knew it was no longer the marshland lad who spoke. A terrible darkness reflected the fear in his own heart as he listened to the voice of the Banskrog, and there was a dreadful desire to give in to the cruel will of the Dark One.

"We shall not surrender! You are defeated now! There will be no turning back from the Middle Islands. We will be reunited there, and that will be the end of your dream."

Another frozen blast of wind shrieked and whirled around the friends.

"Do not be so sure. I have more methods for your destruction than the bungling Worlugh and Varad armies. The Dargol Brem shall be the root of your downfall. They are freed upon Atlanton now. There is no escape from them."

"There is destruction in the Dargol Brem, but they are not indestructible. We have our ways of defending against them now. The Pipe of Ring Parath is with us, carried by the Olthlinden. That is as the Law was written. You have been aware of that all these lifetimes. When the gathering of the clans of Atlanton is done, the shadow of the night of the Dark One is on the wane."

Largo's body writhed in anguished torment as he racked with the terrible black rage of the Dark One.

"Do not tempt me, O ancient fool. I know your race has been since the First Beginning but you are not invincible, either. I know the secret of your power."

"It is the same secret as your own. If you try to destroy me, you shall perish also. You are well aware of that!"

"I don't have to destroy you, you ancient filth. You have wrought your own end by choosing to ally yourself with the weakling forces of the Light. You are doomed!"

Olthar was mesmerized by the confrontation that had been going on between the Dark One and his old friend and companion from the Westing Wood, and he failed to notice that the battle all about them had been slowly dying down;

the Dargol Brem was farther away now, off in the direction of The Beak, where he was circling above another battle that flared there.

"There are other ways to rid the Lower Wilderness of the blight of the Circle. I have the means by which I shall be able to extract that wretched pipe from your little weasel friend you so grandly refer to as the Olthlinden."

A wild, hysterical laugh escaped Largo's lips; for a moment the fair features of the young man took on the frozen beauty of the Dark One.

"When you know that I have all the pieces of this puzzle safely within my grasp, you will understand why it will be of no use to resist me."

Upon saying, Largo fell forward at the feet of Coney, and the tormented face eased into a senseless, glowering stare; above the unfortunate young man, a small green cloud gathered until there was the shape of a figure there that resembled a human form; in a cloud was what appeared to be a picture of something very dim and vague at first, but slowly coming into focus; Olthar felt a great need to stand closer to see what the indistinct images might be, but Coney held him back again.

"What is it, Coney? Let me see! I want to see!"

If it had not been for the positive flow of strength from the pipe, the otter would have been lost; that was a thing he somehow sensed as he stood there, torn between the desperate need to surrender to the Dark One and that equally sure knowledge that he would never give up so long as he had breath in his body to resist.

Still there were the frightening shapes that began to materialize in the greenish mist cloud before him, and as he felt his eyes being drawn irrevocably there, he knew ahead of time what he was going to see; it was as though it had all happened before and he was only now remembering. There in that evil haze were the frank, stubby features of Malcom and the wistful gaze of Morane, looking directly at him from some horrible distance; Olthar could almost hear her voice speaking to him, yet there was no sound.

"These two have given me great pleasure," came the voice from the cloud. "I have felt exquisite moments in tormenting them with the promise I have destroyed their offspring."

Olthar's muzzle flushed hot; he felt the ache in his heart grow into a red-hot bolt of rage that consumed him, and the next moment he was lunging straight for the wraith-like cloud that hung before him; he moved so quickly that even Duirn was unable to move rapidly enough to stop the young otter from plunging headlong into the green mist.

In the wink of an eye, the green form, the Dargol Brem, and Largo were all vanished from the shores of Dreary Lake, leaving the stunned Coney and the leader of the Shanoliel staring desolately at the unmoving young otter who carried the fading hopes of all those who yet dwelled in the dimming light of the world of the Lower Meadows.

Bor Asa and Yvan Earlig

IN the aftermath of the terrible battle, and faced with the rescue of the gravely endangered otter from the steel vise of the Dark One's will, the stunned and much subdued company that remained went through the motions of driving off the rest of the Worlugh and Varad army; without the awful presence of the Dargol Brem, it was a task that was not overly difficult, due to the great numbers that had gathered to the cause of the Olthlinden. Duirn knew that the battle was not meant to be a decisive one, and now understood more fully the true purpose of it—a ruse by the Darkness to trap and carry away the object of her deeper designs.

"It was all my fault," lamented Coney. "I should have warned the lad about something like this happening."

"It's no use blaming yourself," consoled Jahn Spray. "I was right beside him when it happened, and I could have stopped him if I'd thought quickly enough."

"You are both underestimating the Banskrog," said Duirn. "We were all under the Dark One's thrall when this happened. None of us could have done other than we did. And none of us can answer for what went on in the Olthlinden's mind."

The leader of the Shanoliel clasped Jahn Spray by the shoulder and smiled grimly.

"No one could have done any more. It is up to the lad himself now. We are all helpless to do more to aid him."

Linne and Famhart, who had just returned from helping to drive off the enemy bands, pulled off their bloody cloaks and fell exhausted at the feet of the small group huddled around the elfin leader, oblivious to all that had taken place with Olthar.

"We have finished with the last lot," said Famhart, his voice hoarse with fatigue. Linne shut her eyes and lay wearily with her head in his lap.

Jahn Spray handed the two a mug of the healing tea which was brewing on the fire.

"Are you two of a whole?"

"Nothing but scratches and exhaustion. I could sleep for a week."

"I'm afraid we'll have no time for that," said Duirn. "We're going on to the Roaring as soon as we're all gathered back together."

"Surely we have time to at least get a night's sleep!"

"Olthar has been attacked," explained Jahn Spray. "The Banskrog has been here."

Upon hearing this, Linne opened her eyes and sat upright, trembling.

"What happened?"

"The Dark One came."

"But how?"

Jahn Spray looked down awkwardly.

"Largo. She came through Largo. It seems one of the ways she is best at."

The marshland girl broke down into sobs that shook her small shoulders.

"Oh, it was my fault. I should have left Largo with the others. Now the otter is in grave danger because of him."

Famhart tried to console her, but she would have none of it. She shook free of his arms and ran from the fire, going to the small covered litter where the unconscious Olthar lay.

"Let her have a cry first. There is no place she can go."

"Was it really Largo?" asked Famhart, also feeling more than a small pang of guilt, for he had helped the girl bring her brother along.

"It was the Darkness. Largo is gone somewhere. It was his likeness, but the real Largo is innocent. He is held captive in the dark night of Dorini's will. That is where our Olthlinden is now, I fear, struggling to free himself."

"We were the ones who brought Largo. We never thought it would cause anything like this."

"No one could have guessed that this would have happened," said Duirn. "I should have been more wary about the Banskrog. My mistakes grow more costly as time goes on."

"We shall need to get on quickly," urged Coney. "The longer we delay here, the longer we'll be in reaching the Middle Islands. I think from what we have seen and know now about the Dark One's plans, that is the best thing to do to help Olthar. If we gather there quickly enough, and our allies are there, we shall perhaps be able to do the lad some good."

A rousing cheer from a group of otters returning from battle filled the air, and all turned their attention toward the small animal warriors. Hydin led the group, marching triumphantly at the head of the procession.

"We have news! We have overheard from one of the Worlugh that a terrible thing has befallen the Darkness. The two waterkind that she held are free, and are gone from her power!"

Duirn motioned for the group to quieten so he could hear what Hydin was saying.

"The Olthlinden's mother and father have escaped! We heard it from a beast soldier! He was talking to his friend and didn't know we were about."

"They knew we were about soon enough," said a stubby warrior who was standing close by his leader.

"They did, indeed; but they will never know how they gladdened our hearts by betraying that bit of news."

Jahn Spray drove a fist into his open palm.

"If only Olthar had known before he was taken! It might be the very thing he needs to combat the Dark One. I wish he had known!"

"All the more reason to get on with our journey," said Duirn hastily. "Quickly! Gather everyone for a muster and let's be off! Hydin, you and your party have done very well indeed! The Olthlinden needs all the help from his friends he can get, so you will stand guard over him until we reach the Middle Islands."

Hydin went a shade grayer, and his handsome muzzle took on a troubled frown.

"Thank you for the honor, O Duirn. I and my bloodthirsty lot are unworthy of such praise; but we shall stand watch over Olthar for as long as we have breath left in us, and until we have seen him safely back from the Dark One's realms!"

There was a grim and rousing war chant at this, and the otters all lined up gravely at their loading place along the shoreline, where the elfish clans had righted the overturned skiffs and repaired the damages as best they were able. Without waiting for any further orders, the entire host began the loading and pushed off once more across Dreary Lake, on toward the horizon; as the companions had stood talking, the first pale light of dawn had washed the gray-green sky, turning it to a darker reddish gold, and as the last of the skiffs were under way, the full light of dawn burst forth in a clear, golden halo of light that heartened the weary wanderers; it cloaked the litter where Olthar lay in its golden glow and raised the spirits of his comrades, even though their hearts were heavy and troubled by the strange wounding of the Olthlinden.

Linne and Famhart were in the sleek craft that was next behind Duirn, and they were able to talk easily as they ghosted through the stillness that had fallen over the lake; the great noise of the battle was gone now, making it seem even more silent than before.

"If this news is true about his parents being freed, will it help Olthar?" asked Linne. She was still suffering from guilt at having been the cause of Largo's being in their midst to bring harm to her small friend.

"If Morane and Malcom are free, it means that the lad will have a chance to resist. He is very young to be carrying so great a burden. I would have hoped that he would be spared this confrontation until he was more seasoned, but it was not to be."

"I think he's more seasoned than we may give him credit for," said Coney. "He has been through much for one so small and so slight in years."

Coney floated beside the skiff on Duirn's left side, traveling effortlessly with the motion of the elfin craft.

"You are right, in a way," conceded Duirn. "Yet there is still a great danger when dealing with the Banskrog. There is no way of telling what tactic she'll use or what course she'll take."

"I've even heard of times when the Dark One concealed herself in the guise of gentleness and innocence," said Banon. "Somehow that would seem even more cruel and horrible than dealing with her at her very worst."

"That is always the case, Banon. We always receive the most painful wounds from those we think the least likely to harm us."

"Whether she has the pup's parents imprisoned or not, she

260

will certainly say she has," said Jahn Spray. "The only proof against her word would be to present Malcom and Morane to Olthar."

"No small wonder then, except that we don't know where any one of them is at this moment."

"I somehow think Malcom will be making his way toward the sea. All the other woods are full of the beast soldiers; there is nowhere else left to go but to the Roaring. We had often discussed that in the old days when we were traveling together, before all this."

Jahn Spray moved his arm in a wide circle to take in everything about them.

"The Roaring has a coastline that is very broad, my friend," said Banon. "Even if they reached the sea, it would be a miracle if they were to find their way into the camp of friends."

Duirn shook his head slowly, lost in thought for a moment; he studied Jahn Spray closely as he spoke.

"In the past, it might have been harder. Now it seems that everything is coming to a head. They may find it easier to reach someone who may help them. Plus Malcom knows the elves well, and would go straight to them for help."

Jahn Spray nodded.

"He would try that first of all."

"Then it might not be so farfetched to think that somewhere along the coast there are others like ourselves gathering to make the voyage to the islands. It seems as if the Middle Islands are the only safe places left."

"Were," corrected Coney. "No more. Now the Banskrog is poised to deliver a blow even there."

"That's true enough, Coney, but you must remember that the Middle Islands are also the road to the High Havens. It was from there that all our ancestors crossed the Last Ocean into the Straits of Upper Windameir."

The ancient being was lost in his own thoughts for a long time before he replied.

"It always takes a long night to make the day seem welcome," he muttered at last. "What a long night this has been."

Linne agreed, yawning.

"I'm speaking of a longer night than what we've had here, my dear," replied the tree-being. "I speak of the long night that has been full of the Banskrog, and all the times and places we've been to try to see what the Darkness really is."

261

The marshland girl answered Coney by nodding off into an exhausted, fretful sleep. Famhart held her closely to him and looked about as if dazed.

"You two shall have your chance to carry on what I am speaking of," chuckled the Old One. "It is through you and those who follow you that we shall find our way to freedom at last."

"I'd be more interested in finding our way to Olthar's rescue," said Jahn Spray.

"We are going about that as quickly as we can," replied Duirn.

"Not quickly enough, I fear. I wish there were some way to give him news of his parents' freedom."

"We shall deliver that when we shall. First we must reach the Roaring and call up the seacraft of Bor Asa the Navigator. This is our first order of action."

"I hope Bor Asa had fast ships," muttered Jahn Spray.

"Fast enough, my friend, fast enough. Now I shall turn myself to something I have had no time for before. You keep us to our course. I shall return shortly."

"But ..." began Jahn, starting to protest, although the King of the Shanoliel was gone even before the words were out of his mouth. Shrugging his shoulders in resignation, the elf turned to speak to Coney, and was not surprised to find the Old One had disappeared as well, as he often did just when Jahn Spray needed him most.

Upon the growing light, Duirn had raised himself on a golden beam that pierced the blue sky and spiraled away into the distance until there was nothing but a tiny dot of brilliant light that blended into the sun; the leader of the Shanoliel felt time and space disappear, and was in the hallway of his ancient forefathers, studying the crystal-clear fountains that sparkled and turned their fine mist in the golden light. Duirn bowed thrice and entered the homey, simple room.

Inside, he was greeted by an ancient elf, whose bearing was stately and kind; there was another beside him, dressed from head to foot in gray, with a gray, weathered riding cloak that was stained and torn with long wear and bore the look of having been on a long journey.

"Greetings, Bor Asa. My service, Yvan Erlig."

The two tall, fair elves bowed low to Duirn.

"Come in, Duirn. We have expected you since our Dark Lady has taken this new turn in her plot."

"She has confronted the pup. He is with her now."

"We know. Yvan arrived with that news not long before you."

"We have also learned that the pup's mother and father are free. They have escaped the Banskrog."

"We shall need to help Olthar in this time of testing. He has not been fully prepared for dealing with the Dark One. She has moved ahead of us again. We did not expect her to take this tack."

"Nor did I," answered Duirn, a worried frown creeping over his fair features. "I don't know what I did expect. I can offer no excuse for my oversight."

"We have all been remiss in our perceptions of what the Darkness has been doing. Bor Asa and I were going over our past dealings with the Dark One, and we have concluded we've both been badly mistaken at her intentions."

"That is easy to explain, Yvan. We don't have far to look to see the reason why she has eluded our detection for so long!" Bor Asa snorted a short laugh. "We're always too ready to see the good in everyone, and to assume that when someone says something, he means it."

"I know we have been easily duped, if that's a fancy way to put it," replied Yvan. "Every single time we have chosen to believe the best, exactly the opposite has happened. We chose not to believe that Dorini would exceed her boundaries, and she went far beyond her given powers in the Lower Meadows; we thought she would never dare tamper with the structure of the Upper Gates, and she called down the Dargol Brem, turning loose the dragons on the Wilderness; and now we have thought she would choose to confront one of the Circle herself, to demand her concessions and state her case, and she has attacked our youngest member, who has had no experience with her before, and has not the slightest chance of being able to defend himself against her alone."

Duirn sighed softly and said very gently, "There is the Pipe of Ring Parath. He does have that."

"It won't do him much service if he doesn't know how to apply it," answered Yvan, striding up and down the small room impatiently. "By the Sacred Name of the Flame of Windameir, I wish I'd tended my business a little more closely! If I'd been doing what I should have, we'd be free of this troublesome affair by now."

Bor Asa reached out a hand and grasped Yvan by his cloak as he paced by.

"You know you were but acting out the part that had to be

played. If it had not been you, it would have been Greyfax, or Fairenus, or any one of the others of the Circle."

"But it was an elf, and it was me. I find it difficult to accept my failure."

Duirn recalled from his most ancient memory of the history of the Circle the event which Bor Asa and Yvan Earlig spoke of; it was from a time long before, when the Circle was upon closer terms with those of the Lower Meadows, and the times were not as dark. Dorini, the twin sister of the beautiful Lorini, Lady of Cypher, had tricked the Circle through Yvan, by promising her good behavior to him in return for freeing her from the bonds she had been sworn to by the High Lord of Windameir. Yvan had been young and in love with Dorini at the time, for she was, after all, the sister of Lorini, and it was in a period before she had gone against all the order of things and begun to create her own worlds of Darkness where she alone reigned.

That had been the beginning of the Banskrog, the Black Death; Dorini's will was set against the High Lord of Windameir, and her rebellion had begun in earnest. At first, it was thought by everyone that the errant sister would soon see her mistake and mend her ways; instead, as the tale grew more grim, Dorini found a way to renew her attacks on the Light, and she had succeeded so far and so well that here they were all those turnings afterward, couched in a room at the end of the Lower Meadows of Windameir to discuss what was to be done next. Their lives, and the life of a small gray otter, and the lives of all who yet dwelled in the Light of Windameir, rested in the course of the decisions they made and the turn events took. Yvan was never one to look at the dark side of an issue any longer than necessary to see what was there, but he was clearly worried by the new developments that confronted them.

"We could go to Olthar ourselves," offered Duirn. "I don't know if it would do any good, but the lad would at least feel he was not alone."

"We might do more harm than good by that; but it may be the only path we have to go," said Yvan, stroking his beard and looking deeply into the flames of the small fire that burned gaily in the tidy room; he grew silent for a time, and seemed to be a long way off; there were sparks in the fire that popped and sizzled, and the colors there took on blue and gold hues, until there were forms and figures that began to take distinct shapes as Bor Asa and Duirn watched.

264

In the front of the fire, nearest the hearth, there appeared a small form that looked very much like Olthar; he was standing with his paws held out before him, as if he were holding off an assailant. Behind, and very hazy, was a formless cloud that defied any shape, but was very menacing in its presence.

"It's Olthar!" cried Duirn.

"And the Dark One, if I don't miss my guess," added Bor Asa.

Without speaking aloud, Yvan cautioned the two to silence, and went on concentrating on the unfolding drama taking place far away from them, but reflected back in the mirror of the elfin fire of Yvan Earlig.

Shifting his thoughts slightly, there came into view what appeared to be a glade, deep inside a forest of trees so ancient they went beyond the passage of time. Duirn, staring hard, finally recognized the trees as the Brotherhood of the Ancient Ones, the fellowship that Coney belonged to; and there in that clearing was another small, familiar figure; as the leader of the Shanoliel looked more closely, he saw yet another, lying down as if in sleep.

"It is Morane and Malcom," Duirn breathed. "They are with the Old Ones."

Yvan Earlig was very far away in his thoughts, and his body remained motionless there before the fire; Bor Asa nodded to his friend.

"It is indeed the Old Ones. If the two waterfolk have reached them, they are as safe as they shall ever be in those Lower Wilds."

"Hush! Look!" warned Duirn.

The fire flickered and sputtered again, sending out a shower of green sparks that filled the snug room with grotesque shadows.

"She knows Yvan has found her," hissed Bor Asa.

The two friends quickly filled their thoughts with the White Fountain that played at the feet of Windameir, where He sat in the Highest Havens. A shrieking, piercing, bitter wind tore at their cloaks, burning through them to the very quick, cutting through flesh like a frozen blade; it screeched and ripped violently at their thoughts, trying to distract them from the Fountain. After another savage gale of frozen wind, the storm abated, and what seemed to be melodic voices began, as strange in their calm tones as had been the frightful wind.

"Don't pay any attention to what she says," cried Yvan,

coming to himself for a moment. "She is aware of us now. She is trying to lure you into her snare."

Duirn felt himself giving in to the beautiful, calm flow of words that soothed and consoled him and filled up those parts of him that were the empty places where the sadness was, and would be until they were all called Home again to Windameir and the eternal gates were closed behind them forever.

He wanted to hear that call Home, and so it sounded to Duirn very much like it when Dorini assumed the notes of the High King's voice.

"Carefully, lad," warned Yvan Earlig, his tone hard.

"Leave us alone," cried Bor Asa. "You can't keep us from answering the High King."

"It is not Him. You are deceived."

"You were the one who was deceived, Yvan! You were the one who fell." Bor Asa's voice had taken on a shrill note, bordering on hysteria.

The handsome elf ignored his friend and tried to concentrate on the fire all the harder.

"Perhaps if Dorini is busy trying to snare these two, I may get through to the lad with the news of Malcom and Morane being free."

Yvan bent closer to the fire, full of the green flames now, and sent his thoughts arrowing through that dreadful darkness, straight into the very depths of Dorini's frozen fortress. Howling gales of sleet and snow and iron-hard shards of ice devoured him, but the burning flame of the Light never faltered, and in another moment, he was before the small form of the otter again; in a flash, Yvan thought of Malcom and Morane in the glade with the ancient tree-beings, and of the Pipe of Ring Parath; then he hummed the tune to himself, over and over, so the small, lost figure of the dazed animal could hear and remember the haunting melody of the Ring Parath.

The ice and snow swirled again in renewed force, and the elf quickly withdrew from the grip of Dorini's power. She had grown very strong over the past turnings, and Yvan knew he was not equal to her by himself, so he quickly came to himself and cut off the swirling, starry tunnel that spun through space and time to where Dorini was. In another moment, the fire flared again, sending so many sparks out onto the floor that Bor Asa found himself quite busy with stamping out a

266

dozen hot embers that had found their way onto the dazzling carpet.

Looking about in a daze, Duirn turned to the exhausted Yvan Earlig, who now slumped in a chair before the hearth.

"But what shall we do to help Olthar?"

"We have done everything it is in our power to do. From this point on, it is up to the lad himself."

Duirn started to protest, but was cut short by Bor Asa.

"We were very near giving in just now," he said, shaken by his ordeal.

"I'm sorry to have had to use you as bait, but that was the only way I could think of to distract Dorini long enough to get to the lad. She has always had a weakness for snaring those who follow the High King."

"I remember I said something awful to you," stammered Bor Asa. "I don't know what came over me. I'm terribly sorry."

"You have nothing to be sorry for, my friend. The power of the Dark One is far-reaching. The Dark Seed that lies in all of us lies waiting to be awakened by her hand. It is why we must live in the Light so that even the dark flower will eventually bloom in the broad daylight of Windameir's sun."

A faint, faraway murmur began in the room, echoed by itself, then growing stronger. It began again, and repeated itself twice more, causing Duirn and Bor Asa to exchange puzzled looks.

Yvan was beaming when they turned to him.

"The Ring Parath had a song that spoke of the paths of stars through a vast heaven on the way Home to Windameir. You are hearing a very faint melody that is coming from the Olthlinden at this moment."

Duirn opened his mouth to speak, but Yvan Earlig was gone. Bor Asa smiled once, then vanished as well, but his voice hung on in empty space.

"The Middle Islands, old fellow! That's where you are bound!"

Duirn snorted in surprise, very much used to doing the disappearing himself, but taken somewhat aback when his friends chose to perform the same ritual upon him. He felt the least bit of smug satisfaction as he reappeared unexpectedly next to Jahn Spray, startling him badly.

The Sea of Roaring

THE glade in the wood smelled of time and space and moldering sunlight that had difficulty reaching the ground. Malcom sat beside his mate, who was sleeping again; he listened to her slow, steady breathing and felt a great relief growing in him. He had been worried about her until they reached the fringes of the Westing Wood, for until then they had never once been beyond detection by the beast armies that roamed over every trail and river all the way from the ancient delving they had escaped from high up in the Serpent Mountains to the spot they lay hidden in now. There was something in this wood that assured Malcom that the beast soldiers never came to this place, and had never been near the ancient glade. It was a safe enough place for Morane to sleep, for she was very near the ragged edge of her endurance. He smiled and patted her with a paw, then began to feel the exhaustion of their ordeal overtake him. There was not even a chance to fight the coming of the sleep that swept over him then, for he was so far gone he never even realized when it was exactly that he passed from wakefulness to slumber, for even in his dream he still sat guard over his sleeping mate. He was not sure if the sounds he began to hear were from his dream or from the surrounding wood; there was a soft rush of water, chuckling and rippling as a clear stream through a winter sheath of ice would; then there were voices, old and deep and so wonderful that Malcom looked to Morane to see if she were awake to hear them. As he turned toward his mate, he was quite surprised to see her talking earnestly with a large group of beings who were as brown as berries and who wore odd plumed caps that were of a cheerful green color. It seemed that they were the ones who made the pleasant sounds as they spoke.

Malcom tried to speak to his mate, but nothing came; there was a silence then, and the light began to dim until it was a pale blue heaven above, dotted with a fiery sort of white dome that blazed brightly in a growing halo directly over the two otters; in what seemed another drawing of breath, there was a face beaming down at them, one the otters were not familiar with, but which made them feel very good to look upon; then there were the fair features of Duirn before them, which made Malcom's heart skip a beat. The next image was blurred and frightening, and made the two animals shiver in every bone; the light was gone a muddy greenish brown, and a terrible rush of frozen wind howled about their ears, and a dark claw seemed to grope through the dreadful mist, searching for their hearts. It was only for a moment, but Malcom saw the distinct outline of an otter against the awful frozen background, and in that instant he recognized his own pup.

"Olthar!" he cried aloud, and the noise awakened him, to find him still sitting in the same wood, lying next to Morane.

"Shhhhh," she soothed. "You've been calling out his name for ever so long. I didn't know if I was going to be able to wake you or not."

"I was having a wonderful dream, and then it got awful."

"I was having a strange dream myself. I saw a face, but I don't know anyone who looks like that. It was an elf, but I can't remember ever seeing him before."

"Did you see Duirn?"

"Why, yes. Did you see him in your dream, too?"

"I saw Duirn, and then there was a light that looked like a summer night by the stars, but that changed into something awful. That's when I saw the pup."

Morane sighed deeply, fighting to hold back her tears.

"I wish we were able to travel more quickly. I know we'll find news at the sea. Everywhere we've been there's been nothing but beast soldiers and the wolves. There's nowhere left for us to go."

"We shall be there soon enough. If we rest by day and travel the river at night, we should be to the Roaring quickly enough."

"Not quickly enough for me."

Malcom shrugged and changed the subject.

"I wonder who the other elf was in our dreams? He seemed friendly, but I don't recall ever seeing him before."

"It made me feel good to see him, whoever he is. He seemed to be saying something, but I couldn't quite make sense of it."

"Maybe if we finish out our naps we'll have the dream again and can see more."

"I couldn't go back to sleep now. I'm too excited. Maybe we should go on a little farther."

"We can go back to the river easily enough. I don't think we'll be bothered in this wood."

Morane looked about her slowly, feeling the ancient trees' silent grandeur. They were giants, stretching away toward the thin patch of blue sky far above their heads.

"I wonder if there's anything to eat here?" she said at last, only half aloud. The strange dream and the majestic trees had made her feel hungry all of a sudden; she could not remember the last time she ate, but knew that it had been hours before. They had traveled fast and desperately, not daring to slow down for a moment, until they had reached the spot where they now stood.

"We should explore around to see," suggested her mate, who was feeling restless as well, although thoroughly exhausted.

They had not gone far when they heard the murmuring; it was just below the rim of hearing, like faint, rumbling echoes from deep underground. Morane began to grow frightened, but Malcom's dream flashed through his mind, and he thought that the strange voices were more than a small bit familiar.

As the two animals stood motionless in the tall corridor of the ancient trees, a golden beam of light began to descend from the canopy of leaves high above them, and as they watched, it formed a shimmering, brilliant pool on the ground before them. In it were the reflections of the beings they had seen in their dreams, and the low murmur became a voice they could clearly understand.

"Tidings of yore we bring you, waterkind, news of matters beyond your sphere, but matters that concern you in time."

"Who are you?" asked Morane meekly, still in a state of exhausted shock from her recent ordeal.

"We won't have time to repeat our names for you. Your tongues were not meant to say such things as the sounds of what we are called. Know we are the Old Ones, and have been instructed to help you reach the Last Salt Lake of Lowerweld."

"Wherever is that?" questioned Malcom, who knew many places from his travels and reading, but had never come across any mention of the Last Salt Lake of Lowerweld.

The spokesman for the Old Ones went on patiently.

"Your geography is not as extensive as your Older Brothers know. You perhaps might refer to it as a sea, although it is nowhere near the size of a sea, once you've seen the difference."

270

"Are you speaking of the Roaring Sea? Is that the Lake of whatever you said?"

"It is the same, except that it really is merely a lake. You have not traveled enough, little brother, to have seen what a sea looks like."

"Don't argue," whispered Morane. "If he says it's a lake, let him have his way."

She was wary of all the odd beings who had begun to fill her life since that long-ago evening when Jahn Spray arrived at their holt door. It seemed to her that from that time nothing but trouble and tragedy had followed their steps from one catastrophe to the next.

"I'm not arguing," argued Malcom. "I merely asked if we were speaking of the same place."

"Come. We waste valuable time here. Yvan Earlig has spoken to us about you, and we are to get you to the lake as quickly as we can."

"I don't know that I want to go that quickly," said Morane reluctantly. "I want to know where I'm going before I go rushing away."

A slight change came over the voice then, and the next words softened Morane's resistance.

"We are to help you reach your pup. He is in grave danger."

"Well, why didn't you say so right off?" muttered Malcom. "Of course we'll go straight off. Why are we standing around here like a pack of ninnies without our wits between us? Do whatever you're going to do and let's get on!"

"Oh, yes, yes," echoed his mate. "Let's do hurry!"

As Morane finished speaking, the golden light began to form a whirlpool that grew larger and larger as they watched, gathering them up inside a tunnel of spiraling light and sound and flashing stars that burst brilliantly into glowing white diamonds as they passed. Malcom had never been quite so dazzled as he was with that brief voyage, but Morane rather thought it reminded her of things she had seen in her own fire the night the King of the Shanoliel had come to them for the first time.

The otters were lost in their spinning journey for a time, at once long beyond count, and as short as a breath. They were hardly aware of their leaving before they were arriving, although much less quickly than they had supposed, for upon looking at his mate, Malcom saw a very old animal, dark gray about the muzzle and chest, but still his familiar old friend from his lost past.

271

"Why, Morane! Have we gone so far beyond ourselves that we've aged without knowing?"

Morane studied her mate silently for a moment, then said gently, "I can see that we can't go about with all this marvelous carrying-on without paying a price. There is always a score to be kept."

The voice of the Old One came through to them clearly then, although there was no vision to accompany it.

"We could not carry you here without the aging. Yvan Earlig said to bring you as quickly as we could, but without changing you into another life. We only did as best we could."

"Are we still in time to help our pup?"

"You are. Now I must go. If I am to remain in my own time, I have to return now. Farewell. Keep the Light. Adieu."

Morane started to protest, but soon saw that there was no one to protest to. They sat in a small grove of trees that looked like gnarled old men with knotty knees sticking up above a low-lying swamp that stretched on all about them. It was late afternoon, to judge by the sun's position in the sky, and a very light breeze was blowing from across the water, carrying with it a definite salty tang that tickled the nose and stirred the blood with excitement.

Malcom looked at the old animal beside him, at once happy and sad as well.

"I never thought we'd get old like this," he said mildly, looking away across the vast, flat distance of the brackish swamp.

"I've never thought it would be any other way, once I found out what living with you was all about," exclaimed Morane, a trace of her old pepper returning to animate her graying form. "Whatever we missed by getting here this way would have probably bored us to the point of distraction, anyhow."

"I could have used a little more boredom, just to break up all this excitement," said Malcom truthfully.

"Here we are, but no Olthar!" said Morane. "No anybody else, either, unless my eyes have gotten so bad I can't make out anything plainly enough to see an otter when I'm looking at him."

Malcom studied their surroundings more closely. The wind had picked up slowly, blowing little ripples across the face of the water; off to his right, a great white seabird hung effortlessly on the invisible back of the breeze, floating there in the afternoon sky like a pennant. As Malcom looked more closely, the bird seemed to be beckoning to him.

"Look! Do you see the bird?"

Morane nodded.

"It seems to be making some sort of signal for us to follow it."

"I guess there's nothing else for us to do. No one else seems to be around."

The otter found himself stiff and awkward as he moved into the water, but before he could say anything to Morane, the seabird lowered himself toward the horizon and beckoned to them again. It was all the two otters could do to stay up with the stately bird; once they thought they had lost sight of the white figure, but after a long moment's disappointment, they found it again and went on.

Morane complained that she was beginning to tire after they had been swimming for some time, and Malcom could feel his own strange body start to send him signals of fatigue. He was ready to give up in despair, when the bird landed amid a stretch of small, rolling dunes that were just ahead, and Malcom's heart leaped. There beyond all doubt was the roar of the sea, and it was only a small distance away.

"We're there!" he called to Morane, although he had to gasp for air as he spoke.

Morane merely nodded, panting heavily.

Malcom slowed further and clutched his mate's paw.

"Not a moment too soon, either," gasped Morane. "I couldn't have gone on for another stroke if I'd been chased by one of the beast soldiers."

"I hope we've seen the last of their lot."

Morane had stopped and looked distractedly at Malcom, her gray brow drawn into a worried frown.

"Do you think he will recognize us? I . . . we've aged so."

Malcom halted, floating easily on the surface of the water.

"I hadn't thought of that. I wonder if he looks older?"

"If we do, he must."

"Let's go on. I don't want to think about any of this anymore. I want to find Olthar and then we'll know all about everything."

For the first time the two noticed the heavy booming of the surf, and another sound that seemed to be coming from the direction of the sea. The dunes were high and covered with willowy plants that swayed back and forth in time to the wind, and the view of what was beyond was blocked.

"Hurry. I can hear voices."

"Or music! It sounds so strange."

273

Malcom halted again in mid-stroke.

"I hope whoever it is is friendly."

"Maybe we'd better go carefully. I don't think the bird would have been leading us into a trap, but you never know."

"We have been fooled before," said Malcom.

"Then let's hide and see what it all means."

Doing exactly what they spoke of, the two aging mates left the water and cautiously skirted the dunes that rolled down to the brackish backwater that was separated from the sea by the spits of sand. They crawled slowly up the side of the nearest dune, keeping close to the low sea oats that grew in abundance, struggling to reach the top so they could see where the strange sound came from, and who could be making it.

It was a noise as of a great throng, which they had mistaken for the noise of the sea at first; it rose and fell, and there were other sounds there as well, musical and harsh to the ear, as if the two extremes were battling to be the victor over the other. A strange feeling crept over Malcom as he neared the top of the great dune, and he turned to face Morane as she grappled her way next to him.

"Whatever happens, Morane, remember that I've always loved you and thought you were the best ever. We have had a long, full life, and a wonderful pup has been born to us."

His voice was so intense and his eyes so full of tears that it was all she could do not to break down and sob.

"Why ever do you go on so, you silly thing? You know we've had the best life ever, and we're going to go on just as we are."

The words were nowhere close to expressing what was truly in her heart, but her eyes were clear and full of love for her mate, and she knew he saw that.

The two animals were interrupted by a terrible din that began so suddenly they almost leapt out of their skins. The sea noise was drowned out by the shattering roar and screech of some demented demon-being, and a frozen cyclone of sleet and snow whirled about, blowing stinging, icy shards of the frozen sand into their eyes, blinding them. The gale howled on, yet they could still hear the horrible voice above the tempest, rising to an ear-shattering wail.

Malcom struggled the last few steps to the top of the dune and shielded his eyes, trying to see what catastrophe was occurring on the shores of the Roaring.

At first he was unable to pierce the storm, but by squinting and placing his paws before his muzzle, he was able to make out a great mass of beings on the beach before him, stretch-

274

ing away in both directions; there was also a fleet of ships that ran from one horizon all the way to the other. He was barely over marveling at that when he saw the ring of dragons, and the source of the frozen wind; and there was his pup, older, but his pup beyond all doubt, lying as still as death on a brightly covered camp litter that was guarded by a band of heavily armed otters; behind him was the ruler of the Banskrog, the terrible Queen of Darkness, who sought to devour all the Lower Meadows of Windameir.

Malcom impulsively moved to try to shield Morane from the horrible sight, but it was too late, and she was already beside him.

The freezing wind died and left an eerie stillness in its place, broken only by the constant, steady pulse of the sea, which rolled on behind.

A Final Crossing

THERE in time, where there was no way to speak of what had been before, or would be afterward, Olthar found himself locked in struggle with the very deepest shadow that lay at the bottom of his being. The green mist-form of the Banskrog had taken on one terrible cloak after another in trying to terrify him into submission; it was when the wraiths of thoughts turned in another direction that he began to know the true dread of the knowledge of his own inner soul, for there, hidden from all the light that surrounded him, was the Seed of Darkness that was the Banskrog, waiting to spread its black wings and grow; it was apart from the Light, yet still a part of it, but Olthar saw only the horrifying moment as it occurred to him, and he realized that he wanted to become allies with Dorini; the Darkness had offered him more than trinkets or mere objects to trick his fancy; she had offered him the cloak of power that would put him on a par with the High King of Windameir. That idea leaked into his chaotic thoughts, even though he struggled against it; then he gave in for a moment to ponder the unthinkable, of becoming the Dark One's ally, to reign supreme over all the Lower Meadows forever.

As the young animal struggled within himself, the sea about him churned into a fearful storm that fell on the island's shore with a ringing, hollow roar; the ships that were there were tossed about in the gale like bobbing corks, and the armies, the very armies that had gathered together from all the lands of Atlanton, were drenched in a torrential downpour that flooded the sea and sky with blinding fury.

There were Borim and Brian and Trianion, all come to the Middle Islands to carry on the war against the Banskrog, and there were they all in grave danger of defeat, for the trying of the resolve of Olthar was the very key that might spell out their own ultimate downfall.

It was there on the beach that Olthar's greatest danger lay, not in facing the raging hordes of enemy soldiers, but the gentle, soft-spoken, reasonable shadows, which promised him peace, and peace for all the Lower Meadows, if only he would give up the futile struggle he had been waging against the lawful ruler, Dorini the Protector. Olthar seemed to slip away from all those who were about him, who cared for him and stood by him to defend him; in the black nightmare of Dorini's will, he had missed seeing the days when the armies of Borim and Brian arrived, followed closely by the hosts of Trianion Starseeker. They had met and conferred and drawn their battle plans, and been poised to strike to rescue the Olthlinden, when the Dark One and the forces of the Banskrog had arrived to challenge them each and every one; she found them all set against her, except for the youngest of their lot, who carried the Pipe of Ring Parath, Olthar, who was the least experienced of them all; to keep the others at bay and hard pressed with other matters, Dorini set her vast hordes loose across the islands, dividing the armies of the Light and drawing them into a deadly struggle for survival. She then set to work seeking to destroy the Olthlinden's will to resist, for she knew if she could but gain control of the pipe the otter carried, the cause of Windameir would be lost.

This was the scene that Malcom and Morane saw unfolding before them as they looked down from their hiding place on the beach, where Olthar was locked in a shattering, terrifying battle of wills with the Dark One.

Without hesitating any longer, Morane leapt forward and dashed toward her pup. Malcom was caught by surprise, but followed quickly afterward, hating his old muscles that would not move properly, and hoping he would not be too late to catch up to his mate.

Sensing this new threat to the Dark Queen, one of the Dargol Brem raised its terrible form to full height and coiled in readiness to strike; Morane did not slacken her pace and ran on, her aged body trembling with the effort. As the others all about them fought on, powerless to help the stricken otter in the death struggle within himself, they saw the two gray animals come from beyond the dunes behind the sea, dashing and darting between the waves of raging warriors, galloping awkwardly toward Olthar.

Jahn Spray, mute and pale, fought beside Duirn and Emeon. He recognized his old friends at once, even though their appearance had changed so drastically, and he was racing toward them then, paying no attention to the dragon that threatened to engulf them all in its fiery breath.

"Malcom! Morane! Here!" cried Jahn, breaking into tears as he saw how old his friends had become, and wondering if he too had grown so aged without his being aware of the passing time.

"Jahn!" barked Malcom. "Help us, lad! The pup is in danger!"

Olthar, who at the moment was far away in his innermost dungeons of despair, heard a dim name at the very surface of his being. It seemed at once familiar, yet odd; but it came again and he turned his attention to it for a moment.

Immediately the sweet, enticing wind began to curl about him, bidding him deeper and deeper into the pleasant darkness, where he would find rest and peace, and where he would never have to feel any uncomfortable thoughts again. The voice of the wind was compelling and drew him even against his will, although there was a part of him that fought to return to where he heard the sound, away and above him, over the immense distance that seemed to be between himself and where the sound came from.

The dragon was upon the two helpless otters before they could reach Olthar; in another instant he held the elf captive as well, locked securely in the iron grasp of his cruel talons. Morane called out Olthar's name again before she was silenced, which the pup vaguely heard, and for a moment he broke free of the dense shadows that stood between himself and the light. He saw what looked to him like the Dargol Brem holding three faces familiar to him, and an unheard chord struck inside him, freeing him from the very inner depths that he had been plunged into; there where the seed of

277

the Banskrog lay hidden there also lay concealed the Light of Windameir, waiting to burst into flame again.

Dorini recoiled from the pup's inner fire like someone would retreat from a stove that was too hot; she resumed the green mist form, and there was another blast of icy wind that howled over the gathered hosts there on the Middle Islands, where all her enemies had gathered to oppose her.

Trianion at that moment had called out the name of the dragon, and Olthar began a soft melody on the Pipe of Ring Parath; the Dargol Brem relaxed his hold on his prisoners just long enough to allow them to be led to safety by a band of Hydin's otters.

"You are mine, O dragon," repeated Trianion. "You, and all your brothers. You shall return with me when I go to the Fields of Light."

The doom snake set up a hideous howl that tore the ears of all who heard it, but the dragons were powerless to try to escape.

"You will not do that, Trianion, for you will not be able to come back again! You won't leave my precious sister alone!"

"We never leave, my lady. We but rest a moment upon the tide, and then it is all upon the beginning once more. In order to put things back into their proper order, I shall do exactly as I say. I would take you with me, but that would be against the grain."

As they spoke to each other thus, Olthar was fallen upon by the two gray-muzzled otters, who smothered him with affectionate hugs and squeezes until he was fearful of being crushed. Jahn Spray was among them, clapping both Olthar and Malcom heartily upon their backs, and giving Morane more sedate pats upon her head. Duirn and Borim and Brian had rallied their armies and fought toward the cluster of Worlugh and Varads that surrounded Dorini in a protective circle, but she merely sneered at her attackers, laughing coldly at their boldness.

"You shall not be rid of me so easily, fools. I have not done with these ridiculous dolts. My armies are upon the march across the Wilderness, and you shall not find them easily dealt with."

"But you, my lady," replied Trianion, "will be safely out of harm's way for a while. We now have all the tokens of the High King gathered together, and the clans of elf and animal have joined the ranks of dwarf and humankind. That was written as the Law long before, and once it has been done, you will have to begin again from your own beginnings. That is how it has been written."

A blizzard of green fire blew across the gathered hosts then, and a deadening chill struck all those there numb, as dreadful visions filled their minds with the rage and hatred of Dorini, the Darkness, the Banskrog, the sister of the One of Light.

"Then do what you say you will, vile fiend! I do not believe you will give up your precious Lorini so easily."

As the Dark Queen spoke, a hush fell over the throngs there, and a golden-white light grew in strength at Trianion's side; soon it was the Lady Lorini, standing beside the young master, radiant in a beauty that was too painful for the eye or heart to bear. Linne and Famhart had to turn away from the vision, as did all the others except Trianion. The beast armies howled and gnashed their teeth in despair as Trianion smiled at his bride and kissed her gently.

"We shall be at one soon, my love. This is but a moment, this absence. We are not parting, but merely beginning to grow together."

Lorini smiled through her tears and kissed Trianion quickly.

A shudder of fear shook Dorini then, for she was aware of a strength that was greater than any power she controlled in any of the puny beings that dwelled in the Lower Wilderness. It began as a feeling deep within her own frozen black void, that empty place where the Light should have been, but where there was none; because there was none, it was only natural that it sought to be, and drew itself toward the brilliant fire of the Ocean of Windameir; it was dangerously near moving toward that Light, to merge with it, when Dorini gathered herself for a great last escape, and blew herself into a hurricane of shrieking green sleet that covered all there with a sheet of frost and snow, and left them shivering as though they would never be warm again.

As the last of the storm subsided, Olthar saw that along with Dorini, Lorini and Trianion were gone; the Dargol Brem were nowhere in sight, and the dark sliver of fear that was lodged in all their hearts seemed lighter, making the sun appear to be even brighter upon the water, and shine more warmly on all of them who stood beside the sea. The hordes of the Darkness fought on, but without heart, and finally toward sunset the last of them were slain or driven into the sea.

In the strange stillness that came after the pitched heat of battle, the friends began to fall wearily into an exhausted

279

stupor. Borim had dropped in a limp heap amid his closest companions, and Brian and Senja were nearby, resting on their dwarf axes; Duirn and Emeon and Banon, joined by Hydin and a number of his followers, surrounded the Olthlinden and his gray-muzzled parents; Olthar, recovering somewhat, fell on the two old otters, who covered him with pats and hugs and kisses until they were all quite exhausted.

"You haven't changed a bit," muttered Malcom, holding his pup back from him to examine him more closely.

"Oh, he's changed, no doubt of it," chided Jahn Spray. "Much thicker-headed, for one thing."

The friends all laughed heartily, and Duirn exchanged greetings with the long-absent elderly otters.

"How came you to find us here? It is a long journey from where we last had news of you."

"Where are we?" asked Morane. "It didn't seem that we went so far, but when we got here, we looked the way you see us now."

"You covered a long distance, my good friends. You are in the Middle Islands."

Malcom gasped.

"I've always heard stories of them, but I never thought I'd be here."

"But how did we get here? I only remember that last grove of trees, and a funny dream, and then it all got very confusing."

Olthar spoke up then.

"Did you say a funny grove of trees?"

"Why, yes. It seemed as though they appeared to us in a sort of dream. We spoke with them, and then the next thing you know here we are all this distance away, and turned as gray as an early winter morning."

"I think I know who you were dealing with. Coney is here. He can probably explain it better than I can."

Olthar turned and spoke to one of the elves that stood by Duirn's side.

"Can you find the Old One and ask him to come?"

"He's still on the cliff overlooking the harbor where we landed."

"We shall go there then. Come along! We have plenty to discuss as we go."

"What about the Dark One? And the Dargol Brem?" asked Emeon.

"And Trianion?" asked Banon.

"We have seen the Law at work, I think," said Duirn.

"Trianion took the Dargol Brem with him when he returned to the Fields of Light. He knew all the names, so they had no choice but to return with him. It also seems the Dark One got a little too close to the Light here. She had to withdraw or be merged once more."

"Then she's gone?" asked Malcom hopefully.

"Hardly, my good fellow, but she has had a severe setback. The Dargol Brem were her mainstays in these past turnings. Now she has only the beast armies to carry her battle."

"And those whom she has gained control over," explained Borim, his magnificent armor a burnished gold in the dying sunlight. "They will carry the seed of destruction with them until it grows rampant again. We have served our time and held the Banskrog in check as it was given to our lot to do as best we could."

"And next it will fall to those who follow, until there is no longer any need to maintain watch in the Wilderness, and everyone has gone Home again," said Brian. Galen stood beside him worshipfully, and the older dwarf turned to him as he went on. "It will fall the lot of yours and those who come after you to keep the fires alive here, Galen."

"But what of you, sire?"

Brian looked sadly about him, holding Senja's hand tightly. He nodded to Borim and Olthar slightly.

"We shall have to tell them sooner or later," said Borim.

"Perhaps later, not now."

Olthar shook off the heavy look he wore, and urged everyone to hurry on to find the Old One, who was perched right at the highest point of the island, overlooking the beautiful harbor, where the fleet of Borim and Brian lay at anchor; all the boats of the hosts of Trianion and the seacraft of Duirn were there as well, riding gently at their anchors. There was such a number of the lively, delicate boats that the outer harbor was filled as well, as were all the havens around the island.

The smell of death and battle was rapidly fading, and the smoke and stench of the Dargol Brem were blown away to sea as Malcom and Morane walked beside Olthar, worried looks wrinkling their old muzzles.

"What did he mean when he said you were all to leave?" asked Morane. "We've only just found you. Surely you don't mean to leave again so soon?"

The pup's broad muzzle turned a lighter shade of gray, and

he looked anxiously to Borim, who was also walking along in the group nearest him.

"Coney can explain it all better than we," he said at last, seeing the stout form of the bear king seem to grow weary, and the proud bearing looked to the otter to lessen the smallest bit.

"What can this Coney explain that you can't?" persisted Morane. "Jahn Spray, you tell me what's going on here!"

The elf was taken back in time by the tone of voice that Malcom's mate used, and he remembered many times when he had been called on the rug before the irate Morane to explain various disappearances and sudden trips that sometimes dragged on all winter long or through the better part of a summer.

"Well, it's hard to say, really," began Jahn, but was saved by Duirn.

"He won't be able to tell you all of it, my good otter. Coney will explain."

"Why can't you tell us?" asked Malcom.

The leader of the Shanoliel had grown visibly older, just as the otters had, and he walked with a weary tread.

"We are reaching the end of our time here. There needs to be an understanding of it all so we won't have to stay any longer than we have to."

"You mean we won't be in these islands long?"

Duirn looked long and steadily at Morane.

"When the Dark One withdrew, and the Dargol Brem were called back to the Upper Gates, all our journeys were done in the Wilderness. We shall be going on to the Upper Meadows now."

Morane turned to her grown pup, clutching at him.

"You mean to say that the Last Sleep has taken us?"

A strange catch hung in the old otter's throat.

Malcom hugged his mate and looked to his pup for an explanation, but they had reached the winding path that led up the cliff toward where Coney waited and had to concentrate on climbing; the trail was too narrow to walk abreast of each other, so the questions had to wait.

Morane and Malcom followed Olthar, and the rest trailed along behind, facing the sheer living green wall of the cliff on their left and the faraway azure blue of the sea and the harbor on their right. Up and up they went, until at last, right at the top, the animals came to a broad green lawn that ran all the way from the cliff's edge until it reached the peak, where they could see in all directions. The sea was a golden-blue shimmering lake, and the companions saw that there was a strange sight at the mountain's crest; there in all his resplendent glory was the Old One, covered with leaves and blossoming fragrant yellow flowers.

"Coney!" called Jahn and Olthar together. "Is that you?"

What sounded to be a low chuckle came from the depths of the tree-being.

"I see you have found the lost ones," he said. "The others of my Brotherhood said they were being brought here."

"We were brought, but look at what happened," said Malcom. "We got old on the trip."

"That is the Law," replied Coney. "There are some things that cannot be done, and one is that you can never alter the Law of where you are."

"But what has happened to you, Coney? I've never seen you like this."

"I'm staying," answered the Old One. "I'm going to stay right here until it is time to return Home. There has to be someone who can stay and help guide the others along. I have no desire to go back as yet, and this feels really light and airy here."

"You'll be a good reminder," said Duirn.

"I'm also to be here so that when the time comes again for the Banskrog to awake, all those who follow the Light can reach me here to call all the Brotherhood together. If you are needed, I can reach you."

"Or those who will take our places," added Brian. "And there will be those who take the places of the followers of the Dark One. Her seeds are carried away on the wind and will flourish again. We have not seen the end of the likes of Par Hance and Bern and Sigman Col and Famhart and Trane."

"But what is all this rubbish you've been talking?" cried a peevish Morane. "I want to hear something that I can understand."

"We've been trying to tell you, but you won't listen," explained Duirn patiently.

"Let Coney finish," said Olthar. "He can tell it best of all."

"If he just won't be so long about it," interrupted Jahn.

The ancient tree-being seemed to grow taller then, and the fading rays of the sun shone brightly through the thick green foliage and reflected off the brilliant yellow flowers.

"It was written that the Banskrog would fail in the Middle Islands, but all those who defended the Light would be called back to the High Meadows. The circle is closed. The Darkness has come full and waned, and the Light is following its path. The tokens of Windameir have served their ends, and the bearers of those tokens now have earned their rest. You all have a choice in the matter, to stay or go on as you please. I cannot say what you must do, but you must choose now. Trianion is away to the Fields of Light, and the Dargol Brem are gone; Lorini is in Cypher, to help all those who yet need the visions of Windameir in these Lower Wilds. Borim and Brian have gathered the animal and dwarfish kingdoms from their countries, and Olthar has gathered his host. There is nothing now to do but take leave and go on with the chores that await us."

"You mean we have a choice in all this?" asked Morane. "I could go back to my old holt on the Greenleaf if I wanted? And not be old?"

Coney nodded his upper limbs.

"You could choose that, if you wished it."

"Or could we go on with Olthar, wherever he's going?" questioned Malcom.

"You may do that also."

Malcom studied his mate a moment, then turned to Jahn Spray. "What of you, Jahn? What will you do?"

"There are still those left behind who will need warning and looking after," began the elf. "There's no end of silly lumps who have no idea about how much danger they're in as long as they remain in the Lower Wilderness."

Morane began to protest, but changed her mind, and her frown softened a bit.

"And Olthar? Does he have a choice?"

The pup took his mother's paw in his.

"I have to go on. But I am always with you, no matter what you decide. That is for you to say. We all have our parts yet to play."

Morane began to cry softly, and Malcom hugged her tightly to himself.

"We have only to think of him and he'll be with us. It's not like parting at all."

"And you could come along," went on Olthar. "There is no end of things that need tending across the Last Sea of Beginning."

"Are the rivers nice there?" asked Malcom dreamily.

"The best water there is," replied Coney.

"In that case, we should at least give it a try, don't you think?"

Malcom had begun to turn to look at Morane, but in that moment, a flash of stars blinded him and there was a sudden wind that tore past his ears; then there was the brilliant white Light towering away so high above him that he grew dizzy looking at it and lost his sense of balance for a moment.

When he came to himself again, he had just stumbled on a piece of the firewood he had dropped in the kitchen doorway; behind him was a starlit night, soft and silent beneath new snow, starched white and squeaking in the boughs of the trees and under his paws. Morane sat quietly at the table before the fire, and when he got closer, he saw she had gone to sleep over a small piece of knitting.

Something was tickling the back of the otter's memory, and he couldn't remember what it was for a moment, until he closed the green outer holt door and plodded down the long passageway to the snug bedroom where the pup lay, sleeping soundly with his paws drawn up to his muzzle, making small contented noises at the pleasures of his dreams. This was vaguely disturbing to Malcom, and he struggled to remember what it was that was out of place, but he was interrupted by an anxious rapping on the outer door. It came again twice more before he was able to unlatch it. Morane had already been awakened by the noise and put on the kettle for the visitor. Malcom was both surprised by and at once expecting Jahn Spray, who stood before the hearth dusting the snow off his cap and cape.

"Sit down here while I get you something hot to take the chill off," said Morane with finality, forcing the elf down at the table. "You two can entertain each other while I put the supper on, I'm sure."

Malcom looked at his old friend, who seemed as startled as he was, but confused by some baffling occurrence that neither of them could quite remember.

Morane came back with a huge crock of steaming stew, followed by a chubby pup who trundled along after her.

"Read me a story," chirped the pup, scampering hard to land in his father's lap, and picking up a thick, old book that was beside the otter's chair at the fireside.

Without knowing quite what he was about, Malcom opened the book in a daze, and his eyes fell on the pictures there of dragons and beast armies, and a horrible wraith-like cloud that hung over all the other figures; there were four other

285

forms also, each in a corner of the large parchment page; a bear, a dwarf, an otter, and a man, all adorned in battle garb and looking grim and heroic at their posts.

"Read me the story about the Olthlinden," cried the pup, squirming about in his father's lap.

"Yes, do! Read that one again," said Jahn Spray. "We hadn't finished that one the last trip I was here. Let's have the end of that one."

Malcom looked oddly at the pup, then to his friend, then to his mate; they all seemed on the point of bursting with good humor, so Malcom turned to the page that the pup pointed out and began to read aloud; there were the King of the Shanoliel and all the water and wood elves, and the struggle with the beast armies and Dargol Brem; there were the Banskrog in all its terrible savagery, and all the tales that went with the struggle of the Light to survive. There were the exploits of Borim Bruinthor and Brian Brandigore and Trianion Starseeker, and Malcom read on and on, unable to stop; it was like a purge, for the terrible grief and fear that had been within them all began to flicker and leave their hearts as the otter read, and by the time the story was through, all the grief and heartache that had lingered in their hearts was gone. He placed the book on the table and took up his cup of tea. The pup was asleep in his lap, and Morane was busy with her needlework. Jahn Spray looked over innocently enough, and drew out a map he had concealed beneath his vest.

"Here's a place we haven't been to yet, Malcom, that sits on a bank overlooking the river . . ."

Morane frowned over her needles, but when she saw the wistful look in Malcom's eyes, she did not speak.

It was all just beginning again, from the last heartbeat to the next, and the tale spun on and on until they would all be safely Home again at the table of the High King, free at last.

That was a good thing to think of, so Morane went on thinking it.

Epilogue

THEY were all scattered on the winds, in every direction. Borim and Brian and Senja crossed the upper boundaries and were welcomed Home at long last by the High King himself. Trianion was there to greet them, along with scores of their companions from the old days of the Dragon Wars. There was news that Cypher flourished, and that Lorini had borne a child she called Cybelle, who was as beautiful as her mother, which cheered the young master, and he awaited the day with light heart when they would all be reunited again in a time where there would be no good-byes.

Olthar lived on for a great long time in the Outer Meadows, and along with Jahn Spray and Malcom, struggled to bring together the vast hosts of remaining wood and water elves who in turns watched the borders of the Darkness. At the insistence of Coney, the two elderly otters finally crossed the upper boundaries in the year the first child of Famhart and Linne was born.

It was a long wait until the call of the Last Battle which had been written of long before, and which would one day draw an end to the roles they had played; and they would all be returned once more into the Living Heart of Windameir.
The Beginning.